Spirit

Of A

Dragon

Keith Gardner

Keith Gardner

Spirit of a Dragon is a fictional Adult Erotic Crime Thriller. And the first in what could be a series.

Copyright © Keith Gardner 2000

Editing by Keith Gardner

The Limited 1st Edition paperback of this novel was first published in Great Britain on the 1st December 2012 by Keith Gardner, and is still available.

ISBN -13: 978-0957511071

ISBN -10: 0957511078

DEDICATION

To my late parents who simply told me to keep at it - and
one day that I would be able to get my writing out into the
wider world for others to read. As well as to my brother &
sister, relatives and friends for their continued support.

∞

Contents:

Spirit of a Dragon

Acknowledgements

I also wish to thank those people from around the world who already bought a copy of the original Limited 1st Edition run of 150 paperbacks when it first came out. And of which I was proud to sign for them for doing so.

∞

As well as to all of my readers and fans of any genre that I've written so far, for their offered feedback and reviews on whatever retail site where any of my books have been bought by them

Thank You

And to those of you who are on my Twitter, Goodreads, and Facebook pages, for each book which has been written so far - and for any tweets and chats with me in those same places, on how any of you view my different novels.

You can also look out for regular News or Book updates, and other new information on my Website Blog, or on any of those same pages too.

Other Books by this Author:

{See the back of book for more detailed information on any of these:}

* Also available in printed paperback
**Coming soon in paperback

*A Silent Land
(Early Western Adventure/Drama)
----

*Honour The Star
(Wild West Adventure)
----

*Little Haven
(Wild West Adventure)

**The Brotherhood
(Adult Supernatural Crime/Thriller)
----

*Once In A Lifetime
(Romantic Drama)
----

*The Magical World of Cassie Carey
Book 1

(Fantasy/Science-Fiction)
----

*An Unexpected Christmas
(Family Christmas Story)

CHAPTER 1

July 2000

The twenty-two-year-old brightly painted yellow classic car, to which others at various shows and rallies, always admitted looked in an immaculate condition for its age. Had always been very well cared for during its life, despite the passage of so many numerous and increasing years; however, it had sadly taken quite a beating over the past few days throughout the summer heat wave. The two occupants within its old-fashioned and somewhat now outdated plastic looking interior began to plead with the old machine to keep going as the needle on the temperature gauge began to rise steadily.

Much too rapidly it seemed, as it was climbing higher and higher so fast into the red zone towards it reaching the overheating stage. Until barely only a few minutes later, the first danger signals were of white wisping tendrils of smoke as they began to emit and to emerge from the two small vents which were situated on the bonnet. The young male driver of it, whose body now began to move forwards and back in a rocking motion, as if his own efforts would also help it to reach the crest of the small incline they were now trying to climb.

'Just a bit further, baby! Come on, you can make it!' he now crooned to the ancient vehicle.

The car groaned as if in answer to his pleading request, and even picked up a little more speed. Though this only brought more of the same

1

white smoke to blow out from the vents. Yet much to their amazement and surprise, the old car still kept dragging them up the low incline. Until finally, they actually crested the very top, to where it now slowly started to gain some momentum as it coasted down the other side. The straining note of its engine no longer needed for the moment. By now though, the smoke was almost a dense streaming cloud as it erupted from beneath the bonnet as well and drafted back towards the windscreen to hide the road ahead.

'About a hundred yards ahead there's a small parking area,' his female companion said to him with her head now stuck well out of the wound down open passenger side-window.

He listened to her completely, since by now he could barely see a thing in front of him due to the excessive coils of smoke that were now erupting from beneath the bonnet and through the vents. At her word, he indicated a left turn, then began to slow down, and turned in carefully following her direction, and parked in the centre of the lay-by. He switched the engine off quickly and climbed out, after popping the catch to the bonnet. The hiss of steam was quite loud as they now stood in front of it.

The heavy goods vehicle that had had to crawl up the incline so slowly behind them, slowed down as it approached. The electric passenger side window of it already rolling down as it drew up alongside. They both expected to hear little more than abuse form causing what they knew would be a small tailback behind them earlier. But the driver simply smiled and waved. Then as he passed, shouted, "Well done, lad, at least the old girl made it for you, eh!" as he drove slowly past before picking up speed up again.

∞

After five minutes had passed and the smoke began to die away slightly, he raised the bonnet fully and used the easily unclipped metal bar holder to keep the bonnet in its high open position. Then using his hand as a fan, and his mouth to help to blow some of the smoke away so that he could lean over and peer down and inspect the interior. He was able to look down behind the radiator and see what the problem was. As some steam was still emerging from what could only be a hole in one of the radiator hoses . . . and quite a large one too, he thought. Not something that could be fixed by them where they were now. And certainly not by using anything they carried in the boot in case of such problems when they were driving. He shook his head from side to side, already knowing that it would need a spare, if not actually a new hose fitting on to it now.

He also knew that at kind of tape wrapped around it wouldn't hold it long enough until they reached home. They would likely also have to stop every mile or so just to replace it continually, and adding more of the lost water too. He knew that it would be the water factor required for the radiator that would cause the most trouble, since it would just become steam quickly and continue to aim for the weakened area again and again. Every time the tape would begin to disintegrate due to the heat and high pressure of the steam. And since he knew that they certainly did not carry that much spare water in his boot to constantly keep refilling it over and over again. Or had a sufficient enough quantity of tape either, he knew that without a new part being put on now, any other outcome was almost dead from the start!

'Call up the breakdown services on your mobile for me would you, pet. And tell them that we only need a new bottom radiator hose and gasket, and some water to be able to get moving again,' he said from beneath the raised bonnet before coming out.

The girl nodded and reached in through the open window to retrieve her mobile from the small shelf on the dashboard. Then from her purse she extracted the small credit card sized membership card, and followed the thirteen numerical digits on the card as she dialled.

'They're asking if we need picking-up?' she said after speaking for a moment to the call centre operator.

'Not if they can bring the right parts to connect on to it, and some water as well,' he told her, information that she quickly passed on. At the end of the call she gave her own mobile number in case they needed to contact them. Then before disconnecting, was told that it would be between thirty minutes to an hour until someone was with them. Quarter of an hour later her phone rang and she answered it.

'They said that they'll just have to recover us here. As they don't carry any kinds of hoses at hand for our type of car in stock up here, they'll just have to pick us and the car up and take us home.'

He gave a shrug. 'Fair enough, pet, as long as they get us home I can get the new parts tomorrow somewhere and put it on myself,' he replied.

The young girl thanked them and said that that would be fine. Responding with a polite, 'No thank you', when she was asked if they wanted the car taking to a local garage to be fixed. Answering that her boyfriend could get a part for it tomorrow and fix it himself.

∞

It was around seven in the warm summer evening as they sat together on the kerb of the lay-by. And at least a good ten feet away from a metal waste bin which had flies moving inside it, as well as circling around it from what left-over foodstuffs it must have contained. The sky was clear and blue, the clouds which were in sight, were already beginning to tinge with redness, which signalled to most of those who saw it. Only if they knew or had heard the age old lore of, "Red sky at night, sailors delight", that another good fine day would be occurring tomorrow. And with only a gentle breeze to cool them, it meant that there was little chance of any rain again. Though, because it had not rained for the past five weeks, it was also why the usual worried water saving messages were already being aired on both television and radio stations alike.

As usual, they were constantly asking all of their customers to try and conserve as much water as possible, and in any way they could. Just as almost every other Water Company throughout Britain, knew that without any regular rainfall in the summer months, the water levels in the majority of reservoirs would not only begin to evaporate from the daily heat; but levels would also continue to fall through the constant demand and usage for it.

About half an hour into their waiting vigil, she announced to him, 'It's no good honey, I've just got to have a pee!'

He grinned at her. 'So, go on over behind the hedge then!' he said to her.

'And as soon as you've been I think I'll have to go and have one myself as well!' he added with another grin.

She chuckled in a quite deep and throaty way and he grinned at her.

'Go and have your pee while I keep a watch out. If he comes I'll give you a warning shout. Then you can do the same while I'm back there, okay?'

'Geoff?' the voice said from behind him a minute or so later, causing him to turn around but seeing that she wasn't there.

'Where are you?' he asked.

'Just behind the hedge and having my pee where do you think I am?' she answered then carried on, 'do you think there's enough room in the boot for us to carry a bike?'

'Which type, pet, pedal or motor?' he laughed.

'A pedal one, as there's actually a bicycle behind here and it looks quite new and in super condition. Though I haven't a clue why anyone would have wanted to throw it away back here.'

'Why, what are you going to use it for?' he queried. 'Riding to work every day or just for the odd bike ride now and then?'

'Well it would be okay while its warm wouldn't it? For the summer months I mean. Although not that great when it's really pissing down with rain, or when the roads are icy, or if it's snowing. But it would be a shame to leave it here to rust when it looks in such good nick.'

'Should be okay seeing as we're getting a lift back home now. We may have to use some rope to tie it in there if it's going to stick out too much,' he responded.

'I'll go and have a bit of a closer look at it when I've finished then,' she told him.

'You do that, love.'

She then said, 'If it is okay, then maybe you could get a bike too, eh? Then we could go out riding together now and then.'

'Jesus woman, don't you ever give up? What do you think a car's for!'

'You're just a bone idle sod!' she said loud enough for him to hear, to which he laughed at.

A slight lull in the traffic on the road allowed him to hear her zip being pulled up. Then she said to him, 'I'll only be a mo!'

'Take your time. There's no real rush right now, except for me needing to go myself!'

She made her way through some patches of very dry foot high grass towards the shining metal that lay on its side. One particular ray of sunlight was catching one end of the handlebars as it stuck up into the air, similar to a modern day totem. Likely enough, that was must have caught her eye. As she got even closer to it, she thought that it looked almost brand new. So who the hell had left it here, and why on earth had it been left here like this, she wondered? And the nearer she got the more confused she became. As it even had a pair of saddle panniers at the rear and also one over the crossbar at the front too . . . and to her mind that could only be seen as being highly unusual. Her thoughts were now turning to it having being one which had been stolen and just dumped here out of sight.

The lonely gleaming bicycle, which so far had lain untouched by either rain or frost yet, lay on a tiny rise before the earth fell away just behind it. And as she finally stood over the bike, she also caught a glimpse of something that lay barely a few feet away from it also. She screamed out his name once, and then simply just fainted beside her unexpected newly found prize. As what she had just seen, was something which she had never envisaged ever wanting to ever see. Which was that of a completely naked and lifeless woman's body. One barely twenty feet away from her and slightly lower down from her own position there.

∞

The alarm in her voice had quickly caused him to rise from his position of sitting on the kerb. And being unable to see her due to the height of the hedge behind him, he, without thought, jumped up onto the well-polished bonnet of their beloved car to look for her; as he'd already closed it again since she had left him, after having heard that it couldn't be fixed and only recovered. So from his higher vantage now, his eyes went searching over the hedge and beyond until he located her prone body lying on the short grass near to the same glinting metallic object, which he naturally assumed was the bicycle in question that she had found.

Jumping from the car, he charged around to the gap in the hedge where she had gone through earlier and plunged through the small gap like a rugby forward heading for a try. He fell a few times as his trainers caught on some of the high twisted tussocks of grass and which left him sprawling on the ground. Yet within minutes he was knelt beside her, her head resting on his own lap as he tried to work out what had happened to her.

He took a quick glance around them, as he knew her utter dislike and fear for snakes, as she could well have seen an adder or a grass snake. Though from his habit of watching innumerable nature shows on television, his memory told him that snakes didn't like the heat that much except to warm them, and would mainly try and stay in the shade somewhere. And then his eyes caught on something else away from the bike. He raised himself slightly, as he was actually kneeling and reclining on the backs of his legs at the moment. His new position raised her body a little, while it also allowed him to look down the other side of the slight knoll. So that he could also now see what she must have seen, although what was there certainly wasn't a pretty sight to see at all for him now either.

Holding the bile that was rising back in his throat, though it had left a bloody terrible taste in it from doing so, he gently picked her up and carried her back towards the lay-by. Thinking as he now carried her, over the weird fate which had brought them both to this once idyllic appearing place; and of one almost in the middle of nowhere too. Though now, it would only be a place burned within each of their own memories for as long as they both lived. As the place to remember that of a terrible event having taken place.

∞

The police, as could be expected, were already at the lay-by well before the recovery wagon for the car and passengers finally turned up. As he, on his return with his girlfriend to the car, had left her to recover behind the hedge. Since he quickly found out that he was unable to get her through the small gap properly while carrying her. So he'd left her on the grass then went back to the car to retrieve her mobile to get some help to them, since his own mobile was almost dead from earlier usage and required charging.

He was still standing in the lay-by when the first police car arrived at the scene. Watching for them, or the recovery truck with one eye, while the other he kept on her to watch if she came around from her earlier shock. But she didn't come around until just a few minutes before the recovery truck arrived and it couldn't get into the lay-by now. As there were four police cars as well as a van carrying the scenes of crime officers, or SOCO as they were known to those in the force. Who were all now awaiting the arrival of a forensic pathologist to take as many important details from where she had been left in such a way. Even before the body could be removed from the site and taken back to the mortuary.

There to be laid out in a chilled cabinet until it could be carefully checked over in possibly minute detail. But even while they waited for that person to arrive, they were already taking pictures of the surrounding area around her and of the position in which her body lay. And only when they had done that, did they then erect a tent over the body to shield it from any unwarranted viewing.

∞

The police at the scene took their names and address then helpfully aided the recovery truck to get in to the lay-by at the side of the road so as to be able to pull their car up on to its then hydraulically lowered end. But only after making sure that they were both all right after what they had seen, took statements from them, and then they were they let go. Telling them that someone from the newly soon to be opened enquiry would likely contact and then visit them at some time in the near future; or for them to get in touch with them, should they remember any further details at a later time.

So with their saying that they felt that they would be all right now, the recovery truck finally pulled away from the scene of the death. Within it, two still shaken passengers who were now seated within its rear compartment as they were taken home.

∞

Fifteen minutes after they had left, the forensic pathologist arrived to inspect the body in-situ before it was removed by the coroners department. Twelve minutes after that a Detective Inspector who had been detailed to begin the case in hand now arrived on the scene, his work, to about to try to establish and then begin what could be either be a very short - or indeed a very lengthy and very trying ordeal for their force. Until either the case was solved quickly, or had to be left open as a cold case as time steadily passed by, until they, maybe with some kind of luck, eventually made a breakthrough of some kind.

CHAPTER 2

The newest arrival who appeared on the scene was that of a six-foot, tall clean-shaven, and dark-haired man of just over forty years of age. His well-built muscular frame easily visible as he climbed out of his car, and one who already knew that not everything was ever as it might seem. In fact, he already knew by long experience of just how quickly some of the least insignificant facts at the time could turn out to be the major leads to any investigation like this. Especially if it were a murder enquiry, and one that would just about to be started. As soon as he was given some of the more relevant facts as quickly as possible from those who arrived before him, that was.

He stood waiting, patiently, his eyes giving him a slow but detailed close scrutiny around the location outside the erected tent now set over the body; after having already seen the white coveralls of the forensic team who were moving within it. Minutes ticked by as he watched the constant flashing from their camera still capturing even more information regarding the victim. He was on to his third cigarette before a white garbed figure who was already well known to him through their work, appeared through the opening of the tent structure. The clothing which was being worn by the figure, was only to prevent any possible outside contamination to any evidence.

'Ah, Dougie!' said a gentle feminine voice.

'Hi Carmen, what can you tell me about it so far?' he asked.

'Not a lot to give you at the minute, Dougie, though I can say that she was definitely strangled from the marks that are on her neck.'

'Raped and murdered?' he asked, 'or just murdered do you think?'

'It's hard to say at the moment until I can do a full autopsy on her, Dougie. But judging from some marks that can be seen upon her inner thighs and genital area, I'd think I'd have to say that too at the moment.'

'So what *can* you give me to start with?'

'She allowed a shrug. 'Murdered . . . yes, I would say so. Even to classing it as the means of death. Raped or sexually assaulted? I can't tell you that for sure until we've run the usual checks as you know. But it's more than likely *seeing* as she was found naked and she does have those marks upon her. At a rough estimate for you, *at the moment,*' she said with a long look at him. 'I would guess her age to be somewhere around eighteen to thirty, about five foot one to three in height, and of an Asian-Oriental appearance.'

'Chinese?' he queried.

'That is a possibility, or perhaps Japanese, or even something just as similar in that kind of Asian gene origin.'

'Were there any personal effects at all on her?'

She shook her head.

'What about in any of those bags, or on the bike itself?'

'The bike and everything in those three bags will have to be taken as they are in-situ back to the lab as you know, so that we can do fingerprint and DNA swabs on them as we go. Even you know just how careful most murderers are Dougie. Unless it was a crime of passion and whoever done it fled straight after they had done it. If that is the case, then we'll have a good chance of finding something on one of these items. Or if not, then I hope on her body. But, somewhere along the line, we always know that a murderer will make some kind of a slip . . . and if it was an unexpected crime of passion. And if she *was* raped, then there could even be actual traces of his semen, hair, or skin to get. Which as you already know yourself, is all that we'll need to be able to acquire some

DNA results, and those results which you may well need for your new case which has already started now for you.'

He nodded. 'And just how long do you think she's been here, Carmen?'

She studied the man before her, knowing that he was only trying to get a good head start on his investigation. But even so, getting times down to any exact kind of parameter without a good witness wasn't easy, especially when out in the field like this. In the mortuary she would have everything at hand to help her to do this, but not here. So it would have to be at most her best estimated guess.

'Two . . . possibly three days tops,' she offered. Not needing to tell him about any of the stages in a body's rigour mortis and of how decomposition followed a person's death.

He nodded at her again.

'So, I guess I'll have to get on the phone back to HQ then, eh? To get enough manpower out here in order to carry out a fingertip search of this area; just in case our suspect may have left any possible clues for us to find?'

'That might be your best bet, Dougie,' she told him. 'And from the marks around her neck, I can already tell you that the killer didn't use their hands to do it.'

'What then?'

She shrugged. 'Thin rope --- thick string --- a leather strap . . . maybe even twine, I'm just not sure at the moment? I can't be exact for you right now until I get her on to my table, get a good magnifying glass on her. And then if I'm able, to get a better idea if there any fibres or particles which have been left in the neck wound.'

'When can I have some results?'

She glanced at her watch. 'First thing tomorrow morning now,' she advised. 'Will you be there?'

He nodded. 'Sure, I can get the search organised for here tonight if I'm lucky, or very early tomorrow morning if not right now, as I don't need to actually be here while they do that. Right now I'm more concerned about who she is, where she's from, and how long she's been in this country. Unless of course she's a natural?' he said with a slow look at her.

'Dougie,' she sighed. 'I *do* know that I'm actually a *good* Forensic Pathologist, but not a Psychic. T*hat's* like asking me for an answer which even *I* can't begin to guess right now! If I could actually commune with the dead, then just *maybe* I could give you that every time. But since I can't . . . You'll just have to wait until we run some tests on her, and look through her bags.'

He gave a sad smile. 'Only if that is *her* bike and it is also *her* bags though, eh?'

'Go on smart arse - make things even more difficult for yourself then!' she cursed him.

With his hands held in a peace gesture he grinned at her. 'Hey! I'm not being awkward here, Carmen. But until you *do* actually take a look in those bags then we won't really know - will we? And for all we do know, the bike may even be that of the killers!'

'Just left it behind like that after it was done!' she chided him. 'Come on, Dougie!'

'I'm serious, Carmen. It is possible that after whoever done this to her, was so scared that they just *ran* off to get away!' He saw she was already shaking her head.

'Carmen,' he said softly, 'If this was done at some time during the day. And unexpectedly . . .' He then looked behind him and walked back up the slight slope to the lone bicycle, and pointed. 'The road is almost hidden by the hedge . . . But, the farthest lane of the road's not that hidden.'

Her intelligent brain caught on immediately. 'So that whoever done it, may have just been seen by someone passing by in a vehicle at the time?'

He nodded and said, 'Hopefully, if it was light enough, and *if* someone was actually looking this way at the right moment!'

'What if her killer was driving something, and not using this bicycle?'

'Then we may get a lead from somebody who saw a car, van, or truck parked at the lay-by within the last few days. But that might also depend on what time it might have happened too . . .'

'Because if it happened late at night ---'

'Then it's going to be a right bitch to get something to help us, Carmen. As when it's night most drivers are too busy concentrating on the winding road here since there's no lighting on it. So, unless a passenger in one of them saw something parked here, or there's a clue lying somewhere around. Then it's going to be damn hard to even get started on this enquiry.'

'I'll get you as much information as I can, and as quickly as I can too, Dougie. You can count on that from me.'

'I already knew that without having to ask you, Carmen,' he mentioned. 'As one thing that I do know about you by now, is that you're very thorough! And that may be the one thing that we have in our favour right now!'

∞

Just then, a phone began to ring. But each knew that it didn't come from either one of them . . . It was coming from one of the leather saddle panniers on the bicycle. And as they both looked at each other in that one moment, almost the same thought ran though each of their minds, that here and now, there was a possibility of accumulating some facts very quickly indeed.

'Me or you?' she asked.

'It has to be you, Carmen. You still have the gloves on don't you.'

She nodded unhappily. As even he knew that her job only ever entailed investigating dead bodies sometimes found out in the field as a precursor to the main examination, which would then take place back at the mortuary.

Squatting down on her haunches, Carmen began to open the catch of the pannier bag over the handlebars. And as soon as she lifted the flap, the ringing tone became much louder from within it. She used both hands to delve inside its darkened interior. The forearm of her left arm holding the flap away to let the light enter within it, and to where she could locate the ringing mobile telephone. Which she pulled out to then study its display for a few seconds, before her thumb depressed the tiny green telephone display button. Douglas motioned quickly for her to stand up and as she held it to her ear, he placed his own to the opposite side to hers.

'Hello?' she asked in a querying voice.

The voice that answered her was distinctly female in origin, but of a totally foreign lilting nature which she couldn't begin to understand at all at first. Whereas he could and *did* know what the voice was saying in its original Japanese form, as he could actually speak it, and fluently! But that was one of the many varied talents that he had had to keep hidden from almost everyone since joining the police force in 1986. That was only after he had left the Armed Forces due to a medical discharge, forced upon him after what could have become quite a serious injury if he had not left.

'Hello?' Carmen tried again, both their ears now keenly and quite intently listening in to the small mobile.

'Who is that?' the voice queried, and this time in the language which Carmen understood.

Douglas tapped her arm and shook his head, then quickly pulled a small card from his inside pocket, about the same as that which a businessman might carry.

'Ask whoever it is where they're calling from, and for them to call me back on this number here straight away, Carmen,' he said softly into her ear.

The pathologist gave a nod and did just that and gave his number out slowly. And then almost as if uncertain, the empty line lingered open for a close to a full minute before Carmen repeated the number once more and it went dead. She turned the phone off altogether now and replaced it back inside the bag again.

'She said she's calling from Japan, Dougie, and that she was calling her sister. So I'll let you deal with this now and I'll get the bike taken in right away. I'll also have all the contents inside the bags out for you to look at in the morning after they've been checked and tested if need be.'

'What time tomorrow do you want me to be there?' he asked.

Spirit of a Dragon

She thought over that. Knowing that she'd be at work by eight, first needing to do some earlier reports, and then having to make preparations to look at what items might need testing for fingerprints or possible DNA if any. And then she would get to work on the corpse of the young woman. To see what she could find out for the man by her side right now, so that he could then get his investigation started.

'Say nine-thirty at best, Dougie. It may be slightly earlier or later, but if it's the former then I'll call you to let you in time to get there, okay?'

He gave a jerk of his head in reply. 'I'll be there for nine-thirty on the dot then if I can, unless you ring me, Carmen.'

She nodded just as his own mobile phone began to ring, and muttered a small aside to him, 'Rather you than me, my friend!' Then she walked off back to the tent and to those who were still waiting there for her.

∞

He sat down on the grass and pulled out his notepad and pen, clicking the end of it in readiness before using the phone.

'Hello?' he asked.

'Hello? Who is this please? And why do *you* have my sister's mobile telephone?' said the voice in response.

'May I have your name please?' he asked.

'Why do you wish to know my name?'

'So that I know who I'm speaking, *too*, of course . . .'

The silence lasted a few seconds before she replied; 'My name is Hirano Kumiko, and you have my sister Akiko's telephone on your person, that is why!' stated the unhappy sounding voice.

Still hiding his own knowledge from her, he answered carefully, 'My name is Detective Inspector Douglas Hyde, Miss Kumiko, (he offered her own first name back as her surname wrongly to her, in order to keep his own talents hidden still). And I'm sorry to probably have to be the one to give you some bad news . . .'

'Has Akiko been involved in a very bad accident over there, Detective Inspector?' she asked.

He was immediately puzzled by her still very calm voice. As there was no real hint of panic, no crying, no screaming, in fact . . . not a trace of any one of those things seemed to show in her voice from what she had just heard.

'Are you sitting down at the moment, Miss Kumiko?'

'Yes, thank you,' the voice said just as calmly again. 'But my name is actually Miss Hirano . . . Inspector Hirano of the Tokyo Police.'

He wrote everything down on his pad as she spoke to him. 'As I said only a moment ago, Miss Hirano, I'm afraid that I may well be the bearer of some extremely sad news for you today.'

'And why is that?'

He coughed once just to clear his throat. 'Because I'm afraid I'm at what you would also call a murder scene right now, Miss Hirano.'

This time he did hear a gasp down the telephone.

'Are you all right, Miss Hirano? I do apologise if what I just said might have come as quite a shock to you just now.'

'Yes . . . I am quite alright thank you. It was indeed, well, it was just such an unexpected shock to hear of such a thing which could involve your own sister, Detective Inspector. But I also thank you for saying it so painlessly and as kindly as you possibly could in the circumstances. So, I must now ask you, has she been arrested for this murder, or was she the victim of it?'

'I'm afraid she is the victim, Miss Hirano. And I could but only try to give such news to someone over the telephone like this, and with you being so far away right now. Although I'm quite sure that it cannot compensate for what you have just been told by me?'

'That is true . . . I am only pleased that I am the one who is being told this first. As at least with having done similar work myself over here, on occasion, I also know just how difficult it can be to give such details to a family member.' Her pause lasted a good minute before he heard her start to speak in Japanese to someone. Which from what he heard, knew that she was telling a colleague at work about her younger sisters possible murder.

'Hello? Are you still there?' he asked quite unnecessarily, as he of course knew that she was.

'Yes, Detective Inspector, I am still here. Although even *I* am finding it hard to accept that my own youngest sister may have been murdered.'

'I know, and I'm deeply sorry to have to tell you of such a shocking and tragic event so soon.'

'Of course I understand your own problems of having to do this, and if I can help you in any way then you only need to ask . . .' she responded in what he could only think of as an immensely professional way.

'Well then Miss Hirano, or should I really call you by your professional work title of, Inspector Hirano?'

'Miss Hirano, or perhaps even by my Christian name of Kumiko will do fine if you wish to right now, Detective Inspector.'

'Very well, Kumiko, then I would be pleased to do so, but only if you will call me Douglas in return?'

'Very well Douglas, if that is your wish. So, is there any way in which I can help you?'

'Could you tell me more about your sister please Kumiko, only so that I can get as many details about her as I can to help me here?'

'Of course, and where else to start but right at the very beginning, *neh*? My sister Akiko has been studying both English and Computers, which I think is what is actually called Information Technology. At your Newcastle University in England over the past two years within her two three-year courses.

'She is, she was, is, I'm sorry, as it's still a little difficult for me at the moment to even think of her as being deceased.' He heard a deep sigh then she continued again, 'My sister was only twenty-two, Douglas. Her twenty-third birthday would have been on November the thirteenth of this year. By which time she would have finished her studies there, and then have returned back here to us all at home once more.'

'I'm sorry,' he said.

'It is not for you to be sorry, Douglas. You are not the one to have killed her, so you have nothing to be sorry for. Only the person who did this to her should be feeling some sorrow or remorse for what he, or she, has done to her, and to have now caused such grief to come to her family.'

'I know, but even to me, it still seems sad for such a young life as hers to have been lost at such an age.'

'I thank you for your concern and kindness to me and for my family also, Douglas. But can I ask you what happened to her? I mean how she came to die, and just where this may have happened?'

'I can't tell you much at all yet, Kumiko. As we have only been at the scene itself for about an hour at most. And at the minute, apart from your telephone call that came when it did; it will also probably work just like your own police force over in Japan follow the same procedure, too. So right now our forensic people are in charge of the scene at this present time. When you rang up, I had just come to stand beside a bicycle to have a talk with the on duty forensic pathologist here. Over what facts she had managed to ascertain so far, and could hope to give me up to now, just so that I could begin to get my investigation underway.'

'I see. So there is nothing very much which you can actually tell me so far then, *neh*?'

'Only one thing, Kumiko, but at the moment it is only a rough evaluation by Carmen about how she was killed.'

'Carmen?'

'She was the woman that you talked to first on your sister's mobile, Kumiko. She is the forensic pathologist who was on duty when the call came in to our headquarters a short while ago. When the mobile rang, and as she was still wearing her gloves, she answered the ringing phone.'

'I see, thank you Douglas. And does she know if my sister was only murdered yet? Or, I do not even wish to think of this really . . . But I must ask you. Which is, does she think that my sister may perhaps have been raped as well, even if her death was more than enough right now?'

'Kumiko, only because you are in the police as I am, will I even tell you this. Which is that all I can say at the moment to you is this, that it *appears* as if she was strangled - and that it may also be *possible* that she could have been raped too.'

'Why, Douglas?'

'Only because her body was naked when found, Kumiko.' Then he added quickly, 'Which actually does not mean to say that she was . . .'

'Why?'

'Because her killer may just have removed anything from her body that could have left some traces of their own skin, hair, or any other kind of DNA samples for us to find a clue about her attacker.'

He heard her elicit another low sigh. 'I thank you for your . . . Yes, I do indeed thank you for your honesty and candour with me, Douglas. May I give you my own personal telephone number now so that if you wish to, or need to speak with me again about any matter, then you can quite easily do so?'

'Only if you yourself don't mind offering such a valuable aid to me Kumiko, then of course I would be happy to have it?'

'Not at all, Douglas, and if you feel that I may be able to help you further with *anything* you may have need to know, then you only have to call me . . . But now, well, I will sadly have to call my family and pass on this so very sad and terrible news to them too.'

'Of course, I understand, and would you also please pass on all of our own deepest condolences to the rest of your family, too?'

'Most certainly, Douglas, and I thank you from my family and myself for your own compassion throughout this terrible ordeal.'

'If I can be of any help in any further way for you, you only have to call me as well, Kumiko.'

'And I for you also, Douglas, so for now I will say thank you and goodbye for the moment.'

The line went dead . . .

CHAPTER 3

His mobile, placed as usual upon on the bedside table, suddenly began to ring over and over again incessantly. And being awakened from what was a brief sleep of barely three hours at most. Douglas was not really a very happy person. Forgetting of course, that it was his own fault for not turning it off before he'd went to sleep in the first place. Especially after he'd made himself something to eat, and then had a shower before turning in for the night when he'd finally returned to his home at around eleven that night.

He reached out a hand for the offending instrument with his eyes still closed and upon finding it brought it over to his face. His mouth opening to say hello coincided with a yawn at the same time, which caused it come out something more like, "Heh-ho!"

'Douglas?'

'Yes, who is it?' he asked, and yawned again, very loudly.

'It is just I, Kumiko.'

'Oh, well hi there, Kumiko.'

'You sound sleepy? I did not wake you up did I?' He then heard her give out one of her loud gasps. 'Oh! Please forgive me Douglas, I forgot all about the time difference between us!'

'What time is it?' he asked her stupidly.

'I apologise to you again, Douglas. But what time is it there now?'

He cracked an eyelid open to read the face of the digital clock on the table. 'Three!' he said while also scratching at his hairy chest.

'And what time did you go to bed?'

'It doesn't matter now, Kumiko. My fault, I should have remembered to just turn the damn thing off first!'

'Please . . .?' she asked him quietly.

'Around midnight-ish after having a bite to eat and a shower first,' he answered.

'Three hours or less, for that I apologise very much for having woken you up from your brief sleep, Douglas. I will however promise to call you back at a much more sensible time next time!' she said to him, and then she hung up just as he was about to reply.

'Bollocks!' he grunted loudly. Then by feel he turned his phone off correctly this time. Trying twice before finally managing to get it back onto the bedside table with his eyes still closed. He was already well asleep again within five minutes.

∞

When the alarm of his clock went off at seven, his eyes opened instantly and he was fully awake and completely alert. He was thankful for his old military training for that. As quite often while out in the field, he might have only managed to grab a few hours of power nap time daily. So it was not an uncommon event for him to do even now, something that had already helped him out enormously over his many years in the police force. By allowing him to get by on very little sleep at all whenever he may have needed to, while still leaving him fit to do whatever was necessary straight away.

He slid out of the bed and walked toward the shower quite naked. Not bothered at all about his state of undress, since he was single and lived alone. He was not really that bothered anyway, especially not after what his earlier life had entailed for so many years.

His shower over, he dressed his lower half in the clothing he'd laid out ready to wear last night, including his socks and shoes. Picked his shirt, ring, and mobile up and then went downstairs with a towel around his neck while fastening his watch around his wrist.

Switching on the electric kettle on the counter to boil, after first lifting it into the air just to make sure that there was enough water left within in it for his morning cuppa. He then lit the gas on the stove and also the grill with the handily placed lighter, and then went over to the fridge for the eggs, bacon and sausage for his breakfast.

He'd never been a cereal or vegetarian man at any time in his life. And whenever he wanted a meal – he'd wanted something far more substantial inside his body to keep him ticking over. As for one thing, he just never knew when he'd manage to eat again until he got home to make a proper meal. So some days he packed himself with carbohydrates, and other days he enjoyed a full breakfast. And with being quite a good cook, well to his own personal tastes anyway, if not a very spectacular one, he knew just what proteins and minerals most meals would all offer to his body.

So while the kettle was boiling, the eggs were cooking in a pan and his bacon and sausage was being cooked under the grill. He began to towel off his very short-cropped dark hair; hair which appeared like that of simple fuzz right now, especially after its latest harsh self-cutting off it, and quickly dried it off in the mirror on the wall in the hallway just off the kitchen.

Still as pleased as always to see his same hard, and flat stomach and its accompanying six-pack reflected back at him in the mirror, just through the mass of black hairs there. He threw the towel on to the back of the nearest chair in the kitchen for a moment, and posed in front of the long mirror. Almost in the same way like that a bodybuilder would have done. Seeing his muscles writhing and rippling underneath the skin of his chest, stomach, and arms as he twisted and turned while posing. Even to the detailed muscle development upon his shoulders and back which were quite pronounced too.

'Huh!' he grunted at his image in the mirror, 'still not that bad at all for a forty-two-year-old really, even if I do say so myself!' he said while grinning back at his own reflection.

Spirit of a Dragon

Then, with his hair simply rubbed into some semblance of apparent disorderly order only by using his fingers; He returned to the stove to turn over his sausages and bacon under the grill and nudged the two eggs in the pan slightly, before he pulled his shirt on and buttoned it up. Not once making the effort to tuck it in yet while preparing to have his breakfast. A daily thing for him, as he knew that by the time he'd eaten and stood up again he would need to redo it before leaving for work.

Taking a plate from a shelf and cutlery from the drawer, he placed them on the counter right beside the stove. A glance at his wristwatch showed that it was only seven-thirty, so he still had plenty of time in hand yet. Another check on his breakfast, and he slid the eggs from the non-stick pan out onto his plate without the aid of the spatula, then pulled the grill pan out from underneath and deposited them on to the plate also. He turned both gasses off and carried his plate over to the table. Lastly, after making some tea to drink with it, he finally sat down and began to eat and drink.

He wasn't a perfectionist or neatness addict by any sense, but still hated to leave anything he'd used just lying around. So he quickly washed whatever items he'd worked with, wiped any grease from off the hob caused by frying his eggs, and then cleaned off the residue in the two pans before tucking his shirt tidily into his trousers.

He turned his phone back on and then put his grey leather jacket on. Which didn't exactly go with his black casual trousers at all, but he knew that *that* was the one of the benefits of being a DI now. No more uniform wearing, except for the very rare and strict code at formal occasions that might come up now and again. And within what he hoped was only another year or two, his promotion to Chief Inspector would maybe appear. It was what he'd counted on when choosing to make the police force his next career instead of that of becoming either a bodyguard or some kind of mercenary.

∞

He took his time driving in to headquarters since he, as usual, had left himself with a good fifteen minutes or so as an extra window in case of any unavoidable problems.

Looking at the clock on the dashboard he knew he would be there in ten minutes or so now, depending upon the traffic. Not one minute of his allotted extra time being needed so far. Then his mobile rang.

'Hello?' he answered while driving with one hand following the traffic at a steady thirty miles per hour.

'Douglas? It this a more opportune time to talk to you now?'

'Kumiko?' he responded.

'Yes, it is I once again. What are you doing now, eating your breakfast or are you at work?' she asked.

'I'm on driving in to work now to get things started on the case.'

'So you will not have anything further to tell me yet then, *neh*?'

'No, I'm afraid I've nothing more for you at present. I'm just going in to work to get a search of the area started from yesterday. And after I've done that, I'll be going over to the mortuary to find out if Carmen has any news for me.' Then he said to her, 'And where are *you* Kumiko, at work?'

'No, Douglas. At the moment I am on a plane with my Father even as we speak, and we are flying on our way over there.'

'Why?'

'Why . . .? Because she was my own sister and my Father's daughter of course Douglas. And as such we could not allow her remains to fly home quite alone, could we?'

'I wish you'd told me you were coming, Kumiko. As I would have told you that it could be at least a few days yet. Or perhaps even more before she will be released for you to even be able to do that yet.'

'Oh!'

'I know, and I'm sorry to have to tell you that, but it may take even longer than that what with it being a murder investigation.'

'That is quite all right, Douglas. It is our own fault for being in such a hurry to get there to be beside her that's all.'

'Have you made reservations to stay in a hotel anywhere? What I meant to say was; do you know where you will be going to when you do finally get here? As if you tell me which internal flight you'll be coming up from London on, then I'll drive over to meet you at Newcastle Airport for when you land here.'

'London?' she queried, 'Douglas, we'll be landing at Newcastle.'

'But that's impossible! Our airport doesn't have any scheduled straight run flights from there to Japan, or the reverse, as far as I know!'

'But we are not on any scheduled flight, Douglas.'

'You're not?'

'No. We're using the company jet to get there.'

'Ahhh, now I can see what you mean, the people who own the business where your Father works has allowed you both to use it to do this because of the usual difficulty, eh?'

'Oh no, Douglas, my Father is the president and owner of Hirano Electronics - so of course we are using his own company plane.'

'Douglas?' she queried into the long silence.

'I'm still here,' he said. 'I was just surprised to hear that your Father actually owned a company and had his own plane. But I thought you said that you were an Inspector with the Tokyo Police, Kumiko?'

'I am, Douglas.'

Almost giving his hidden knowledge away, he mentioned, 'But I thought that Japanese children usually followed their Father *into* their own family businesses if there was one?'

'I guess in many cases that that is usually true, and also very astute of you to know that too, Douglas. But as my parents had seven children, it can be typical that not all of them were expected to do so. My two eldest brother's work for the company, just as my two younger sisters do also, While my youngest brother is a bit like you, and is a Detective in Tokyo. Whereas Akiko was going to join the company after her studies had ended.'

'I apologize to you, Kumiko.'

'Why, when there is nothing to apologize for, Douglas.'

'For asking questions that I don't really need to know about.'

'A typical police officers thinking, Douglas, to get as many facts as you can about someone more than likely.'

'Maybe, but it doesn't really have anything to do with the case does it? I mean it just sounds as if I was prying.

'I am not offended, Douglas.'

'Thank you, Kumiko.'

'You are welcome, Douglas.'

'Anyway, as I was saying earlier. Have you already made reservations at a hotel for when you arrive here?'

'Oh, no, we will just take one of your taxis to a good hotel nearby and book in to it and then just wait there to hear from you.'

'If you wanted you could stay with me at my place?' he said before he'd even thought about it.

'Certainly not, Douglas, as something like *that* would be too much of an imposition. As well as possibly also being an inconvenience and burden for us to place upon you to do that. It could even be seen as an invasion of your home privacy . . .'

'Not really, Kumiko. My own place has three bedrooms and can accommodate you both if you wish while you're here. Call it professional courtesy from one police officer to another at such a time if you wish. The only thing that it will cost you is for any different foods that you both may want to eat. As long as one of you are able to cook the kind of food that you are used to that is? As I don't think my own culinary skills could offer either of you what you might want.'

'That is a very kind offer from you, Douglas. Indeed it really is *very* kind of you to have offered something like that to us both. If you will wait just a moment I will ask my Father what he thinks.'

The seconds began to tick by as he waited, and once he even had to steer the car with his knee for a few seconds as he changed down a gear due to the traffic ahead of him slowing down. But he had already safely changed back into fourth gear again before she came back on the phone.

Spirit of a Dragon

'My father gives his thanks to you for your very generous offer to us, and said that he would feel honoured to accept your personal hospitality. If even only for a short while. And as far as cooking goes please do not worry. I can cook whatever we need to eat with your permission, and of course we would never hinder you by asking you to provide food for us while we are there. We will shop somewhere to find what we need.'

'That's great, Kumiko. Now I know that we do have some stores or supermarkets that sell a few types of Japanese ingredients and food. So when I get into work I'll ask around to see what I can find out for you.'

'Oh, please do not worry yourself about us like that, Douglas. We will just ask someone at the airport where we can get such food.'

'I don't think that they'll know, Kumiko.'

'Then one of your kind taxi drivers will be probably be able to take us to a shop there.'

'I don't think that will work either, Kumiko. It's probably just not something that a taxi driver would know. If we had an actual Japanese restaurant now, then he'd probably be okay. But just for shops that sell what you'll want to buy is another matter. As I said, just leave it with me and I'll see what I can find out before you arrive.'

'Very well, Douglas. But I think that we are *already* becoming that stated burden to you, is that not so?'

'No. I made you the offer in good faith, Kumiko. So I'll do some more detective work before you get here to find out where you can get some of your own kinds of food supplies.'

'All right, if that is your wish.'

'Good, that's settled then! Now then, how long before you get to the airport?'

He had to wait again while she went to talk with someone, and when she returned said, 'The pilot told me that we should be there in a little under four hours now, depending on things such as headwinds or tailwinds he said.'

'Right, well if you'll give me a call when you're only about an hour out from the airport. I'll head over there and pick you both up.'

'You are being much too kind to us, Douglas.'

'Think nothing of it, Kumiko. As I said earlier, one of your own people would probably have done exactly the same if the events had happened the other way around.'

'That is quite possible, Douglas, though in all honesty I would not be able to swear to it.'

'It doesn't matter now. I have already offered and it has been accepted, so I'll just wait for your call and then meet you at the airport, okay?'

'Very well,' she said and gave one of her sighs.

They both hung up.

∞

On his arrival at headquarters he asked to see the Chief Constable, the man personally in charge of this area; and gave him what information he could about the murder so far and what resources he might need later to get his enquiry off the ground. Not forgetting to tell him about the murdered girl's Father and sister arriving within a few hours, and more importantly, that her arriving sister was an actual inspector within the Tokyo police force.

The Chief Constable listened as he spoke, taking in the man seated across from him, and one who he had helped promote upwards from an ordinary constable over the eleven years of his fourteen years of service that he had personally known him himself. Not done so through any favouritism either. As it was only by his dedication, sheer hard work, and the effort which he had put into it that had allowed his rise within the force to became possible. And now, as he sat opposite listening to what he was being told, he was still able to recall almost without much thought the background of this one particular individual under his command. One who had come into the force after his initial, but probably very tame kind of training to what he'd been used to. Down at their Hendon training unit, where every new rookie copper would need to be sent for evaluation before being passed out and being judged fit to go out on their usual beats, although under some supervision at first.

Spirit of a Dragon

As a training establishment it was already very well known to other police forces throughout the world, and as one of the best, if not *the* best in the world, for training up and coming law enforcement officers. Which was often why they occasionally also received cadets from many other countries to be taught. Even to some of their top brass coming over just to see how it was being ran, in the hopes of being able to get something similar up and running in their own countries at some point in time.

He smiled to himself as he listened and thought over the report filed on this man. As during his unarmed training session he had flattened three of their own instructors at the time, but couldn't tell them why he could. Apart from fabricating a story and stating that he'd done some martial arts many years ago. It was really all down to the Governments Official Secrets Act, to that which only a very select few were entitled to know about his past; and just *what* a past record it had been he mused!

'So what do they know about you so far, DI Hyde?' he now asked, giving input into the mainly one-sided conversation.

'Only that I'm the Detective Inspector who is on handling the case, sir.'

'And you've actually offered your own home for them to use while they're here?'

He nodded. 'I thought it would be good, sir. As a bit of professional courtesy between us as we say, what with Miss Hirano actually being an Inspector herself.'

The Chief Constable nodded. 'The first thing I'm going to do is check up on that fact, Hyde. Just to be sure that she is telling the truth.'

'Yes sir, though she also said that her youngest brother is also an officer in the same force, but he is a detective.'

'I'll check up on *him* as well while I'm on with it.'

'Very good, sir, what about the resources I might need to proceed with this case?'

The chief nodded. 'After what you called in last night before going off-duty, I left a two-man marked car over there last night. And this morning I dispatched twenty officers to do your requested fingertip search of the area.'

'I only asked for that in case the item the killer used to strangle her. Or anything else which may help us had just been thrown away nearby afterwards, sir.'

'A good point, though it must be said that there *is* a lot of ground out there for our limited resources to try and cover Hyde. And even you know that we can't search it all. Especially if the murderer dropped it a few thousand yards away, possibly even miles away. As if he or she drove away from the scene then there'll be nothing left for us *to* find out there. Will there?'

'I am hoping that we may discover a few things, sir.'

'Like what exactly?'

'Like what happened to any of the clothing she was wearing at the time of the attack, sir? Did the murderer actually take them away with him or her whenever they left the scene? Or were they just stashed somewhere nearby in the hope that the body, and everything else would never actually be spotted back there due to being where it was!'

The chief nodded again. He was quite astute, he thought.

'All right, Hyde. You get started on you invest---'

'Excuse me, sir,' said Douglas as his mobile rang. 'Hello? Right, I'll be there in about ten minutes Dr Stone,' he answered and hung up. 'Sorry, sir, that was Dr Stone. She was just calling me to tell me that she would be starting the post-mortem examination of the same woman shortly. And I asked her to call me so that I could be in attendance to get all the possible related facts for the case straight away as it happened.'

'All right then, Hyde. Go over and do that, and then ask her to send me a brief report of her findings until I get far more detailed ones from you both later on. I'll also have you notified if anything which may seem important comes up at the crime scene. And, since you have decided to take responsibility for our two guests who will be arriving over here soon; *and* seeing as you are going to lodge them at your own expense. If you keep any of the receipts from their stay regarding food bills and such like, then we will recompense you for those costs incurred.'

'Well, thank you very much, sir.'

The chief grinned at him. 'Don't mention it, Hyde. Just think of it as -

as a professional courtesy being extended by us to them, eh?' His grin was wider. 'We can't allow young Detective's like you to make offers like that off your own bat, now can we? As it wouldn't look good for the force if we didn't share some of the courtesy involved in doing so.'

'Very well, sir.' He smiled back. 'If you don't need me anymore right now, then I'll be on my way over to the mortuary?'

He shook his head. 'No, Hyde. Things are starting to move on the investigation now, and it's a beginning anyway. Now though, we can only hope for some kind of a quick breakthrough in any area that deals with it!'

He left the chief's office and returned to his car and drove over to the mortuary where Carmen was patiently awaiting his presence.

∞

At the mortuary itself, and in the coldness of the examination room with the eight shining metal tables appearing so clean and clinically sterile to the eye. Not counting all of the handy metallic trays filled with a vast but differing array of surgical tools and instruments along with the bottles and tubes and scales still awaiting use. The one not so nice feature there of course, was that of the small naked figure of the young Japanese woman who had just been wheeled in and now lay face up on the table and was being examined.

Here and there as she spoke into the microphone while she worked, Carmen Stone, the Forensic Pathologist, either asked for a photograph of some aspect of the still body. Or placed a ruler beside some mark for a detailed measurement to be taken and then photographed.

Douglas stared down at the naked figure laid on the table, and as usual began to think over what made someone *want* to kill someone else like that, without any regard or thought. She had been a *very* pretty young woman, he knew an only by what features he could still see clearly, and maybe that was the reason behind it. As Carmen's own low clinical voice kept up a constant flow of information for the microphone as she worked.

The colour of her eyes, her hair colour, height and weight, skin tone and nationality, no information was omitted before the more detailed internal examination would begin. So he watched almost with a sense of now being a part of the examination itself as she continued her work on the inert form.

He watched as she took both blood and urine samples, and then swabbed within and around her genital area and inner thighs also before placing those into various sealed tubes as well. All of these things would soon be inside the lab being stringently checked for any unusual characteristics. A few pubic hairs and a few hairs from her head with their roots still attached also went into separate tubes for yet further tests.

He then watched as Carmen went over the inert body with the aid of a large pedestal mounted and articulated magnifying glass next. Checking over the most expected areas of skin where any signs of drug abuse would show up. But when that failed to give her anything, she began to look over other more unexpected places on her body where it could have been done. But still there was nothing to find.

She turned to him after switching the recording microphone off for a moment. 'So far it just looks like an everyday strangulation to me, Dougie. As up to now, there have been no signs of any needles being used on her, either for her own use, or by the person who killed her.'

'Any sign of anything under her fingernails?'

'Like if she'd scratched someone you mean while attempting to fight them off?'

He nodded.

She shook her head. 'Her body, apart from mark around her neck at the moment, and a few marks between her inner thighs, doesn't appear to have any retained bruising on it at all. Meaning that she may well have been either unconscious when she was killed, or drugged somehow, or, perhaps just too weak to fight off someone. But there's no trace of any needle holes on this side of her body and all of her fingernails were remarkably well manicured and clean except for two on one hand.'

'And?' he asked hopefully.

She shook her head again at him. 'So far it just looks like dirt from where she was lying at the time. But as I spotted those were dirty on site, I brought a sample of the earth beside her back with me to test against it. To see if she was killed there, or killed elsewhere and her body was actually left where it was found. As her hand could have clenched in a muscular spasm during it, and they may just match what is there? It is even possible that as rigour began to set in, her nails may have scraped into the earth also . . .'

'So it's still possible that any marks, or bruising, or puncture marks may be on her other side and still unexamined as yet?'

'It's possible, Dougie. But if there *are* any puncture holes on that side, then you can be sure that she didn't do it to herself!'

'So we'll just have to wait and see, eh?'

'I'm afraid so.' She looked up at him. 'Did you get much information from her sister yesterday when she called you back?'

'Only some trivial at the moment, you know, her age, name, what she was doing here and why, etc.'

'Well how old *was* she? I've only got her down as between eighteen and thirty right now which is a bit skimpy even for my own records, Dougie! And you likely know what I mean with her being Oriental, eh?'

'She was twenty-two, Carmen. Though what did you mean by that comment?'

'Dougie, have you ever looked closely at an Asian or Oriental woman and *tried* to guess their ages! Unless her face is lined with wrinkles to show her old age, most of the time they can be taken for as much as twenty years younger than they really are.'

'Yeah, I guess that much can be true.'

'Damn right! Now what other details do you have?'

'Her name was Akiko Hirano, spelled, A-k-i-k o H-i-r-a-n-o, and she was a student in her final year at Newcastle University.'

'What damn bad luck!' she cursed aloud herself, even as she wrote down the information that he was now passing on to her.

'You're right about that, Carmen. When she'd completed her courses in Information Technology and English here this year, she was going home to Japan to join her Father's company before her birthday on November 13th.'

'As I said, Dougie, damn bad luck - Or maybe it was the old saying again, huh? That she was just in the wrong place at the right time?'

'Likely enough, Carmen, but when I get a chance to speak with her sister shortly when they arrive I'm going to try to find out exactly what she was doing riding so far away from where she was living?'

'So you've already deduced that it was *her* bike that was found on the grass then?'

'I'm only assuming as much as it was her mobile that was ringing in the leather bag on the handlebars.'

'Do you know when anyone last spoke to her yet?'

'Nope, though I'll ask her sister if she can remember what time and what day any of her family last talked with her. But Carmen, when you do check over her phone, just take a look in the calls received section in its memory for me and write any of those numbers down for me would you?'

'Sure, but why?'

'A little bit of selective reasoning, my dear Watson.' He grinned at her.

'You sod! Come on Sherlock, spill it then!'

'Isn't it obvious?'

'Not at the moment Dougie my lad, and just remember if you will that I'm carrying out Path work here right now . . . So just tell me so that I don't have to rack my brains for the answer – or beat it out of you!' she stated.

'Okay then, Watson.' He grinned again at her unhappy expression. 'For one thing the memory in it should hold any numbers of calls that she'd missed, yes?'

She nodded. 'I guess so!'

'So that would also possibly help you to maybe base your time of her death on, yes?'

'Ye—es?' she said a little guardedly.

'Of course it does! Whatever calls she missed within the past few days will help you to narrow her time of death down even more. And then with the other numbers I may be able to find out who her friends were over here that even her family may not have known about.'

'Ah-ha . . . but, you may have forgotten just one thing, Sherlock!'

'Which is?'

'I didn't want to say it - but I thought I'd better mention it to you just in case it may have happened.'

'What?'

'The person who killed her, Dougie, there's also a slight chance that if their number was on that memory then they may have already erased the log held on her phone altogether.'

'It wouldn't help them, Carmen.'

'And why not, may I ask?'

'Because I'll just ask her service provider for a list of any calls she made or has received over the past days, month, or such.'

'You can actually do that now?' she asked startled.

'In the event of a murder investigation, Carmen, it's quite easy to get a court order if necessary, or even just a warrant to get that data. Which I'll probably set in motion anyway when I get back to the office, as really, it doesn't pay to overlook *any* means of information gathering, does it? As her killer might even have been a man who didn't like getting the brush off from her afterwards.'

You certainly have a suspicious mind, Detective Inspector Hyde,' she said in mock awe.

'That goes with the job, Watson. Steady now, or you'll make me big-headed!'

'Hell, it's too late for that already!' she announced smugly.

'Cheeky bugger!' he responded, then got back to the task in hand. 'When will your lab people know if there's been any other foul play on

35

her?'

She gave a slow shrug. 'As soon as it's possible, Dougie, you know as well as I do that any murder case immediately gets top priority over everything else to get the results to you fast.'

'Which actually means in plain English?'

'We might have something later today for you, or tomorrow latest, Dougie. It takes *time* to run a full analysis over everything that we have to check you know!'

'I know, dear heart, that you will all do your best like you always do for us. It's just a bitch having to wait to get a first piece of evidence for something or other so that I can get things rolling!'

She rhymed her usual response to every detective who was in such a hurry like this. 'Time saved is time gained, Dougie. And you already know, that if we do try to hurry too quickly, a simple mistake could be made and then, poof! All those hours of hard work all go down the toilet!' She then turned to her assistants. 'Turn her over please boys.'

Then a low whistle left her pursed lips as she looked down on the reverse side of the young woman. 'Quite beautiful isn't it!' she said to Dougie as even he leaned closer to look at what they could now see.

'It's bloody fine work, too!' he added.

Carmen went over the new finding with her magnifying class slowly. 'It's goddamn *very* fine work I'd say, and some parts of it are so highly detailed and very intricate looking too, Dougie. It must have cost her a fortune for something this good to look at – not to mention how long it must have taken to have done, too!' she expounded.

'You and your oh so silvery tongue, sweet thing.'

'Ah, bollocks to you!' she cursed him.

He looked at the three smiling male assistants who were all awaiting the next command from her mouth. 'That such a mouth would spout such sweet nectar!' he said.

The three men gave a low chuckle at his words. As they knew Carmen better than most with working with her nearly every day, and a sweet mouth certainly wasn't one of her main characteristics. Vulgar and coarse perhaps, but since she did her work extremely well, and in any topical talk, be it sport, general knowledge or whatever. They knew that she could definitely hold her own when it came to the extreme sport of profane cursing. One day making even a female Chief Inspector blush, from using some of the far more choice words at her command. But that was Carmen, you just had to take her or leave her as she was - And most people liked the way she was. Since it was her own way of blowing off some steam from the tasks she had to carry out almost every day.'

'Get a few good close up pictures of her tattoo, Carl,' she told the one with the camera, 'and then take two final ones showing the entire thing across her back just so that it shows exactly how big it is in comparison to her body too.' Then she moved the remaining strands of shiny long black hair away from her back and neck for him.

'Right you are, Carmen,' he replied and began to do that while she moved up and down the body with her glass looking for any tiny puncture wounds again.

Finally she rose up and stretched her back. 'Nothing . . . and I've even looked under her finger and toenails just to be on the safe side, Dougie.'

'Any chance of it being injected in her face or head, as it would be hard to see amongst all the hair roots.'

'Just a bloody blazing ray of sunshine you aren't you!' she grunted.

'I'm only asking.'

'I'll do that after I've done some other work, Dougie. But all that I *can* safely tell you for the moment until any of the lab work comes out. Is that she was definitely strangled by *something*. So, if you'll now just go and get stuffed, and pop-off and do whatever it is that you're supposed to be doing, and what you're expected to do. You can then leave us poor devils to be getting on with our own work, eh?'

He grinned at her and took the hint given. Returning to the side room he replaced the green overalls and hair covering and rubber boots and lastly threw the mask into the bin. Replaced his own shoes back on again and his jacket, then left the mortuary.

The hour from landing at the airport call was received by him just as he climbed into and started his car. And after he had replied to her call, he cursed quietly after he'd hung up, as of course he'd forgotten to ask if anyone knew where they would be able to buy any typical Japanese food items locally. He drove back to headquarters quickly to find out what he could in what was now left of the allotted time being he had to meet them.

CHAPTER 4

He arrived at the airport with only ten minutes to spare before their small jet passenger plane was on its landing cycle. And after speaking with the airport duty manager and its customs and immigration managers, was allowed to drive his car right up to the plane after it taxied and came to a halt slightly away from the runway on a side parking apron.

As through his talk and then additional backing of the Chief when he had then asked for permission, in order to offer such an unusual procedure. As it was normally only heads of state and very high ranking VIP's who were allowed such extraordinary measures to do so.

But, as the Chief Constable had informed them at the airport, the man arriving on the plane was not only the president of a very large corporation in Japan himself. They were also members of the family who had flown here to be able to recover his own daughter's murdered body after their investigations had begun; and he added, they hoped that she could be released for them to take her home with them with the smallest inconvenience possible.

And so, with the Chief's backing, most of the formal procedures had been waived or actually bypassed for them. So much so, that there was even a customs and immigration officer on hand waiting for them when they disembarked from the aircraft. To do what was necessary right there and then, simply so as to allow them to get on their way with the minimum of fuss and red tape being required upon their initial entry into the country.

And with the usual required formalities quickly seen to, Hyde introduced himself to her father and then to the woman who could only have been Kumiko.

'Welcome to England, Mr Hirano, Kumiko. I am only sorry that it had to be in such deeply saddening circumstances as these now are.'

'Thank you, Mr Hyde,' said the slightly greying man, quickly grasping hold of his outstretched hand, as did the woman when she was greeted by him afterwards.

'If you're both not too tired right from your flight over right now. I thought that I would suggest that we go shopping for what food you may require first of all. Before I will then take you to my home where you can relax as much as you may need to after that?'

They looked at each other and her father nodded to her. 'That would be quite acceptable Douglas, thank you. But are you still entirely certain that our presence within your home would not be far too much trouble caused to you? As we can quite easily stay in a hotel if that would be so?' she asked in her precise English.

'No trouble whatsoever, Kumiko. I've even been advised by my boss to tell you that any food or other items which you may need or require, I will buy for you and I will then be reimbursed by our office.'

'That would be *much* too generous of your police force, Mr Hyde. Especially when we can very well afford to pay for those things ourselves,' said her father.

He shook his head. 'As I agreed that you could stay with me at my own house, the Chief told me himself, that in this case they would pick up the bill for your food, as a matter of courtesy from one police force to another.'

'That is very kind of your Chief also then, Douglas,' said Kumiko, as she watched him placing their now re-closed cases of luggage into the boot of his car. After customs had quickly vetted some of them. And with their passports attended to and stamped by the immigration officer also at hand. The two men left after seeing to the pilot, co-pilot, and the one extremely attractive stewardess at the bottom of the stairs of the plane.

Spirit of a Dragon

Hyde gave a nod past Kumiko towards them. 'Where are they staying while you're here? Do you want me to find other places to put them up as well while you're all here?'

Her father said, 'No that is quite all right, Mr Hyde. My office, after you spoke with my daughter on the telephone earlier, called and booked them all into the nearest hotel that was as close as possible to this airport. So that when we are, in all sense, finally ready to leave, then they will have ample time to get here before we do. And so they can begin to get things moving in readiness for our departure.'

Closing the boot, he asked them both to climb into the car and they would leave. Her father went into the back, while Kumiko decided to take the passenger seat next to him in front. Finding the electric window control, her father called out to those at the stairs. But without showing it, Hyde listened as he said to them in Japanese, "*I will be in contact you as soon as I know what is happening here, or when we will be leaving for home again.*" and watched as the three of them all bowed low to him.

'Do you need to speak with them any further, or is it all right for us to leave now, Mr Hirano?' he asked her father by turning his head slightly.

'I have given them their instructions, so we can leave whenever you are ready, Mr Hyde,' her father informed him.

As they drove off Kumiko said to him, 'Is this your own car or a police car, Douglas?'

'It's a police car Kumiko, though just an ordinary looking one so that I can go around on my work unnoticed. Although it does carry the usual lights and siren on it, but these are hidden away and only used when it could become necessary. As I leave my own car at headquarters every morning and pick one of these up for my work duties.'

He was also was pleased that he'd driven the same car for almost two months now. As he looked after the inside of it just like he did his home, it was neat and tidy inside. Unlike many he had seen where the back seats and sometimes even the front passenger seats ended up being littered with all sorts of things. Making them sometimes appear more like a refuse vehicle than an unmarked police car on duty.

At the shops where he'd been told they would find what foodstuffs they may need to buy. He paid for their purchases with his credit card,

41

keeping the receipt for means of recouping his money later, and then the three of them lugged the carrier bags back to the car which almost filled the boot. As like any normal police car it also had to carry all the emergency and safety devices which may be required at any time. More or less like any normal patrol car would have to do too.

∞

At his house he parked just in front of the closed garage door and turned the engine off, pulled the lever inside the car beside the driving seat to open the boot and then climbed out, his two guests copied his own motions. He gestured for them to follow him to the front door and after opening it, pointed to the beeping alarm on the wall.

'The code to switch this alarm on or off is 1-4-0-5-5-8,' he told them. 'Which is my date of birth if you're wondering? And I'm giving you the code in case you ever want to go out somewhere if I'm not here at the time. I'll also give you a spare key for the house, and write down a few taxi numbers and this address for you as well. So that if either one of you, or both of you decide to go out somewhere, then one of them will be able to bring you back here.'

'You are being very open with us, Mr Hyde. Especially to tell us what your private security code is!'

He grinned back at them after feeding the same six digits into the box and the beeping stopped. 'You only have twenty seconds to turn it off after opening the front or back door. And I'm quite sure that you are both trustworthy enough to have my code . . . I mean, after all, Kumiko *is* also a Police Inspector!'

She smiled back at him. 'We thank you for saying that you trust us, Douglas. But really, not many people would offer something like that to two total strangers as we are I would think?'

He shrugged. 'As I said, I'd rather that if you did go out you put the alarm on for me, rather than leaving it only locked-up and unprotected. So I can do nothing *but* to give you my code for it, yes?'

'Your reasoning for that is quite agreeable of course, Douglas.'

'Well seeing as you're in now, you might as well go right in and have a look around while I bring in your luggage and supplies.'

Her father shook his head. 'We will *both* help you to bring everything inside, Mr Hyde. And then *you* can personally show us around your home - so that if something is here which perhaps you do not want us to see, then we will know of it from you.'

He grinned again. 'Probably only my dirty washing is something you wouldn't like to see!' he told them with a laugh.

With their shopping taken into the kitchen and their cases brought inside and left in the small passageway leading to both the upstairs and downstairs. After then putting what groceries had been procured into either the fridge or freezer as may have been required. He then set the kettle away to boil while showing them both around his house, where from each of the three bedrooms, even to where he also left his laundry to dry in the small cupboard after having ironed it. To the large colour matching bathroom where he'd had installed an unusually large white Jacuzzi family sized type bath along with a double shower cubicle, toilet and washbasin. The tiled floor was done in a way and colour that caused it to appear as if only floorboards had been laid down.

The two toilets were on separate floors. One being inside the bathroom upstairs, and the second smaller one just off the living room where he'd had a conservatory built on at the rear of the house. The kitchen was just off the front door and its window looked out onto the road where they had driven up to it. The conservatory at the rear of the house, where it had been attached on to the living-room, had enlarged the room, and also now allowed plenty of light to come in. And apart from a few chairs placed randomly to catch the sun, the conservatory was more like a mini gymnasium, with having a treadmill, exercise bike, and a multi gym all inside it.

They then looked out through its long vertical windows on to the garden outside the structure; A garden that by any means would not be classed as huge, except in many cases in their own country where space itself was always at a premium. It appeared to have been laid out quite nicely and showed many signs of it being attended to quite often. They saw that just right outside the conservatory was a small area of wooden decking and beside it was a various coloured stone laid patio area. The rest of the garden was all green with grass.

'Do you sit out in your garden much, Douglas?' she asked him. Liking the way it had been both thought out and planted, seeing the roses, chrysanthemums, carnations, tulips, and other varieties she had no idea about. The small shed which due to its weather-beaten colouring, and maybe also because of its age seemed to just belong there. Then next to it there was a small greenhouse at one side, with a large water-butt between them, with pipes running into it from each to catch any rainfall. Even the shaped small pond in the centre looked as creative, and just as well looked after as the rest of it appeared. Although it did have some kind of unsightly green netting strung across it in a slight dome shape, which was about the only odd and unattractive thing in the garden to their eyes. A tiered kind of waterfall sent ripples down into the water beneath; though there was no sight or sound from the hidden pump that worked it.

'Now and then, Kumiko,' he answered her, 'usually only when I have time to do so, or I'm working out there and take a break. But if either of you wish to do so then just take either of these bamboo chairs out onto the small decking, the patio, or onto the grass and use them, which is what I do.'

'And I must ask why you have the unsightly netting, Douglas. I mean why do you have that netting over the pond, as it appears to detract from the beauty of the rest of your garden here?'

'I have a few carp in there so I have to keep a watch out for any sneaky cats or birds that were trying to get at them sometimes for a quick free feed. And most likely just like yours, my own working hours can vary from day to day. So I tried the netting above it, just so as to try to keep them off them while I'm out at work,' he told her.

'Listen Father!' she then quietly said to him at her side.

They watched as he turned his head from side to side trying to listen for what she had heard. 'I can't hear anything, Kumiko?'

'Exactly . . . It's so peaceful here isn't it?' she sighed. 'None of the continual noises of people or traffic all the time . . . It's almost like we're in another world!'

'But it's almost as quiet as this at our family home, Kumiko,' he said to her softly.

'Yes, *almost* as quiet!'

'Yes. I do know what you mean, daughter. With more people there in our own home than there is here, of course their voices can intrude into your own thoughts sometimes. But we are still lucky to also have a family home outside the city as we do. Many other families can only wish for what we have when we're there!'

'Yes, that is true, Father. I don't know how I would be able to cope if I had to live in the city every day without a chance to get away for some peace and quiet now and then. I almost feel some pity for those who are unable to get away like I am able to do.'

'But many of those very same people *prefer* the sounds of city life to the country, daughter. Some of them would even begin to die day by day without the constant sound of noise and commotion being all around them. Perhaps even in the same way just as we all love to get away to the rural area whenever we can. We are just lucky to have the best of both worlds, I feel, daughter; one where we can either accept the noise of the city, or the serenity and calming peace and quiet of the countryside. We as a family ourselves, are indeed fortunate to have that choice when so many do not.'

She nodded and was thrilled at the lack of sound again. She sniffed, as if she could actually smell all the different smells of all the flowers outside in the garden in front of her.

Unwilling to disturb them right now, he had no choice but to say, 'Would you like a cup of tea or coffee? Or would either of you prefer something a little stronger?'

'One of your Scotch whisky's on the rocks for me if you have any, and ice. Only of course if you do not mind my asking, Mr Hyde, As I have indeed taken quite a taste to its flavour over many long years.'

He gave a slight nod to the man. 'Certainly, and what would you care to drink, Kumiko?'

'A cup of tea would be nice, thank you.'

'Would the same tea coming out of teabag feel the same for you?' he asked with a smile.

She smiled sweetly at him and then grinned. 'It will still be made from tealeaves, would it not? And yes, I would still like a cup even if it is only from a teabag, as you say!'

'I'll get on with that then,' he said as he unlocked and then opened the pair of patio doors on the conservatory. 'Feel free to have yourselves a nice long stroll around my botanical garden while I'm getting your refreshments, if you so wish,' he told them.

'You do not mind, Douglas?' she asked.

He shook his head. 'A garden like mine is really there to be walked around, enjoyed, as well as being looked at, Kumiko. And sometimes it's nice when others can do the same and also appreciate its beauty and various flower displays and their scents, too.' Then he left them, and Kumiko slid her arm into her fathers as they walked outside onto the grass.

∞

Coming back with a tray carrying their three drinks, he rested it on the small table on the decking next to the open doors, and then having picked their two drinks up from it headed towards them.

He looked consciously at her as she bent over deeply to place her small and pretty snub-like nose into one of the carnation flower heads, and heard her inhaling its fragrant scent. His own thoughts on that, was that she was damned attractive - and probably knew it! One hell of a fine looking body on her, and her face . . . well, her face had an almost angelic quality to it. His smile faded as he then thought of just how much she *did* look just like her lost sister. That young girl; who he had last seen lying stretched out inert and naked upon a cold metal table in the mortuary. As they turned to him as he approached, he switched his smile back on and pushed his last thoughts out of his mind for the moment.

His eyes fixed on her as she took the proffered cup from his hand after her father had taken his glass. How old was she? Carmen was spot-on with what she'd said, he thought. If her younger sister was only twenty-two, then how old was Kumiko herself actually. He now knew that she still had two sisters younger than herself, likely both older than her recently lost sister. So as the eldest of them all, was she twenty-five, thirty, thirty-five, or maybe even forty? It was just so difficult to tell! He saw that she wore no rings on her fingers to help him. He didn't even know if she was married or not . . . Although that was something which *he* shouldn't even *want* to know, he quickly thought. Yet it did bother him, and he knew it because he *did* want to know. As he already knew that he was very much attracted to her.

Spirit of a Dragon

He walked back to the house from the far end of the garden to get his own cup of coffee. While her father moved very close to her.

'He appears to be very interested in you, my daughter.'

Her eyebrows arched in surprise at his words. 'I cannot believe so, Father, since in truth we hardly know each other at all.'

He nodded back at her. 'There was definite interest from him. I could even see it in his eyes as you took your cup from him.'

'It would make no difference, Father, he is not Japanese is he?'

'You know that I do not mind that, as long as you are happy, Kumiko. And as a clan I have also encouraged our members to look outside for potential suitors for almost the past two decades to improve our own clan's bloodline.'

'He is quite nice I suppose, even handsome in a way too, for a non-Japanese man,' she offered hesitantly. 'Though I don't know very much about him at all, apart from what work he does and how he looks after his home and any guests.'

'Well I'm telling you that he is definitely interested in *you*, my daughter. And since you are now my *last* remaining unmarried daughter, I will leave it to you to decide one way or the other. Although I will have to have our good friend in our government see what he can find out for us about him. As we do need to know his background before any further decisions can be made for him. Although if you do have any feelings for him already, then all I will say to you, is that his bath is large.'

She emitted a tiny gasp. 'You are asking me to actually *bathe* with him, Father, and so soon!'

He gave a small shrug to her. 'I would say only if *you* may personally feel anything towards him, my daughter. As while you are bathing together you can also discuss things that you will both *need* to know about each other, *neh*? And if he does not return to work today, then you will very much be distracting him while I telephone our mutual friend about him.'

'Oh, but I thought that you wanted me to marry *him*?' she said to her father, meaning the man in government.

He shook his head. 'Only as a last resort for yourself, Kumiko, as I know that he likes you. But you were never really, shall we say, that overjoyed about wanting to marry him.'

'But I would if you ordered me to.'

'I know that,' he said softly, 'but I also want you to be happy in your marriage, and not feel as if you were forced into it by me or anyone else. Your own happiness is now very essential to me, Kumiko. So if you feel that you do like this man, and who it appears seems to like you so much already. Then all I can say is do what you can do and see what will come from it.'

'But for me to do something like that, Father. To bathe with a man that I have not even known for less than a single day is - well, it is almost beyond any thought.'

He shrugged again. 'Such an event may well even lead you into having sex with him, too!'

'Father, I *could not* do something like that!' she gasped.

'Father, could not what?' he replied.

'We are only here to pick up our dearest Akiko and then to return home again. And you are talking about me not only bathing . . . but also maybe even having sex with this man. It --- it's just not right at such a time.'

'Kumiko,' he sighed, 'my own dearest and eldest daughter, your sister, and my youngest daughter; is as you know now already lost to us. Her soul is now waiting to either be reborn and to hopefully place itself within a member, or potential member of our clan. Whereas we also know her spirit from her untimely death cannot rest now until her killer has been found, and we have returned the same fate upon him, her, or them. Maybe *he* is the one who will accept our Akiko's soul as our newest member, maybe not. But unless you are able to find out one way or the other, then we'll never know will we?'

'But to go and sleep with him just like that Father, when you know that I have held my own virginity secure and pure until I did meet and then marry my husband in life.'

'And he just may *be* the man you will marry, Kumiko.

Spirit of a Dragon

She looked extremely unhappy at the moment as Douglas made his way back to them. 'But what if we do have sex and then he *doesn't* wish to marry me afterwards, Father?'

His shoulders moved again. 'Again, only last week I'd have probably said that something like that *would* have mattered a *great* deal to me and also to the members of our clan, Kumiko. But, as we have now *lost* our own Akiko just so suddenly in life like this; and because it was also just so unexpected too, and worse at such an even younger age. Also because she had also never actually sampled the enjoyment of having sex for herself yet either, my own mind is feeling much freer and far less clouded than it usually is. And your own normal everyday work is also quite dangerous, daughter. So we could lose you just as easily as we have lost your sister, though likely in far different circumstances. So, in order to allow you to experience what your young sister cannot now, just in case it may ever happen, then I am prepared to give you my blessing and to allow you to enjoy such a thing as this. And if you do end up married to him, then all will be well and good. But as I have already told you, it will also depend on what information I receive from our friend shortly.'

She nodded her lowered head in silence as the man they were talking about approached them again. She was not only still shocked by what her father had just said to her, but almost disturbed. As year after year she had saved her body in order to give it freely to the one man who she hoped that she would fall in love with and then bear his children. Especially with their clan being almost adamant about how things like this were actually supposed to be done by them all.

Yet here was her father, who, though luckily enough was the head of their clan, so he was usually the person that made any new rules that they all had to abide by. And it was now he who was the one now also telling her to forget all her years of carefully waited chastity, and not only to bathe with him but also to have sex with him if she wished. Her mind was spinning at the events now taking place already here. She had only come with her father to take her sister's body home again for it to be given its usual funeral rites. Yet now she was being given the chance to have real sex with an almost unknown man to them both. It was making her feel both cautious and also very much wanton at the same time.

∞

In any event further discussion was not possible as the mobile in his pocket rang even as he reached them.

'DI Hyde?' he said after recognising his own department from the number on the display of who was calling him. 'Right you are Terry . . . Okay . . . I'll be there in about half an hour then,' he finished and closed his phone. 'I'm sorry,' he said to them both, 'I'm afraid that I'll have to go back in to work for a while.'

'A development maybe?' she queried.

He gave her a nod. 'Yes.' then glanced over at her father and back to her again.

She understood. 'My father fully understands the nature of your work, and that what you may have to say at any time to us may sound unwelcome, Douglas. But since it concerns Akiko, and because of that both of us we are willing to hear whatever news you may have.'

'All right then, if you're sure?'

They both gave an affirmative nod to him.

It was his turn to sigh now. 'Well, that was my department on the phone. To tell me that only a few minutes ago and only about a hundred feet away from the scene, they came upon some signs of digging or else some kind of a hasty excavation. So they carefully dug into it and came up with clothing and a pair of sunglasses.'

'Female clothing you mean, Douglas? And Akiko's you think?'

'Some of the apparel that came from the hole would suggest that very thing, Kumiko.'

Her brows almost knitted together as she tried to work out what he was saying from his careful wording. 'Ah!' she said. 'You meant from the underwear found there, *neh*?'

He nodded. 'We would also like one of you to confirm her identity very soon, as well as checking over what belongings we've found so far. Just to make sure as far as we can that it is all hers. If there is something there which you aren't sure of, then we'll check those items over even more carefully, just in case it belonged to another party.'

'Her killer being the party to who you are referring to by that Mr Hyde, aren't you?'

'Yes. Anything that we can do to get a lead on any suspect in a murder case we'll take!' He looked at them closely. 'While I'm out please feel free to use my home as you would if it were your own. Have yourselves a meal and take a bath or a shower if you wish. Even go to bed to catch up on your sleep if you can, unless your body clocks are way out at the moment. And I'll be back as soon as I can.'

'You do what you have to do, Mr Hyde. We will both be quite fine while we wait for your return. Perhaps you would care to join us when you return by sharing our own meal?'

'I don't know when I'll be back, Mr Hirano. So it may be better that if you feel hungry just to have a meal yourselves. If I'm back then I'd love to join you both, but if not then I'll just make myself something when I get in.'

The older man bobbed his head. 'Then we shall just have to see how it goes, Mr Hyde.

Douglas left them both in the garden and returned to his department where various facts and files were already filtering their way through to his desk. It took him a few good hours of writing on the computer before he had a good enough written report composed that he could actually pass upstairs for the Chief Constable to read.

He wasn't even able to head for home again until just after six. As some work from a few previous cases he'd worked on needed some cross-referencing doing to help them out. Then only an hour before he went home, he received the news from the lab that he'd been waiting for all day from the samples in the test tubes.

The very short report so far told him that she had indeed likely been raped, and that enough semen had been found for them to begin DNA testing of it; though that could take at least a day or more to come through. While the second part of the report now stated that some slight traces of a barbiturate and also that of an aphrodisiac had been found in both her blood and urine samples. Drugs, which he finally now knew from their breakdown, had shown that both substances had somehow been administered and ingested by her in some way. And both *prior* to her death, which were now also his first real clues as to how it had taken place.

Douglas added these small reports on to his own report for the

Chief Constable, now knowing already that she had likely been enticed into eating or drinking something by her killer that contained these two substances. And then her killer had only waited for her to feel very drowsy and quite amorous before taking full advantage upon her unresisting body.

And he was now sure that it was a man they were looking for. All he needed now was some further clues which could lead them to get much closer to his identity . . .

CHAPTER 5

After he'd left them to their own devices, Kumiko went back into the conservatory twice to carry out two of his bamboo chairs, which she then placed close together out on the grass. They both were now able to sit down with their drinks and talk together quietly, while savouring the sheer peace and quiet which dwelt within the colourful garden.

But even their low voices must have been overheard, as a voice from the other side of the left hand fence then cooed, '*Yoo-hoo, Douglas*?' and then a silvery head of curly hair began to rise over the top of the fence.

'Oh! I'm ever so sorry! I thought that I'd heard Douglas out here?' she mentioned. Her eyes roamed around the garden as if looking for him.

Kumiko said in response to her, 'I'm afraid that Douglas received a call for him to go back into work only a few minutes ago. So we are just taking in the air and the peacefulness of this lovely garden of his while we wait for him to return.'

'Then I do apologise for disturbing you both,' she replied and began to vanish.

'Wait!' she called out, and as the head reappeared again, she added, 'would you care to join us for a while?'

As the old woman nodded and said, 'I'd love to and won't be a moment then, my dear.' And as she suddenly disappeared from their view, her father turned to look at her and gave a questioning look.

'We may just be able to get some information that we may need about him from her, *neh*?'

Her father smiled, she was a clever young woman indeed, he thought. Then his head swung around as he heard a grating kind of creak, and was surprised to see quite a large portion of the fence swinging away from them. With the same elderly woman of who, they both now saw was quite plump along with a rounded face. Though who now looked even smaller than they had both thought at first, and who right now, was attempting to bring her chair through the opening. Across over to them from within her garden, but with some difficulty it had to be said.

Kumiko was amazed at how quickly her father left the chair he was sitting on and took what he soon found out was a much heavier chair than they were sitting in, out of her small hands. Though it had surprised him at how she had been able to actually move it that far herself!

'Facing us or beside us?' he asked her.

'Placed facing you both if you don't mind, my dear, as it saves me from having to turn my neck too much. Arthritis and bad eyesight all due to my old age now you know,' she told them.

Her father set her chair down only when he had decided that it was centred correctly between their two chairs, though facing toward them. They watched the old woman take her seat with an amazingly long drawn out sigh of what could only be called, pleasure.

'Are you both guests staying here with Douglas?' she asked politely then gave a very slow shake of her head. 'I do apologise, I shouldn't be so nosy really. Only I've baked some pies and scones for Douglas, like I usually do. As I'm quite sure that he never gets enough to eat the poor dear, not with all the time he spends out at work.'

'You must know him quite well then to be baking things for him?' Kumiko said, already testing the ground carefully to begin with.

'Oh, only for about the past eight years since he moved in next door, my dear, though he used to get on very well with my late husband you know, what with them both having served in the Royal Marines once.

Spirit of a Dragon

And as my own husband was a young man during the Second World War and Douglas was about the same age when he served in those Falkland troubles, so they used to compare various things together.

'Nowadays though, ever since my husband passed away, just under three years ago now, I've actually come to rely on him to help me out a bit now and then. Which is also the reason why I indulge in some baking for him in return, and I'm very pleased to say that he does seem to like my cooking!'

'We were just saying to each other that he has a beautiful garden,' said Kumiko.

'Oh, that's nothing, my dear. You should see what he did in mine when I asked him, as I just couldn't manage it myself, mainly because my husband Bert used to do all that when he was alive. Oh yes, he's a very lovely boy to offer so much time and help to me, and my gardens almost twice the size of his own. Yet he still checks up on me every day or so, just to make sure that I'm all right; especially if we haven't seen each other for a day or more. And now and then I'll see him in here or in mine, either weeding, planting, or watering, just to keep it in good order for me. Heavens, I just don't know what I'd do without him now!'

'He sounds like a very good friend or neighbour to have,' said her father to her.

'Oh, he's a real dear to me, almost like the son we never had. Always willing to help me out if something goes wrong in the house, or if something needs repairing.' She gave a little laugh. 'He even changes any of my ceiling lights when they go off. As he says that I shouldn't be climbing so high upon any ladders at my age now. Are you both over here on holiday?' she then asked changing the subject. 'As I'm surprised he didn't take some leave if he knew that he was having guests staying with him.'

'No,' she answered. 'We're here on family business.'

Her old eyes crinkled as she looked at the young woman across from her. 'How silly of me for not guessing, though I must say he has kept really quiet about it.'

'Quiet about what?' she asked, confused.

'Well that you've brought your Father over to meet him of course, my dear. As I said, I'm surprised that he never even mentioned you once to me, even about getting married.'

'What?' she gasped aloud while her father did little else but chuckle.

'Oh, you're a very pretty woman indeed and will make a lovely wife for him I'm sure . . .' she told a bemused Kumiko. 'But if I was fifty years younger, and still a single woman, then I might have snapped him up even before you had the chance of doing it!' she chuckled upon seeing her face.

'Though you'd better be kind to him, or I'll want to know the reason why. But I do think that you will do him nicely, my dear, and I also hope your Father likes him too? As I just can't believe that he's managed to stay single all the time that I've known him. In fact, I can even tell you that I've never seen many women in that way here at his house until I saw you here, my dear.'

'Never, are you saying that not a single woman has ever been here with him?'

'No not one, well not in that way anyway, though he did once tell me that he found it hard to find the woman he would like to marry. As he really doesn't like these women who are always going out drinking, and some of them even getting very drunk every weekend. No, though he doesn't mind if she smokes mind you, due to him doing it himself mainly through his work, he says. Though I know he's even tried to quit doing that on a number of occasions, but what he does always causes him to start up again. And I know just how stressful his work can be, I only hope that you do *too*, my dear?'

'She does indeed Mrs . . . I'm sorry we do not even know your name.'

'Oh, how silly of me, I'm Mrs Glover, Edith Glover.'

'We must also apologise for not introducing ourselves Mrs Glover.'

'Edith, please.'

He nodded. 'Edith then, my name is Koichi Hirano, and this is my daughter Kumiko.'

'Are *you* married, Koichi?' she asked.

'For the past forty years, Edith,' he replied.

She sighed, 'Just my luck! I thought it was too much to hope for to meet a handsome man like you who was single.'

It was Kumiko's turn to laugh now. 'Just wait until I tell Mother that you received a marriage proposal Father!'

'Don't you dare young girl, or she'll make me sleep on my own for a week if she even hears about it.'

All three of them laughed at his jocular aside.

After a few minutes had passed, Kumiko said to her, 'I almost expected him to have a dog or a cat, as I keep hearing that English people always seem to have animals?'

She tilted her head to one side before answering with a wicked glint in her eye. 'And I have heard that Koreans like to *eat* dogs?'

Her father nodded and responded with a grin. 'Yes, I have also heard that they consider it quite a delicacy in their country. So we are thankful that we are Japanese and prefer to eat just raw fish instead.'

Edith's head now moved to tilt on the other side and the same wicked glint appeared in her old eyes which they both noticed - and wondered what she was going to come out with next. But not for long they soon found out.

'And by any chance do you eat whales and dolphins?'

He shook his head at her. 'No. I did try them both once, but I couldn't quite get used to their taste so I just stuck to eating raw fish. Though a lot of our countrymen do enjoy eating it,' he said and waited for her reply to that.

'Yes, it is sad that one mammal group has to live by eating another don't you think so?'

'Do you not eat beef and lamb and other such foods, Edith?' he asked her in return.

'Ah-ah-ah, Koichi, you won't catch me out like that you know,' she laughed shaking a finger before him from side to side. 'Those animals are actually bred for slaughter with which to feed us. Whereas the whales and dolphins are actual wild free roaming and breeding creatures, and possibly even more intelligent than we ourselves think we are!'

'That may well be true,' he conceded. 'But as our own country doesn't have the room to grow or breed all the food that we would need to sustain us. It is why many centuries ago we had to look to the sea for other means of feeding our people.'

She shook her head. 'As we did too in our own history, and I'm not condemning your people at all for doing it, Koichi. As we in this country used to hunt whales, too, but for us, it was mainly just for the oil to light our lamps with, the rest was usually just wasted. All that I am saying to you is, that in this modern age where electricity and food is so easily acquired. Why on earth is it still necessary to hunt the poor whales and dolphins for food, when in most cases we know that it's not really needed anymore? I know that there are some places where they take a few whales and such to feed a colony for the rest of the year. And that is fine by me, as they've been doing it that way since time immemorial for their survival.

'But they are not what we could even call modern by any standards. They don't have electric like we do now. In fact some still even use the whale oil for lighting in just the same way that we used to. It's the modern countries who don't hunt them for their own needs – meaning they harvest them on a grand scale, termed as being of a scientific nature, though really it's still just hunting for food and for profit.'

'I couldn't agree more, Edith. Although even Kumiko here prefers to eat burgers and various other western foods more than our own more typical plain Japanese fare now.'

'But that's impossible! I mean just look at her - she's so thin! I only wish that I would be able to do that like her and not gain any weight.'

'Ah, but she also does a lot of running and walking Edith, which takes care of her eating habits.'

'Oh, are you some kind of an athlete then, my dear?'

Kumiko smiled and shook her head. 'No, Edith. I'm an Inspector with the Tokyo Police.'

'Ahhh, no wonder they fell in love with each other then, Koichi, eh?

What with both being the same kind of work and all that.'

'Father, *please* . . .' she almost begged him.

He gave a loud sigh, knowing that she was becoming quiet bothered about what was being said about her and this Douglas.

'Edith,' he said to their elderly woman before them. 'The reason that we are both here now is that my youngest daughter, and Kumiko's sister, was found murdered yesterday.'

'Oh, heavens above, I am so sorry for you both to now hear that. I simply had no idea that you were here because of such a tragic . . .' her head dropped, and she couldn't go on as tears readily filled her eyes.

'Thank you for your sympathy, Edith. You see, we are only staying here because of Mr Hyde's kindness too,' he told her. 'Instead of us having to go and stay in a hotel. He actually asked us if we would rather stay here in his home with him as a courtesy. Which I can only say to you was very considerate of him to offer.'

'That's Douglas for you, forever kind and always willing to help anyone in need.' She sniffled into a handkerchief which had suddenly arrived from somewhere upon her person.

'Mr Hyde is also the policeman in charge of my daughter's investigation. So we are here to help with any formalities that need seeing to before we take her home to rest.'

'Again I apologise to you both for just rambling on about silly things when you must be so exhausted and feeling so sad at the moment.'

'It is quite all right, Edith. Really it is. Our talk together like this was actually even beginning to take our minds off what we were both here for.'

The elderly woman then gave a loud gasp as she looked straight at the younger woman across from her. 'And there was I prattling on about you two getting married. I'm ever so sorry, Kumiko,' she offered to her.

'You were not to know about it Edith, so I am all right about it.'

Edith gave a sad nod then said almost from out of the blue, 'Though I must still say to you that I *do* think you would make a lovely couple!'

Her father's lost laughter returned as the same look appeared again on his daughter's face at her words. There was just no holding back with this woman, he thought.

Over the next hour that the three of them spent together, Kumiko made tea for them all as they sat and talked. While Edith vanished back into her house and returned with the large plate of pies and scones that she had baked earlier for her neighbour Douglas. They ate some of these as they talked and drank their tea in good company. The two newcomers were astounded by the utter deliciousness of her pastries as they tried them out. Both of them quite happily consuming and also becoming genuine fans of her baking skills. She even went back into the house to get some of her home made preserves for them to use, which they also found only added to their newly discovered flavour filled tastes. Their singing of her cooking praises brought a smile to her face.

When their hour together was about up, Kumiko took through into the kitchen what remained on the plate for Douglas. Though with three of them eating what she had originally brought out, it hadn't left a great deal to carry in anyway. Which gave the elderly woman some cause for concern, and as such, she said that she would need to bake more of each of them to make up for their unexpected disappearance.

So while she then went off to do that, her father carried her chair back into her garden for her. And stood looking almost in wonder at what had been done with *her own* garden, before he returned back through the fence again into Douglas's and latched the gate closed.

As he came inside the house to call up his friend who worked in the government back home, he looked at his daughter as she came back through, and eyed her somewhat speculatively before saying to her, 'I think Edith was right about you two you know, Kumiko.' He grinned at her shocked face again. 'In fact, just as I think she would probably put it so bluntly. I think you should bed him and wed him!'

He chuckled even louder as he saw what he had seen appear on her face at that statement.

'*Father*, for goodness sake!' she admonished him, flustered.

∞

The hours passed slowly for them in the house, and to pass some of this time they both even stripped down to their underwear and began to use his gym equipment. Her father quickly had to change the weight settings on the bench press machine, since he found out that he couldn't even budge it; certainly not at the setting which Douglas had left it at for his own personal use. While close beside him his daughter was happily jogging at a steady pace on the treadmill in her bare feet. Since neither one of them had even thought of bringing training shoes, or any kind of workout gear with them. As they had expected it to only be a very short stay. So they now knew that they would have to buy some while they were over here so that they could use the equipment at hand properly.

After at least a good hour at that, which included them occasionally swapping over to take turns on each of the various pieces of equipment he had in place in the conservatory to use. They were both soaked with sweat by the time they had completed their tiring but well enjoyed workout. They both then took a quick shower and emerged dressed in light and bright *yukatas*; which were very lightweight silk kimonos, and mainly for usage around their own homes back in Japan. Although originally, these same items of clothing, had been packed only for their expecting to be worn in the privacy of their hotel rooms or suites; dependant on what may have been available for them upon their arrival. It was also due to their hasty packing being done, only after finally deciding to come over here to be with their recently deceased family member.

And so, while her father settled in a chair with yet another of his now favoured glasses taken from out of Douglas's whisky bottle, with ice. He was soon feeling quite relaxed while talking on his telephone to his wife back home. Kumiko had eventually, after close to fifteen minutes of studying, managed to get the washing machine working with their clothing and undergarments inside. Only when she saw the clothes within begin to turn and the water begin to fill within it, as then the suds from the small detergent tablet start to be produced. Did she give a nod to herself and make herself another cup of tea. She smiled, and done yet again with just a teabag.

∞

Barely an hour and a half later since they'd parted in the garden. Edith was rapping at the front door and was invited inside by Kumiko who had answered it. She was holding her recently delivered evening paper in her hand. Kumiko invited her through into Douglas's living room where her father was resting his full length in one of the two large reclining chocolate coloured leather armchairs, one hand holding his third. Yet now only a half-full glass of vibrant and alcoholic amber coloured spirit which he had come to love.

'Hello again, Edith, back again so soon?' he began, 'Is there something you need some help with next door which we can help you with while Douglas is out?' he offered.

Edith moved over to him with a shake of her head and passed over her paper to him. 'No, Koichi, but thank you. I came round with this for you only because I know that Douglas doesn't bother with an evening paper himself. And I thought that since some of it concerns your late daughter, that you may want to read it?'

Kumiko moved across the floor and with her arms resting on the back of the thickly padded chair, looked over her Father's shoulder as they both began to read the news story now covering Akiko's fate.

Edith's eyes widened as she saw from the young woman's new position quite a revealing amount of her breasts as she bent over the chair to read. It made her wonder if either one of them actually wore *anything* at all beneath those thin appearing gowns . . . And if that was true, why not?

'They've somehow even managed to get a picture of Douglas to add to it while he was there. He won't be very happy about them doing that either I can tell you . . .' she told them both.

'Why not?' asked Kumiko upon looking up sideways at her.

'Because he usually says he's not what he would call photographic material? I guess he means good looking? I'm not sure. Yet I've always thought of him as being very good looking - in a rugged and roughly handsome kind of way. The other reason being, I suppose, is because he's always telling me that what he does is not a one-man job. That there is a *team* of them working together to do what they do, and for one man to get the publicity, or most of the credit, doesn't seem right to him and never has.

'You'll see that from the small piece near the bottom of the story where he's given a short statement to them. Where he's actually saying that only by good *teamwork* and with some help from the general public will they be able find the attacker of the young girl.'

'Maybe it can only help if your press here have done this,' said Kumiko, 'as with your public's help, just as Douglas has stated in his interview, that maybe they will have people calling them up with some valuable information that he may be able to use soon?'

'That would seem to be very unlikely yet, my dear,' Edith responded.

'Why?'

'Well, if you look better at what Douglas *has* said in his statement to the press. You will see that in it, he hasn't given a time or date out for when it may have happened. So any calls that might come in to them at the moment could just be spurious or hoax calls. It also means by what has been said at the moment that they haven't been able to narrow it down yet to get an exact enough time of her death, which of course is very much needed if you're going to ask the public for help. As you have to be able to say to them . . . Something like - were you passing by this particular place at such and such a time, and on such and such a day, and if so, did you happen to see anything suspicious happening? If you have then please ring this number and contact us with any information.'

Her father looked up at her now, and thought. As old as Edith may be, her brain is still working very well for her. 'So to get a true investigation started it will need such facts as those to be found before anything can be done?'

Edith gave him a nod. 'Facts are facts, Koichi. Kumiko should certainly know that with her doing the same thing.'

'Yes,' Kumiko said. 'What you have said is quite correct, Edith. Even *we* have also to rely on the same facts to deduce our own times and use it to gather or to collect information about something.'

'Well, you can keep it now since I've already read it through myself. And it's possible that Douglas may also want to see it when he eventually gets back home.'

'Are you sure, Edith?' he asked. 'As we can easily go out and buy one of these papers ourselves for him if need be.'

She smiled. 'The newsagent's is a good few miles away from here, Koichi, which is why I have it delivered every week night, to save me having to walk there, or get a bus to get one. Douglas always pays my paper bill for me every week when he gets his own Sunday papers. And that is another thing you'll have to be careful about while you're over here too, my dears.'

They looked at her with expressionless faces as they waited to hear what she was going to come out with next.

She didn't fail them, though it did appear to be given as a warning to them more than anything. 'Anything like this happening usually ends up in the national papers, too. So for the next few days, or maybe even for a good few weeks now, you could well have reporters from the national papers really searching for either of you, or any other of your family members just to ask *you* or they questions about your daughter Koichi, and your sister Kumiko.

'The one good thing in your favour is that they may find it difficult to find you where you are, since you're already here in Douglas's home, while they'll be searching around all the local hotels first to try to find out if any of you are over here already. But, if you ever do leave the house at any time to go out with Douglas somewhere and are seen by just one of them. You can be quite sure that they'll somehow manage to follow you back here and start knocking on the door until you do finally decide to talk to one or all of them.'

They looked at each other before turning their eyes back to her again. 'So what would you suggest we do then, Edith?' he asked.

Her eyes crinkled. 'Talk to Douglas about it straight away when he comes in. As I'm quite sure he'll know what you should do about it,'

As Kumiko went with her to let her out, though this time saying to her that it might be better if she returned by means of the back way so that no one saw her at the door. Edith agreed with her quick thought, as those living opposite to him would also be wondering what a Japanese looking woman was maybe doing appearing at his door. Then if they read the paper might put two and two together a little too quickly for their own good. So she was more than happy to help out. Even to saying that she would use the back gateway to come in again while they were staying here.

After Kumiko had reached over to raise the latch that locked the portion of fence in a secure position. And had then opened it for her to walk through into her own garden. Edith paused as she went through and turned back to her.

'I do like those gowns you're both wearing Kumiko,' she told her. 'Though I just to have to ask you something, if you don't mind?'

'Of course, Edith, what is it that you would like to know?'

'I wanted to ask if you were actually wearing anything underneath them . . . And if not why, and also why you were wearing them now when only a short time ago you were both dressed?'

Kumiko smiled at her. 'To pass some time while we waited for Douglas to return, we decided to try out his exercise equipment. And we became so hot and sweaty from doing so that we both required a shower afterwards. These gowns we are wearing, as you call them, are what we normally wear at home after work and for us just to relax in. I do not know about my father, but I rarely wear anything beneath the silk as it always feels so cool against your skin, and Japan is usually a much warmer country anyway. So this helps me to stay cooler.'

'I thought so. As when you leaned over to read the paper behind your father I was very sure that I caught sight of your breasts. It did not bother me so much however, with being a woman. Although I *wouldn't* let Douglas see you like that Kumiko, or else you might light his passion for you - and phew! Even I don't want to think about what might happen after that at my age now! As sometimes when *I've* seen him exercising with his shirt off, or just working in the garden like that. It can still give *me* a warm glow!'

'Even at your young age still, Edith?' Kumiko grinned.

She nodded. '*Especially* at my age, Kumiko, as Douglas is one fine hunk of man to look at, which is also why I sometimes wish I were so much younger than I am, so that I may have had another chance in life. But at eighty-five now, such times as those have now simply just passed me by.

'But for you, my young friend. At your young age of - I'm sorry, but just how old are you, Kumiko, as you only look about twenty?'

'I am thirty now, Edith.'

'And are you married or single?'

'Single. I've never been married, Edith.'

'Then don't wait much longer if you want that in life, my love.' Her head began to tilt over. 'I would be extremely happy to have you as a neighbour to me now you know, Kumiko.'

'What?'

'I know that you like Douglas, as I've seen it in your eyes when his name is mentioned. And he is a truly lovely young man who would make not only a fine husband, but also a wonderful father to any children you may have, too. So if you do have the chance, then I'd tell you to grab onto him with both hands while you can, and hold onto him dearly, love. As there just aren't many men like him around these days now.'

'She shook her head. 'I'm afraid I barely know him, Edith. So what you are implying between us will likely not even have a chance to start, as we'll be going home soon with my sister when we are allowed to take her.'

Edith smiled a warm smile at her. 'May be Kumiko, may be . . . but just remember what I've said to you that's all, as he's a gentleman through and through. Though certainly also a *man's* man by any sense of the word! He's also kind, polite, and very charming too.' Then she actually tittered like a young girl. 'And what a body holds all these things within it! Oh, Kumiko, I know that you are from different countries and all that. But I just feel it inside me that you would both be ideal for each other if you just gave it a chance. You are both quiet people and quite reserved, but there's just a thing about you both which seems to make it an almost ideal matching!'

They finally parted company and she waited as raised the latch to lock the doorway. Edith's words had actually left her mind busily thinking over what she had been told. That she was thirty and he was older at forty-two mattered little to her anyway, as she had already worked out his age as soon as he'd given them his alarm code. And something like the small amount of twelve years difference between their ages meant nothing to her, as her father's friend in the government was much nearer to being fifty than forty anyway. It was just the thought of her marrying a foreigner, not one of her own kind as others may well say, which was making any choice so hard to make, that she knew. Even with her father's already given blessing, she knew that she would have to think even deeper over what she should do now.

CHAPTER 6

Douglas finally returned home that evening at seven-fifteen. Leaving the garage even as the door began to roll down automatically behind him. He opened the front door when the handle turned easily under his hand. Which told him that they were still inside - or had they simply gone out and just forgot to lock it all up?

But even as he entered inside, he heard an unusual melodic singing in a female voice coming from his kitchen. So he went there first and found Kumiko now on ironing the clothing which she'd washed and dried earlier. Her back was to him as he looked in, and her body was swaying gracefully in time with her singing as her hand moved back and forth over the ironing board. Why she was standing there in a kimono he didn't know. But what he did find unusual was that her feet were now encased in his slippers; slippers that must have been between five to ten sizes too large for her very small feet.

He leaned against the doorjamb and just stood there watching her. Watching as the iron was placed to stand on its base, as she now deftly folded the clothing up and placed it on to a small pile of others that were already laid upon a chair. She then half shuffled and half dragged her feet within the slippers towards where she picked up the next piece of clothing to iron. He shook his head, thinking that it was just like watching someone trying to move around with a pair of those amazingly elongated clown shoes upon their feet!

As she started to iron, she began to sing happily away to herself in Japanese again. He wasn't sure of the song, though it did have a kind of pop rhythm to it. But really he wasn't what you could call "up to date" with any Japanese pop songs at all.

He left her there to amuse herself in two different ways, and walked through to his living room, which was where he found her father resting in one of his reclining chairs/ Or rather almost lying prone in one, with the footrest being raised up where it was. On his lap was a laptop computer, and on the coffee table beside him was what appeared to be a small printer connected to it. Hooked on to his ear was a new device that had only appeared on the technology market recently, and one that he had only become aware of himself over the past year - an earphone microphone. It had a tiny microphone coming from the small set around his ear and placed close to his mouth. He followed the lead running down from it and saw that it was connected to a mobile phone beside the printer, or whatever it was.

Her father gave a wave to him. 'Just checking up with my son's at home, Mr Hyde,' he told him. 'I have to make sure that they are running my business well enough while I am away from it.'

'No problem at all, Mr Hirano. But you could have plugged your laptop into the socket to save its battery life if you'd wanted to,' he told him.

Hirano senior shook his head. 'I actually forgot to bring a compatible socket voltage changer with me. So I'll just have to hope that the battery inside lasts long enough while I'm here.'

'I'll find one tomorrow for you somewhere if I can.'

Koichi shook his head. 'You will likely find it hard to locate any over here, Mr Hyde. Your own overseas adapter sockets here are typically made or stocked for when *you* go abroad to connect something you may take with you there, just as ours are. Anyway, I have already been on to my office to have one sent over by courier, and hopefully it should be here within one or two days if I am lucky. But just as with any business around the world Mr Hyde, you have to keep your finger on its pulse in order for it to continue working to its fullest extent and potential.'

'Won't you please call me, Douglas?' he asked him. 'All of this Mr Hyde calling you're doing is making me feel a lot older than I already am?'

Spirit of a Dragon

He nodded and smiled. 'Only if you will also be pleased call me Koichi, in return?'

'I would be quite happy to do so, Koichi.'

'Then I will be pleased to call you Douglas - Mr Hyde.' The lines upon his forehead then wrinkled together en-mass, as he understood what he had just said, as it had sounded quite stupid when he thought about it.

'Would you like a top-up?' asked Douglas, gesturing to what was his empty glass on the table.

He smiled at him. 'Only if *you* do not mind, Douglas. Although I must admit to have been sampling your bottle many times already, and may have to buy you one in return before I leave.'

'Don't worry about it Koichi, you're my guest here.'

'But you would have none to drink yourself if I was inconsiderate enough to do that!' he argued.

'I rarely drink myself, Koichi. So really, I only keep supplies of this and any other spirits in the house for New Year. And that's only in case any of the neighbours I know, or if any of my work colleagues come around; only if I'm *in* the house at the time and not at work, of course!'

He broke off to refill his drink as her father began to talk into his mouthpiece to one of his sons by the name of Hiro, who had just come through to speak.

'That sounds all right to me, Hiro,' he said to his son in Japanese. 'Though to get that order out we may have to step up production just a little bit more in order to manage its completion date on time?'

As Douglas returned with his drink, he saw one hand gesticulating even as his head was nodding as he made yet another reply to his son.

'Well, I'll leave it for you to decide on while I'm away, Hiro. Just don't bankrupt us all whatever you do, *neh*?' He laughed down the mouthpiece.

After setting the glass down, and having kept a straight face from what he'd heard said. Douglas returned to the kitchen, and to where

Kumiko's swaying form was still singing. He passed by her this time and went to the fridge and opened it, then closed it again when he saw the tray with some pies and scones lying out on the counter top.

'Has my neighbour Edith been around?' he asked her.

She stopped singing and swaying to talk with him. 'Yes, Douglas. My father and I were sitting outside in your garden when she looked over the fence, as she thought she'd heard you. But we told her that you had just left to go back into work again. Anyway she soon joined us at our invitation and we all chatted together, and later she brought that tray out. Though I am very sorry to say that she invited us to try some of them, and at first, we only did so for politeness. Sadly, we then found them to be just *so* delicious, that it was only when we were quite full did we finally stop ourselves from doing so. As her jam and marmalade made them taste even better than without. And we just became so greedy that I'm afraid we both gorged ourselves on them. It is also the reason I'm afraid, why there are now so few left on the tray for you. But she did say that she would bake a few more of each to replenish what we have eaten for you, Douglas.'

He smiled at her. 'I thought the plate looked kind of empty from what she normally brings around to me. I don't mind in the least though, Kumiko. As Edith always makes so much for me that it can take me days to get through all of them usually. Sometimes I even have to take some of them with me to work to have for the odd snack when I can.'

'We both found her to be quite a delightful woman.'

'She's certainly that!' he said.

'And she also appears to have a slightly more than a little romantic crush on you herself, Douglas.'

'Ah, well, at least it's always nice to know that someone does then!' he said unhappily.

'I am sorry, Douglas, did I say something wrong?'

'No, well, not really, Kumiko. It's only - well, it's only that one of these days I would like to be with someone in a good steady relationship. Do you know what I mean?'

She gave a nod in understanding, as often she had the same

thoughts herself, although for her, she felt like that at least once a week.

'But, with what I do, and the unsociable hours I sometimes have to keep . . .' He said, and then shrugged expressively. 'Well, it will be hard to find someone who can put up with such an arrangement as that. As any plans made in advance could be broken at very short notice, which would of course cause untold grief on any relationship. And that would also make it harder for two people to be together as much as they should be to make it work.'

She nodded again. 'Surely someone in your own line of work, and who works the same hours as you do could perhaps be a possibility, Douglas?'

'No, I wouldn't think so, Kumiko. As they rarely allow married police couples like that to work at the same station or on the same shifts.'

'But why, that sounds rather silly to me?'

'Because of any possible marital problems which may follow them into work sometimes, or because if one is in need of help while at work, then the other may leave whatever task they are on with to go to their aid. It is also why they mostly end up on different shift patterns so that they *won't* be working at the same time to hear anything like that over the radio. It is another reason why most relationships that involve two police officers here, rarely work out unless they can handle the constant daily shift or station separation.'

Now she began to understand why some of those same relationships, which had appeared to start out just so happily enough back home in her own precinct, had also begun to deteriorate over a certain amount of time. She now knew that it was mainly due to them worrying about their respective partners when they were at work and facing unknown dangers every day.

Kumiko looked at the man in front of her quite studiously. 'I also sometimes feel this way too, Douglas. As at my own age of thirty now, I also feel as if passed over in terms of a relationship ever happening for me.'

'You're thirty!'

'You thought that I was older perhaps?' she enquired unhappily. As no woman liked being thought of as a lot older than she actually was, no matter in which countries society.

'God, no, Kumiko!' he muttered. 'I only thought that at most you were a just few years older than your sister was!'

'Thank you, you are very kind, Douglas.'

'Kindness has nothing at all to do with it, Kumiko. You're an attractive - No, I'll take that back. You're an amazingly attractive woman totally! And I can't even begin to understand why you don't have admirers knocking on *your* door every day of the week even just hoping to go out with you!'

She smiled, showing her even white teeth. 'You are being quite charming to me Douglas, and I thank you for it. But, just as with what you have stated, my own law enforcement work also keeps me involved. And with the exact same identical problems to those which *you* have already spoken of, and so very succinctly.'

And does your career mean more to you than marriage, Kumiko? Or would you be prepared to give it up for that?' he asked.

Her head bowed gracefully as she thought over what he had said, as that certainly wasn't something that she'd envisaged ever having to do to simply become a wife. When she raised her head again, her eyes peered right into those of his.

'I suppose, Douglas, that for the *right* man. I would be quite willing to give up my career. But, just to be at home all day with nothing like what I am now doing. What I mean is, I can focus my mind on one or many issues each day as I am able to do now. So my *not* having something ike that to do could make me become a little bored. So I may also need some kind of other stimulation to keep me happy as a wife.

'A different job is always possible, Kumiko, unless you have some hidden talent which hasn't been unearthed yet?'

'Talents like what, Douglas?'

'Oh, I don't really know. What about painting, or writing? Or designing and making clothes like this?' he said reaching out to feel at the material she wore. 'Wow, its pure silk!' he said, then quickly averted his eyes when his own touch upon it actually just caused it to part and fall wide-open; Now displaying her quite naked body beneath, which had previously been hidden to him. 'I'm terribly sorry, Kumiko. I had no idea that you were --- er --- like that under there!' he tried to explain.

Kumiko was just as stunned. His shyness at what he'd just seen of her naked body had immediately caused her own heart to begin to thump almost painfully within her slim chest. She didn't know what was happening to her, but it felt both amazing and very strange at the same time. Through that happening, it even took her almost a full minute to finally react to what had happened, and draw the two side of her *yukata* back together again and tie its loosened sash tight.

'Again I can only apologise to you for that, Kumiko,' he said quickly when he was able to face her again.

She was able to see the remains of his blush on his cheeks when they looked at each other. 'Do you *still* think that I am as attractive as I was before that has happened, and after now seeing my old body?' she asked him.

'I didn't see that much of it honestly, Kumiko. I turned away even as it fell open. But what I did see I *very much* liked!'

'Just what are you implying to me by saying that, Douglas?'

She watched as he was on the verge of just being about to say something to her, then didn't. 'I think I'll just go and have a shower before I have something to eat and drink,' he said, and left her standing there on her own, her mind now working in deep thought.

Her heart was still pounding heavily even as he withdrew from her, and if only he'd looked more closely at her. He would have actually been able to see the beating of her own rapid pulse upon her slender neck.

As she heard him climbing the stairs slowly, she went through to speak with her father and told him what had just happened between them.

'To have that happening to you, Kumiko, to me means that *you* must also actually feel something for *him*! Otherwise, you would never have felt like that at all, *neh*?'

'But I still barely know him, Father. So how could something as innocent as that happening between us do that to me?'

'But do you *feel* that you like him?'

She gave what he thought was a tiny nod.

'And where is he now?'

'Gone to have a shower he said, 'before he comes back down to make something to eat and drink.'

Her father smiled what appeared to her as a very knowing smile.

'What is *that* smile for, Father?'

'Well, Kumiko, if just think about it for even a moment. He caught a brief glimpse of your own very naked body only a moment ago, and now he's gone for a shower! What does that suggest to you?'

'That he may have liked what he saw . . . But I know that because he already told me that. We even talked together about our own relationships.'

Koichi's brows furrowed. 'But you haven't had one yet.'

'I know. And from what he said, I don't think that he has either, Father. Well maybe no long ones since becoming a policeman anyway.'

'He's gone to cool himself off after seeing your nakedness, daughter! That is all it can be!'

'So you think he likes me then?' she asked quickly.

'I have already told you that he does Kumiko. But now, to me at least, it also appears as if you share similar feelings for him now too . . .'

'After only less than a day, that is impossible, Father!'

'Love can happen in very odd and unexpected ways, my daughter.'

'*Love* . . . I have never experienced being in love before, Father, so I wouldn't know what it felt like.'

'It's like having a deep thumping pain beating away in your chest when you look at someone that you feel you may care so deeply for, daughter. As my own did when I first saw *your* Mother as a young woman.'

She shook her head even as the same pounding began inside her again. 'This cannot be. I simply cannot *be* in love him already, Father, surely?'

'Only *your* own heart can ever tell you that, my daughter.'

∞

After her talk with her father, Kumiko climbed the stairs in her bare feet, but only after leaving his oversized slippers at the bottom of it due to their size. Feeling utter trepidation within her mind, and with her palms beginning to perspire, she edged closer and closer to the bathroom. Where she could then hear the same sounding water running quite forcefully as it had for her earlier.

At the open doorway to it, which she thought he must have forgotten to close with more used to being on his own. She peeked around it, feeling like a mischievous young schoolgirl. Knowing that what she was doing was totally wrong and almost inexcusable. Especially for a woman of *her* age to be doing. But now. she also wanted to know if that what she felt now was truly real, or whether it was just an actual desire and yearning for her body to have not only love, but sex. And as much as she was still trying to deny it, even to her own mind, she was constantly finding herself not only being drawn to him as only a woman could be. But also consciously hoping that he was also just as attracted to her as she now felt towards him.

Sliding inconspicuously into the bathroom just as he turned around inside the cubicle away from her within the unclosed shower, she froze instantly like a statue. Where once more she had been thinking to herself. That he must have simply forgot that he wasn't on his own within his home. Her heart began to thump terribly again as she openly looked upon him, as he stood completely naked this time. At his broad shoulders and arms of which now lay unhidden by his clothing, both showed a very definite amount of muscular development to them. His shoulder development and tight buttocks caused her to catch her breath. And what was even worse for her, was that to *her* eyes they looked even better with the water and suds now rolling down them.

As he began to turn around again, Kumiko almost ducked backwards out of the room. It was only her *need* to stay and look at him which transfixed her in that place, and halted her feet from moving. She thought her heart was going to literally burst from out of chest as she stood and watched him turn. His hands had now risen to rub at the shampoo that was upon his sparse head of hair, above his closed eyes. And she saw his muscled hairy chest and his flat tapering lined stomach beneath her gaze.

Her gaze dropped even lower and she felt as if she was about to faint. As his thighs, which to her seemed almost thicker than that of her own waist, she now knew supported that powerful body of his. But, her eyes became almost transfixed upon his manhood, as streams of shampoo rolled down from his head on to the skin of his chest, stomach, groin, and further.

She muttered a low voiced, 'By all of my ancestors!' And then could only watch as the foam like streams either continued to roll right down his body and legs, or ended abruptly where they fell from the end of his large appearing appendage. She was almost mesmerised by its size as it hung there, and without a clue even as to what to do next.

Until finally, her brain must have been able to eventually thrust one single thought through her by now quite tangled mind. And with that one thought now in it, she slid the *yukata* from her body and hung it from the inside door handle. Then, she walked up to the shower as brazenly as she now hoped she could manage to do, and stepped inside the compartment.

For Douglas it was quite a shock, and he almost knocked himself out against the tiled wall when he felt someone else's hands suddenly placed upon each side of his waist. Only from not actually knowing at that particular moment, whether it was the father, or the daughter beside him. And after shaking his head for a moment to clear it, he looked down at the face that was now looking up at his. He watched as she drew even closer to him and her hands went behind his neck to pull his head down to meet her own and then their lips locked together in a passionate embrace.

Their bodies were so close now that there wasn't a gap to be seen between them. Her breasts, with their already stiffening points were rubbing against him, which also made quite sure that it wasn't long before his own ardour showed in return to her, as she felt his very solid erection now pressing against her. They kissed hungrily again, and then she held on to him so tightly with one side of her face pressed against his chest. It was as if he was the last safe thing in her world.

Spirit of a Dragon

The cool water from the power shower pummelled their two embracing bodies relentlessly. Her own rich and soft long black hair being pushed away from her face to lie wetly against her back, though right now, she didn't care. She was just allowing the new warm feeling she now had whirling around within her body, and was very pleasantly just enjoying everything that was happening to her right at this moment.

He reached for the upside down hanging bottle of shampoo again on the small counter, and pressing the button on it squirted some into his hand. Then moving forward a little, just so that he could then take the brunt of the jet of water upon his own shoulders, he actually began to wash *her* hair for her.

With a smile on his face, he after a few minutes, watched as she personally finished off what he had started for her. Then she pushed him back slightly until the water came over his shoulder and hit her again. He studied her movements in a state of almost unbelievable concentration as the powerful jets of water literally bounced off her face and head.

The sight of her small, but very firm breasts getting goose pimples on them, as well as her nipples hardening and becoming fully prominent once again, due to being back in the cold flow of water. Left him once more becoming even harder below at the sight of her, and what they were actually doing together; and almost within hearing distance of her own father in the room below.

Then it was her turn. So she turned him around until *he* was now facing the nozzle and the water was bouncing off him and hitting her head and shoulders. After that, she then turned him to face towards her again, and made him back right up until his spine was touching the tiled wall beneath the high shower. Glancing quite often, it appeared, at his erection before asking him to take up a squatting position on the floor of the shower with his back against the wall. As she knew that she wouldn't be able to reach *his* head and wash it, as he had done for her, which after getting some shampoo from the same bottle, then did so very carefully and deftly indeed. Although he was now much closer to her than he could ever think of being, since her black triangle of pubic hair was now situated almost right in front of his eyes!

After that, she asked him to get to his feet again for him to rinse his head. And as he did that, she turned their bodies together, and she gently pushed him backwards towards the far end of the shower now. He then watched, as her beautifully tinted naked form headed back beneath to where the nozzle still spewed its contents on her once again until she finally turned the water off. Her dense and long black hair was spread out in an amazingly wide fan shape across her back covering it completely, with its near vertical lower lengthy straight ends reaching just below the cleft which separated her also very cute buttocks.

As Kumiko returned to him, he was asked to squat once more, and here again she stood before him; her triangle of hair was certainly less than a foot away from him again! When she was there, her hands made movements upon his head at first to brush off any excess water, but which then appeared to change to something akin to a scalp massage.

'Why are you doing this, Kumiko?' he finally asked.

'You do not like me doing this to you, Douglas?'

She felt his head shake beneath her hands. 'I'm enjoying it very much if you really do want to know. But I still don't understand *why* you're doing it, especially with your father sitting just downstairs from us.'

She parted her legs to either side of his still closed knees and sat down upon his thighs. At which point she stared almost eye to eye with him. And as her hands began to gently stroke at his chest and shoulders, he ran his hands back and forth along the outside of her thighs constantly. They were, so it seemed, very much enjoying being in such very close contact with each other right now.

'Honestly?' she said.

He nodded. 'I like honesty above all things,' he replied.

She kissed him deeply again before saying, 'My Father told me that he thought you were quite attracted to me earlier, though I myself wasn't that sure. Are you?' she queried, hopefully.

He nodded. 'More than you would have ever known, I guess. Until now maybe ...'

'Good. I also felt something for you too, Douglas. But was not entirely sure what it was. And as you say that you appreciate honesty, then I will be honest with you because of this. I also began to feel something similar for you too, Douglas, which I admit did surprise me. Though my Father even said to me that I could be in love.'

'*He* said that to you!' Then he shook his head at her. 'No, I don't really know that much about your country at all Kumiko, but I do know that any relationships between foreigners and your own people are more often than not frowned upon.'

'But if you feel the same way for me in the way that I already feel for you, then I would not care what anyone said, Douglas!'

'But what would your family say?'

'They do not care who I marry so long as I would be happy. And right now, you are making me happy, Douglas.'

'Marry!' He blinked his eyes. 'Are you actually talking about marriage between us already now, Kumiko?'

'Yes, but only if it would also be your personal wish for us both soon, and that you would also be willing to do that with me, too, my Douglas?'

'But your sister . . . and your career that's still awaiting your return over there for you?'

She slid herself even further up his thighs until both of their chests and faces were almost touching. 'Of course I would have to return home with my sister for her funeral ritual and ceremony, Douglas. Yet perhaps if you would happily wish to marry me, then you could come back with us, and we could be present at her funeral together. Then we could be married, and then I could even come back here with you as your new wife, *neh*?'

She waited while he digested all the amazing news she had just given him. As by now she was feeling so good from just being with him, that she may even disregard what her father might say if he was not up to his own expectations after he'd been checked out.

'Are you sure?' he said again without knowing. 'You would actually be willing to leave your family, your home, and even your career this quickly just to be over here . . . with me!'

She flicked her head at him strangely, which to him either meant he had said something wrong right then, or that she was just moving her hair. Her next words helped him to know.

'If I have found true happiness now here with you, Douglas. And right now I am sure from this feeling that I indeed have! Then I would be willing to give up *everything* I have and am just to be with you. You must also understand that it is becoming much rarer for a woman of my age to still be single there. Unless the only thing on her mind is a career before all else! Whereas I just never seemed to be able to meet the right man - perhaps this was the reason why, *neh*? Maybe my own fate was that I would fall in love with a foreign man - from this particular country, in other words, you!'

'But what will you do over here, Kumiko?'

'I will need to speak with my Father about that if you do want me to be with you, Douglas. For the time being I'm sure that he could call up some of his contacts and manage to have me seconded to your police force for a short while, or something, maybe even to working with you for a while on this case, *neh*? Afterwards, well, just as you said, I could always perhaps begin to design, make, and then sell both *kimono* and *yukata*. As I have made my own before now you know. And I already have my first buyer of one of them.' She smiled widely at him.

'And who would that be?' he asked her.

'Your Edith, as she said to me earlier that she was quite taken with the one that I was wearing, and that she would really like one for herself, so there you are! So, Douglas . . . would you wish to become my husband or not? That is the only answer that I now want to hear?' Then she just sat there upon him, her arms draped around his neck and shoulders and awaited his answer.

He thought over the pros and cons of such a hasty thing occurring. Though found little in her words that put him off, if anything. He also suddenly found himself feeling quite happy right then yet didn't know why that was. Of course he'd heard of true love before, as who had not . . . It was just that he'd never expected that *he* might ever be one of those caught within its spell. All of this took only a few seconds to mull over in his mind, as she sat there waiting for his next words.

'If you do feel and think that you will be happy with me, Kumiko. Then I am also quite happy to be with you, too,' he told her.

Her smile broadened immensely at his acceptance. She nodded her head rapidly in front of him. 'To do so will finally make me feel complete as a woman, Douglas, therefore tonight I will sleep with you in *your* bed, which will soon become *our* bed. And we will also make love together tonight to seal our new bond of love.'

'But your Father . . .?'

She pressed the small index finger of her right hand against his lips to silence him. 'I will speak to my Father about us shortly so that he will not mind, Douglas. You see he only wants me to be happy in my life too, and by my being here with you, I do think I will be. And tonight, my Douglas . . . when I feel you enter me for the very first time within my body and take away my own virginity, only then will I finally know all of the desires and feelings that a woman with her love and lover can have!'

'You're a *virgin*!'

'Yes. Why, does that bother you?'

'God no, in fact---'

She grinned. 'Yes, I can even *feel* how *you* feel about me now, Douglas.' She kissed him hard. 'But *tomorrow* night we will share a warm bath together, instead of a cool shower, *neh*? As I am not used to any cold water except rain and it's never ever *this* cold!'

'I'm feeling happier than I ever have before,' he said to her somewhat awkwardly.

Her eyes glinted wickedly as one of her hands vanished and ended up holding him, which made him draw a deep breath. 'I too am feeling very happy now, Douglas. More especially when I think of where this lovely thing of yours will be visiting tonight!'

As her hand slowly slid upon him he gasped, 'Roll on bedtime!'

She kissed him even harder again, and offered, 'I also cannot wait for that time to come around very soon now too, my first ever lover!'

CHAPTER 7

When the alarm clock on the table went off promptly at seven. Which was about normal when he was working on the day shift. Douglas's eyes opened on to a sight that he would never wish to forget even as he reached out to halt its abrupt noise.

Beside him, or rather amazingly enough, almost lying fully on top of him he thought. As she was snuggled so tightly into his own body. Was the same woman whose intense passions had almost killed him outright by way of a possible heart attack fairly recently. Although her face right now, showed little of the effects of it from their lengthy physical joining. From her very first time, right through to the very last time as they had made love together, her own newly awakened passion for more, and then yet even more pleasure had kept them going for close to three full hours. Until finally they had both lain inert upon the bed, spent and utterly exhausted, *or at least he had been!*

His own style of basic foreplay he used with her, he soon found out appeared to be almost rudimentary. If not indeed quite lacking in technique, only by what she, through helping him, was able to teach him. Things which also came as something of a surprise when she, who said she was still a virgin earlier to him. Still appeared to know a hell of a lot more about how to please not only his, but also her own body so openly.

Which was also another reason why their night of love together had seemed to last for so long, because as one frenetic bout of lust filled pleasure ended; and just as he thought that he'd be unable to continue. She had somehow managed to do, or was able to cause *something* quite unknown happen to his body. Which only kept on arousing it back to where it had all initially began, time and time again. Until their bodies could no longer match what erotic thoughts their minds still wanted to carry out. So it was about at that point when they both just fell into a deeply languid and restful sleep beside each other.

As he used a hand to push some of her black hair away from her face, her eyes opened to look back at him.

'Good morning, my love,' he said.

Her returned smile was nothing if not the same as those he'd seen on her face most of last night, even as she squeezed his torso in a hug. 'Good morning back to you, my love, too.' Her eyes moved and fixed on the readout on the clock. 'You will be leaving for work very soon now, *neh*?' she asked.

He nodded. 'Up at seven so that I can shower and shave, then get dressed, have breakfast, and get to work in plenty of time every day.'

'But what time are you actually supposed to start work on a morning?'

'It's roughly about nine at the moment, Kumiko. Though with my routine set out for me every day as I usually do. I usually make it in with ten or fifteen minutes to spare - depending on traffic or any other problems on the way.'

'So if I got up and prepared your breakfast ready for when you came downstairs . . .?'

'It would probably save me another quarter of an hour or so.'

'That sounds very good to me, Douglas,' she said, and then smiled at him again quite suggestively and openly, with her pair of sparkling almond-shaped eyes fixed upon those of his own. 'So, in that case, maybe we could. perhaps . . . just one more time, do you think---?'

∞

It was the first morning that he had ever been late for work in close to three years that day. And he'd driven his entire journey there with something like a stupidly inane grin plastered upon his face. He felt as if he was locked in a kind of daydream cycle on his drive in to work that day.

His new found happiness could not last however, and was about to become a very short-lived one. Because almost as soon as he reached his department and entered. The people already working there within it appeared to be rushing around in an apparent state of near confusion.

'What's up, Terry?' he asked one his team on the case. 'Has a good lead come in for us already?'

Terry's eyes went to the clock close by first in surprise. As he had thought that Douglas was *already* in the building before he arrived, since he always was. And to hear him asking him something that was already common knowledge in the department had left *him* a little confused now.

'I know,' he said, then lied quite admirably, 'I had a bit of car trouble this morning.'

Terry gave a nod. He knew that it couldn't have been much to stop *him* from coming into work early, or even right on time. Seeing as their teams leader had an almost near perfect if not spotless record. In fact most of them thought that it would only ever happen if he suddenly became hospitalised! Even then, they would expect him to be chomping at the bit to get out and get back to work again.

'We only just got some news in from the Durham force, Dougie,' he told him. 'It seems like their people have just come up with a similar kind of finding as regards our own!'

'What, another body? Another young woman found naked and with a strangulation mark around her neck?'

'Yep, just that - a woman out walking her dog decided to go a different way this morning to make it longer one for it, and simply came upon the body. Though from what little info has been given to us so far, it could be that this one was also before our own, Dougie.'

'And if ours was close to being three days old, which would put it back to the Friday sometime. It will depend on what their findings come up with too. As their times will then give us a range of possibilities, wouldn't it? Either that they were being committed during the week, or on a weekend, or in a worst case scenario, that it was just someone passing through each of our patches on their holidays, or whatever? And if the former *is* what's happening, then it's going to be a right swine to get a lot of good information coming in. We can also only hope that the two are separated by something, or else we could have ourselves a serial killer out there to hunt down.'

'Christ, you could be right!'

Douglas shrugged. 'As I said Terry that was our worst case scenario, although only having a single killer out there would be far better for us than multiple ones. As with only one person to look for, the more attacks he has already made - or will make - will no doubt make a costly error at least once which will give *us* the chance of learning who it is!'

Terry, who at only five-feet-six, slightly overweight, and who already had the beginnings of a centrally located bald patch starting on top of his head. Which was unusual to say the least since he was only twenty-nine, but the stress of work was showing itself that way with him, with his receding hair. As some people could cope with the job without becoming over-stressed at all over what they saw, and *did* most of the time. Whereas others, just like Terry himself, almost considered it to be a personal battle in not showing their own weakness and lower tolerance levels to murders. And to also be witness to some very grisly scenes which they just had to attend on occasion. While certain other people, could and had even ended up with mannerisms or body movements which showed off their own anxiety levels as they rose higher occasionally.

'But some murderers can go on for years without one making a slip-up and finally being caught, Dougie!'

'I know that, and that's why we can only hope that he *has* made a slip-up if these two murders *are* linked in any way!'

'And that'll probably all come down to the forensic people trying to find that out for us?'

Hyde nodded, then muttered, 'Which is also making me start to wonder if our killer really *is* just a newcomer and starting his run of killings---'

'Or, what if he's actually been doing it for far longer - perhaps even for years, and we've so far never made any kind of a link to any of them!' Terry interjected.

'Well done Terry, you're catching on.'

'Not really, Dougie. The real reason why this place was in such a state when you came in was because the *Boss* decided to come downstairs and have a talk with us before you got here this morning.'

'He *actually* came down, *into here*!'

'You're damn right, Dougie, I can tell you, it scared the shit out of all of us when he just waltzed in through the door like that. He even terrified some of the poor buggers here who never even seen him since they first came here.'

'I can well understand that happening!' acknowledged Hyde.

Since it had to be close to two years since his last unexpected visit to their department, as he normally stayed up in his lofty office throughout and just dredged through every single report that was sent up to him to read about how each department under his control was working. As he was definitely more of a hands-off boss with them, by allowing them all to just get on with what they were supposed to be doing here at headquarters, and all without him having to continually bear down on one department or another to get things moving. And it was usually only whenever an unexpected problem arose in any department, that a call would be sent out – or even a very curt summons would be sent to one of the floors below for someone to go up there to see him. This told all of the people who worked under him, that He was in fact, still in total control over them all and was very much a hands-on man in every way!

But such a thing wasn't done often, and typically only happened when he wanted to know something at first hand. As it had been when Hyde had been called up to see him. It was basically just to give him a quick update and briefing about what had been found out about the murder already. Limited as any knowledge may have been at such an early stage. But that was the Chief Constable, and they all knew it, from the ordinary constable's right up to the far higher Chief Inspectors. Not one of them doubted that their boss upstairs knew almost as much about their own working cases as they did. The thing was that he seemed to know what was happening in all of them. While they only saw what was taking place within their own much smaller departments; as they were ran almost like separate units from each other.

'So what the hell did he come down for?' Douglas queried.

Terry gave him a smile that as usual showed his one slightly crooked tooth that marred it. 'It seems that he heard about this other murder enquiry just before we did Dougie. So now he's got all of us ringing-up other forces around the country, to see if any of them have had any similar currently on-going, or waiting and now cold investigations that could also correspond with this one of our own.'

Hyde started to nod as he thought about it. 'Just in case our killer *has* been doing his dirty work elsewhere in the country as well, huh?' he said.

'I think that was his idea.'

'So, how are we doing so far?'

'Some of them are already checking up for us on their own databases to see. While a few others are a bit low on staff right now to make our own new request a priority search for us. Although they did say that they'd do one as soon as they had the time or the manpower available to comply.'

'So it's mainly a case of waiting to see with some of them, and wait in hope with the others, eh, though none in vain I'm hoping!'

'That about sums it up for the moment. So is there anything else you want us to be doing as we finish with this, Dougie?'

'Has Carmen sent a list over yet of what names were in the deceased woman's phone's memory? And have they had any luck with everything else at finding any clues?'

Terry was already shaking his head before he finished speaking. 'From her mobile, Carmen took two lists from its memory file for you. One had the numbers for those who she must have called herself on it often enough, so they were either good friends or family to her. And the second list she sent over contains the numbers from the people who were the last ones to call her. As the particular memory on her mobile file automatically deletes the tenth and last number in that list as each new call is received. She also sent a transcript over for you of who was on her own personal file of numbers on the mobile too.'

'Well, it's a start. But if it's been deleting numbers all the time, then I think we should call up her service provider and ask them to list her last calls for us, for say----' He paused for a few seconds as he thought. 'Say backdated for the last three months so that we can start and match them up and then try to cut out the more often repeated similar numbers first. And with any kind of luck end up with a number that might be that of her killers. Though even now I have to say that *that* is also just wishful thinking on my part, Terry, but, you just never know what can happen when you do things like this, do you?'

'You know yourself that they'll probably not give us that list, Dougie.'

'Maybe not, but luckily with the service provider of her mobile being based here in the UK, when you do call them up for me shortly. Just say that if we do need to present them with a court order to get the list, then we will definitely go through that procedure if the need arises.' He then grinned at his younger team member. 'But just add that with it being a murder investigation that we're dealing with here. That their *co-operation* in this matter would be of a very great help to us, especially if they decided to do so without one needing to be requested; as for us to have to do so, would only slow our investigation down while we waited for it to come through.'

'You're a bloody cunning one I have to say that, Dougie!'

'There's little need for cunning here, Terry. All these service providers are big companies, who should be more than willing to provide us with help in solving such a crime. As, in due time, their help might also offer them what they would see as being quite an opportunity for good public relations.'

∞

'Well, daughter?' her father now enquired of her upon entering the kitchen over an hour after they themselves had both got up.

And also after Douglas had had to take a much quicker shower than normal, even to having to use his electric razor to shave with while he ate his rather rushed breakfast. A breakfast which had finally been made by her just as she had offered earlier; who also knew that she could easily have been blamed by him for his being late for everything that morning. As in the end, she knew it meant that he would have got into work unusually late too. But for once he hadn't cared --- as what a morning it had been for him. An experience he now wasn't too bothered if it was repeated most mornings, and especially if he felt like this every day as he had told her with an enormous smile.

'Yes, I'm *very well*, Father, thank you,' she replied happily.

His eyes narrowed as he looked at her as he sat down in the chair opposite from her. 'You know very well just *what* I meant, Kumiko!'

'I know what you mean. And I will say again to you that I am feeling *very* well this morning, Father!'

'Did he please you?'

She smiled rather coyly in return which surprised him somewhat, and that worried him slightly.

'A great many number of times, Father.'

'And did you also please *him*? When I say that Kumiko, you also know that I mean by your using some of our own very secret sexual techniques that we have at our disposal . . .'

'Only once, Father, when I'd almost forgotten just who I *was* with for a moment. But I don't think he noticed it when I did it to him.'

'You are quite sure of this? Did you also tell him that you were a virgin before you had sex?'

'Of course, although I think that he was very surprised when I told him about that.'

'You don't think he really believed you when you said it you mean?'

'Oh, I'm sure that he did, Father. As not many women would readily admit to still being untouched by any man at my age would they?'

'Some types of women will go to any lengths to lure their prey, Kumiko.'

'I apologise as of course you are entirely right, Father,' she said, giving a bow of her head so to show humility to the leader of their clan. As was expected by any one of them if what he thought he said was right.

'I know that I am, Kumiko. Just as I do also know that some women can be very devious when they are truly after something, just like a spider can be with its waiting web - always ready to catch the unprepared.'

'But I am no spider in that sense, Father. We have even already discussed our marriage together.'

'And you also want this to happen now, Kumiko?'

Her shoulders rose then fell as she emitted a low, yet long sigh. 'Even I cannot explain to you how he already makes me feel, Father. And even I cannot believe how much I actually do feel for him now, even if what I think is this love you spoke to me of? As if what I am feeling is love ... then I can only tell you that I have never felt this way in my life before.'

'Was he good at sex?'

'Very good I thought, from what I have ever only *seen* happen personally already; and especially since he has never had any of our own training to aid or guide him. The only time I used my own skills upon him were after almost two hours had passed. When I wanted to feel him within me just once more, and then again. But sadly by then even his own limits had already been reached. That was when I administered a pressure touch on his body so that he would be able to satisfy me just a few more times before we rested.'

'I see. Well, as long as you are happy with him, and he is happy with you, daughter. All I need to know now is what background he has before inviting him to join us.' Her father looked at her closely now. 'As well as you can know him by now, do you think he will be willing to participate fully with our clan? And I mean by that, in everything that we do?'

'I think to know that much about him in only one day is really asking a little too much, Father. If you are actually asking me if he can come to terms with being trained to our levels and even to being as tattooed as we all are already, then probably yes. But as to the usual ritual of the gifts of pleasure that may be offered to him on the night prior to our marriage, as well as to what can also happen afterwards too – in answer to that question, I just do not know, Father. As how could I, as a woman, and one who has just made love with a man for the first time now, really know how *he* might feel. If between two, or I dread to think of it, even up to one hundred or more of our own female members from our clan willingly offer their own bodies to him just for the sake of his and their own pleasure the night before it; and then also any time after we are married as freely too?'

'You think he may even refuse any or all of their offers!' her father said becoming almost wide-eyed and open-mouthed in surprise. 'But such a night as that is. Is also almost a once in a lifetime moment for any newly married man within our clan. It is during that brief moment in time where a part of each of their essences becomes at one with another member - even if only for a few seconds, if such a feat can be managed.'

She sighed again. 'I just do not know, Father. He is still quite a shy man in all respects. I found that out when my *yukata* fell open in here yesterday and he was able to look at my entire body for just as long as he wanted to. But even then he shyly averted his gaze until I had covered myself up again.'

'Strange . . . yes, that I must say sounds very strange indeed, my daughter, as I had always heard and thought that western men had little else upon their minds *but* for naked women and wanting sex all the time!'

She grinned happily. 'Though I am more than pleased to say that he wasn't as shy in the shower later, when I joined him there.'

He nodded. 'Quite understandable really, Kumiko, as that was when you caught him totally unprepared and off guard, as well as his being naked would have left him feeling very vulnerable! And how is he in size?'

Her smile widened even more. 'From those which I have already seen at home Father, I can only say that his is *much* larger in every way than *any* of the other men that I have already seen.'

'*So* large!' her father enquired.

'Last night I sometimes found it difficult to breathe when his erect penis filled me inside, Father. In fact, at the very beginning, I became quite worried that I would not actually be able to accomodate him!'

'By the heavens!' he stated. 'If word ever got around our clan about this when you get home with him, Kumiko,' He said while giving her a wink then a shake of his head, 'then he might have *every* female member of our clan all praying to be accepted as a partner for him on his pre-wedding night.'

'Could I not just spend it alone with him myself, what with him being non-Japanese, Father?' she enquired hopefully, though knowing that it was very unlikely.

He shook his head firmly at her hope. 'You, as my daughter *should* know our ways by now, Kumiko, knowing that it has been done this way for at least two centuries already. As I have said, it allows a kind of sharing to take place between them. You will know that back in the olden days, when some of our clan would certainly be likely to perish while doing our extraordinarily, and sometimes very hazardous work. This same opportunity taking place for them, sometimes allowed some of those women whose husbands had perished to again be with a man quickly. And for some of them, this same gift they were allowed to offer, then gave them the seed to bear one, or perhaps even a few new members into our clan again months later.'

He smiled at her again. 'And if he *is* as large as you *say* he is, Kumiko. Then I am quite sure that there will be some very hopeful women around on that night. Your other two younger sisters will likely be the first in line to sample his pleasure stalk if I'm not mistaken. As we both know already how small their own husband's shafts are, don't we. And if I hear that they won't go to him as a gift just because he *is* a foreigner . . . Then I'll personally *send* them to him myself as an order, and hope that he makes them both weep as he thrusts his enormous shaft into them. As I will certainly not stand for any of my own daughters refusing to offer themselves as a gift to him; especially as he will be a man who will indeed be becoming a part of our own family as their brother-in-law!'

'But what if they enjoy it just *too* much, Father? If they do, then they may want to try to have *even more* sex with him after that!'

'I wouldn't be at all surprised if they didn't request more, daughter. I know that even I myself am not endowed with what anyone with good eyesight would call a large shaft. Yet I always managed to, I hope, satisfy your Mother most of the time. Having seven children should tell you just how much *we* always enjoyed having sex together. But I also know of how thrilled she would have been if someone owning a much larger shaft than my own is was invited to reach into her own depths with it.

'You must also remember this, my daughter. That in the future, after you told to me that you would be returning to live here with him, that you will benefit from this shaft of his on an almost daily business after that. Whereas only a member who may come over to visit you here, or if you both come back home again for a holiday or other necessary event, will again be able to request a sexual session with him. As they may not see him again after you have married and left to come back here for maybe a month, or even a great deal longer maybe.

'And you know that the sharing of bodies in our clan is only for training purposes foremost of all, and secondly sometimes just for the pleasure of it. As we are not controlled by any of these stupid outside sources or politically correct forces who say that the matter of sex is a moral issue and should be strictly kept between those who are in a marital relationship. As if we all did that, then how would our training in the many varieties, and *various* art forms of sexual manipulation *ever* be made to work correctly?

'So, when he does finally become a true member of our clan, Kumiko, then you will have not only the *honour*, but also the added *privilege* of becoming his personal tutor and teacher for us. And unless you come home sometimes with him, or some of us are able to visit you over here, then he will have to rest entirely upon your own teaching skills while having to do all of this for him. Which may be extremely hard for you to accomplish without any additional help at all; but if you ever think you do need more aid, then just give me a call with whoever you may think will be suitable to help you out for a short while. Then I will see what I can arrange for you.'

She nodded her acceptance. Knowing that if Douglas would indeed be going to become a full member within their clan, and with everything that such a step would actually entail in doing so. Then to have to actually begin training him as a novice in all of their clan's secret ways all on her own, could very well take her quite a long time to accomplish. Although she was looking forward to starting some of that training with him, and in particular those skills that she would have to teach him which would involve their having a great deal more sex together.

As ever since her own first time with him the previous night, she knew that she was already hooked on it and as such would like it to continue for as often as possible even while they were still here. In her own mind, she knew that her no longer living youngest sister Akiko, whose body they were actually only here to carry back home again. Wouldn't mind what she was doing so with him while they were waiting for this to happen. As she was quite sure that her sister was even now around her in spirit and watching what was taking place. So that even she, while alive, might have been allowed the pleasures that she now was feeling. Then thought that maybe, in some kind of way she *was* experiencing this new delight - through her . . .

Her father broke into her own thoughts by asking, 'Do you think that we will be allowed to visit the place where her life was taken, Kumiko?'

'I do not see why not, Father, though as Edith told us only yesterday when she brought the newspaper in for us to see. That we must be aware of the many reporters who may wish to speak with us over it . . . which will probably involve us being asked how we feel about what has happened to a member of our family in their country.'

'What *can* we tell them about it, Kumiko? Except for saying how much sadness there is in our family at having to come to their country for this reason, and of what feelings it has caused in us, *neh*?' he responded. 'We are not under investigation by their police force ourselves are we? So perhaps after a brief statement given by us to them like that, then we will be allowed to become invisible to them again. As we will have no more to say after that, will we? Any further details about what happened they would have to get from their own police.'

'I will give Douglas a call and ask him for us, Father, *neh*? As just like at home, we would only be allowed close to where she was found if they have finished their actual search of the area involved and are satisfied.'

He nodded his approval of her suggestion, so she withdrew her own tiny mobile telephone from the pocket of her *yukata*, and then dialled up his number from its own stored memory page.

∞

'Hello?' said Hyde in response to his mobile ringing. 'Oh hi, Kumiko, what was that? Well I'll have to check here first to see if they've finished down there. Then I'll also have a word with the Boss just to be on the safe side, in case. If everything's okay and the Boss agrees to you both being able to visit it, then I'll pick you both up myself and take you there,' he said into his phone with Terry looking on.

'What? Yes, I'll also check to see if there are any reporters still there. And yes, if there are some of them *still* over there, they will no doubt be hoping to interview one or both of you to ask you some questions regarding it.

'A prepared statement for them just in case . . . Well, you could do that if you wanted to, I suppose. But if you wait until I find out what's what first, then if you want to you can do one while I'm on my way there to pick you up and then I'll check it over for you too. Okay, right then. I'll call you back as soon as I can find more out for you. Bye!'

'That was a good one-way sounding conversation, Dougie.' Terry grinned at him.

'It was Kumiko and her father asking if they could visit where she was killed, or where she was just left on the ground,' he told his colleague.

'So I came to understand from what I heard. But do you think that it's wise for them to see it?'

Hyde raised his hands into the air. 'I haven't a clue, Terry. But as far as I know there's nothing left for them to see there now is there, unless some of our lot are still doing their search. Their relative is over in the morgue, and her bike along with all of the contents from the three bags are all over at the lab still being checked over; including the clothing which they found buried there. So I really can't see a problem with them wanting to see *where* it happened now - can you?'

Terry shook his head. 'Nothing at all, and I think the reporters will have headed over to Durham by now anyway, to where the second body was discovered only this morning.'

'Good point! It should be safe enough for them then. Although I'll still have to ask the Boss his views about them doing this.'

'Good luck, mate.'

Hyde grinned at his shorter colleague. 'The Boss *isn't* as terrible as everyone thinks he is Terry. In fact he's one hell of an organiser here if what I've heard about him over the years is right. He has his finger on everything that's happening in this building minute by minute, although we don't think he does. That's why he knew about the second body even before we did down here.'

'So he's not actually a hands-off Boss then?'

'Far from it really, he already had twenty officers in place ready to do the search at the scene for us. So, as you can see, he can get things going himself before you've even thought of asking him for it.'

'I'd better watch myself from now on then,' said Terry.

'It *always* pays you to do that with him!' he answered stoically.

CHAPTER 8

Indicating, and then crossing the road so as to pull up in the lay-by. Behind the two police mini-buses, and the one remaining patrol car that were still in evidence at the scene there. He waited until he'd turned the engine off before facing the woman in the seat beside him. Who with now also being so to near to the scene of her younger sister's murder, had a face that had gone just that little bit paler in colour.

'You don't *have* to do this you know, Kumiko,' he told her.

She looked back at him. 'I will go there with my father if *he* still wishes to visit the place where she may have last been alive, Douglas.'

'But there's really nothing to see,' he tried again. 'Only bare grass and where some officers are still searching around for us.'

'I only wish to have stood once at the place where she last lay, Douglas,' her father Koichi informed him from the back seat, "for me personally, it is more like a spiritual journey you could even say; To have been able to go to the place where possibly she was last alive, and breathing.'

He understood, as he had already told them that the police laboratory was still checking to see if this was actually the place, or not, where her murder had taken place. While also telling them both the

97

results of her earlier samples, that she had indeed been raped, if indeed she was. To which they had both replied quite quickly that she was. Stating that just like Kumiko herself, she was also a virgin in body with not having found her ideal partner yet. At which point Hyde averted his eyes from her father's gaze, wondering if he knew that he had slept with his eldest daughter only the previous night.

When his breathing slowed down again and he felt more in control of his features, he then told them about the two substances which had been found in her fluids by the lab people.

Her father had nodded unpredictably. 'That would explain some of the facts then,' he'd said. 'Drugged not only to make her unaware of what was happening to her body under this narcotic, but also drugged again in another capacity to make her mind feel sluggish and unresponsive to what was actually taking place *with* her. As we all knew that she would never have given herself freely to anyone without any of us having known of this person in her life already Douglas!'

Her father's very next, and forthright words almost stunned him completely, as he then now stated in such a matter of fact way. 'As of course you will know, a vagina for intercourse is always much easier to be enjoyed when it is lubricated during sex. So her attacker must already have known this; and as such he used those combined drugs that you mentioned. Of which we now all know, were used to make her body pliant, as well as easily accessible to his desperate needs. As of course, even someone wanting to do *that,* would never want to injure *his* own person in any way while forcing his attentions upon her!'

∞

Without much further talk between them, Hyde led them both over to the gap in the hedge, which had been made much larger for ease of moving equipment in and out of the scene the first day. Very close beside either of the two openings into the entrance, Kumiko and her father noticed the many bunches of flowers leaning again the hedge and each other as they neared it.

'Who are those from, Douglas?' asked Koichi.

'People who have heard what happened here just leave flowers like this at any kind of tragic event, Koichi,' he told him.

Spirit of a Dragon

Kumiko squatted and began to read some of those that had small-attached notes to them, her father bending at the waist to look over her shoulder began to do the same too.

'But why do they do it? When this crime upon Akiko does not involve any of them?' he said.

Kumiko turned her head to look up at him. 'It was just like this when we watched what happened at home on our news on television after your Princess Diana was killed in the August of 1997, I think. People that were truly unknown to her in life even left so many flowers for her.'

Hyde nodded. 'They each have their own reasons for doing this, Kumiko. Some feel sad at any senseless loss of life like that, and this, while others just want to show you their own feelings at what has happened.'

As she pointed out one of the more poignant notes to her father that was lying there, a handkerchief came from somewhere out of her sleeve, that she dabbed at her eyes and then her nose with before returning it.

She gave a tiny sniff as she got to her feet again. 'To think that they did not even know my sister, Douglas, yet they still made the time, and effort, to not only leave some flowers here for her, but also some very nice messages.'

They all heard the car when it pulled up not far from them in the lay-by, and turned to watch as a middle-aged woman climbed out and began to walk towards them. In her hand was another bunch of flowers waiting to be placed with the others.

'Was she your relative?' she asked softly as she reached them.

Her father could only nod his head, still a little dumbfounded over what he was seeing.

Kumiko said, 'Yes. She was my *sister*, and was my Father's daughter.'

'So tragic,' said the woman to them. 'I am deeply sorry for the loss you have suffered here. I only hope that you won't think we are all like that here in our country.'

Kumiko was already shaking her head. 'Of course we do not think that, and thank you for your sympathy to us. Our family has always enjoyed visiting this country over the years and has never once experienced any problems here, except for now. Which of course was so regrettable, but we know it was not the work of your country as a whole, just one person maybe. Just as we also know that the same thing occurs in our own country sometimes, as well as every other country right around the world each and every day.'

The woman gave a slow nod, even gave Kumiko a hug then handed her bunch of flowers to her before walking back to the car. As the car pulled back out into the road, Kumiko waved to her with her free hand, while the one holding the flowers was up at her face trying to brush away her tears. Koichi just bowed as the car went by him.

Hyde, after Kumiko had regained her composure, then took them through the gap in the hedge and over the grass to where he had first come into contact with the bicycle. Which was where they all came to a stop, and only the two newcomers looked around the area.

'If your daughter rode a bicycle that day Koichi, then this is the place where it was found,' he told her father.

'She rode very much while she was here,' he answered. 'As just like at home in Japan, she enjoyed riding in your countryside, and down the much quieter roads and cycle tracks outside your cities; even to visiting some of your old buildings and places. She also did the same further away when she had a longer break from university, taking her bicycle down by way of a friend's car, even by train to reach more to the south of your country.' He looked at his daughter then, 'I think that was last year when she visited your Aylesbury and also took one of those Shakespeare tours.'

Kumiko nodded. 'Yes, that was what she did last summer before coming home for a short while before her latest term began again. She quite fell in love with your country you know, Douglas,' she said to him.

'And just as your people in the west like to hear about the days of our samurai and geisha from Japan. She had begun to fall in love with your history and traditions . . . Of all your Kings and Queens and your parliament, and of your playwrights and poets, writers and fashion. She was even one of those people who actually understood and truly enjoyed your very own special sense of humour! Although when she *did* come home occasionally and told us some of your jokes, and also about some of your comedies that were showing upon your television - I'm afraid that much of it left us quite lost!'

He shook his head. 'I wish I'd had a chance to meet her, Kumiko,' he said in response to her thoughts over her sister, 'as she sounded like a very happy go lucky and very nice person to have known.'

They both nodded, though quite aware that only by her loss had he been able to meet them to actually hear these things.

'Akiko did leave us with one very special gift though, Douglas,' and then she saw that he was waiting for her to explain. 'On her first year, and second trip home after starting at your university here, she began to tape those same comedy, and various other shows that she had told us about for us, which we were all soon watching when she brought them home for us.'

Hyde was puzzled. 'But I thought that *our* video systems, just like those here and in America, were incompatible?'

'That is true,' said her father. 'But we took them to someone we knew who was capable of converting what was on the tapes which she brought back, on to those that we could play on our own systems.'

'But surely you could just have bought the same programmes over there without all that bother?'

'The foreign videos which have been *allowed* to be released for sale in Japan, Douglas, are nearly always dubbed in Japanese for our own internal market. To which Akiko said that it would never feel the same to us unless we actually heard it as it had been meant. Which of course was in your complete English language from from beginning to end . . . and certainly without us having to use Japanese subtitles so as to try to understand it.'

'So what did she bring over for you?'

'Oh, I really loved to watch those episodes of your very weird Fawlty Towers, and especially some crime films called Prime Suspect!' said Kumiko.

'And I liked your Sweeney - I think it was called, and also your Professionals,' added her father. 'Though since she had got us so interested in them from what we had seen already. That I had installed, what you would likely say, was a quite substantial satellite dish at our rural family home. So that we would be able to pick even more of them up ourselves and just tape them as and when they came on. It has become such a feature at our house now, that I'm afraid my own wife would die if she didn't get her regular supply of some of your own soaps called Emmerdale Farm and also of a one called Coronation Street, too. Though we found out that she wouldn't even start to watch any of them, at least until they began to show both of those series right from the very first episodes!'

Kumiko was nodding her head. 'She becomes so engrossed in these that she won't even talk to anyone until she has not only watched it, but also taped it while doing so. The rural life of this Emmerdale Farm appealed to her own young life so much, that she almost hangs on to every word that Annie, who is the mother of this Sugden family ever speaks. And the gritty drama of the black and white series set in your Manchester here, can honestly keep her glued to the television for hours and hours as she watches what your Ena Sharples is going to do next.'

'She's going to have a long time to spend catching up with everything then,' he told them.

'Why is that,' asked her father.

'Because the series Coronation Street is *still* running now, after well over thirty years I think. As I'm sure it began in the sixties. And Emmerdale Farm as it was then, I think began in the seventies some time, and the last I remember of it was that it is also still running but just called Emmerdale now.'

'Good God!' muttered Koichi. 'Kumiko, I think we'd better explain to your mother just how far behind them all she is right now, or else try and wean her from them and just tape them for her?'

'You could very well be right, Father. As if either of those two are actually on television on the day and evening of my wedding, then we would almost have to drag mother away from it just to come!'

Their conversation came to an end as they all watched as a man dressed in a white covering suit emerged from behind a bush. Who then began to walk up the slight bank, until he finally came to a stop in front of all three of them where they were all still stood on top of the higher part.

'DI Hyde?'

'Sergeant Crawford?' he returned.

He gave a nod. 'Exactly how far do you want this search of ours extending to, sir?'

'How far have you reached now?'

Turning to face the area where he had been, he raised a hand and waved it at various positions as he spoke. 'We've been doing a half circle sweep over the area since we began here yesterday, sir. We started one way for about fifty yards, or until we need a break for refreshment or rest and marked where we got up to. After the break we sweep the same size section beside it until we reach the same mark. We do that until that half circle search is completed, and then we start from where we'd finished the very first one.'

'So how far out are you now from the main scene?'

The sergeant looked just below him to where the officers were still moving on their hands and knees out of their view. 'At a rough guess, I'd say about four hundred yards out now, give or take a few.'

'And how far out were you when the clothing was discovered?'

'About halfway through section seven, sir, say about a hundred and seventy-five yards.'

Hyde did some mental work quickly and wasn't sure if he liked what he'd just heard. As the clothing had been buried away from the body and the main road from that. So he now knew that it was quite possible that her killer didn't drive and park at the lay-by to this place.

'Okay, sergeant. Only go as far as you have on every other section up to four hundred yards. After that, stick with your section seven and keep searching along its track.'

'How long for, or for how far, sir?'

'Either until you finish tomorrow evening or until you reach around seven hundred yards that way. If you haven't found anything else unexpected by then, then just do another final slow fifty-yard walkover the ground for me after that. And if you still find nothing more, then we'll call it quits. As after that I think we'll have to count on it being a vehicle used and parked in that direction, and also see what our lab people can come up with for us.'

The sergeant nodded. 'Do you think that the two may at all be connected in any way, sir?'

'We won't know that until our colleagues over in Durham can find out what they have themselves, and then let us know. After that happens, well, all we can do is to wait and see as usual.'

The sergeant left to continue with his task, and to follow his orders from the man in charge of their own investigation. While Hyde had to quickly fill the two of them in with what he up to now knew had transpired over in Durham only that morning.

'So he may have already killed another woman before killing my daughter, Akiko?' asked Koichi.

'It might be possible, or they may not even be connected to each other Koichi. Their pathologist will get in touch with ours if anything looks the same. Just as they will also do anyway, if any of their own lab work corresponds with ours. As I've already had copies of our notes sent over for them to see if they might match-up in any way, or not. And my Boss after hearing about this new crime this morning has already begun to ask for information from other the other forces in England, Scotland, and Wales, at the moment too.'

'For what reason are you doing this?' he asked Hyde.

But Kumiko answered her father. 'As if there are, or there has been a similar murder in *their* areas, Father. Then that would lead Douglas to suggest that they all may be the work of just one man – which will then be that of a serial killer! Am I not right, Douglas?'

'I'm afraid you may be right, Kumiko. Though I only hope that any DNA that we do get shortly, *will* match someone who is already on our database.'

'And if it does not?'

'If not, Koichi?' He shrugged. 'Then it could be a long hard road to track down whoever is responsible for these crimes. Unless of course a mistake has been made by this person unknowingly, as that would help us to narrow any search area down and close in on him until we finally get him!'

There was little else for him to show them at the scene, only as there was nothing still there in place to do much. The best he could do for them was to stand at roughly the spot where he'd remembered the tent had been erected, and that was all. At this point they both bowed their heads for a minute or so as they prayed for her life, her soul, her spirit, or whatever, they were praying for. Then following her father's lead, Kumiko copied his bow.

Returning to the car again Hyde then drove them back, though first going with them to the mortuary where an identification of their relative needed to be carried out. Which was also where they both met Carmen for the first time. And as Kumiko decided to be the one to identify her sister and look through all of the belongings found on the bicycle to see if they were all hers. Her father asked Hyde if he would, if at all possible, be allowed to meet with his superior for a few private minutes. Only so that he could express his daughter's and his own thanks for how they had been treated since their arrival.

∞

His surprising request was summarily granted almost immediately by the Chief Constable, and leaving Kumiko to help Carmen where she was. He drove her father over to his own headquarters. Where even as they were shown into the Chief's office by his secretary, he immediately informed Hyde to return to the mortuary to collect what information was being given out by the sister as it may be very relevant to his case. As while she looked over what objects had been brought in, that he should be there on hand in case anything of great importance came to light. While also telling him just before he left, that he would have an officer escort Mr Hirano back over to them there when they had finished.

The few minutes of his visit to the Chief Constable's office came closer to being that of half an hour. Until her father was escorted back by a uniformed officer in a normal patrol car; while they were both now just waiting for him to arrive.

Kumiko's initial identification of her sister was harder than she would have imagined. As from her chin down, her body had been covered by a crisp white sheet, which left only her face open to view. But after lying out in the hot sun for possibly a few days as she had been. Its strong rays over all that time had had enough time to burn and blister the skin of her face until her features had become a little distorted. She was pleased that she was the one looking at her, and not her father or mother as she looked down. Simply as her own police background and experience in similar matters, had somehow managed to allow her to do what was required of her. As she had to control and push her own very personal thoughts away to one side for that brief moment. Almost to the point of becoming totally uninvolved at just whom she *was* now looking at.

Carmen had watched her face throughout as she had done this. And had also seen and noticed, not only the courage, but near professional detachment she was showing as she attempted to identify the body. But even she could see that she was having some trouble doing so. So had asked if her sister had any distinguishing features, or marks upon her body, which would leave her in no doubt. When she described the large tattoo that her sister carried upon her back, Carmen had told her that a positive identification had now been made of her. And while her sister was wheeled away from the room to be placed back into one of the cold storage drawers for the time being. Carmen led her through the building to where the other items waited for her examination in the lab, which was where they were when Douglas came back.

Kumiko actually recognised nearly all of the items they had in the lab that had belonged to her sister, although a few items remained unknown to her, since she had not seen her sister after she'd last been home for Christmas and New Year. And of these unknown items seen by Kumiko, of which each one of them could have been bought by her sister over here after she had returned. Along with those items of a more feminine nature, were presumed to have belonged to her anyway. He and Carmen had to leave it at that, as she couldn't offer any further information regarding them.

The officers in his department were already starting to track down her friends and acquaintances from her call list. And as Carmen had shown her a copy of what she had taken from it. Quite a few of them were quickly scratched through as Kumiko told them which members of her own family back in Japan those same numbers on the list belonged to. The rest of them that were now left would all be checked up on by his enquiry team. Finally, after all had been finished, and her father had returned to join them, Hyde took them both back to his home.

∞

When they had returned, after thanking him for taking them to the very place where she had lost her life. He had to leave them there while he returned and got on with his job again. To where Terry had already been sent to talk with some of her fellow students about what men she may have known, or had been quite friendly with. And they also had arranged to meet up with her three roommates at the house they shared. A house he'd then found out, which had originally been purchased for her by her father for her own use while she was over here studying at university. But the actual loneliness of her having to live there on her own, had led her to advertise for roommates and companionship.

Which would not only give the house a feeling of it having some additional noise and life inside it, but that it would also provide a small remuneration back to her Father, by way of them paying rent also. Although when she had finished her courses at the university and returned home, he would then be left with either having to sell the property, or leaving it to be rented out. He had still been undecided as to which thought to take right up to her death. And so, as he left them both to their own devices again, he went off to do what he was paid to do by the public.

Her father quickly settled in the reclining chair, his feet up again, with his laptop in position and a drink on the table. While Kumiko began to make a meal for them both from what provisions they had brought home the previous day. She rapidly checked over all their use by dates, only to make sure that none of them would be wasted, and decided to make a meal from most of those carrying the earlier dates anyway. From the packets, boxes, or sealed plastic wrappers, she selected various foods. Tiger prawns, noodles, one pack of fresh fish, herring. From those she selected, the ingredients would allow her to make their own watery looking *miso* soup. The fresh vegetables she found in a small rack in what Douglas had called his "pantry" when he'd showed it to her. As well as their own more widely used vegetable types that they had also bought and which he had placed in the small rack beside his own.

Even as she had everything sorted into the correct order for the various stages to her starting to cook. She hunted through his drawers until she found a pair of scissors to open some of the bags. The various sized knives that he used often enough as and when he needed them, stood nearby in a wooden block on the counter. Thinking over what else she would need, she went through the cabinets until locating his pots and pans that she would also have need of. And with those, she filled the largest first, then the smallest of them with water from the tap.

As she read over the instructions actually printed in both English and Japanese, just to see if they would differ from what she would have used back home. She heard her father's mobile phone ringing over in the living room. And as she got on with what she was doing, heard her Father start to speak with whoever had just called him.

'Hello, Yoshi!' said her father to the caller, who was the man from yesterday who worked quite high up in their government back home.

'I have not called you at an inconvenient moment I hope, Hirano-san? And that you are unable to talk with me?' he asked.

'Not at all, my friend, Kumiko is just making a meal for us while I checked up on the business back home. And our police friend has returned back to work, if that is what you actually meant?'

'Yes, that *is* good news, Hirano-san. However, for what you required of me to help you out with what you asked of me yesterday. I have had to call in some rather large favours to get you exactly what you wanted.'

Koichi was quite puzzled by that. 'I do not understand, my friend. Surely it should have been quite *easy* for you to get what information I told you that I required?'

He imagined he could almost see the other man slowly shaking his head at the other end, as he voiced, 'It was actually *extremely* difficult for me to *get* what you wanted to learn about him, Hirano-san.'

'I do not see any reason why that should have been so difficult, Yoshi . . . We have already found out that he was in his country's military forces as a Royal Marine, and is now a policeman. So what could have been so difficult?'

'Mainly because of what he *had* been and was, Hirano-san! This was where the problems began when I contacted my counterpart in England for a background check on this man. I *even* had to personally tell a *lie* a few times to get you what you wanted. So, if you are called up unexpectedly by one his own government officials, then this will also have to be your story to keep my position safe.'

'I'm listening, Yoshi,' Koichi answered carefully.

'Your story, through me, was that you were thinking of maybe hiring yourself some personal bodyguards back home due to some serious Yakuza problems.'

'Yakuza?' he said. 'Yoshi, my friend, I have no such trouble as that. Nor will I ever have such trouble, as well you know!'

'*I* know that, Hirano-san, but *they* do not. So I had to think very quickly when I was asked *why* I wanted such information about him. Information that I soon gathered was actually described to me as being of what they called it - quite highly classified material!'

'What?'

'That is exactly what I was told, Hirano-san!'

Koichi began to nod to himself as a sudden thought struck him. 'But of course Yoshi, he must have worked as an undercover policeman sometimes, *neh*? So that is why some of his details have been hidden, for security reasons.'

'No. These details I finally managed to find out go back to his earlier military service.'

'Are you telling me that he may have been thrown out of his army and not left through injury as he told us?'

'Not even that, Hirano-san. Through my counterpart there, and by him also having to ask for favours above his own station there as well, I *finally* found out *why* his background information was so difficult to get for you.'

'And the reason being was?'

'That he actually served in one of their elite regiments, Hirano-san. A regiment that people throughout the world have heard talk of, even I, but rarely of who they were . . . He has actually been a member of their much feared SAS, Hirano-san!'

'*Was he indeed!*'

'Yes indeed he was, Hirano-san.'

'And were you sent a *full* record of him?'

'I was.'

'Then if you would please forward a copy of it by e-mail to me for my own private reading and consideration. I would be very happy to receive it from you.'

'Do you mean right now, Hirano-san?'

'Now would be as good a time as any, my friend, since my laptop is here beside me and is already turned on.'

'Very well, Hirano-san. But I must also tell you that this information must be erased straight after you have seen it. As if any leak did occur, then I would be the one held accountable for it happening. I was also told this by my counterpart before he sent it to me. As with only those from myself to those who managed to get it for you . . . only I would be suspected of having done something illegal with it. As the rest of them have a high enough clearance level to not be suspected of giving out such typically undisclosed knowledge.'

'I will of course do as you have asked my friend, as you are much too important to me to allow something as dangerous as this obviously is to escape into the outside world.'

'Thank you, Hirano-san. I am sending a copy of it to you right now before I then delete it here, and will look forward to meeting you again upon your return home.'

'Yes, thank you, my friend. I will also enjoy meeting you once more where we can have a drink together at some time, or a meal perhaps, *neh*?'

'I would indeed be honoured by that, Hirano-san,' offered the government official as their call finally came to an end.

Koichi lay reclining in the chair waiting, until a small message appeared on the display in front of him in Japanese characters. Informing him that he'd just received an e-mail message. He clicked on the flashing icon, which took him straight in to his mail site, upon where after he'd inputted in his own e-mail address and password, he selected the new piece of mail almost as soon as his mailbox came up with its entry into it.

As he slowly began to read through what was on the display. His lips pursed and a very low whistle escaped from between them. My God, he thought. It shows you just how wrong you can be about some people! He moved the arrow over to the top of the menu board and clicked on the print icon. Seconds later, he watched as the small machine on the coffee table began to emit a light noise as the same details were quickly printed out on to a sheet of paper. When it was finished, he transferred those same files into one of his own very personal mailboxes. One that he knew was very much secure from any unwanted reading, as it was highly encrypted, and no data on it actually showed anywhere. He had even had incorporated into it three separate passwords before it would even show up on the screen and allow you to select one of the files within it. Only when it was cleared and safe, did he turn the laptop off and unclip all the equipment from it and put it down beside the chair. Then picking up the print out began to study it in even closer detail.

As he came to the end of the paper, his head began to sway side to side in amazement at what he'd just read. He sat in silence for close to five minutes as his brain mulled over the facts of what he'd just read. And then turned his head and called out for his daughter Kumiko.

CHAPTER 9

Kumiko stood beside the chair her father was reclining in. And he actually saw her mouth just drop open in surprise by what she was now reading on the printout herself. Even her head was shaking as she read down the sheet. If asked from what little she knew of him already, Kumiko knew that she would never have actually believed he had done something like this.

Her brain was rapidly taking the details of her soon to be husband, even as her eyes continued to scan over them. Aged twenty-three to twenty-eight he had served with the SAS, who even *she* had heard of in Japan. And over that short five year period had been additionally trained in armed combat, and karate and judo for unarmed combat, and able to use a wide variety of weapons from a knife to a mortar. His talents on paper noted that he had been trained as a sharpshooter, frogman and diver, a field medic, demolition and explosives disposal. But what had surprised her most of all, was when she learned that he could actually speak and write Japanese fluently . . . as well as both Malay and Thai. He had even been almost finished studying both Chinese and Burmese just before his injury had caused him to retire from their armed forces.

'I just *cannot* believe this of him, Father,' she told him as she stood there with the printout now just dangling from her hand.

'Believe it well, my daughter. Though just as you did, I also found it quite hard to accept. That this very same man who has been talking so calmly and easily to us as he has been doing, has in fact actually killed over twelve men personally. And from that, I can also now remember a short documentary that I saw on our television late one night at home. Which must have been bought from one of their television companies over her to show in Japan. If I remember something about it, it was that there actually not any real ranks as such in this unit, apart of course from their commanding officer. And that any of the volunteers passing the training, and also the many, very, very, hard tests did, after getting through it. Then they had to start further training and learning as many of these new skills as they could manage; to equip them better so as to be able to fit into any needed small team. Including foreign languages, of which they had hoped to try and learn at least two fluently.'

'But he shows very little outward sign of what he has once been, Father. How can he possibly do that?'

'I can only guess that he must been a natural to it, Kumiko. Either that, or he has simply been able to close his mind off from it all, especially if what he has done in the past never comes back into his mind to ever haunt him as a vivid nightmare or bad memory.'

'So would he actually be acceptable to you as my proposed husband now, Father? Or has what he has been in his past life mean that he is not quite worthy enough for you?'

He peered at her. 'Kumiko, your Douglas has actually disposed of more people himself than any one single member of our own present day clan, and that's including me and my own late father too. So to say that he is not worthy enough to become one of us, is so stupid as to be almost unnecessary. As just as we all have so much to teach him now, he also has a lot that he can teach us by way of a family duty too. And yes, my daughter, I would also now actually not only be proud, but also feel quite honoured to accept him within our family after seeing what he has *already* done within his life.'

Kumiko was happy. The man who she now felt she had loved for less than two days was at least now actually being recognised by her father. Recognition which also now meant that her own dream of becoming his wife was still possible, in fact, by the way her father had now spoke of him, her forthcoming marriage sounded almost like a certainty. She walked back almost as if she was walking on air, back to the waiting food in the kitchen with her heart brimming full of happiness.

As she sorted out the ingredients as she prepared them, some going into one of the two pots, while others lay ready on the counter. A sudden thought began nagging in the back of her mind, of which she wanted to know the reason.

'Father . . .' she called out loud enough for him to have heard her. And by his reply knew that he had, then said to him, 'Why did you want to see Douglas's boss earlier?' She waited, and then waited a little longer for his response, but none came. '*Father?*' she called slightly louder.

'Yes Kumiko, I am right here beside you. I can also hear you very easily now, so there is really no need to shout so loud.'

'Sorry.'

'So what did you call out to me?'

'I asked you why you wanted to see Douglas's boss earlier, when we parted company at the mortuary, if only for a short while? Was it about some information that Douglas himself could not have told you?'

'I really only wanted to know when Akiko's body would be released to us. So that we could make our arrangements to pick her up from where she is, and for her to be transported to our plane to take home.'

'I'm sure Douglas could have told you that, Father. Since he *is* leading her investigation - and also would have known when her body was no longer required by them too . . .'

'I did *know* that, daughter. But I also wanted to ask this boss of his if Douglas could come back with us when we left, to be just like an ambassador for this country and their police force to attend her funeral.'

Her brows knitted together as he watched.

'And also because I told him that you two were going to be married after it had taken place. So he might actually be requesting a leave of absence, only for a short while anyway.'

She blew out her cheeks at her father's actual impudence of telling his senior officer that. 'And what did *he* say about two people who have only known each other for less than two days going to be married?'

Her father grinned. 'I told him that *I* myself had also been just as surprised, if not quite *shocked* by your sudden announcement. Although just from seeing how happy you were together, that I had happily given my blessing to it happening anyway.'

'He believed you when you said that to him?'

'Certainly, as you do know that I am very skilful when it comes to only showing upon my face what I want to be seen shown upon it, *neh*? So he was none the wiser about my little untruth to him.'

Her eyebrows now rose well up into a double arch just as quickly. 'But if that is so, Father. Then you were already going to allow me to marry him, *neh*! As you didn't receive that printout about him until we got back here.'

He nodded. 'Yes, my daughter, I had already decided upon doing that anyway, after having seen how your feelings had altered so much for him so quickly. Though these new details we now know have only added even more to my wanting him within our clan.'

'So when do you, or perhaps even *I* myself personally confront him? I mean, about these many new facets of information about him that we have, Father?' she asked.

'Not until we get him home, Kumiko. Right now we must both try to forget what we already know about him. And I mean everything . . . including the fact that if we speak Japanese to each other, or to someone on the telephone as I did before, that he actually *knew* what was being said.'

'So we will have to extremely careful in what we say to each other then, Father. Is that what you mean?'

'Not entirely. As if we start and try to think of what we are going to say *as* we are speaking. Then he may quickly work out that we know something about him that we really shouldn't have been able to find out. And now know. So for now, we must just try to simply forget that he can, and act just as we have done until finding this information out now.'

'Doing that could prove very difficult to do, Father.'

'I know. But his boss did tell me that Akiko would hopefully be being released to us by Thursday at the latest. Which is only two days away now. And he did also tell me during our talk together that if he did come to ask him for some time off for personal reasons. That he could allow him to take up to two weeks off. As there was someone working within one of the departments there that he could have take over for him while he was gone for that long. Who could if necessary, also ring him up while he was with us to ask for advice or anything else; only if he needed to do that was. Whereupon I did ask his boss, a little presumptuously I thought later to myself. To remember the variable difference in time between our two countries before such a thing was done, just so that he wouldn't be calling him up at some time through the night or whatever.'

'And he still agreed?' she asked uncertainly again.

'Of course, daughter, he even said to me that with him finally becoming a happily married man like himself. That it could only end by possibly bringing some extra and beneficial changes within a good officer's life. So you see, Kumiko, all we have to do is get our family to get Akiko's funeral planned for this weekend in readiness of our return. And then have your wedding planned for a little later that same week, so you will also have time for a short honeymoon together before you return here with him.'

'You have everything already planned, haven't you, Father?'

He nodded to her. 'Things like this usually cannot be rushed into being, daughter. But this time it must be done this way. When he comes home later we must have a talk with him about your wedding and such. And I have already been on the telephone, just before you gave me a call, to the Japanese embassy in London. As we will have to call in there first for him to pick up his waiting visa to allow him to visit our country on such short notice, before we can continue with our flight on it to Japan.'

All she could do was to nod a reply to him, and as always, she had again found out just how very organised and rapidly her father could get such things worked out and moving. It seemed as if everything that was, or had needed to be done, was already well in advance, preparation wise. She knew that there would actually be little other planning required to set things in motion once he got started on something. Then she looked at him. 'What about the casket that we will need for Akiko? I know from what I do that a very unusual one is often required when transporting and repatriating any persons remains back to their own country again?'

He smiled disarmingly, which told her again that he was already way ahead of her once more, and then said, 'I spoke with his boss on exactly that subject as well, Kumiko, and also with our own embassy. The details he gave me about what kind of casket their own services could provide for such a task, also matched those given by our embassy. So she will be laid into one of those special zinc, lead or steel, or thermostat controlled or such like. One of those kinds of sealed ones anyway before we come to collect her.'

'So we could definitely be leaving on Thursday then?'

'Yes, Kumiko, so make the very most of your time here with him while you can. As when we get home I will definitely have to speak with your Mother straight away, I think. Before she would even think of allowing you to sleep together before you are married.'

'If she does not wish me to, Father, then of course I will follow her offered advice.'

'Don't be silly, Kumiko. If she decides that she does not want to allow you to do that at home. Then all you have to do for a few short days is to take him to your apartment in the city until you *are* married. So you can still have whatever sex you wanted to have with him while your impending wedding day continued to approach.'

'You would not object if I wished to do that, Father, and even to go against my Mother's own wishes in this matter?'

He smiled somewhat benignly now at her. 'Since you have already sampled what impressive goods he has to offer you, my daughter. Why should only a few more days of your having so much passion filled sex while you are still a single woman bother me now? As you yourself know that he may have to do the same for other female members of our clan before you are married.'

'Only if he will agree to it though?' she responded.

His head began to shake on his short neck. 'I have already told you this once before, my daughter. That there are few actual straight men living in this world of ours who would truly and willingly, *refuse* any such offer as that if it was being made. A chance for their shaft to penetrate and enter so many other women's velvet pavilions! And especially with what you have already told me about his quite large genitalia. He, as a man, would I think be most stupid to refuse so many willing partners . . . As I know myself from the night before I married your Mother. That I received so much pleasure and enjoyment from the many women partners who did wish to offer their bodies to me that night. That afterwards I also enjoyed other times later with many of the same women again, and not only in training with them - but just for our own mutual pleasure together also.'

'I just do not know how *Douglas* will see it, Father. That after we are married, he will actually be able to have sex with any other woman within our clan if they both desired to do so. Just as I myself, from the day that I become a married woman, and as I would no longer termed as a virgin within our clan. Can also, if I ever really wanted to, enjoy sex with any other man who was not my husband within it as well.'

He shrugged at her. 'Our rules are very different to those of the normal outside world, Kumiko. And therefore because of that it allows us all to enjoy various things which to any outsider's eyes would seem shocking, if not actually perverted in some way. But our own clan's actual openness in the very meaning of the acts of sex, to me personally, have always been seen as more of a help than a hindrance.'

'How so?' she queried.

'Well, for one thing, daughter. If any of our wives are pregnant and either do not *wish* to indulge in any sex for a while, or perhaps if their time of the month of menstruation is occurring, or that of a birthing experience is approaching very close at hand. Then usually any sex before that time will come to a halt with it being, or feeling, quite uncomfortable for her by then. So, the opportunity we have always had, with being who we are, allows us to indulge ourselves with another partner within our group. In that way the wife is happy by not having to have sex until she is feeling ready to do so again. While her husband can happily shaft with other willing women until she is.

'For those women themselves, they know that there is no actual pressure upon them to have sex if they do not wish or want to. And that their husband will readily find another willing partner quite easily from someone else in our clan. Be it member or servant. While it can be almost the same for our women too, if they simply want a change from their husband being their usual partner all of the time.'

'I do not think I would feel happy about seeing him do that with any other women, Father. Even if I already know them very well,' she replied quite honestly to him.

Spirit of a Dragon

He gave a long sigh. 'It can be very difficult at first to come to terms with this part of our clans ways, daughter. But you should have no trouble so long as you can keep him content in both mind and body yourself.'

'That is one thing which I will *always* strive to do, Father.'

'I know that you will *try* your very best to do so, Kumiko. But you must never also forget that other members in our clan will also have the *right* to ask this not only of him, but also of *you* as well! You already know that your two younger sisters have had other male partners since their marriages, just as you yourself may have need to accept someone now and then, too. As to train in our special skills requires you to take various partners in order for you to aid your own training as well as theirs. And now, at the point where Douglas would only be classed as a bare trainee in our ways, would mean that even *he* at this early stage, until he was given the necessary training involved. Would only be any good at giving what we would likely call, *ordinary* pleasure to our women, as he has none of those other basic skills which are required yet with which to bring on or prolong an orgasm for them.'

'So in respect he will only be seen as little less than some kind of a male stud. As someone with a large penis and so only there to be used for our own sexual satisfaction and gratification?'

'Yes. Until he has some of our own vital knowledge imparted to him, which will also become one of your main duties by the way, daughter. As until then, he will only be seen as little more than a large shaft on the side-lines of our clan, and as such, readily available to all who wish him to fill their voids whenever he may be needed. But only *if* he agrees to it, of course!'

She shook her head very sadly. 'Oh my poor darling, Douglas,' she murmured, 'what have I gone and got you into with me!'

'Or one *very lucky* Douglas if you care to think about it for even a minute, Kumiko?' her father said as her head tilted over in her usual questioning way of which he knew so well by now, 'especially if he is more than willing to accept *all* of our ways in this, that is!

'As with him being *like* he is right now, he may have just as many willing partners only wanting him *for* this basic pleasure. Just as you yourself have already enjoyed with him so much.'

She turned away to think over what he had said to her, and also to wonder if Douglas would be able to understand the various nuances which lay deep within their ancient clan's history. She went back to her cooking for them as her father returned to the living room.

∞

Over in Durham, at the scene where the other body had been found, quite similar facts had already being established by the attending forensic pathologist. An almost identical marking around the neck, though a little harder to determine due to the slightly longer length of time the body had now been left outside to the elements. Yet she had been left just as naked as the first one had been. Again showing no actual means of transportation beside her either. The country lane a few hundred yards away from it offered possibilities of *how* she had got there, but as yet not of when or why.

An unexpected attack on her had immediately come to the thoughts of the man overseeing an almost identical crime scene to that of Hyde a few days earlier. And with Hyde's teams' own report in his hands, he quickly had officers supplied by his own superior to carry out an almost identical but search procedure. But with him already fearing that his own could be either the first or second to have been found now, his superior had also offered even more people for him to use in the search. After an almost similar scenario whereby all very careful details and pictures had been taken, the body was removed to their own mortuary. It was only a little later in the afternoon when the apparently hasty burial site of her removed clothing was located less than a hundred yards away once again.

And to Andrews himself, a Chief Inspector who had been detailed to attend the scene and take the case, the worrying signs of a duplicate type of murder enquiry were already running through his mind. The same unclothed condition of the body, the probable marks around the neck of the victim; told to him by the pathologist after some careful study and checking the sent over helpful files. And now the finding of her buried clothing not being that far away from her. Began to tell him that, what had started to be suspected by the actual officer in charge, Hyde, was now coming together - and that they were indeed being carried out by the same person. Only some study at the autopsy and from their lab people would answer a few other questions left remaining in his mind . . . Had this girl also been drugged in the same way. If the answer to that was going to be yes, then both teams were going to have a great deal of work ahead of them to find the culprit responsible for them both. Though the emphasis would lie with Hyde.

∞

Hyde was surprised when he was asked to go up and see the Chief Constable upon his return to headquarters, after he'd just returned from dropping them back off at his home. Not actually knowing why he had been summoned to see him, unless the chief had heard something from Durham about the new murder, which hadn't filtered down to his own department yet. And to his astonishment found himself being invited to sit down by a somewhat *smiling* Chief Constable. Another rare occurrence.

'Well how are you progressing so far, Hyde?' he asked, and almost as his rear end touched the chair seat.

'Kumiko has now examined every item found at the scene, sir, and *most* of them she remembers belonging to her sister. There were a few discrepancies of course, as expected. But that could be because she'd bought them here after returning from her last visit home. So Kumiko wouldn't have seen them anyway.'

'And how is the little lady?' he queried with a smile.

'She appeared to look at everything in a very professional manner, sir,' he answered, interpreting his question wrongly.

'She is also quite pretty I have heard?'

'I do believe that that is so, sir.'

His boss began to nod to himself, knowing that he was getting nowhere quickly. 'So, what have you got planned for the next few weeks, Detective Inspector?'

'Not a great deal, sir, until we receive some information which may help us a bit more from Durham. Though I have got some of the team out talking to some of the students and any faculty members she may have known over at the university. And I was going to go out to meet up with Terry to talk with her flatmates myself before I received your call to come up.'

'On a more *personal* level I meant, Hyde.'

'Not that much is happening right now really sir. Although I could be getting married quite soon.'

'Good grief!' he said feigning an utter look of surprise. 'And when did all this start to come about?'

'Only in the last few days, sir,' he offered grudgingly.

'So you'll be after some time off during this new murder investigation to accomplish this then Hyde, eh? Which as we both know is a damn tricky time to even think about getting married, if you were to ask me.'

Douglas nodded. 'I know that it's bit inappropriate right now, sir. But I do have a lot of leave time that has been lying unused for months now---'

'Lots of time in hand, but which for some strange reason, you rarely ever seem to want to take it off, Hyde.'

'I just like what I do, sir,' he said quickly.

'Of which I am extremely glad *about*, Hyde, believe me! Not many officers like you would be prepared to miss out on holidays when they could just as easily have taken them. And just how long is it now since you actually *were* on any leave?'

After a moment's thought, he said, 'My last leave was probably a few months ago now, sir.'

He shook his head. 'Try *eight* months ago now, Hyde. That would be much nearer the right figure involved.'

'As I said, sir, I enjoy what I do so much that it never seems to bother me that I may work so long without one.'

The Chief gave a long sigh. 'Well I think that it *does* matter, Hyde. Especially when you're dealing with such cases as you do. A good rest now and then can not only help to de-stress you, but it can also help to recharge your batteries once in a while too. Don't you think so?' Then before he could offer an answer said, 'Which is why I making you take an enforced break from this Wednesday coming for at least two weeks so you can do just that!'

Spirit of a Dragon

'But---'

'Give me no buts, Hyde. I'll be placing DI Jennings in temporary charge of this investigation until you return from your break. So for these next two days before you leave I want you to familiarise him with your case up to now. Get him up to speed with whatever facts you already know. As well as what you might now suspect, think, or even just be thinking. And any other relevant information that you think he may need while you're not here at work for that amount of time.'

'Yes, sir,' he said unhappily.

'Now go back down to your department where he's waiting to meet you,' said his boss. Then, just as he was about to leave through the door, he added quietly, 'Have a nice wedding and honeymoon in Japan while you're there, Hyde, and give my regards to the young lady Kumiko too . . .'

Douglas was almost halfway to his department when he suddenly came to a sudden stop. An abrupt stop which must have caught the following uniformed policewoman readily off-guard, since she walked straight into the back of him. A quick apology and then she was around him and gone. While he could only stand in the bright corridor with a wry grin just starting to appear on his face, that sneaky old devil! He thought. He already knew about Kumiko and me, and I bet that it all stemmed from his meeting with her Father earlier. He then quickly assumed correctly, as how else would he have known exactly *when* it would be taking place.

CHAPTER 10

On Thursday morning, Hyde was woken-up as usual by the ringing of the alarm clock. Only because this time he'd actually forgotten to switch it off altogether before going to sleep. And only as he just wasn't used to *not* having to get up to go in to work. His companion in bed alongside him was also awoken at the same moment by the shrill sound as it buried itself into their inner eardrums.

'Sorry,' he apologised to her as her head lifted from the pillow beside that of his own. Then reaching his hand out he depressed the mechanism to halt its ugly and rather insistent wail.

'That is quite all right, Douglas,' she responded rather brightly, and then stretched her body almost sensually beside him to get her muscles working. 'I am usually awake before this on a morning myself, although . . .' she then chuckled quite seductively. 'I *am* usually alone in my *own* bed in my flat in Tokyo when I do so!'

'Would you rather *still* be alone in bed?' he asked her.

Her smile was warming to him. 'Oh heavens no, not now anyway, Douglas. As waking up right beside you for these past three days has been so . . .' She had to ponder for a full minute before she could extract the word she wanted from her brain in Japanese and say it in English to him, '*fulfilling*, for me in so many ways already.'

Spirit of a Dragon

'Me too,' he told her.

'Why so is it for you, too?' she asked, woman-wise. Wishing to know why he also felt as she now did.

'Why? I suppose because just my being with you so much has also been quite wonderful for me too, Kumiko. As I had no idea at all that you would attract me so much all of the time.'

'Do I make you, as you English say it, "*horny*", yes?'

His own chuckle was loud. 'Yes, you always make me feel *very* horny indeed now, Kumiko!'

'And especially at night and in the morning, *neh*?' she asked. 'As from your thrusting within me on those times, or just when we hold each other, I can also say to you that you make me feel very horny, too!'

'I'm pleased to hear it,' he said with a smile.

She returned it automatically. 'Well Douglas, you have started your holidays now. And so, as we are both now wide awake. So, *what shall we do*?' she said with an impish grin on her face.

'What would you suggest?'

'We-ll - I would *like* to have even more sex with you again of course . . .' she told him with flashing eyes. 'But if you would prefer me to bathe you again, which you also seem to enjoy so much now. Then we could always do that instead,' she replied, although her face said that the former idea appealed to her much more than the latter did.

'Well we can always bathe then come back to bed again for that,' he told her.

Her head began to shake. 'Always sex before bathing, Douglas, since it makes us so warm and we perspire. So bathing first would be rather foolish, don't you think? As then we would have to bathe all over again.'

'I don't mind if you don't mind,' he said with a grin. 'Though I hope you're not only doing this now, and after we are married it will come to a complete stop!'

She leant over his upper body and kissed him very hard on the mouth and murmured, 'If you desire us to continue with that after our marriage has taken place, Douglas. Then of course I will continue to do so with you until the time you request for me to stop.'

Which may be a good fifty years off!' he said with a wink.

'You like us bathing together as we do?' she questioned.

He smiled. 'Whatever could be better than lying back against a beautifully exotic, and erotic, woman, while her hands moved all over your body in such a way?'

'Maybe, if it sometimes happened the other way around once in a while too, *neh*?'

'Hey, I'd like nothing better,' he answered to the beginnings of a frown coming to her face. 'What now?' he asked in response to her now tapping digit upon him.

She prodded his chest with a finger. 'I think I know you quite well now, my Douglas!' she told him off. 'All *you're* thinking of is me sitting on your lap while you do this to me.' Her left hand suddenly snaked round to grasp hold of him beneath the covers, as she then added, 'while *this* which I now hold is also deep inside me at the same time, *neh*? You are only thinking of having *sex* with me while we bathe now!' she stated with a rather stoic expression.

'Now that's a really great idea, Kumiko!' he told her. 'I wish I'd thought of that myself!'

'You mean you were *not* thinking of that?' she asked.

'No. Only of being able to enjoy washing you, as you washed me. With my hands being allowed to roam all over your back, your shoulders and your breasts, and then also moving between *your* legs, just as you do it to me.'

She gave a little shiver. 'Oh, I see . . . Well, in that case, I think that I would also like that very much as well, Douglas.' She began to wiggle her hand holding his flaccid member within it, which of course caused it to stir. 'I wouldn't even mind if this were inside me at the same time, too, if I am honest with you. As I do love for it to be in there so much now. And since I can feel it becoming hard now . . . don't you actually think that we really might as well use it now since---'

Spirit of a Dragon

Their talking came to a sudden stop as he rolled her over on to her back and began to do just as she'd asked.

∞

That same morning the new man in charge of the on-going investigation, DI Jennings. Was on the telephone talking with the Chief Inspector from Durham. Who himself had only just received the report's that he'd patiently, although quite anxiously been waiting for from their own laboratory.

∞

On the previous night, Wednesday, just after the fall of dusk had finally taken over from the long hours of July daylight. In the later darkness of evening, and due to it being helpful. A quite nondescript coloured Transit Van, with no lights on and with no engine running now. Sat parked up off a main road outside Berwick and around half a mile down a narrow unlit lane in the moonlight.

Inside the van was a young girl who had been walking home from a pub. And who, after having had too many drinks in her system to recognise the immediate danger of accepting a lift from someone she did not know. Was sat in a quite relaxed way in the passenger seat beside the gallant knight who had offered her a lift home. She had enjoyed whatever was in the thermos flask. Which when he had asked her if she was thirsty as they had driven off, had offered it to her to see if she liked the taste. With the flask only feeling about half-full in her hand to her, she guessed incorrectly that he was offering her some kind of alcohol to drink from it. Through her quite inebriated mind though, she still enjoyed the tasty concoction that was basically only well sweetened coffee. But, she had no clue that the sweetness was in fact only to hide the far more dangerous additions which lay hidden within it.

His voice and friendly manner, notwithstanding his rough good looks --- At least they were to her quite drink filled eyes, had caused her to accept his kind offer. She had already drunk half of the liquid in the flask before he unexpectedly turned off the main road and drove down the dark lane. She had wanted to say something to him at the time, as she knew it was the wrong way to take her home. But her mind by then was already fogging, and her body felt as if it was literally on fire inside.

Stroking the nape of her neck with his gloved fingers, which began to turn her on so much she couldn't believe it. He said to her calmly and gently, 'You've had a bit too much to drink tonight, Susannah, eh?'

She only nodded an answer to him even as she held the flask to her lips and poured yet more of the same unusual brew down her quickly parched throat.

'Won't your parents, boyfriend, or even your husband be unhappy about you being out so late and returning home so drunk?' he asked.

Her shrug was over-expansive, relating just how drunk she had been to begin with, and of just how drugged she was now becoming. 'They won't be very pleased about it, Murray, let's say that!' she announced with just the hint of a low Scottish burr to her voice; and also in an even more pronounced slur than she would have expected. 'And I'm not married . . . I mean to say, not at my age since I'm only nineteen, why should I be!'

'Because you're very pretty, that's why?'

'G'wan! I bet you say that to every girl just to get into her knickers!' she chuckled throatily.

'Sometimes . . .' he said, in truth. 'Though I've never had much luck with any women like *you*,' he said. His different toned *you* to her ears, came out as if she was truly special in his eyes, just as it was meant to do.

'What is this?' she asked finishing what remained in the flask off with a final gulp. 'Mmmm, it tastes so good!'

'It's just my coffee.'

'Just coffee, are you sure?'

'Well, there are just a few of my own special ingredients in it, but only to give it a little more taste and flavour . . .'

She was licking her quickly drying lips even as she finished it. 'It's lovely. Do you have any more?'

He shook his head even as his fingers gently stroked her neck. 'I'm afraid not - you've gone and drank all that I had!'

'Sorry, did you want some of it yourself?' He heard the slur in her voice gradually deepening and getting worse now as he listened carefully.

A few minutes later whatever she was saying became almost unintelligible as the administered drugs finally took their separate effects on her. And his hand moved from her neck to begin to stroke gently on her leg, slowly moving back and forth over her smooth skin. She gave a weird sounding giggle first at what he was doing. Then she began to moan deeply, her tongue continually darting out to wet her dry lips much more often as his hand moved higher and higher up her thigh each time.

'I think you need to sleep your drunkenness off,' he told her casually, and watched as he halted his hands own movement upon her. To which she quickly grasped hold of his hand and pulled it further than even he had done himself. Until it was soon dragged well in-between her legs, to then be pressed firmly against her own groin. He could see that in the moonlight flooding into the windscreen of the van's interior, just as he could see the flimsy underwear she was wearing.

His soft warm smile at her suddenly turned ugly right then, almost deviant in nature, as he thought. 'Yes, my lovely young thing, you *certainly* won't be wearing *those* for very much longer either now!'

Managing to release his hand even from her amorous grip, he climbed from the van and went around to the back of it and opened the rear doors. With those now ready, he walked up to the passenger side and opened that door, where she almost toppled out of the cab into his barely ready arms. As he held her, he closed the door with his buttocks then carried her around to the back and got her inside, closing the double doors behind him. Although he wasn't able to see or hear what did fall out on to the thick grass beside the lane along with her.

His breathing was harsh, and his erection that pushed against the left leg of his jeans easily seen. If she had been awake enough to do so that is; but she was already well sedated by his drugged cocktail in the coffee. He stripped her body quickly, placing each piece of her apparel into one growing pile in readiness for later.

Only when she was quite naked, and as her bare body lay on the thick carpet within the rear of the van, which was actually so soft that she gave a kind of luxurious sigh from it. Did he then rid himself of his own clothing, and placed it to the opposite side out of the way. Then opening her almost limp legs he spread them carefully apart and bent her knees up. Then, he released a self-fashioned very soft lined tool from each side of the van's inner walls. Which he himself had devised, built, and fitted to it for this very purpose. Which as they were quickly placed to hook around either side of her ankles, it was able to keep her legs in that same open position.

He then moved inwards towards her groin and knelt there momentarily before lifting one of her hands and enfolding it around his erection. He masturbated himself quickly by using her limp hand. His other hand went between her own thighs at the same time and his fingers touched, fondled, and delved within her until she was very damp and breathing almost as hard as he was.

'You *want* me to fuck you, don't you, *bitch*!' he now ranted at her.

Her own sigh at what he was doing to her drove him on. And then he threw her hand away almost in disgust from his now rampant member. Bending over her in one easy movement, he then thrust his penis deep into the confines of her young body.

Her head shook from side to side as he relentlessly forced himself into her over and over again. Her louder moans driving his sick urges more and more as he thrust harder and harder in response to her own cries. His first ejaculation speedily burst from him in a torrent and he collapsed on her.

For close to two full minutes they were breathing just as hard as each other. He *knowing* what he was doing, whereas she had no idea *whatsoever* of what was taking place. Raising his head after his brief rest on her fulsome breasts, he began to suck and lick around her hard extended nipples until he was aroused and became hard inside her again.

'Do you want me to do that *again* to you, *bitch*?' he asked, uncaring, then dragged his teeth over one hard nipple so gently that it made her entire body shiver. 'Oh you do want me to then, do you!' he barked. And again he began thrusting into her unresisting body time and time again until his end came again.

Satisfied so far by what he had accomplished, it was now time for him to move on. So first moving her arms, he then slid his own legs up the side of her torso until his knees were in her armpits. Then just from knowing what was coming next, his already hard penis sank into her mouth. And he was overjoyed when only for the second time in his perverted ambitions, her mouth closed around it like a seal. But this time he wasn't so rough, since she was pleasing him by helping out. He came again, and as she coughed and almost choked from it, he then moved back to his first position with a wide smile on his face. And once again he rested. His body just like hers now carrying a light sheen of perspiration upon it.

He began to harden again, though mainly only through his own perverse desires, as usual. He leant over to kiss her on the lips; his erect penis rubbing against and between her sexually heightened and swollen vaginal lips as he did so. Then he settled back again on to his calves and controlled his breathing until it settled.

With that done only his penultimate act was yet to be played out. His hands raised her buttocks high enough so that he could get his knees beneath them and his engorged penis sank slowly out of sight into her anus. As he deftly slid it in and out of her, her head rolled back and forth and her closed-eyed moaning became very low and deep.

A final ejaculation some minutes later finally satiated him and he slid out from her altogether. Standing up, but in a ducked head down way due to the height of the roof above him. He then slowly walked around to where her head lay. He knelt down, with his own head angled the opposite way to hers and kissed her once more deeply. Then, after wiping his now flaccid member of any faecal matter upon it with some waste cloth waiting ready for that purpose in the van. He now knelt behind her, easing himself gently beneath her head, then her shoulders, as he edged under her, until her body lay against his.

His hands went under her limp arms around to her chest, where he rubbed and fondled her breasts for a few minutes for yet more pleasurefor himself. Then, from the small toolbox near the inside wheel arch, he pulled something from it, flicked it around her neck, tightened it quickly, and strangled her. The terrible sounds of her retching and choking caused him no ill effects whatsoever. In fact, from his face it could be thought that it only turned him on even more! And then, from mostly slight movements being given off by her, any of those struggles ceased, and she was dead.

His grin now could only be termed as sadistic, if not evil. As he returned between her parted legs and entered her dead, but still warm fleshed body once more. His last and fully-fledged vigorous attack upon her was now finally being unleashed. Knowing that this time there could be no outcry of pain, or any scream due to his violent intrusion could be given. He flopped on top of her at the end once again, but now, even *he* was finally and utterly spent.

A few minutes later he dried himself off with a ready towel, redressed back into his clothes, then held one of the rear doors slightly ajar as he looked out cautiously at first. But it was pitch-black where they were, and so there was no sign of anyone around as far as he could tell. After loosening the tools which had held her ankles in position for him, he then dragged her halfway out until her bare limp legs dangled over the edge of the van. He gathered up her clothing and stuffed it up inside his T-shirt, giving him a pregnant look, or like a man with a large beer belly. Her shoes he stuck into each of his jacket pockets.

Another quick glance was taken around him, with his ears trying to pick up or hear any unexpected sound. But there was still nothing to hear. He nodded happily, safe and sound yet again he thought. Then, he pulled at her legs a little more until her body began to slide over the edge. He caught her, ducked down, and allowed her limp corpse to fall over his right shoulder where it hung like a sack. He gace a grunt as he took on her full weight. Then closed the two doors gently before walking off into the nearby woods.

Fifteen minutes later he returned. Not coming out from behind a thick bush until he was sure that it was still safe for him to do so. He grinned inanely. It was all just so easy – *'As easy as fuckin' pie!'* he said while laughing out aloud to himself. He climbed into the driver's seat and sighed with both pleasure and exhaustion. Started the engine and switched on the interior light which made him blink. The small round key-fob on the ignition key spun around from the movement on it. There was a name inscribed upon it that flashed as it turned. It did begin with an "M", but it was only four letters in length not six, so he'd even lied about his name to the young girl anyway.

His hand lifted and he pulled down the sun visor in front of the windscreen. A smile began to form as he picked up a pen from one of the small storage units, and pulled the top off and then raised it upwards. He wrote on it: *Susannah - Berwick - 19 - July 2000. Great Fuck!* And then followed it with four stars, and that to him meant vagina, mouth, anus, and vagina again. But the last star made was only when done with a dead body, of which he knew that it was termed as having committed necrophilia.

Above her name were already seven others, all with their first names, places met, their ages, and each had a date of his attack – as well as lastly, the stars. The first dated was of November 1999, the second the December of that year. March and April of the year 2000 were not included, but until July he had rarely attacked more than one woman in a month in this way. This month was very different though, as there were now three of them already. And the seventh name that appeared down on that list of eight was of one young Japanese girl. Called by the very unusual name of Akiko, and who also had four stars at the very end of her details as well.

∞

The Hirano Electronics Corporation's sleek jet landed at Tokyo's International Airport among the many small airliners and Jumbo's already there. *Their* engines being far louder in comparison, as their thrusting jet engines were opened up fully in order to propel and lift their full weight from off the runway, or to decelerate them just as rapidly upon landing. Douglas was watching from one of the small porthole windows with Kumiko sitting happily beside him, as they landed after what could only be called a very smooth and amazingly quiet, yet long flight. And for once, there was legroom to spare, and an amazing on-board service had been included. He watched as the jet finally turned off the runway and taxied over to a small hangar which was actually emblazoned with her family's name. He felt the mere slightest of jolts as the brakes were applied just outside it.

It had been quite amazing right from the very start to him. Watching with them as Akiko's casket had been brought to, and then loaded gently inside its small cargo hold and strapped in. And joining it in what was quite a tight space that he could clearly see, were two similar reclining chairs to those of his own at home, which her father after using one, had wanted to take back with him. As he had found the comfort levels in them *so* good, that he just *had* to take one back with him, but had decided on two, just in case. So a hasty trip to the same shop where he had bought his own from had had to be taken.

Luckily, the same type as his was still for sale, though sadly the same colour as his at home was no longer in stock right now. And as her father didn't want to wait for them to be ordered and shipped over to Japan later, so he took one of jet black, and one in a cherry-red colour. Paying for them with his credit card, and asking if they could be delivered quickly to his plane at the airport before they were due to take-off. To aid the manager with his decision, he then said to him that, if those he was going to show them at home liked them also. Then quite a few more of them could also be heading that same way very soon too. Without much more needing to be said on the subject, the manager stated that if given enough time for delivery that they would both be there for him in plenty of time . . .

They were, and then with everything readied, they lifted off into the sky. Yet returned back down quite soon, in order to land at the quite new but much smaller inner London City Airport based on the Thames, which was easier for them to get to the Japanese Embassy from. But instead of them even having to go there to complete what was necessary to be done; a member from the Japanese consulate staff was already at hand and waiting at the airport for them to arrive, and simply handed over the necessary documents.

The jet was already being refuelled in readiness for the long flight ahead even as they accepted them. And the same beautiful flight attendant, resplendent in her very elegant fitting uniform, served drinks or food to them whenever they were asked for. With such grace and very little sign of tiredness throughout the whole flight that she could indeed have been a robot. Although his first visit to the toilet though had left him just staring. As the toilet itself was nothing like those in any other aircraft that he'd ever travelled in before. And with it also being a private aircraft, it was fitted out with mostly luxury items inside it, unlike commercial airliners or military transports. There were buttons all over the place on it, and it was only with Kumiko's already knowing help was he able to learn what they were all supposedly used for.

Lastly, as they finally disembarked down its own built-in short staircase to the ground at Tokyo, a spotless looking dark windowed silver Bentley quietly materialised next to the plane. So quietly that he looked once at the back of it to make sure that it hadn't just been pushed there! Only because he hadn't heard a sound coming from it as it had rolled up.

The minister, who the Hirano's knew as Yoshi, came out of the hangar at that point and walked straight over to them all until only a few feet away. Then he bowed low to them.

'Welcome home, Hirano-san, Kumiko-san,' he said as they returned his bow, though to Hyde's surprise not as low. 'If you will give me all your passports I'll have them taken care of for you right away!'

He gathered their three and the three from the crew of the plane and just passed them behind him without looking. 'See to all these immediately!' he called out as a man trotted up and took them from him with a dutiful bow. 'And I want no problems that may cause *any* delays whatsoever!' The man ran off with them like a trained athlete.

'As you requested Hirano-san, I called your office to request your car and driver to be in attendance for your arrival here. As well as a hearse from the company you instructed me to call on your behalf, to come and to pick up the coffin of your late daughter for you.'

Hirano's nod was habitual. 'Thank you, my good friend. I was sorry to have to bother you with such rushed tasks as these. But as always, I *knew* that if I did ask you, then I could just forget about it and count on everything I needed being done for me.'

Yoshi sucked in his breath and bowed even lower. He was being given very high praise indeed for his work to him and their clan 'It was my *honour* to have been the one chosen to do this for you, Hirano-san . . . '

The three now shook hands, after having to wait until Hyde had finished shaking those of the crew also. Which to say the least had not only surprised them, but also those who had watched it. And only after he had done that did he come over to their group to do the same with Minister Yoshi. After a short greeting passed between them, Hirano senior asked the crew of the jet if they would wait for the hearse to collect his daughter after the plane was stored in its hangar before they went home. Only if it didn't arrive while he was here, he informed them. To which they all agreed to, just as he knew they would. As they were all servants to their clan so would be expected to comply with any such request from him anyway. Though they did all carry their entire luggage from the jet and place them into the large boot of the Bentley as they stood in front of it.

The man sent with the passports and also Douglas's passport and visa returned at the same running pace, and well out of breath. Bearing them and handing them over, with no foreseen problems having been said to his superior. Though Douglas from arriving this way into Japan had no idea whatsoever of the strict rules and checks that had just been waived on Minister Yoshi's own personal guarantee for him.

The hearse still had not arrived, but one of his company trucks had for the chairs. Hirano senior watched two of his own employees as they entered the small cargo hold. A deep bow was given by them both to the still waiting casket containing his youngest daughter. As of course the whole company had known why he had left for England in such haste. With their respects now paid, the two men carefully manhandled the twin items from the hold and into the back of the truck. They knew that they were to be taken to his main rural home outside Tokyo. So just as soon as they were inside and secured, they bowed to the assembled group stood beside the front of the large Bentley before driving off.

Yoshi's face showed puzzlement at what he had just seen coming from the cargo hold. 'Chairs, Hirano-san? But surely there was no need for you to bring any such items as those back with you. We have similar ones, probably even far better ones in fact that could have been bought quite easily here?'

'Yes I know that, my friend. But while we stayed at Douglas's home, I found that I just could not believe their levels of comfort when I used them. So, instead of trying to seek out similar ones over here upon my return, I simply brought two of them back with me. I hope that will not be a problem for you either, my old friend?'

He shook his head almost violently. 'Certainly not, Hirano-san, I have known you long enough now to know that that is all they are and nothing else. If you have a problem at *any* time with doing so, then please just let me know and I'll sort it out for you if I can.'

As they chatted away in Japanese to each other, Kumiko watched her soon to be husband as he looked around the hangar space from outside. Apparently taking not the slightest bit of notice of what they were saying to each other. But now, since they knew he understood every word that they were saying. Was he actually listening to them all of the time, or actually taking no notice whatsoever just as his face showed? It was slightly disconcerting as well as unnerving to her with knowing this highly secretive information about him now.

A few minutes later, with still no sign of the hearse's arrival becoming evident as yet. Her father decided that they might as well leave. At the sign that they were going to leave, the mainly unseen chauffeur so far, quickly stepped out and held a rear door open for them. Hirano, his daughter and then Hyde climbed inside it to recline within its opulent luxury and waited for the driver to take them away, which he did. Yoshi and his young personal assistant could have left then, but he had decided to only finish with his duties when the casket had been collected from the aircraft. His duty would have then been carried out to his erstwhile leader to its full completion, and to the best of his ability. He was already disappointed that it had not arrived in time to do that while thy were here. As that, of course, would have shown his efforts off even more on his behalf. But even he knew what the traffic was like in the city all the time, and an empty hearse driving along received little in the way of sympathy or help from other motorists on the road. In fact they almost dreaded being stuck behind one which was in use, due to the slower and typically safer driving of their drivers.

CHAPTER 11

After close to an hour of driving in stately elegance, and with over half of that time spent just trying to get out of the busy city streets of Tokyo itself. The quiet luxury motor at long last, purred up in front of what appeared to his eyes to be; an elongated bungalow shaped house. As he clambered out of the armchair-like quality leather seats inside, he stood for a moment just to enjoy the panoramic vista around him, as the house seemed to have been set into an almost idyllic piece of countryside.

Behind the house itself various types of trees rose upwards with an incline like a small forest, as if some type of a small hill lay beyond it. The differing shades and colourings of the leaves upon the trees only added to its already picturesque image quality. The only downside to its apparently old elegance was the extemely large satellite dish at the side of the house. As without that, the house would have looked as if it had been from a much older period of time. But that one piece of modern technology took most of it quaint charm away from it now.

He saw the open decking with a tiled roof above it filling the entire front section of the house. Though for him it could just as easily have been a type of veranda, since there were three different places where steps rose up from the ground to join to it. A much larger one was located centrally to the house itself, while the other two smaller ones were positioned at either end.

Spirit of a Dragon

After his view had passed over the house to look at the rest of the surrounding area; the three other sides appeared quite flat, resembling much of the farming landscape which they had recently driven past. Kumiko tapped his arm to gain his attention, and nodded to where her father was waiting for them both at the pathway leading to the widest set of steps at the front of the veranda. Walking around the car with her, and only brief seconds before it silently moved off. To reach him, they went around to the front side of the house where the satellite dish's static and unlovely appearance was soon missing from his sight. Her father was already at the base of the steps and removing his shoes one at a time. Placing the first upon a little waist high raised stone block until he could hold both shoes in his hand. Then he walked up the dark wooden steps in his stocking feet.

Kumiko held on to his arm while she slipped each one of her own flat-soled moccasin type of footwear from her feet. Although after the first had been taken off, that foot went on to the first step, then the next on to the second step when the other was uncovered. With those held in one hand, she now held her empty hand out for him. So he took one of his own shoes off and handed it to her, placing that foot onto the step, and copied it with the last. At which point he'd expected her to hand them back to him to carry. But she just gave a smile and a small gesture of their now moving on again with her head. With that, she began to walk up the steps in the same direction as that which her father had already taken, and had since disappeared.

Douglas followed her through the first doorway after she had placed their footwear facing away from the doorway beside the many others already located there on a mat, and had then opened the shoji screen. And he was shocked it had to be said. As it was just like one of the same type from most of the olden style Japanese films he'd watched. The outside wall covering was indeed literally "paper thin", as that was all that stood between those inside and the elements without.

He could see no bricks at all, or perhaps there were a few somewhere, though must be hidden. Only a few places here and there also had some slats of dark wood, apart from the much thicker main beams for the structure itself, and there were only a few similar wood-surrounding windows if he remembered correctly, as he had looked at the house from the car. Which he then deduced, must be set into the wooden framework of the building itself if only to offer further integral strength.

∞

From one door to the next he followed Kumiko, as she parted what he thought had been actual walls, but each time they revealed other doors. Each room just as sparse as the next, set in an almost in a kind of minimalist way; without being cluttered with too many objects to mar its very openness.

His feet moved over floor matting which even he knew were called tatami. But it was the sheer length of it that he was shaken at. Of course he'd heard of an open plan house before - but this was a very different kind of open plan he was looking at now. As one room was just opening into another as they went along. He kept following her, as there was little else he could do, as they passed through one similar room after another, until he was certain that he could hear talking, and in English. No, not proper English, he thought as his ear picked up the sound better.

As she opened yet another doorway up for them, the sound was much louder, and he actually then heard a theme he remembered so well. Which was that of Coronation Street whenever it was having a break on the television. Abruptly the sound came to a sudden silent halt, and he now heard a low muttering taking place instead.

Kumiko's opening of the next double doors showed him that this was what they must use as their living room. Where a very large television set in one corner of the room was on, but with no sound coming from it, so he deduced that it must just have been muted in some way. Not that he had time to ask anything.

As Kumiko immediately said, 'Douglas, this is my Mother, Shinko.'

Her mother gave a bow to him and then held out a hand. Which not only to her surprise, but to theirs as well, he raised her hand to his lowering mouth and kissed the back of it.

'It is my pleasure. And I'm very pleased to have finally met you, Mrs Hirano,' he announced. Then without trying to show it, he studied her carefully. She was barely more than five feet tall at most, slim-bodied just like her daughter, her hair was still completely black, unlike that of her husband's own now. Which may have been dyed to do so, but he doubted it. As he'd understood that Japanese women as they grew older were not that characteristically vain or bothered about their changing faces or odies as old age crept up on them. In fact, it was as if they were proud to show off their older status to those around them. Definitely unlike many of their western counterparts, who would be straight to a plastic surgeon as soon as one wrinkle showed anywhere upon their body, if they could afford to do so, that is.

And she was watching him in return, just as he studied her.

'I can't believe that you're Kumiko's Mother, Shinko,' he told her, 'as you barely look a few years older than she does right now.'

She smiled. 'You are very charming and *gallant* if I may say so, Douglas. But I am indeed her mother, and of the six other children of which I have had,' she responded in heavily accented English.

'You certainly wouldn't think it to look at you, Mrs Hirano . . .'

Her smile was quite genuine to him. 'I can actually see now why my Kumiko found you *so* acceptable now, Douglas.

'Pardon me?'

'So charming, so gallant, and quite attractive for a non-Japanese, isn't he Kumiko?'

'My husband-to-be is very *handsome*, Mother. Not attractive,' she said in an attempt to alter and help her with her wording.

'Was I wrong to say attractive then, *neh*?' she asked with deep frown that caused her eyebrows to sink low.

'Women like *you* are attractive, my wife, whereas men are usually called handsome in the English tongue,' Koichi said, guessing that she had got her words slightly muddled.

She shook her head at his answer. 'I do know what handsome *is* you know, my husband. And I still say that he is attractive . . .'

With all the greetings soon over, Kumiko decided that it was time for her to show him around their house, so led him from the room and closed the double sliding doors behind them.

'Come Douglas,' she said happily to him, 'just as you showed us around your own home that first day, then I will do the same here for you.'

'It won't be too much trouble will it?'

'You are a guest here with us in *our* home now, so of course you should also know where everything is that you might need.'

He grinned as he placed his arm around her waist. 'Everything that I do need I now have right here, Kumiko.'

She smiled in return. 'I do hope so, Douglas. But I must show you where our bathroom, toilet, kitchen and bedrooms are, so that you will be able to find your way around them if required while you are here with us.'

He nodded, so she un-wrapped his arm from around her waist and placed her hand within his and then led him around her family's home to view it like that. She showed him their family bathroom first, and he could only stare at it. As there was no bathtub at all, just a large and well tiled sunken pool with clear water almost so high that it was lapping around its edges.

'It's a bit large just to have a soak in, isn't it, Kumiko?' he asked, comparing it to his own at home.

'This bath itself is not to wash in Douglas, it is only there to be used to soak our bodies in *after* it has already been washed and rinsed thoroughly.'

'But so much water just for one person seems a waste, Kumiko. So I'm hoping that you will join me in it just as you did in my own back home?'

'Of course I will. And so will everyone else,' she stated with a very white toothed smile.

'Eh?' he gasped aloud.

'But of course, Douglas. This is our way not to waste the water after it has been heated-up for our use by our servants.'

'You mean you actually have servants as well? *Real servants*?' he queried. Then what she had just said finally hit him. 'Hold on a minute there, my lass, what exactly did you mean by what you just said, as in, *everyone*?'

'We, unlike many other people in so many other countries, are not so ashamed of our bodies, Douglas. It is also why we have all bathed this way since we were only children together, just as both my father and mother regularly say to any new children that come into our family. That a naked body is nothing to be ashamed of since we each have one, and though some things may vary with each one of us, in truth, it is only that of skin tissue surrounding bone, muscle, and the liquid elements which make us who and what we all are . . .'

'You all bathe *together*!'

'Of course, just as do any of our family, relatives, or those of our clan, if they are here with us, my love. Or at their own homes, and there is absolutely nothing to worry about it for---'

He interrupted her right then, 'Are you saying that you will be expecting *me* to actually join all of *you* in there when you bathe!'

She nodded. 'Yes. As you will very soon be a member of our family, Douglas. So of course we would also *expect* you to enjoy the hot water along with all of us at the same time, too.'

'*Naked?*'

She smiled up at him. 'Of course very much naked, my love. Otherwise, you would hardly then be able to call it a bath with clothing on. Would you?'

'But . . . with your father and mother in there!' He was stunned.

'Yes, and also with any of my sisters and brothers, and any of their own children if they are staying with us here at the same time too, Douglas. And also anyone else who may be a guest, sometimes the servants who may also be at our home at any time too, if there is room, or they are not working.'

'Good God!' he muttered shaking his head.

'There is no problem, Douglas.'

'Maybe not for you . . .' he said.

'Nor for you either. Once you've seen a naked man or woman once, or perhaps just a few times, then there is little else to see, is there? The sheer beauty of the children with their still young firm bodies - to those who are now more elderly and have some wrinkled skin, is nothing, my love, nothing at all.'

143

'But I've never done such a thing, Kumiko. In fact I've never ever even thought about doing such a thing before. And if I were to bathe with other women in it too - Well . . .' he looked down at himself.

'Ah,' she whispered, 'you are worried that you may get one of your wonderful erections in front of them, *neh*?'

'She could see his embarrassment even as he nodded. 'Please, you do not need to worry about that at all. If it happens, it happens, my love. As our younger boys, or men, who have not yet managed to gain control over their own maleness so far, also have that same difficulty too. But, all I can offer to help you is this, which is that any other female in there, including myself, will really just be looking at your erection with such vast pleasure.'

'What?'

He couldn't quite believe what she had just said to him.

She nodded. 'It's true, Douglas. They will of course wonder why it has risen like so, and each one of them no doubt hoping that they are the single reason for it happening. Which may well be the case, I suppose, since my sisters are all far more attractive than I myself am.'

'I very much doubt that!'

She smiled, raised herself up on her toes and kissed him on the mouth. 'Your thoughts for me are so warm, Douglas. That you are making it hard for me to have to wait until tonight to lie with you again.'

'And all I can say in answer to that, my darling, is waiting so long may also be a problem for me too.'

She studied his face for less than a moment, and then with a grip that closed even tighter upon his hand, she began to drag him through one door after another until they were finally in her own bedroom. She turned to him, her breathing heavy and rapid. 'I'm afraid that now I just *cannot* wait for tonight, Douglas. I want you now. I want to feel you inside me again just to know, to be sure that you are truly soon going to be all mine very soon now.'

He was just going to speak when her fingers were placed over his mouth, silencing his unspoken words. He stood rooted to the spot as he watched her now shed her clothes before him. Then he watched again as she went to a wall and somehow slid part of it open to withdraw some quilts or something. It was actually a thick, but very soft futon, which she used as her own bed whenever she stayed at home. As she laid it on the floor, and settled it properly while on her hands and knees. Her casual glances at him were if not coy, then definitely sensual. And her unclothed body moving so much around and about so near to him, could do little else but begin to stir his blood. Something Kumiko knew was happening very well indeed, as her eyes had spotted the tell-tale bulging occurring inside his trousers. Which, just as *she'd* expected, caused her own heart to beat and thump so hard it terrified her somewhat. The dryness in her throat and the imaginary lump within it also told her only one thing . . . That she had found out that she was now just as desperate for him as he was for her.

With the soft quilted bedding completed ready on the floor, Kumiko turned on her knees and then got to her feet almost liquidly, ready to help him undress. But there was an oddly strange look on his face now, as if he'd just seen something that had put him off the idea totally.

'What's wrong, Douglas?' she asked.

'Your . . . your back . . . I mean the mark on it, it's just like an identical copy of the one I saw on your sisters!'

'But I thought that by now, you *must* have seen it already, Douglas? I mean since we have showered, bathed, *and* even slept together?'

His head shook. 'In the shower you had your back to me, and your hair must have covered it up. And in the bath you always sat behind me when we bathed.'

'And when we made love?'

'I guess you were either flat on your back, or you were on top and facing me, Kumiko. So I've actually never seen it on you until now. But what I do need to know now, is why do you have the very same, or an almost identical design like it on your back as well?'

As they talked together her hands were already loosening the buttons on his shirt, and then the belt, catch, and zip of his trousers until they fell down around his ankles. This of course only left him standing there from the waist down quite naked, since he more often than not never wore any briefs or boxer shorts of any kind as underwear. He watched her tongue slip from her mouth and slowly moisten her parted lips, as if in anticipation of what was about to happen between them . . . once again.

After taking his shirt off too, she picked his black casual trousers up from the floor and carried them over to the same lone chair where she had laid her own clothing. All fastidiously folded and placed one on top of the other, and where after doing the same with his, placed it on top of those.

She led him over to the futon and they sank down on to its deep and very soft cover. 'I will explain as much as I can to you while we are making love, Douglas. As I would much rather be doing that than anything else right now,' she said with her usual smile.

And so, while they lay on the soft quilt, with him on his back, arms behind his head. She was moving ever so gently above him, and began to tell him of the significance of her own tattooed back. He listened as she spoke quietly, very much amazed that he could actually listen to what she was saying to him while he was being enclosed so deftly within her.

∞

'The clan, to which our family belong to, began a very long time ago, Douglas,' she began for him, 'for at least over the past three or four hundred years now; only at least that long ago however, as that is as far back as we can know from the old written writings we have of our own family history. Almost from birth we are all always told of, *who* we are, and exactly what we as a clan then belonged to. And our training begins from when we can first understand speech and can walk. All of our training finally culminates when we can manage everything that has been taught us, including martial arts.'

'Karate?' he muttered as she slowly ground her body against his.

'Yes that, as well as many others, my love, as we have to know them *all* . . . and many *other* things as well. *Ka-ra-te, Ai-ki-do, Jiu-jit-su, Ken-do, tai-kwan-do*, as well as their various styles,' she said naming them in their correct forms. 'The Iron Palm, The Crane, and the Closed Fist are but a few of so many of these various styles that we each have to learn; and of the correct way in which you must breathe exactly in order to summon all of your inner spiritual forces, or as we call it, *Ki*, for any such efforts that you may want to use. You may have heard of the Chinese version, which is, *Chi*?''

His face was a study of emotions she saw, until he asked, 'And you know all of these styles already?'

She nodded and her hair fell around her shoulders to lie on his chest and face. She, *almost,* halted her movements upon him, as she used her hands to lift her hair away from him. Though while doing so, her lower body was now being lifted and raised by her knees alone. While she twisted her hair into one single thickly braided strand of hair, which she then wrapped around her neck like a long scarf. Only when that was completed, her hands were replaced up back beside his head and she was once again in full control of her body's motions.

'We need to be very proficient in them all, Douglas, to enable us to know how to counter any attacks and defences, as well as potentially the most difficult and dangerous one of them to learn too.'

'And which one is that?' he queried.

'*Nin-jit-su*, my love, because you see, we are all *basically* just following on from our own generations from those who went before us.'

His eyes peered into hers, very carefully. 'But it's just another martial art as well, surely?'

Her head shook. '*Nin-jit-su* is no martial art, in truth, my love. *Nin-jit-su,* when it is being taught and learned in its rawest state of teaching and principle as we all must do, is known to us as the "Way of the Assassin" or, of the "Silent Killers". Our clan is called "The Black Dragon Clan", which is also centuries old. Because my love, we are all *Ninja*!'

'Fucking Hell!' he said with a shocked gasp.

She bent over and kissed him. 'And to be with me, my love, you must also *become* a part of us now.'

'Good God!'

'I know that it is a lot for you to take in so soon, Douglas. But you did ask, so you must also know this before any more of our other teachings are passed to you.'

'And will I also have to have one of those same tattoos of yours placed upon me too?'

'I'm afraid so . . .'

'Neat!' He smiled. 'But I don't think we'll be here long enough for me to get that done,' he told her.

It was her turn to smile. 'Your tattoo will be completed in just two days or less, and the third day you will just rest to allow it to heal.'

'That'll be quite a painful two days then?' he muttered.

Her smile was fixed as her head shook again. 'You will feel nothing as it is done for you, my love.'

'Nothing, nothing at all . . . I can't believe *that*, Kumiko.'

'You won't feel anything you see, because you will not actually be *awake* while it is being carried out. One of our own drugs that we use on occasions such as these will literally knock you out so that the required work can be carried out very swiftly.'

'But two days, Kumiko? What about going to the toilet and eating, or drinking, things like that?'

She smiled beautifully at him one again. 'All of your needs will be provided for and taken care of, my love. I will be with you as much as I can be while it is being done, but if I am not, then there is always someone at hand to do these things for you while you yourself are in the land of dreams. You will be fed mostly soft foods like babies eat, though ours are, by far, even more nutritional just to keep your body strong while you are there. That kind of food is used, simply so that it will slide easily down your throat with no difficulties. All of your limbs will be stretched and manipulated every hour or so by someone, if not by me, to keep them remaining supple and allowing no cramping to form. And you will regularly be bathed and dried, your toilet needs seen to if the need occurs. In other words, everything about you will be carefully monitored throughout. This I *can* promise you, Douglas.'

As she saw him thinking over what she had just told him, and was just about to add a little more information into what his new life would soon entail for him. The shoji door to her bedroom then just slid fully open with a gentle hiss. A young woman was kneeling outside her door with head bowed.

Spirit of a Dragon

'Excuse me for interrupting you, my mistress, but your father has asked to see you,' said the woman in Japanese to her.

'Thank you, Raiko. Please tell my father that I will be with him in say---' Her mouth widened into a pleasing grin, 'about another half an hour or so, *neh*?'

The other woman's gaze raised to look at them without a hint of shock upon her face as if she'd seen it all before many times. Which she had of course. Though not here with the eldest of the four sisters; and especially not with a *gai-jin* like him. Though she was looking very happy at what she was doing with him in her room. 'I'm sorry, mistress, but I think your father meant now, as in right away . . .'

Kumiko emitted a long drawn out sigh. 'I'm sorry, Douglas. If I have been asked to attend father, then I must go at once.' she said in English as she moved and he slid from within her as she got to her feet and stood up. Ultimately leaving behind his stiff erection as it stood there in full view of the other woman. 'I will try not to be very long for both our sakes, *neh*?'

Raiko's eyes at the doorway had opened very wide at what she saw now in the bedroom. 'If your man would wish to use my own poor body's services until you came back again, mistress. Then I would be quite happy to help you both out?' she offered.

Kumiko looked at Douglas to ask him just that, only to see that his face had turned beetroot red. It was the first time that it actually hit her that he of course *could* understand *every* word the servant had just said.

She gave a sudden gasp in mock alarm. 'From that look on your face I just know that you must be able to understand Japanese, Douglas. You can understand it, can't you . . .?'

All he could do was nod. Until he then finally said, 'Yes,'

'That's great!' she told him, 'though I must also report this new development to my father too! But if you would also care to accept Raiko's happy offer to you while I go and see what my Father wants from me, then that would be quite alright to do?'

'You just *have* to be kidding . . . aren't you?' he asked in shock.

'No, my love, I really do not mind in the least . . . really I don't. As I was just about to tell you that in our clan we also need to have sex to train, as well as also just for pleasure whenever it suits us. We are quite free with our bodies here, and due to that, none of us actually care in the least what our partners may wish to do - mainly because it has *always* been allowed that way.

'So do not ever feel guilty if you wish to entertain any of our female members, *with your member!*' she chuckled lightly, 'just as the very opposite may occur if I ever wished to enjoy another man also. Both wishful parties *must* consent to the act though, or it will not happen, Douglas. And if you *would* like Raiko here to help to please and entertain you until I get back again, then I have no problem at all with it, honestly.'

'Are you sure, Kumiko? It all seems a bit . . .' he was it appeared, quite stuck for words now.

'Loose . . . Carefree . . . Lustful . . . Shocking . . . Even filthy to your eyes? Then do not think of it in that way, my love. Our bodies were created in their separate forms like this in order for them to engage together. To accept one part into the other since time began – as if a key into a lock. So in our own way a long time ago, they must have thought it to be stupid not to indulge in it. So sex is really just a basic requirement of the human body, yes? And in our own way we have found the ideal solution to that very problem, which is to have sex whenever you require it. If any night when you are here and I cannot be bothered to do so. Although to be honest, I also now wish that I never will say no to you! Then your sexual urges can always be spent with someone else that night. That will keep your body not only feeling healthy, but also your mind will feel relaxed and complete.

'Please, remember that we here in our clan are quite different from anywhere else. We would each die to save another of us . . . just as we would also kill to do the same too. It is bred into us and fed into us from an early age, my love, that our clan is the ultimate passage of our lives. This is why we have no preconceived notions of sharing things with each other. Whether it being actual beds, bodies, clothing, money, food, water, or bathing.' She tapped a finger beside her head. 'Only here is where there are any differences in us all, nowhere else. Our bodies can vary from thin to large, from short to tall, and from heavy to light. But only in our minds, my love, is where we are all very different to each other. A body is only that, a conductor for our life's tasks, and as similar the world over as our own two are here now. Skin tissue covering muscle and bone, with liquid elements contained within. No more no less.'

Spirit of a Dragon

'You are actually saying that you wouldn't mind if I wanted to have sex with other women? Or if some women that *you* knew actually wanted to have sex with me?' he asked, literally dumbfounded by what she was telling him.

She shook her head and smiled again. 'Of course I would be a little jealous of it, my love. But then, what woman would not feel that way about her man, *neh*? But then again, I have no doubt that you yourself would feel the same way if I wanted to enjoy another man's body some night?'

'But with any woman . . . Well, to me that seems to need a lot of trust being used.'

'Not just with *any* woman as you have said there, Douglas, only with those women who serve our clan. Either as members or servants as I do, and also soon as you will do too.'

'Why are only those allowed?' he asked.

'Because none of us have ever once slept around outside of our own clan, Douglas, and every single man and women of ours was checked medically before the age of five, for any kinds of diseases both medical, sexual, or for any genetically debilitating genes, which may be lying dormant in them. Including that, we all still have to have an annual check carried out too, just to keep us completely safe. This is the way we know that it is quite safe for all of us to enjoy any amount of sexual intercourse together even if only for the sake of pleasure. As if none of us have sex outside of our own clan, then no sexually transmitted diseases can enter within it. There was even psychological evaluation testing carried out on each of us, simply to see if those who were coming up to the age of training would be able to handle it well enough.

'But, I must go now, my love, and I will tell you more of our clan and of our future life together when I return to you. So for now, I advise you to accept Raiko's generous offer and allow her to sit on that lovely tall and hard shaft of yours for a while as I have just done. And since I now *know* that you speak Japanese, I will tell everyone that you can, and you can even talk to her while she enjoys herself with you now too, *neh*?'

He nodded, though was still unsure about it all yet, as he then watched as Kumiko as she just began to walk away towards the door. 'Hey, don't forget your clothes!' he called out.

'I do not need them in the house, my love. Have you already forgotten what I told you? That we always bathe together when we are all here, so there is really no need to now hide what any of them have already all seen so many times before.' At the doorway she looked down at the servant. 'Climb aboard him, Raiko, but just make sure that you look after my husband-to-be very well now!'

'I will do my very best to keep him readily available for when you return again soon, my mistress,' she responded.

Kumiko chuckled sweetly. 'Raiko, you know that I can actually *make* him hard any time that I want to. So if you feel that you want to feel the full power of his thrusts, and then enjoy his flow at the end, then do so . . . I can tell you now that you will enjoy it very immensely indeed!'

Then as Raiko entered her room and slowly slid the door closed, Kumiko looked back through the closing opening and winked at him before the shoji closed fully. Let's see how he enjoys that? She thought to herself as she walked off in search of her father, her own nudity not even bothering her at all in the slightest, just as she had told him.

∞

A few hours prior to that, the driver of a by now quite filthy light grey transit van. What with all the muck and dirt of a few months dust, dirt, grime, and traffic fumes all over it, resembled more of a dark grey, more than its former colour. Was driving steadily along the motorway, he was now on his way to Aberdeen. Although still furious, and occasionally beating his clenched fist against the steering wheel. As he now knew he must have already made what could be his first very costly mistake.

He had looked carefully, very carefully indeed, but he just couldn't find his flask anywhere in the van the next morning. He'd sweated a lot because of that, worrying if he personally had ever touched it without his gloves on, or if there were any remnants of either of his used drugs still inside. His only hope was that someone would find it and take it home to use it themselves; and hopefully with some luck, well before the body was discovered.

CHAPTER 12

Kumiko's father had only sent for her as he wanted to ask her what she thought about the idea of cremating her sister in the old tradition at their own family shrine nearby. Which as all expected, would likely be attended by a few of the usual priests to carry out the required formalities. As well as however many of their clan's members who would be able to attend such a gathering, and some local invited guests. But that it would be staged in the much older traditional ways of their clan again, as usual. Kumiko's own naked entrance into where they were talking together didn't even make either one of them raise an eyebrow, never mind bat an eyelid. Although they were wondering why she was undressed like that.

'Did I interrupt you, Kumiko?' he asked.

'We were just having sex when Raiko came to tell me you wanted to see me right away, Father.'

'You didn't just *leave* him there halfway through it did you?'

'No, Father, Raiko offered to take my place while I came to see you here, and from his blush I finally caught him out on his knowledge of Japanese. So he knows that we *do* know that much about him now. At her word, she said that you wanted to see me now, so what else *could* I do but not obey. Anyway, Raiko seemed quite pleased that I would allow her to take over for me . . . In fact, she couldn't close my bedroom door quick

153

enough from what I saw, just so that she could get started with him.'

'Was he very shocked, Kumiko?' asked her mother without averting her eyes from the screen, and without missing what Annie Sugden was doing in the Emmerdale Farm kitchen with her old father, Matt and Joe.

'Maybe just a little bit, I suppose. Which isn't that bad really, when you consider what we know already and of what he still has to find out about us yet.'

'You haven't told him anything then?' he asked.

'I only managed to explain some things to him, Father. About some of our training methods in the martial arts, our tattoo's, and who *we* actually are and *what* we are. But it was about then when Raiko arrived, so any more that I was about to tell him will have to wait until I get back there.'

'You do not think she will exhaust him before you get back?'

She smiled at him, and said, 'Thankfully not, Father. As with Raiko being only a *servant* in our clan, she really still knows nothing at all about the very arts and *essences* of pure sex like we do. Though she will still be a quite good sexual partner for my Douglas, however, so she should please him a little while I am away. But if my Douglas can last almost three hours with *me* alone, then it would probably take all six of our house servants to finally satisfy him in that way. Whereas only one us, simply by using the very knowledge that we each possess, could make him very soft within only a few short minutes. And even without the need to have sex with him in the first place.'

'You would want that to happen to him, daughter?'

'Oh good heavens no, Father. I enjoy my sex with him just as immensely as he does now, I'm sure. And I would always do my own best to completely satisfy him every time that we now do so. Without having to revert to using my skills upon him, or from having to soften him that quickly.'

'Noriko and Makiko will also be as pleased to hear that, Kumiko,' said her mother.'

'I know that . . . But do they really have to?'

Spirit of a Dragon

Her mother gave a low chuckle while her eyes were still transfixed on to the large screen, to say, 'If he is really as large as your father has already told me he is, Kumiko. Then they would both be fools *not* to wish to enjoy it! Don't you agree? It has even got me thinking of also offering *myself* to him as a gift on his pre-wedding night as well since your father does not mind my also seeking a little extra pleasure still.'

'I think if my own *Mother* asked him for sex as *well* as my sister's . . . it would almost scare him to death!' she replied.

'Are you really only saying that because you think I am too old now to arouse a man, my daughter? Or are you just worried that due to my age he would be unwilling to give me pleasure?'

'In all honesty I just cannot say, Mother. You must remember that what he is being told by me now is already quite a shock to him.'

'What is?' her father asked.

'Well for one thing he's just found out that we all have to carry tattoo's. And due to that he would, when we are married, also require one himself with him then becoming part of our clan. And as yet, I still haven't managed to get around to telling him about his pre-wedding night of pleasure. Or of just how many of our clans women may or may not ask to be there that night with him. Not only members, but including servants as well – especially if Raiko happens to tell any of them about him after she has been with him.'

'It is also any servant's prerogative to be there on any man's pre-wedding night offering as well, daughter. That very special night is not just for the benefit of our main clan members alone you know. So it entirely their own choice if they wish to offer themselves to him, or not,' he told her.

'That I also know, Father. But what if she begins to call up each of our members houses and tells them exactly what it was like - I mean just how good it was for her - Then they may *all* want to come to see him!'

'But she may not think him *that* good herself, daughter.'

'Only if she bases it on some of the younger untrained boys who have enjoyed some time with her, maybe. And if *she* doesn't like it from him then she is a fool!' Kumiko said harshly.

Her parents both smiled. One who of who was looking at her, while the other ones eyes remained glued to the television screen; but who was still listening intently to their discussion.

'Such jealousy over his big shaft, Kumiko . . . It suits you very well already I must say!' her mother chuckled. 'But again, it is indeed something which is making me even more certain that I would like to sample it now.'

She looked at her father for help, but he just shrugged. She knew that he could do nothing to prevent her from offering herself to him. Only by Douglas refusing her offer kindly himself, could end that possibility from happening. Though she could almost guarantee that he would happily accept her remaining two sisters' offer, as even she had *always* thought of them as being far prettier than she ever was. So *they* would both certainly be having sex with him, as if they were not, then her father had already told her that he would request them both to do so. Which in their family, or clan, was tantamount to an order being given, and as such must be followed without question.

But *they* were not her real problem. Her problem was in not knowing just *how* many women *would* turn up that night to offer their bodies to him - and if would he accept any of them or refuse them all? Or would he become so terrified at the thought of having to please so many of them? That he would just vanish from the house on some sudden whim due to the pressure being placed upon his shoulders of then *having* to attempt to please so many of them! She didn't know, and doubted if he did yet. So she knew that that would be the very next thing she would have to tell him all about when she returned.

∞

After agreeing with her parents that her sister's cremation in the old way at the family shrine would indeed be perfect and fitting end for her. Kumiko was allowed to return to her room and her first ever lover. Yet even before she reached the door to her room she could hear Raiko's voice escaping in moans and groans. Until she opened the door that is, which was when everything inside came to a sudden stop. She held a hand to her mouth to hide her smile as she saw a panicked look on Douglas's face and Raiko's own very evident frown at her hasty return.

'If you have returned then I will leave you, mistress,' said the woman beneath him as she looked at her and began to move.

Spirit of a Dragon

Kumiko smiled sweetly as she closed the door behind her. 'Don't be so silly, as there's really no need for you to rush off straight away, Raiko. If you are not finished yet then I will just wait until you both are.' And with that she sat down, at most only about a foot away from them both, crossed her legs, rested her chin in her hands and waited for them to continue.

'What are you doing?' he asked.

'Waiting for you both to get going again of course, as I want to watch you make love to her.'

'You must be kidding?'

She shook her head. 'I *have* actually *seen* a lot of sex performed before me already in my life, Douglas. But never as near as this, and never with a man who will soon become my husband. And as I told you before, as this will likely happen with you either occasionally, or perhaps even quite often now and then, I just want to see what it is like for me to *watch* it happening, instead of being in the main leading role with you, so to speak. So please, do carry on.'

'But . . . I mean you can't feel comfortable watching this, Kumiko . . .' he protested.

'It is only sex, my love. For both your pleasure and for Raiko's right now, and that is all. So why should I be concerned? She is simply enjoying your body for a few brief minutes like this, where I will have many *years* of such times with you, I hope. So please, just carry on with what you were doing for me.'

He couldn't quite believe it, even if he had seen and heard it. But her nod as he looked deeply at her told him to go ahead. So he did. Raiko's mouth opened as soon as he did and the same moans and groans began to exit from her mouth again.

'Are you enjoying it, Raiko?' she asked the young woman servant.

'Very much so, mistress,' she answered breathlessly. 'And though it is my very first time with a *gai-jin* person like your husband-to-be, I must just say that his very length and width is causing me such pleasure that I would like to offer my services yet again to him on your pre-wedding night if I may be so bold?'

Kumiko's shoulders rose and fell in a shrug gesture. 'I cannot *prevent* anyone from asking to do so with him, Raiko, you know that. But my word is not the one you need for acceptance, is it? And I haven't had enough time to explain to my husband-to-be here yet; just what actually *is* involved with one of our pre-wedding nights yet.'

'Oh, I do apologise very much if I have caused you a problem with my saying that right now then, mistress.'

She shrugged again, and then also added a sigh with it for good measure. 'Only Douglas himself can choose on that night who he wishes to have sex with.'

His head turned rather quickly, just as his thrusting motion into the young woman came to another sudden halt. 'What's that you said?'

'Oh please, don't stop, master!' Raiko murmured to the very first foreign man *ever* to have lain in-between her own parted thighs.

Kumiko laughed aloud at her desperate plea to him. 'My husband-to-be must be pleasing you *very much* right now then, Raiko?' she asked her.

'Oh *very* much so, mistress, thank you,' she replied. '*His* shaft feels just so much different to *any* of those that I have already accepted before.'

'But why then did you not wish to have sex with the American, Robert, when he married my cousin a year or so ago, Raiko?'

She shook her head. 'No mistress, *then* I was scared of what may have been said about me by any of the other servants if I had done so.'

Kumiko was bemused by that actual statement from her, so asked, 'Then why are you doing so now with my Douglas?'

Raiko lowered her eyes as if too shy to speak. To where she could now see his hairy groin pressed firmly against her own. 'When your own body left his mistress, so that you could go to see your father. Well, just my seeing *it* standing there so stiffly erect made my body feel so excited, which is *why* I just had to offer to take your place. Of course, my mistress, I had to find out for myself, too – for other reasons.'

'The size of his shaft actually caused your juices to run, Raiko?'

Spirit of a Dragon

The servant nodded. 'Yes, mistress, and luckily for me they did when his shaft filled my body up so very much, too, I think.'

'Would you two please stop talking about me and my shaft as if I wasn't here in the room with you!' he grunted.

'Only if you get back to what you were doing, my love. Could you not see the actual enjoyment on Raiko's face, and also hear her own vast excitement while you were thrusting yourself into her?'

'Give over, woman!' he cursed. 'You're making me get even harder by doing that!'

'You mean you are *not* hard at the moment, master?' said Raiko. 'Then what on earth is that huge thing inside me already?'

'That is only his half shaft, dear Raiko,' Kumiko told her. 'When my Douglas is really hard it can almost take *all* the breath away from your body!'

'Oooh, could I try that as well, please?' she asked him hopefully, while gazing pleasantly upwards into his face.

'God Almighty!' he croaked. 'This is a bloody impossible thing to even imagine!' Then that same immense hardness began that made it appear as if his manhood *was* in fact made of iron began to occur. And so desperate did he become from it that he was soon thrusting into her even quicker than before, which only apparently left the poor woman beneath him literally gasping for more, while also begging for him to stop in the same instance. Kumiko simply looked on at the highly erotic scene below her. Though now more of an actual keen observer. Never before having ever needed to watch just one certain man in particular wo she felt so connected to: and more specifically, the one who she now knew would soon become *her* own husband very soon. And who right now was happily ramming his hardness into another woman right before her own eyes. It was nothing at all like she'd ever thought or imagined it would be she now thought. As she was, in fact, becoming quite excited her own self just from watching them.

So much so that she changed position from her seated one into a kneeling one alongside them both, and beside Raiko's right leg. A sudden twinkle lit her eyes and she reached a hand over to rest it on his clenched buttocks. His head spun to the side to see her kneeling beside them now, a wide smile on her face as she watched him perform very closely indeed. He still couldn't believe that this was happening to him. A threesome with his very new fiancée, as well as with a servant of their home ... it was just too weird and too wonderful to imagine something like that ever likely happening to him. It was almost like every man's best ever dream come true!

Kumiko then leaned her body over them, her right breast now touching his perspiring back and shoulders. Her mouth dropped closer to his ear and she whispered excitedly into it, 'Go on my Douglas, show her just how good you are and fuck her good and hard!' she said in an attemot to excite him even mnore. 'Thrust yourself into her with everything you have left for me now, my love!'

And then less than a second later, one of the fingers from her resting hand on his buttocks slid into the cleft of his buttocks to stroke around his anus. Raiko wailed aloud at the hammering blow he sent into her from Kumiko's sudden touch. Kumiko kept it up and Douglas couldn't help, or was just unable to do anything else *but* to keep the same forceful thrusting from happening now for some reason.

A few minutes later, with her noticing that his furious rocking rhythm was rapidly reaching a crescendo of sexual urgency, Kumiko then actually slipped her finger inside him now, with two of her other fingers moving lower to press against and around his peritoneum. Her unexpectd additional touch on his own never used before and well hidden nerve endings. Sent an uncontrollable sensation throughout his body, a sensation of which he had never before felt or experienced in his life. And the ejaculation that came from her administered touch, felt like the longest and most copious one, *ever*. And after that, his body was so utterly spent that all he could do was to slump upon his similar shattered partner below.

Kumiko left the room for a moment, and the two exhausted people on the futon, to wash her hands after doing that to him. Yet when she returned they still had not moved much, he had only rolled from Raiko to lie beside her on the quilt. Both of their chests rising and falling rapidly as if they were still connected by the same heightened state of passion.

'What the hell was that!' he panted out to her as she now came and knelt in-between them.

'Just some of the many sexual techniques that I have been taught and know how to use, my love,' she responded. 'Ways to make any man or women excited, aroused, harder, softer, orgasm or ejaculate, cry for more and, or, plead for less. Our bodies you see, have so many large and small bundles of nerves hidden within them that, if you know just *where* they all are, then you can quite easily accomplish so many things.'

'Like what?' he asked, his voice recovering only now as he began to cease panting.

'Well, say for a woman, you could always do this . . .' she said, then as he and Raiko watched her, she spread her fingers over the woman's groin and pressed down. Each of her fingers offering a varying amount of pressure. Whereby the young servant woman's body began to quiver and shake as she achieved a very fulfilling and unexpected orgasm in only a matter of seconds. Then she smiled, her white teeth shining at him. 'And for a man, my love, there is always this if it is ever needed.' He and Raiko now watched as only the index finger of her left hand arrived at his groin and was then pressed into it. His limp penis jerked up into the air into an instant erection, to which she quite happily, now began to run that same hand up and down its damp, long full length. 'I think I will enjoy using *this one* quite a lot on you very soon, my love,' she said looking into his amazed eyes. Then using the same finger, but in a slightly different spot at his groin. She pressed yet again and it fell limply, and so quickly even. That to him, it appeared as if it had been mortally wounded by her in some way.

∞

On the Saturday morning, after having spent the past two days together just quietly enjoying each other. Or walking hand-in-hand together in the small hills behind the house and around the nearby area of it. That, even then included a few additional sexual encounters between them while they *were* actually outside in the open air too; which was a novel experience for them both. She had also taken him along into the nearest village only a few miles away from it too.

The funeral of her sister was soon about to take place. Hyde had of course offered to help them with any preparations that were needed, but he was informed that with his not being an actual member of their clan, as yet. His help would not be required by them with their usual rituals. And it indeed was a, *them*, he soon found out. When on that same Friday evening, a lot of men and women, some with children, just seemed to appear at their house from nowhere in a variety of vehicles. The men there mostly all dressed in business suits. Which had also seemed a bit strange to him at the time. But as Kumiko had told him later, most of their men either ran their own businesses, or held places of authority very high up in others. And all were strictly legal enterprises, unlike what he may have heard about how a criminal group called the Yakuza operated.

So, as he and Kumiko passed some of the time together by walking around and about more. As well as enjoying their new found sex life. They regularly saw glimpses of the pit which had begun being dug into the ground at their family's burial site. Which was also where their own family and clan shrine was based. After a few more hours of walking through the trees and down to the village, they returned by the same route to find that the pit was now finished. A surprisingly deep hole, close to eight feet deep and eight feet long, by five feet wide lay ready and waiting. Above its yawning gap, thick timbers had already been placed across it from side to side, with two longer ones stretching from end to end.

He had asked Kumiko how it would be carried out, with his not having ever seen one take place in real life. So she had told him that when her sister had been returned to Japan. Her body had been finally picked up by the hearse, which had not turned up while they had waited for it at the hangar. And from there it had been transported to the nearby village, which they had just been to recently themselves earlier.

She tried to tell him in a way that he could understand that their usual way of a funeral was by cremation. But, she said, with them being what they were and are, and because of their own long history involved. Her father and mother both still wanted to cremate her in the old traditional way out in the open. She then described how she would either be laid out, or if it was at all possible still to do, to have her in a kneeling position within her funeral bier. As was quite common centuries ago for ladies of high class, which of course they all considered her sister to be, as she was of course the daughter of their clan leader. Although, simply due to where her death had occurred, and the many other time factors involved. The main thing being length of time since she had died would likely prevent such a position from being attainable. So it was likely that she would sadly have to finally depart their world laid in a prone position.

She told him so well that he could almost visualise it in his mind as she spoke to him of it now. Of the Shinto priests who would be there to intone an old ritualistic chant observed by their clan, possibly even from its very beginning. To the raised platform that they would be preparing soon for her large formally carried funeral bier to rest upon when it arrived. Of the rites which would be required to carry out before the wood beneath the platform could finally be set alight. With four separate gateways built of wood to see which way her spiritual soul would choose to leave. The one main gateway, which was the hoped for exit, would have her favourite dishes of food laid out for her to be able to partake of a spiritual meal of as she passed through.

As the offered fire took effect and ate into the wood just below her bier, which would already have been liberally doused with much flammable liquid; In order to make the fire burn hot and fast. And as a finale, not only the wood laid across the pit would give way, but also everything above it would then drop en-mass into the waiting pit. Then later, when all the flames and smoke had finally ceased to be. Anything that remained would be pushed into the hole. A hole which would then be refilled once more as if to leave no trace of it ever happening whatsoever. To appear the same way as it had all begun. And the only epitaph of her younger sister's short life would be written in preparation upon a black stone tablet, which would shortly be erected beside other members of her family that had already passed onwards.

One thing she did tell him though was when she said that any clan member attending it would eventually end up bare-chested from head to waist. As it was their own way of showing due honour and reverence to a fallen member. Their unhidden tattoo's were simply shown like that, as a final mark of respect to her by all of them. She told him that he could do the same thing, if he wanted to. Though none of them would care if he did do so, or did not. Seeing as he was not classed as *being* of their clan yet. As for any outsider, it was only when the tattoo was finally placed upon your body, when you were then fully considered as belonging within it. To be one of them for the remainder of your own life, no matter for just how long that eventuality may be.

During their walk together she told him even more about their clan. Of how they were all trained in the most lethal arts of killing - or of assassination as it were most likely better known nowadays. That those who had been instructed in *all* their ways could kill by means of various weapons at their disposal. Or even just by getting close enough to someone with enough time to touch someone in one of the three so very deadly nerve centres which could literally kill a human being instantaneously. There were also many poisons and other serums as well, all made from a variety of common everyday plants, flowers and vegetables, and other things - which she did not mention to him. That when made in the right measures and quantities, could actually be very potent and untraceable. Not just difficult, but almost impossible even to any of the highly skilled and qualified modern day autopsy coroners or technicians to acknowledge.

'Even todays scientists, chemists, and the largest pharmaceutical companies still have little idea of what so many naturally based combinations can produce, and of their causal effect, Douglas,' she informed him. 'It has to be said that even we do not know when this knowledge dates back to – or how they ever found out *what* they could do back then. Perhaps it may have been by simple trial and error. Even live subjects could have offered themselves as test subjects? It was a very different time back then as we know, possibly when even duty to your clan may have meant even more than it may do now! We do not really know, Douglas, only that what has been handed down through the many generations since then, works just the same!'

∞

Just before the funeral was about to take place, Hyde finally reached a decision and decided that she was right. Since he still wasn't a *true* member of their clan as yet. He could be deemed by many of those who would be attending it in their own formal manner, to not be suitable at all for him to join them.

In her bedroom after they had all bathed together in their huge sunken bath. He later watched her as she dressed in a very sombre looking kimono of almost entirely black silk. Only the large gold silken emblem of a dragon spread upon its back took the sheer deep hued darkness away from it.

Coming from her room, he saw that the rest of family also now wore the exact same type of kimono. And then outside the house, all those members who were attending it had also dressed in the same fashion too. He saw Raiko, dressed in a similar black kimono, but unlike those who must have been deemed as being full members within the clan. Her own attire only had two tiny golden dragons placed above each of her breasts; unlike her own personalised tattoos, which he'd now seen during their love-making. Hers were small, but were still just as intricately crafted as Kumiko's and the others far larger one were. There was no change in the detail of them, only their actual size.

So Raiko's, and all of the others servants' tattoos he'd since found, and been told about. Were actually applied to both sides of her body on her shoulders, front and back. They were true identical miniatures of the far larger ones that all those in the clan, who had been given the same training as Kumiko, all wore with so much pride. She had told him that all servants to their clan, be they male or female; were each given similar markings as well. In order to denote their *own* proud affirmation of belonging to the clan, and to those within it. From his own very detailed slow look at both Kumiko's and Raiko's on his first day when in her bedroom together with them. He had been able to study both of them, to note their similar artistic skill levels.

He had questioned her on how some were trained like she was, and why some became servants instead, as Raiko had. Her answer was simple; they chose what they wished to become when very young, at around the age of five or so. To become a servant required quite different training to that of becoming a highly trained assassin. As where she had studied martial arts from a very early age in order to create a supple enough body to be able to acquire it all. Then taught how to use the many various and varied weapons. Also then learning nerve techniques and poisons, or a few potent stimuli for other reasons as her skills and talents progressed.

They as servants were also taught many of the martial arts too, but for reasons only to do with safety, security, and also for physical fitness also. But alongside that, their *main* training regimen was very different. They were training to learn how to serve any house or person to which they could belong to for just as long as they were needed. To bathe people properly before they entered the hot water, various massage skills and techniques. To only shave men or women by means of using a cutthroat razor for the closest shaves possible for hygiene and superior removal. To be able to wash and style, and to wax and remove hair, also that of men too, If they so wished it, and also to manicure and to pedicure, as well as that of many of the usual household duties which were also required.

She informed him that sometimes some of them were so good at cooking, or other similar types of professional work, that they were even sent out to one of the clan member's restaurants, or businesses in order to become completely trained as chefs, mechanics, electricians, plumbers, etc. And for any servant in their clan that was almost an ultimate position, as they would then do nothing else *but* those tasks after that, if that was their wish. Any of the other more ordinary duties would then be taken over by other servants in their place.

And so, as he walked beside Kumiko and the rest of her family, heading up the small incline to where they had seen the pit dug into the earth the day before. He was now able to see her three brothers and her two other younger sisters for the first time. That Hiro was the eldest of them all at thirty-three, and the accountant for the family company. Yoshio who at thirty-one, was only a year older than Kumiko was, and he was the senior lawyer for the company. Kazuo was the young detective she had spoken about when they were in England. He was twenty-seven, and at five-feet-seven also the tallest of them all.

Noriko was twenty-eight, now married for five years with two children, and who walked along beside her husband and two young daughters. She was an electronics engineer for the company, helping to redesign old existing materials, or developing new products for them. And lastly was Makiko, twenty-five and again married, but as yet only with one son, and she was walking with him and her husband within the large group. Her position at the company was as the assistant to the marketing and research development manager, who she would take over from when he retired, or if he ever left.

From taking glances around him, he estimated that Makiko was the tallest of the women at about five-feet-five, or about an inch taller than Kumiko herself. Whereas he remembered that Carmen had said that Akiko was only five-foot-two. Noriko looked a few inches shorter than Kumiko, and their mother was the smallest of them all and barely tipped the five-foot mark. But Kumiko had been right about one thing - her sisters were both quite striking looking women, just as she herself was.

As they all reached their places and knelt, a few minutes later the funeral began to take place. Her bier was already in place, seated upon the wooden trestle like structure above the hole below. He listened as the white garbed priest began to chant, and seemingly, without ever needing to take a breath. As a few times, he had caught himself while listening actually holding his own breath in as he followed the incessant chanting. Though when he found out what he was doing, had to inhale a few good deep breaths just to steady himself. So he could only wonder at how the priest was able to keep up that same virtual monotone monologue quality to his voice, and without ever apparently breathing was beyond him.

What felt like it had lasted close to an hour was only half that length, at most. Until it then it came to rather a sudden and abrupt end. He then watched as her father slid his arms from out of his kimono and folded it down to his waist, revealing his own tattooed back to all of those who were positioned behind him. Everyone else except for himself and the priests, who he now saw were already leaving the site. As their work was now over and done with, had quickly followed his actions. Which only left him feeling a little self-conscious, as he was really now the only person who was still wearing something that covered his upper body. Apart from a few old men and women who must have been village guests. Everyone else beared their flesh, from the old, up to and including all of the young children he had seen. Those of who were actually baring no tattoo at all yet with being too young for one right now. He could also spot those who were known as servants to their clan simply by their shoulder markings.

But in their case, to him it just appeared as if they were already showing their own kind of loyalty to their clan group. As well as to a once highly regarded, but now suddenly deceased member of it. Yet they were all now kneeling in silence with bared chests, breasts, and backs. His eyes widened as he turned his head to look around the clearing, as he'd just received something of a shock. As there actually were a *hell* of a lot of people kneeling here right now around him, and they were just so closely packed together, that he soon estimated that there must have been at least a *thousand* of them here at the small funeral site. *If not more!*

His head turned sharply as he heard a crackling of flames from in front of him as two torches were lit. That was when he saw Kumiko's mother rise from the ground to go across to join her husband at the pit. At which point he handed one of the pair of lit torches to her. He watched as they both bowed from the waist to the bier itself, when they were stood close enough. Beside and around him, he saw that every other head also fell forward almost in one single movement as they all paid their final and deepest respects to one of their fallen clan.

He was only about a second or so behind them to copy them, and kept his eyes looking constantly to his right in order so that he could copy whatever Kumiko might do. Though even as he did that, he also saw a few adult hands here and there. Which were placed on to the backs of some of the youngest children's heads to keep them facing down. He also, from his own position, was able to see that Kumiko own eyes were tilted upwards so that she could see what was happening at the main focal point ahead of her.

As the first loud crackle of flames began, she raised her body back up and he copied her. Her parents quickly moved back as the flames easily found the flammable liquids used to coat the wood below it, and then it suddenly just whooshed up in a large flame. They regained their positions at the head of the mass of mourners for their youngest daughter, and then began to sing; a low mournful song which soon began to ripple through the entire group as they joined in. Apart from he himself and many of those same very young children, who like himself, perhaps didn't know it yet.

He listened to the words as they were sung aloud by them all, the deep vibrant lows and highs from both men and women stilled his thoughts and made his still hidden flesh erupt with thousands of tiny goose-bumps. Just as if a sudden cold breeze had washed over him. The song must have been very old he thought, as it spoke of utmost honour and duty to each other and the clan above all else. And of a warrior spirit in action, and the quickness of death for themselves or of an enemy.

The song continued on, and rose and fell in a tempo of waves as the pyre in front of them blazed ferociously. As the wooden struts beneath the bier itself began to crack loudly from the intense heat now eating its way through it. Their voices rose to an even higher intensity above it, as if trying to drown it out. The gate with the food standing just before it then appeared to combust with an enormously loud bang and a flash of flames without any reason whatsoever. And their voices all rose again in a manner of something akin to triumph; for as yet he didn't understand why. As to all of them, they now knew that Akiko's soul had chosen the right way to leave her mortal life. Then, when an almost amazing in its effect secondary explosion occurred before all of them, the entire display unexpectedly fell into the waiting open maw of the pit below. Their singing now came to a sudden unexpected halt right there and then, and a large sigh arose to take its pace.

His entire body suddenly began to shiver uncontrollably. He had a strange feeling of nausea afflicting him just then. His forehead broke out with a sudden sheen of perspiration. His eyes, he now found, were unable to focus – on anything! His body began to shake very badly now, almost as if he were feverish and having convulsions.

He felt not only dizzy, but also light-headed and close to fainting at the same time . . . and so even as he just felt himself falling forwards, a complete darkness had already claimed him and filled his mind . . .

CHAPTER 13

On that same Saturday back home, Douglas's own new investigation leader, Detective Inspector Jenkins, was already having a torrid time. As not only had Durham's own results finally been returned by their pathologist and laboratory. And that their own similar testing had shown the exact same links and match ups. That sexual intercourse had indeed taken place. Also that an identical drug identification had now been positively identified. Along with the same means being used as the cause of death; as well as the same DNA from their victim coincided with their own.

But that wasn't all, which was why he was in such a depressed mood at that very moment. Belated calls from some of the other forces areas had at last been offered to their team. And these results were the main problem for him, as they had also shown corresponding evidence when placed beside their own report queries which had been sent out earlier. So yet another four murders had now been attributed to the same killer.

He was not only confused by what was happening so suddenly to him, he was also close to losing what previous thoughts and experience over what he could possible try and do about it next. Jenkins had suddenly found himself placed in charge of attempting to try to find a killer on the loose. To then find that it was not just a one off murder that had been committed - but far worse, which was that of it now being the work of a serial killer.

So this was the true problem he was facing. He had always thought that his own detective talents were forever being wasted and unrecognised. Since he had never previously been allowed to run any investigation like this personally yet. Nor having ever been placed in sole charge of one before. So to his mind, his skills were always hid away and being seen as limited. His own personal strengths also never being used for what he imagined his own capability was surely merited at, but previously left unused and untried.

He had only ever been there as the second-in-command in any earlier kinds of murder enquiries such as these, or to him, known as the sidekick. Which typically meant that the person there above him, was always the one who made all the necessary decisions about what they should be doing next. So of course, at the end of any successful outcome to an operation. *They* were the ones who usually received any of the accolades or plaudits that may have been given out.

And now, when it *was* finally down to him to do it, he just couldn't make his mind up about *what* he should be doing next. He really felt like a fish out of water without a leader to tell him what to do. As each additional new murder added itself to only the single one he had at first been sent to run. The investigation was growing in size at an alarming rate, and for him, possibly *too* alarming some lesser mortals may have thought. But Jennings simply couldn't believe in his own mind that *he, especially,* didn't have what it took to do the job. That he simply couldn't cope with the pressure of the new demands which were starting to arise from someone else's enquiries. *He* hadn't been the one who asked the other forces for any of these incoming extra details. So why the hell were they all now coming back here to this unit and putting it all of this on to his shoulders!

Terry could only watch him while he waited to be told what his new team leader wanted them to get started on next as all the extra information was arriving. Yet from his countenance in front of him, he wondered exactly what . . . if anything that is, was actually going through his mind. As he had stood waiting for a good four minutes now and there was still no sign of any decision forthcoming from his new leader. He was already wishing that Dougie were back, or that he'd never even left in the first place.

'Boss . . .?' he said again to the frozen faced man in front of him for what had to be the fourth or fifth time in as many minutes already. Who as yet had still not showed any sign whatsoever of even having heard him once. He emitted a low sigh and waited patiently, wondering just what the hell was wrong with him. Those in the room looked at each other wondering, then shrugged and carried on again. But they all knew it was a very unusual occurrence taking place.

After another minute he tried again. 'Boss, what do you want us to get on with now?'

Jennings's then appeared to snap out of whatever had taken him so long to hear him. 'Huh?' he muttered.

'I asked *what* you wanted us all to get on with now.'

It seemed to take another minute before his eyes focused on the younger man before him. 'I'm just mulling everything around in my head at the moment, Terry. Really just trying to get a clearer picture of all the difficulties that are now lying ahead of us due to the new information coming in. And to then try and formulate our next best move on it all!'

He lied quite admirably in the circumstances. Finally just beginning to understand in his own mind that he was actually way out of his depth here, and by a long mark. *Way out of it!* But also, he was entirely averse to seeking any kind of help from anyone who *he* felt was beneath him.

He now knew that he was only a very able second-in-command of any team or unit. As in being led, but not as an able full leader of one. He had now just found this out at his first chance to fully prove himself, though not in a good way at all, he now knew. Knowing that *he* just didn't have the true leadership qualities, or natural flair: even to the talent of reasoning that would be required for him to be in charge of one of these investigations. Nor did he have the various mental abilities that were compatible, and always required along with it. To know almost without fail what *should* be needed to be done next.

'Just carry on with what you were doing before, Terry,' he told the much younger detective. Who it seemed to him now, really knew a lot more about what they should be doing than he himself did!

'I'm just going to have a word upstairs with the Boss first. As there are some details I want to clear up with him right now before I get you all started on what to do next, okay . . .'

'Fair enough, boss. While you're gone I'll try and get everything laid out into much clearer patterns for you to look at on the boards.'

Jennings nodded his thanks, and as Terry went over to it, he felt quite close to running from the room in utter despair. However, he was just able to contain his panic long enough to maintain his dignity. Appearing to those inside the department to saunter out quite casually from it. Little did any of them know just *how* close he was to breaking down and running out right now.

When the door closed behind him, the somewhat long silence that had started, and then lengthened as Terry had continually asked him over and over again for a response finally ended. And talk erupted from them all in unison about what had happened.

'He's bottled it!' announced one of the much detectives.

Terry was nodding. 'I was just thinking that too, Gary,' he admitted.

'What do *you* want us to do then, Terry?' he asked, as the same waiting silence returned again.

Smiles came to every one of their faces as the same young second-in-command on the investigation to Hyde began to spout his orders. He, *in particular*, had coped very well with the sudden leap thought the older man to himself. As he now listened to the flow of rapid ideas and suggestions coming from the well-known to them, young underling DI.

Jennings' non return as the time passed ever onwards, left them knowing he wouldn't be coming back to them at all, unless by some miracle. And within around a quarter of an hour, the Boss himself was once more striding through the door to their department. Expecting from what he had just heard from the man upstairs in his own office. To come and find all of them just still sitting in here awaiting his return to tell them all what to do next. Instead, he found that the department was almost its usual busy self just as when Hyde was down here.

His gaze travelled over the room to the old detective, who gave a quick glance towards Terry, then actually stuck a thumb in the air to him. Which to Ramshaw, as he stood there taking in the almost beehive like activity of the department. Was saying to him that the man thought another replacement was really quite unnecessary, as young Terry had already got them all working on his own.

'DI Boyne,' he said aloud. 'Can you take over this investigation here until DI Hyde returns from his holiday?' he said, then paused. 'If you need any further help, or suggestions with the case then just come and see me if you need to, or just give me a call upstairs.'

'Yes, sir, thank you, sir,' said the young man. Then he cautiously asked, 'Is DI Jennings all right, sir?'

The Chief Constable gave a nod. 'He's fine, but he's also told me that he would prefer to only be used as a second-in-command at most in any similar investigations such as this in future. As at this moment, he does not consider that his own style of working as part of a team would suit being a complete leader and tactician of one. Not for a department which is running a case like this one is right now anyway.'

'Very well, sir. Of course I'd be happy to take over here for you on a temporary basis at the moment - but only until DI Hyde gets back again.'

The Chief gave another nod and turned to leave, while just before closing the door heard new orders being issued from the same young man. He gave a quiet smile as he headed back to his office upstairs again. One sadly just *not* good enough - and one clearly who does have the makings of becoming *much* better under Hyde's supervision. And if he's occasionally allowed to spread his wings a little maybe, on more tasks like this . . . he thought to himself, as he then moved in his usual purposeful marching stride out of the room and returned back to his office upstairs.

∞

The killer had left a parting gift to the police of Aberdeen after he'd concluded his business there, after earlier buying a similar flask to the one he had used previously. As yet another body lay just waiting to be discovered by someone, just as the one in Berwick had been discovered on Saturday afternoon; and by a small group of shocked local children from a nearby double row of cottages. Who, on the weekends, viewed the small forest nearby as their own private playground. Using it for various games such as hide and seek, or more typically cowboys and Indians, even simulated war games.

He never felt any remorse whatever about what he was doing - or of what he now knew that he was; that of a serial killer. In fact, he was actually enjoying every new turn in his own sexual escapades. For some reason he himself had remained a frustrated virgin in his lonely lifestyle. Until his first attack had taken place, that is. The unexpected outcome to what should have only been a rape, along with the added rush of adrenalin from what it had finally ended up as. Had changed to more of an accident, when he's killed her instead. His different pattern had now, up to date, racked up a grand total of ten. Although he was hoping that much higher double, or even triple figures would be made by him before he was caught - *if he ever was* . . . As he was actually enjoying what he was now doing more and more each time.

His own life and lifestyle only happened because of how the young girls of his younger age, and then women in later life continually spurned his advances. At school, any girls who he had fancied and asked, left him in no doubt of what they thought about going out with him as his girlfriend. Their somewhat spite-filled turn down comments were not only passed on to their friends, but also ended up going around his school, too. It soon made him become a loner, and one with no friends there at all. Even after leaving school, his luck never changed. He was older now, but the responses were still the same from them. Sometimes even harsher than before as well! The only female companion who had *ever* actually loved him had been his own mother throughout. But she was now gone from his life. Killed by a drunk driver late one night as she returned from work. And so a total life of loneliness had descended upon him. No family or friends to speak of, so only his work sustained him.

Even his mother, and he himself had never known that he had become slightly psychotic from when his father had just up and left them one day when he was only a young boy. He quickly became deluded, blaming only himself for his father's sudden disappearance from their lives. Seeing his mother struggling to cope with him on his own. Her now having to go out to work to earn money for them, instead of being there for him all the time. For a mind as young as his was - he was the one who had caused all of this to happen. Not either of his parents. An effect like that soon gave him a distorted look on actual reality.

A doctor could well have termed him as becoming slightly schizophrenic from it all. But as his mother never knew of the chnge in him, so no doctor was ever seen. And so his state of mania gradually grew as he did. At school others saw him as both strange and odd. The reason why no freindships were forthcoming. And also why no girls there wanted to go out with him either. The way he acted sometimes had pushed any of them away who may have felt something for him. This had then continued after school and beyond. It was also the main reason why his own odd thinking mind had finally told him to get some payback on women for how they had treated him for so long. And that was what had begun his attacks!

From the very beginning of his thoughts, *he'd* wondered if he might get away with the rapes he was going to do. But by now, and after so many had fallen victim to him already, he was actually thinking of years to come, and not months. His hopes all lying mainly due to his to his own personal lifestyle and working methods. The fact that he didn't own or rent a house to live in had given his mind the very first idea of what he *could* get away with. As his van was used in dual combination, both as his home *and* as his working environment as well.

The mobile telephone seated on the dashboard in its holder was his only office. While a simple PO Box number back down in London easily handled any mail that he was sent, either in the way of cheques or bills, or reminders when anything to do with his van or taxes needed paying. An accountant dealt with everything regarding hos work, and even *he* had to contact him either by phone, or through a message in that very same box too.

So, in a way, he was an almost non-existent person in the country as he worked as a homeless transient courier, moving from one job to the next wherever it took him. And with few or no worries about needing to live like most other people did. Occasionally he would stay in a hotel or guesthouse when no work came in for a day or two, which also allowed him to rest in a real bed, eat a few good meals, and manage a few baths or showers. As when without them, he lived on fast food, sandwiches, or prepared meals bought from any shop, supermarket or garage that were easy to buy, heat-up in his microwave in the back of his van, and eat.

His personal flask was, just like his toilet habits, usually controlled by the times he rested at any truck stops. Where a morning wash, and shave if he bothered, along with the typical breakfast fare set him up for most of the day. Most nights he would be eating and sleeping in the back of the van. Sometimes watching the little portable colour television which he had fitted there, which was fixed to run from the vans electrical supply. As was his tiny fridge and microwave for any meals if he could not reach a parking depot where there would be something to buy.

He lacked for nothing since he was in all terms a strict loner. He worked when he liked, bathed when he wanted, and ate when he was hungry. But most of all – his job also made him very difficult to find. As the only people who had his telephone number were his accountant, or those from the businesses who used him constantly, and passed their recommendations of his courier service on to others in the same field. As it was well known to all of them that, even if he was in Scotland or Wales he would happily drive to London to do a pick-up and delivery for them with no bother. Six, or even seven days a week unless his van needed some repair work doing at any time. Which he made sure was as rare as possible so as not to lose his clients, as well as the valuable money he earned from it all. Even though, it was really only on weekends when he could have managed to get a few days proper rest into his body.

And from Aberdeen, he was already on his way back down, and would then head right across the country. As his next pick-up, received only hours after he had carried out his latest attack, was now to go to Cardiff. So that's where he was off to now, with the usual thoughts turning over in his mind as always . . . Would he be just as lucky there in Wales too?

∞

On the following Monday morning, and only five days since his usual boss Hyde had left to have some very belated personal holiday time. Terry himself was almost close to panicking, as the reports had begun to filter through by other forces who had been contacted by the staff in this very room. As instead of the previously arranged five crime boards arrayed along the far wall of the room - there were now eight. So he was wondering if that was the end of it, or if this was just the tip of the iceberg and a hell of a lot more were going to come in before long.

Terry walked along each one of them as he studied their locations . . . As they just appeared to be springing up just so randomly to him, almost haphazardly in a strange kind of way. They were now even dating back to November of the previous year, and because of that, the boards had required switching around into new positions just to try and keep track of them all. As apparently, or at least so far, one reply from down in the London Metropolitan Police Forces area had actually been the very first of them all. Then over to Dover for the second, with the third taking place miles away up near Lincoln, and then the fourth was down country again at Norwich. He moved further along. Then back up north again to one at Barnsley in the Midlands that now appeared to be the fifth. Durham was the sixth while their own was the seventh. Then heading northwards his next attack had come at Berwick.

Spirit of a Dragon

Where was he going? What was he doing? And why the hell was he moving around the country so much when he could probably have done the very same thing in one place wherever he came from? Terry mused, but was certainly not amused by it at all. But he was staying hopeful, as he knew that with what he was actually doing, and was now becoming known, that seven other police forces would also now be hunting him instead of just their own.

'Gary,' he said, then waved a hand to the older man.

He crossed over to him after leaving the desk. 'Yes, Boss?'

Terry grinned and shook his head. 'Terry'll do just fine, Gary. I'm only in charge for a short while, not like Dougie is.'

'Our own *Boss* would have put you in charge of the investigation until then if he could have. And now, the main Boss upstairs has done so, so until he does return now, *you're* the Boss in here, *Boss!*' he stated with a grin.

'Okay, fair enough then, Gary,' he said, then waved at the boards in front of them. 'You got any ideas yet?'

Gary was pleased. As unlike Jennings who had tried to do everything in his own way and style right from the off. It seemed as if Terry had picked up some of the right moves from Dougie over the few years they'd been together now. One of the right moves being, that of a willingness to ask others their opinion, and also to *listen* to their answers. Even if they were way out of touch. And then judge from what he heard if it was any particular use to the case they were working on, or not.

'He gets about a hell of a lot does our killer,' he answered, 'so, that gives me a couple of ideas really, Boss. The first is that his work *takes* him around the country all the time, and that is what's allowing him to cause nigh on every one of our patches a problem. So he could well be a truck driver, travelling salesman, or a delivery driver of some sort or other. My second thought was that he could just be some unemployed bloke wandering, or driving around the country looking for his own freaky kicks. Remember, that although in each case we've found the girls' handbags or purses hidden close to their bodies. Inside them only the credit cards were not taken, any money that *was* inside we must assume was. So if the latter, then he could well be funding his later travels by using their money.

'Have you noticed anything else, Gary?' Terry asked him.

The older man nodded. 'Yep, he just doesn't seem to care who he rapes and kills, does he? So long as they're not too old that is. The London one was a young Indian girl, the Barnsley one was a young black woman, and our own was Japanese. The other five out of the eight were young white women. So we know that he's not a true racist, or he'd never have attacked the white girls anyway. And then again it works the opposite way if he was a non-white man with racial tendencies, too.

'But they weren't, all of them were born locally to where they were found murdered, apart from ours. Easily found out since each one of them . . . or I should say, the bags or purses used to carry their gear in had some means of identity on them which was always left behind. They were all found stripped as well, just like ours and the other new ones were – so that I am now guessing is also apparently his *modus operandi* each and every single time.' He looked at Terry under his thickly greying eyebrows. 'But what do *you* think, Boss?'

'I personally think the bastards a bit of a psycho myself!' he stated firmly, 'I mean to say Gary, just why else *would* he be doing something as sadistic as this to so many of them, if he wasn't? Although I'm also wondering exactly *why* he appears to have only just begun to do this in the November of last year, and not any earlier, or later than that. Which could possibly just mean that he may only have got out of prison around then, maybe? So I guess we'll just have to start checking up on that information as well now, Gary. If only to see if any former convicted sexual attackers, or possibly unknown but guessed at serial rapists may have been released around then. Or even just people who could be *thought* to might be rapists fit into this anywhere. What do you say?'

'Sounds like a good enough place to start for me, Boss. I just hope that it does give us a lead somewhere?'

'Why?'

'Because, if none of *those* can tally up with what we want. it'll mean that someone who we actually have no information on at all is the one who is doing it. And will just keep on doing it until we do manage to catch him!'

Terry looked grim. 'In which case could also mean a hell of a lot more murders could be taking place. Before we might even get an inkling of the person who's committing these killings, and only with luck, running him to ground.'

'We definitely need *something* to help us,' admitted the older man. 'Just one small clue as to what he drives, where he lives, what work he does, or just *anything* about him at all would give us a break. Then at least we might get a starting point for our search.'

Terry's head shook ponderously. 'And that's the real problem so far Gary, isn't it. We just haven't found a single clue yet to give us a head start, or any lead on finding this bastard, have we?' It was not an actual question that required an answer coming from the old detective, which he instinctively knew. Though it did have the real guts of the matter contained within it. Which of course was that, *without* any actual clue to help them, they could be searching in vain for this multiple murderer forever.

'Well I'd just finished what you asked me to do, Boss. So I'll get on to the computers now and look through what prison records we can find to see if any of those types have recently been released. Or if some are out on parole prior to November last year.'

'Cheers Gary. I only hope that we can at least get one lead from doing that. As at least it will give us *something* to be going on with. And as long as I don't make a complete balls-up of it all before Dougie gets back!'

'We can but hope,' he replied with a hopeful tilt of his head, before he added just before walking away, 'but I have a sneaking suspicion in my own gut that this bloke's a newcomer to it. So we'll not find him on it, and until something crops up that we can easily spot. That we won't have a bloody clue as to who he is, or what he does either!'

All Terry could do was to nod and then turn back to face the eight laid out boards. Trying to do exactly what he knew Dougie would do in this position, which was to look out for any similarities between them that hadn't been spotted yet. But he could recognise nothing as he looked. That they were all young was easy to see. All aged between seventeen and twenty-three. None of their racial backgrounds appeared to help him out either. Seeing as the killer was apparently being totally indiscriminate about any of those *who* he was drugging, raping, and then finally killing.

A few had been students, two were unemployed, and the rest worked for a living. So that was no help to him either. He shook his head as another idea came to him and then just as quickly left. That it may have been hair colour which attracted him to them. But he knew this was also not the case seeing as four were dark-haired, or brunette's, one was a redhead, one brown, and two were blondes.

Their heights and weights only varied slightly, with barely only a few inches difference between some of them, and at most twenty-five pounds difference in their weights. The heaviest girl of them all being the very last they had been informed about from Berwick. From what he saw and could picture from the boards, all he got was that their killer must be quite a fit guy, as he must have carried each of their inert bodies to where it had finally been dumped. Not dragged, as no such marks had been left at any scene. Which he knew was not really an easy thing to do, as a dead body was literally, *a dead weight* to to move around. And at any scene of death he'd ever attended, it had always taken two assistants from the Coroner's office to move them. So he had to be either fit or quite a strong man just to be able to do that on his own.

'Shit! Dougie, Dougie, Dougie, what on earth can I do to make any headway at all here?' he muttered aloud to himself as sudden of wave of depression hit him. 'I hope that it is only one man doing this and not two of them working together now! Or worse still, two separate killers battling for the highest count!'

Terry glanced at his wrist to his watch, 9.30am he thought to himself. What did Dougie tell me before he went? He stood thinking for a moment until it finally came to him, and he began to nod. That's right, Dougie said that I'd have to *add* eight or nine hours on to our time to know what time it was over in Japan at any time. So it was about 6.30pm over there now today, which was fine, he guessed, as even he knew that Dougie would be unlikely to be asleep at that time of day. He walked over to his own desk, sat down in his chair and pulled himself nearer to it. Then after lifting the phone from its base, began to dial Hyde's mobile number from his memory.

His fingers made a drumming motion on the desk as he waited for the ringing to begin, but there was nothing. And then a kind of message quality voice came over the earphone. Which was telling him that the number he had dialled could not be reached. He put the phone back into its base and sat staring at it.

The voice of the old detective Gary Mooney said quietly at his ear, 'Trying to reach Douglas are you?'

He nodded without much thought it seemed to the older man.

'He's in Japan, my lad, not in the UK now, so of course you can't just call him up that way. He may have his mobile switched off, or there may even be a difficulty reaching him that far away!' Terry looked up at him.

'If you have the number of the house or hotel where he's staying, then you will also need to have the international dialling code, and maybe even an area code for a different country other than ours for starters, just so it can be passed on somehow! If his mobile isn't accepting calls – then it's likely just switched-off at the moment. Remember, he's on a kind of holiday, so he may not want to be called up at just anytime we would like to be able to catch him over here. You could maybe send him a text message though – then he'd just call you back when he saw it?'

Terry snapped his fingers together. Of course! That was what else Dougie had already told him, Kumiko's home telephone number. But he hadn't written that or the code down and had now forgotten it. 'Did you get the number where he might be staying before he left? And do you know the international code for Japan, Gary?'

'Hell, no, I've never had any need to ever call anyone over there before. But if you call across to our operations room I'll bet that they can tell you what it is. Or, maybe even if Douglas had left a different number for anyone to get him there too!'

'Way to go, Gary!' he told the older man. Who smiled and now returned back to his walk over to his own desk, which was where he'd been headed originally until he'd seen his young leader's sudden plight. Terry picked up the phone again and pressed button eight on the handset.

'Operations room?' was spoken into his ear this time.

'Hi there, this is DI Boyne from Department M3 and I'd like to know if Detective Inspector Hyde left any call number to be able to reach him in Japan. If so, what the international dialling code for Japan would also be please, mainly for getting a call through to him over there,' he asked the young woman at the other end. Who was in fact only three floors up from him in the operations room and seated in her chair in front of her console.

'Hold on a moment please, while I see if I can get you that information, sir,' she responded. And then he could actually hear her fingers as they were tapping away at the keyboard in front of her as she sought to find the information that he now needed.

'Are you still there sir?'

'Yes, go ahead.'

'According to the details on my screen sir, Detective Inspector Hyde has not left any additional contact number with us. But we know where he is, somewhere near Tokyo we were told, or have heard said. And the international dialling code for Japan is +81 if you do manage to get a local number to reach him by. That's a plus sign required in place before the eighty-one number sir, and they are also nine hours in front of us over there, time wise,' she told him politely. 'For contact via a mobile from a service providing company here in the UK, nothing apart from the usual mobile number should be needed to reach someone from here as long as it's switched on. Although there could also be a delay if a call is being routed through more than one service provider in order to reach that particular country.'

'Thank you. I already knew about the time difference, it was only the code and local number that I couldn't remember if he'd left it with anyone. But thanks a lot for your help anyway.'

'Pleased to be able to help you out, sir,' she said with assurance.

Now without any additional help in his hands, all he could do was to redial Hyde's mobile number again and again as the time steadily passed. His cheeks puffed out in relief and his breath escaped through his pursed lips as it finally began to ring this time at his umpteenth attempt at the other end.

'Thank God for that,' he finally muttered aloud, 'at least he's finally turned his mobile back on again now!'

CHAPTER 14

Hyde apparently found himself waking up to the sound of some low voiced female chattering. More strangely, chattering that appeared to be coming from all around him. He felt warm, actually very warm indeed, but wasn't sure why this was so while being outside at the funeral. His eyes, seemingly of their own accord, now began to flicker towards opening, and a sudden hushed stillness now came to those same voices.

Upon them finally opening, he gazed down from his head-raised point of vantage to just below him, only to find that he was now lying prone within a room. Kumiko's by the look of it, he thought, as it looked like hers to him – though he could easily be wrong. His lower body was covered by a thick warm covering, but only up to the point where Kumiko's own head rested upon her forearms over his stomach, and from a position immediately between his legs and also from beneath the same covering.

'Wha ---? How in hell did I get here?' he muttered.

'You do not remember, Douglas-san?' a voice over at his left asked.

He turned his head upon an amazingly soft pillow to look that way. And blushed when he saw Kumiko's sister Noriko there. He only just managed to shake his head in reply.

'You collapsed while attending our dear sister Akiko's funeral, Douglas-san,' said another voice now from the right side of him. His head turned again to look that way now. Though while still luxuriating on the sheer softness of the pillow that his head was reclining on. It was her other sister at that side, Makiko.

'Jesus! Just what the hell's going on here?' he said vehmently.

Kumiko tapped at his chest with a finger to gain his attention.

'Just after our sister Akiko's bier fell into the pit Douglas. You suddenly fell forwards and appeared to pass out beside me,' she told him when he'd looked at her.

'I did? Why? I can't remember doing that at all?' he said with a frown coming to his face. 'Then how did I get here?'

'You were carried back down to the house here by some of us, my love. I was also a little bit worried about you since your head did really hit the ground with such a terrible thumping sound too. Though I'm pleased to say that you only sustained a very small cut and bruise from it. And one of the healers in our clan said that apart from that, you would be fine if kept nice and warm. Which is of course why we are all here with you now.'

He tried to move his right hand up to his head but found that he couldn't budge it for some reason.

'Do you wish to use your hand, Douglas-san?' asked Makiko.

'If I can do that now, please?' he queried.

She released her own grip upon his arm, an arm which part of the time she had held tight against her upper torso and stomach. His hand had been positioned between her own warm thighs in order to also keep it warm while he had been out cold. Even then it seemed a little difficult to extract both from its hidden place, but he managed. And as he raised it out from beneath the thick covers, he saw it fall slightly off her, and the bare breast of the same woman at his side emerged, and he blushed.

He laid his palm on his forehead, then back through his hair, and the tips of his three longest fingers touched something behind his head, which he then prodded them with to test its texture. Something that was so soft to his touch that he now had to try to bend his neck backwards a little upon the cushion, in order to see just what he had touched. Only to find out that he had not been resting on any cushion or pillow at all . . . As Raiko was there, and bent her body forward until her small breasts were almost touching his face.

'It is only I, master,' she said as she bowed. 'After having been told by my mistress to support your head and neck with my own warm legs to aid your comfort while you recovered.'

'But why are you *naked*!' he croaked. 'You must be freezing!'

'I am quite warm master, thank you. And I am more than happy to help you in any way I can now. After you pleased me *so much* on the day you arrived here.'

His face reddened again from knowing that he knew that others had heard what she'd said.

'We are *all* very much naked under here, my love,' Kumiko now advised him. 'For the touch of bare skin against bare skin is by far the most conducive means of generating and passing heat between our bodies. So for that reason, I am where I am to warm your lower half from within, whereas my sisters have been keeping each side of you nice and warm for me. While Raiko who is my own maid, has pillowed your head so carefully for you. My sister's maids have kept *their* backs warm for them, as well as the backs of your hands occasionally.'

'What?'

She smiled widely at him, as did her sisters while they all now began to nod as if their heads were tied together. 'Of course, my love, our duty at our father's order was to take very special care of you. And theirs is to take good care of us, too, *neh*? So if we have to do something that requires us being unclothed as we all now are, then they have to follow suit in the same way.'

'You - You - You're mean you're *all* naked!'

She nodded, then said, 'Michi, Akiyo, please come out for a moment to pay your respects to a soon to be new master within our family household if you would.'

His eyes swung from side to side as two large bumps began to appear in the covers formed behind each of the two women against him.

Heads popped out and then their bodies followed, until they were both kneeling on the floor within his view. His eyes could do little else but move from one of them to the other and sample the very nakedness placed before him, even while they bowed and greeted him. Then with similar fixed wide smiles on their faces they vanished back under the covering and back to their original places again.

'Jesus, what else could be next?'

'They are both just as pretty as Raiko was to you, are they not, my love?'

'Yeah,' was about all he could say to that.

'I thought that was what you thought about them my Douglas. As your shaft is growing quite hard beneath my own breasts now.'

'Oooh, can I see it?' asked Makiko.

'No way!' he grunted.

But Kumiko herself, as usual, had other ideas about what was correct to do, or not. So she raised her own body upwards after placing her hands at either side of his outer thighs. Just as her two sisters made more room for her by curving their own bodies a little.

When he saw what they were more than able to see now, he closed his eyes in fright as yet another flush lit up his face.

'My word . . .' whispered Makiko, 'that is a truly lovely vision to see at any time. Is that not so, Noriko?' she asked her sister opposite.

'Very, *very*, much so, Makiko, and I can even already imagine just what wonderful things it could do inside my own body very soon too . . .'

'Would either of you like to hold it?' she asked them.

'*Kumiko!*' he groaned very low.

'I would be more than pleased to accept your offer, my sister,' said Makiko as her own hand gently encircled him. 'Heavens!' she whispered excitedly. 'It just feels so immense within my hand, that I also know I must sample its very pleasure within me soon now too!'

Kumiko bent her head forward over her younger sister's holding hand and kissed its very end softly. 'I can only say that the feeling it gives within you is truly vast when it is there. Is that not so, Raiko?'

'Oh yes indeed, mistress, I can only agree with everything what you have said. As it really is just *so* filling when it is inside you, that it truly can take all the breath away from your entire body.'

'Then I must also enjoy this new sensation myself,' said Noriko. As she then brought her own hand across and replaced her own sisters upon it. Her grip on it tightened into a squeeze and she gave a smile. 'It is just like a rod of thick iron, Kumiko,' she told her.

'I know full well what it *feels* like, Noriko, as after being allowed by father to enjoy it within me so much already. I also know just how wonderful it is to be taken by it also.'

'When *are* you both getting married again, Kumiko?' Noriko asked a little breathlessly.

'Monday afternoon our father said, and has arranged it to be so. As he wants us to have some time here for a honeymoon before we go back to England to live together. And my new husband, Douglas, will then return back to his work.'

'That's great,' she said, 'that means his pre-wedding night will be tomorrow then, *neh*?'

Kumiko hid her own feelings and smiled at her sister as she nodded happily. 'Yes.'

'Then I for one will be staying here for the weekend now so as to actually sample what I have seen. Only if Douglas-san would allow me to do so.'

Kumiko's face lit up as she watched his manhood jerk in her sister's hand. 'I would say that that is now a foregone conclusion, Noriko. Or as my husband-to-be has already told me since seeing most of our female members and servants,' she said with a wink to Raiko kneeling behind his head still. 'That he finds almost all of us decidedly *very* horny!'

Makiko was puzzled by the word. 'What on earth does that word mean, Kumiko?' she asked.

'It means, my sister,' she chuckled, 'that my Douglas has a rather very high passion level when it comes to Japanese, or just any Asian or oriental women possibly. I have heard such things baout Westerm men and Asian women - just as there is similar talk of the opposite way, too.'

'He does, really?'

She grinned at Makiko as she nodded.

'Then I will certainly stay the weekend too now to enjoy something as large as this now is inside me!' she uttered very excitedly.

'That I will also be there is accepted, I hope,' said Raiko after them.

'Me too!' came from two very separate sides of the cover.

Kumiko wiggled the end of his penis until his eyes opened to look down at them her. 'Well, my love, that's five offers to you already for tomorrow night,' she told him, and then began to tickle the end of it with her tongue until he groaned again, and lay there not only red-faced, but also highly aroused now.

Which wasn't hard when he considered what had, and was still very much happening around him. Kumiko's sister Noriko was slowly sliding her hand upon him, and giving the odd occasional squeeze during it. His other hand he now knew was still trapped between Makiko's soft warm thighs as yet. Kumiko herself was flicking at it with her tongue. And all six of them were now actually watching what was going on, since the two outer maids were now looking over their own two mistresses bodies too. He knew Raiko was also becoming excited now at what she was watching, as he could feel her own thighs beneath his head quivering. He just wasn't expecting her to bend her body almost double right then, and whisper a little breathlessly, "I'm sorry but I just cannot help myself, master", only moments before her mouth was pressing very hard against his.

∞

'*Why* did I pass out, Kumiko?' he asked her almost an hour later when they were alone again apart from a still quite naked Raiko. Who was kneeling beside them both without a care and was actually serving them tea.

From her position now lying beside him on her side and using an elbow beneath for stability, she answered, 'Because my sister Akiko's soul chose to enter *your* body at its release, my love. So now to our clan, in truth, you are also part Japanese to us all now.'

He began to smile in return, as he knew that *that* was quite a far-fetched, if not impossible thing to have happened.

'You appear not to believe me, my love.'

He shook his head swiftly. 'I just don't believe in such things as those Kumiko. If you are saying that it is basically some kind of reincarnation event happening?'

'In a *way* it's a bit like that, but not fully, Douglas,' she responded, and saw that his head was just about to start shaking again, so added to it, 'Akiko was a *fully* trained *warrior* of our clan Douglas, as we all are. And in *our* personal beliefs and thoughts of our hereafter life . . . A warrior's soul, it is said, whenever the time comes that it must leave its own body. *Must* find another resting place within that of another suitable body of similar standing to it. And she, so it now appears, has chosen *yours* as being of a similar warrior of kindred spirit to her own in which to enter.'

She saw that he was still not convinced. 'At every clan members funeral I have ever attended, my love. One person has always collapsed close to the end when a cremation is almost over. I know this may sound strange, or perhaps even stupid to you. But that *is* what always seems to happen at one of them. As from becoming a member of our clan, so much has already been instilled into each and every one of our minds throughout all our youth; and the many hard years of training and learning afterwards. That at the end of it all, we finally became what we were intended to become known as, which is warriors of the night, or as we were known by in the far older days by the names of either, *Assassins of the Night,* or, *The Silent Killers.*

'We have, through all the time we have done this, finally become a name of *truly* feared legend. Of the name known as *ninja*, of whose souls were only regarded as being only one thing. That of being black-hearted killers, of whose inborn duty it was to eliminate a specified target; or to die whilst attempting to do just that. While also having to be prepared to take our own lives if ever we failed to fulfil our objective; and that is exactly why we were feared so much, and still are by some today. As we are simply without fear when it comes to thoughts of our own deaths.

'I have personally even seen my father collapse five times during a few of these same events, so we all know that he carries six souls within his own body, with only one of those being his own. This was one of the reasons why he took over as the clan's new leader around fifteen years ago, when our previous clan leader, his father died. He collapsed at *his* funeral for his fifth time, which is why everyone assumed that our leader then, Toshishiro, had chosen to send his released soul into that of my father. Allowing him the right now to lead us, and this must have been correct, since prosperity and good fortune have been with us ever since then until Akiko's sudden and untimely death.

'My father was the one who suggested when he took over almost fifteen years ago now. That our clan base had become much too limited in its basic structure, what with it being kept solely in Japan. He was the one who said that our members should, if they at all possibly could. Marry suitable men and women from outside our own country. Only so as to promote new groups and bloodlines in other countries. Because as you likely know, our own country is not much different to your own in size, Douglas, perhaps even being just slightly larger with it being spread out over four islands as it is.

'Anyway, over time, the possibilities for younger members to begin new businesses within our clan to promote any further wealth, became much more difficult for us to accomplish. As so many began doing the same here. It is also why we had to now evolve much more as a clan, into something akin to a society. One that is now becoming stretched as far as possible around the world. And in those past fifteen years some of our members have slowly scattered out of Japan into the New World to begin to found these outside clans for him.

'We've the beginnings of these clans in twenty separate countries now, so we are now becoming, just as my father wished - a world-wide force. When *we* return to our new home, we will only be the third couple to be located in England. And I, as the daughter of my father who is also our leader at this present time. I will now become fully in charge of the small group thre at first, while it continues to grow and extend over there.

'We also have new formations in America, Australia, Mexico, Argentina, Germany, France, Spain, Italy, Russia, and believe it or not, even in China and Hong Kong! Some of the others are large, or almost as large as our own is here on out hom soil. While some are based in quite small countries too, but which are also being taken into our new force of movement.'

Spirit of a Dragon

'As in spreading out to conquer?' he asked with raised eyebrows.

'Never!' she said abruptly. 'We are not here for that, Douglas. We are only moving into other areas of the world to solidify our own new *society* and to help improve our efforts for wealth to enable the continuation of our clan. And so far from home as we will be in Europe, I will also have overall charge under my father of all those members and their families, my love.'

'Which actually means what, in effect?'

'That if a job ever comes up over in Europe, then it may well be my duty. Or perhaps even to providing the person, or persons, necessary to carry out that requisite mission.'

'Mission?' he queried now.

'Possible assassination, Douglas, seeing as that is what we have all being trained to do. So if it ever needs to be done, then it *will* be done just as it always *has* been done since ages long past.'

'Christ Almighty!' he muttered quite forcibly.

'Do not be too angry with us, my love, please,' she begged him. 'We are what we are and always have been so since our clan first began.'

'But *who* do you actually kill?' he asked.

'Those who know of us pass word to my father through our assigned intermediaries. He then decides if the target is a truly *viable* one to us. Such as a known terrorist, drug smuggler, or perhaps a dictator or tyrant of a country. He would never accept any target that *he* may judge to be what I suppose you would call an innocent though. Someone who to him, he feels does not actually deserve to be marked for death. If this happens he will sometimes even arrange to have them guarded secretly by some of our own members.'

'*For free?*' he said acidly.

'If he knows they could not afford our protection, then yes . . .'

He was quite stunned. 'So what do you actually charge for these things? I mean for a killing, or if you are needed for protection?'

She was very hesitant to discuss it in front of Raiko, what with her only being a servant. But she also knew that she trusted her implicitly by now, since she had served her so dutifully for the past five years. That being when she had just turned sixteen, and had also been classed as becoming fully trained in her new role of servant.

'A *typical* assassination contract will cost somewhere in the area of five million for one of us to be used. Although, the price itself would also depend on how hard the target is to get at, and then if it could take more than one of us to accomplish it.'

'Are we talking Yen here, Kumiko?'

Her head shook at him. 'We normally do our contracts in your own much higher Sterling based currency actually; or whatever the best currency could be at the time. Though sometimes the equivalent in just gold or diamonds can be preferred now and then. Any money made in this way goes straight into the clan's own coffers for further uses.'

'And for protection?' he now asked.

'That usually depends on for how long and just how many of us are required, Douglas. If the client can afford it, then the costs for it can also be quite steep too, sometimes it could be around a million per month for each one of us that is needed. Especially if the subject involved required a twenty-four hour watch.'

'And have we ever lost anyone that we were guarding?'

She leaned over and kissed him. 'You actually said *we* then, my love,' she told him.

'I know. I'm in it for good or bad now, Kumiko, as I will *have* to be just to have you, won't I?'

'You make me feel so warm inside when you say that to me, my love.'

'I hope you mean that in only one way right now!'

She chuckled delightfully. 'Yes, just in my heart at the moment, but somewhere else a little later, I hope. And as to your question, the answer to it is no. Though at these times we have had to, let's just say, had the need to *defend* ourselves from time to time.'

'Which means those doing the guarding were being attacked and managed to survive the attack upon them?'

She smiled. 'We have only ever lost *one* man on a mission in the past sixty to eighty years, my love. This was well before my father's time, and even before his own father had taken over. Our member back then was sadly shot in the back while aiding in the escape of someone that we were guarding. Since that time we have all come through unscathed, so far. Our deaths these days mostly occur only through either old age, an extreme illness, or at worst from some kind of accidental death. The only other exception being as what happened to Akiko. Another clan record of which my father is very proud of right now. Our well trained for duties in these modern day times are, I must admit, very rare indeed! But, we will continue to be trained as we always have been from long ago, just in case any of these missions do ever come up for us to do.'

'So why were you never asked by anyone to take out any of those brutal dictators in countries in the past few decades?'

She barely managed to give a shrug in her position. 'I suppose, simply because we have never been *asked* to do so, my love. As I have told you, we are a secret society, and as such, not a lot of people still know that we even exist.'

∞

It was now Sunday afternoon, and after a fine meal, Hyde found himself sitting cross-legged in one of the rooms of the house along with twenty other males. Not one female being inside the room with them. Her father, Koichi, sat with his back facing away from the door and at the very opposite side of the room to it. While Hyde himself sat with his back to the doorway, towards her father across the circle of men.

'This is Douglas Hyde, my friends,' began her father to thir group at large. 'My own eldest daughter Kumiko's husband-to-be tomorrow as you all will already know. And from what many of us all witnessed, also the new holder of my late daughter Akiko's spiritual soul. A soul which has now been transplanted beside that of his own at the time of her funeral. As those of you who were there must have observed at the time. And, he can also speak *and* read our language very fluently indeed.'

Varying degrees of head nodding went on around the circle to him, from men aged quite close to seventy or eighty, and some barely as old as thirty at most. Kumiko's' three brothers were there and seated close to their father as was expected at such a council gathering.

'By now you may all probably know that Douglas-san here is a Detective Inspector within the police force of his own country. And was also the man handed the task of finding my daughter's killer until he came back here with us for this short period.'

One of the very old men placed his two clenched fists on to the tatami floor and waited.

'Yes, my old friend, Kozo-san?' Koichi asked him. As his demeanour of placing his fists like that meant he had something to say or to ask. So he was recognised and now offered that option.

'When Douglas-san returns home from us here, will he *still* be the one in charge of your daughter's murder, Koichi-san?'

Her father looked over at the man himself for knowledge.

'Yes Kozo-san,' said Hyde speaking in Japanese to the old man who had asked the question. 'Due to my coming here with Koichi-san. I was temporarily relieved of command on her case. But when I return shortly, I will indeed be back in charge of it once more.'

The old man gave a brief nod of happiness. 'That is good, Douglas-san, as my friend Koichi-san has already told me that you are a very good policeman. And that you will do your very best to find our deeply regretted lost members terrible murderer.'

'I will do that, just as all of my colleagues helping me there will do as well, Kozo-san; which is to do whatever we can to find any murderer in our country. Though as you may know, some cases can be ended very quickly indeed when the killer has made a mistake in some way. But at the point up to when I had left, he had not. So no matter whether it may take us weeks, months, or perhaps even years to do so. Her case will never be completely closed while her killer is still at large.'

'I am pleased to hear that,' announced the old man as he raised his fists from the matting beneath. His questioning they all now knew was over and done with.

'May I tell them something more about you, Douglas-san? Just so that they can feel for themselves exactly what kind of man you are, and will become in our clan from your impending day of marriage to my daughter. As I already know from Kumiko herself, that you stated you would be more than happy to wear our own private mark upon your own body with pride.'

Douglas gave his acceptance with a small nod.

'What you may not know about this man here with us, apart from the fact that in such a very short time he and my daughter are very much quite in love now.' At which point Koichi saw his face redden in embarrassment, and grinned at him.

'Is that he himself is *already* a true warrior in both heart and spirit. As he has also been a former member of his own country's armed forces, including the SAS . . .' That unexpected statement caiused Douglas's head to jerk up in shock at his words. As he had no idea how he could ever have know that, or have found out. Since there was nothing in his house where they had been to give them any idea at all about his past like that.

' . . . And as such a warrior he has already dispatched twelve or more enemies, *himself*!' Koichi had said without halting at his look of shock at his words.

The men around the circle muttered various words between them as they looked upon him anew now. Along with many fists already being clenched and resting on the matting wanting to ask questions about this new information.

'Hiro-san?' said father to son beside him.

'Douglas-san, could you please inform us of your previous service life?'

With that question a few fists were quickly removed, as some of them had wanted to know the very same thing as well.

Unexpectedly though, and with already knowing just what kind of group all of these men around him were involved in. He began to talk to talk to them quite easliy.

'I joined up at the age of sixteen from leaving school with the Royal Marines, which was in 1974; I served with them for seven years. But I actually saw very little action with them apart from some peacekeeping duties. So, in 1981 when I was twenty-three my initial five years of service time was coming to an end. I was unsure whether to leave to become a civilian again, or to sign again for a few more years. Then the chance came up to apply to try out for either the SBS, or the SAS, the chance for the latter arrived first. So I decided to go for that, just to see if I could pass any of *their* very extreme tests to get into it.

'Luckily I guess you could say, I managed to do that with the SAS at the first testing I had. And so I was more than happy enough to stay in that unit with them until 1986. Due to that, I was also sent to the Falklands with many of them.

'After that brief action was over, we did various tours and training initiatives around the world. Until lastly when I injured my leg on a climb during a training exercise we were having. After that, sadly my leg just couldn't carry the same heavy weight, usually of being well over seventy pounds or more any longer. Those were just the typical weights that you had to be able to carry, in order to do any job that you may be tasked with. So sadly, I ended in fact, as being classed as medically unfit due to that same injury suffered.

'With that part of my life now over with, and not really wishing to go back into service with the ordinary armed forces again. I came out, and decided to join the police force, to find something with what could be a different long-term career. Instead of just becoming the more usual mercenary or bodyguard when leaving the unit. Like some of the other men from those units sometimes went on to do.

'I've now been in the police force for fourteen years. And as Koichi-san has stated, I've now reached the position of that of a Detective Inspector within it. I am hoping that in the not too very distant future though. That I may be recommended for promotion up to the position of Chief Inspector - and possibly even Inspector or higher one day.'

Koichi nodded, then, 'Kazuo-san?' This was his youngest son and who was also a detective himself.

'Douglas-san, I know that we have never really spoken to each other much as yet, and for that I only hope that you can forgive me. Though I do also hope that can only change for the better while you *are* here with us, and in the many years ahead after you have become a member of our family. But right now, and only if you do not mind talking about it to us, I would very much like to know *how* you actually took those lives.'

Spirit of a Dragon

Hyde was quite prepared to talk to them about that part of it with knowing just what they all were themselves. Though his mind was still really trying to fathom out how her father had found out so much about him so quickly. He was also pleased to see that all but one pair of fists had disappeared from the floor.

'As some of you may, or may not actually know. My own government has for many years; well, as matter of fact it's really been a *great* number of years now. We sort of retained a special pact with some of these other countries; even when many of them had gained their independence from ours. Along with a few other non-independent ones, too. These pacts with them still allow us to do what is known as *real training* when needed. For us to brush up on our actual skills when needed, such as extreme jungle or winter survival and the like. For which of course our own country rarely has that particular climate or terrain to help us do that ourselves at home.

'And well, in some of these certain countries which have rebels or terrorists who cause so much trouble, we are allowed to *practice* our techniques to great effect. With Malaya and Thailand being the most used, and since Burma has become more of a military rule there. We haven't been allowed back in again, *legally*, that is.' Hyde smiled. 'Though we do pop in occasionally by other methods if we ever have the need to do so . . .

'Regarding Kazuo-san's question to me, I eliminated three of them by means of using my rifle from about half a mile or more away, or as we basically call it, *sniping*. Four of them were closer where I used a very well silenced semi-automatic machine-gun or handgun. And the remainder either went out by knife or by hand.'

'You can kill with your hands, Douglas-san?' Kazuo asked.

'In some cases it can be much quicker to deal with them in that way. A quick grab at the head and twist and the neck is broken almost silently - or by using your arm around their throat. With a knife of course, a hand over the mouth while the blade slips through the ribs from behind usually into the heart, or any other vital organs or artery is usually enough to finish them quickly.'

'Thank you for being so candid for me, Douglas-san,' said Kazuo with a bow to him.

His father nodded happily at Hyde's quite open information now being offered, then said, 'Ichiro-san?'

The middle-aged man in question gave a nod then faced Hyde. 'My two daughters Emi and Aya have already heard so much about you since your arrival here, Douglas-san. And as such have asked me to ask you at some point while you were here, if it would be possibkle to allow them to visit you over there whenever they could . . .'

Hyde was quite nonplussed for a moment. 'If they only want to come over do some shopping in London, Ichiro-san. Then I'm afraid I am nowhere near that city. My own nearest city of Newcastle is located up in the north-east of England, which is about 300 or so miles away. And around a six to eight hour car journey between them. As yet, we do not really have the same kind of designer shops there as they do down in our fashion capital of London. Although little by little some of those major chains are steadily opening up new stores further afield now.'

'They do not wish to come over to, *shop*, as you say, Douglas-san.'

'Then why would they want to come over?'

'After seeing you with Kumiko they both think they may also find a husband for themselves over in your country too now, Douglas-san. While of course also enjoying a short holiday with you both of course.'

'No problem as far as I can see with that, Ichiro-san. I do have a three bedroom house and two of them will be spare still.'

'Only one, my friend,' said her father.

'Eh?'

'Raiko is, and always has been Kumiko's maid, so of course she will be living there with you too.'

'You're kidding! What the hell will she be doing there anyway? She'll soon become bored to death from doing nothing.'

'Not at all, Douglas-san, Raiko is her servant and housemaid. So while with you she will look after your house, keeping it clean and tidy for you while you are both at work, or whatever. I know that your own bathroom is also very different from many of our own. But also as a trained masseuse, she can also see to retaining the health of both of your bodies too.'

'Strewth,' he said in English. 'I'll definitely have to put in some long overtime hours then just to be able pay her a good wage.'

Koichi's face broke into a grin and his head was already shaking as the rest of the men began to smile or laugh quietly. 'No, my friend, our servant's wages have always been extracted from out of our clan funds. Which is one of the reasons *why* our own businesses must always do very well, and also make good profits each year for us to keep this situation working so well.'

Hyde turned back to Ichiro. 'In that case Ichiro-san, if your daughters would be happy to share the remaining bed together then it could still work.'

'But then where would their own maids sleep?' asked the man.

'They'll want to bring their maids with them as well!' he croaked.

He gave Douglas a sharp nod. 'But of course! If *any* of us go anywhere for longer than say a few days to a week or more, we *always* take them with us.'

'Then I have no idea at all where they will sleep, unless they're happy to try and share Raiko's with her?'

He gave a shrug. 'None of them are very large really, so a little discomfort for a week or so shouldn't trouble any of them for that amount of time. So I would say it is also acceptable.'

'Well, I'm pleased about that,' he said slightly *sotto voce*. 'As I'd began to imagine that they while there they going to want to have sex as well!'

'No Douglas-san, neither of them is yet eligible to engage in having what is termed as, complete sex. As their status of being unmarried still prevents and forbids them from doing so as yet.'

'And maybe they *will* actually want to do that, my friend,' Koichi said to them both, and who both looked aghast. 'Because as you all know, my youngest daughter Akiko died without ever *once* enjoying or experiencing any of the truest kinds of loving sex in her life with someone; apart from that of her killer, which certainly wasn't that kind of mutual agreement. And that happening was also the main reason for my allowing Kumiko to do so with Douglas-san here. From that offered option, and also from what has transpired between them both now because of that. I can only say that it has made my eldest daughter very happy indeed already, just it has also brought to us a new and also very important member into our clan.

'So, I have therefore decided to alter the rules forbidding our younger men and women from not having, or being able to engage in our sex training prior to marriage. From now on they can both feel free to engage in such acts with any member of the opposite sex whenever they wish to. As this will not only allow them to train quicker, but also to feel the pleasures much earlier than it may have happened for all of them. But, as well as that, it will also add a further chance of new partners possibly linking up within our clan faster as well.'

'From what age?' gasped one of the younger men seated there with gritted teeth.

Koichi gave some thought to that. 'They *must* be at least fifteen, and *mature* enough within their own minds to be allowed to make their own decision as to decide what they wish to do.'

'And what about the girls?' asked the same almost distraught man.

Koichi looked at him. 'I *meant* both sexes, Masaya-san, was I not speaking plain enough for you from the very beginning there!'

The younger man lowered his head and bowed abjectly. 'Forgive my bad manners in this matter Koichi-san, please. I was only shocked at your words because of my four daughter's ages.'

'And how old *are* they all now?'

'The eldest is only seventeen, then sixteen, fifteen and fourteen, Koichi-san.'

'Well what are you so worried about then? Only three of them are old enough to be able to decide now if they wish to have their first taste of male shaft, aren't they? And that is only if they *wish* to have it anyway. We all know that sex is never allowed to be pressed or forced upon anyone within our clan. Is it, *neh*!? And look what it has brought to Kumiko and our own family, in the shape of our Douglas-san here. My own incoming son-in-law to be . . . '

'Yes, Koichi-san, I understand that completely. But by *law* in our clan they are not even allowed to marry at under eighteen, and certainly not until they have gained all their respective training.'

'No, you are right there, Masaya-san,' said her Koichi. Who watched the man then sighed as if he was off the hook now, with the last new rule been given out as law. 'However, I can also think of an arrangement to cover that as well since you said that to me. That from this day on as well, another new rule has just been laid down. Which will be; that if two of those same children like each other more than enough for them to actually then *imagine* a hopeful marriage existing between them later. Then a type of bonded marriage agreement of engagement can be held between them both and each of their families. Until such time as they finally come to fulfil it completely, or unless they cancel it. And that will also mean that even while they are classed as engaged, that they can still enjoy both the training in sex and the pleasures derived from it just as we all do right now.'

Masaya's almost white-knuckled and still clenched fists were already placed back on to the mat.

'*Yes?*' said Koichi with nearly half-closed eyes now.

'Allowed sex with whom, exactly?'

'Anyone in their mind who *they* personally may wish to ask to enjoy it with of course. But our same clan rules must still apply even then. Meaning that it must be a joint decision between them both for it to be allowed to be carried out.'

For the rest of that afternoon, along with the frequent arrival and departure of servants. Who kept bringing in fresh pots of tea, or warmed bottles of sake at the correct temperature required at her father's calling. They sat around the floor and talked of various things and events. Hyde being drawn in to many of them now. As after what he had said to them earlier, had shown him to indeed be a quite invaluable resource to them now in his own right.

Those who were qualified by their own acts of prior marriage also advised him about the night still to come, or better known to the men there as. *"The Main Event"*, and that he should enjoy any who offer themselves to him as much as he possibly could. In the same way which they all had when their own time to marry had arrived. But her father had scared the daylights out of some of them by saying that not only their wives, but even some of their own single daughters could already now have a chance tonight to try out their first sex session with a man. Douglas's own worried thoughts weren't far behind any of *their own,* when he'd heard that being said himself . . .

CHAPTER 15

Douglas's pre-wedding night of pleasure was to be taking place in the largest room of Kumiko's parents' house that evening or night. All depending upon just how many women would make the decision to offer themselves to him. As far as Kumiko and her own family initially thought, it could be as low as five or ten, possibly even upto twenty if more servants wished to join in.

But then, from around six that evening to almost nine Kumiko either sat in an unhappy frame of mind in her own room, mostly wondering upon just how he *was* faring barely just a few rooms away from her. Though after its starting phase had begun, she'd gone to the kitchen to make herself a snack, and found her mother and sisters already there and doing the same thing. She didn't quite know what to say to her mother or either of her sisters yet. As they were all happily chatting away to each other about their times already spent with her man, so she just made herself a large salad sandwich in a bun and left again.

Later, she sat on the wide steps at the centre of the veranda for a while, and then even took herself for a walk for almost a mile and back along the darkened roadway from her home; while she finished her food off. Returning to her room she found it still empty and so left again. She had to pass the kitchen again as she left, and heard a great deal of excited chattering between many women who had already been with him. Outside the house once again, she must have paced around the house at

203

least a hundred times as her own envy over what was happening within it; soon led to a state of quite unexpected, but unknown kind of jealousy beginning to rise from deep within her breast.

She could not understand not only what, but why, she was actually feeling like she was right now. As she sat down on a small wooden bench seat at the rear of the house, only as an aid to halt her own incessant pacing. She knew that when he became her husband the very next day, that it would be a truly life changing event and experience for her personally, as well as a very separate way of living.

She would no longer be single, but at last, finally, living her dream in life as that of a married woman. A position which had been something she had hoped and wished to happen for so long evert since her own youth. Then, as time had passed, she had watched two of her younger sisters both marrying, and had begun to doubt it ever happening for herself. Minister Yoshi always was an option to her - though she would only have done that under an express from her father. As she simply had no real feeling for the man.

Now though, all that had all changed in the shape of her meeting Douglas. She now knew that she would soon, actually within a week now. Also have to leave behind, her long career, her home, as well as her family. Even all of her friends and associates at work when she moved to another country just to live and be with him.

But deep in her own mind she knew that she wasn't bothered about any of that happening to her. She had found love, and knew in her heart already that she truly loved him. Why this was, she didn't know, or actually when it had really began and happened to her - only that it had. She leaned against the backrest of the bench seat and emitted a soulful sounding sigh that seemed to have risen from the very depths of her own being.

She was just totally shocked *by* what she was feeling right now, at the very thought of him in there having to try and please so many of the women who had offered themselves to him. Well, she quickly thought, his *having to*, was not quite the correct word to use since he wasn't actually being *forced* to have sex with them all . . . It was really just, *expected* of him. So it was also about then that she began to wonder about the time he had spent earlier that afternoon alone with just her father's male dominated council. Had any of *them* actually said something to him during their long time together? Simply to encourage him just to accept what he was required to do this very night, without any worries about *what* he was now doing?

She sighed again most unhappily. As she knew that she should *not* be feeling the slightest touch of envy or jealousy at all. Since from her being a very young girl, she had *already* known the strange ways of their clan. Along with what was permissible, and what definitely was not within it. And she certainly wasn't a young virgin woman now either, even that a teenage one and heading for marriage. She'd even been, if not pushed, then certainly given a free option by her father just to have sex with him before they were going to be married. Which was probably an actual first ever for their clan too, as no other girl or woman that she knew of in their clan had *ever* engaged in any total sexual act at all. Well at least not until after the marriage rites had been performed. Whereas she knew, their servants were not kept to the same restrictions – and could enjoy whatever they liked with whoever they liked in th clan at any time. Only as per their rules, and if it was offered willingly, of course!

She had heard her father's new rules for their clan after they had been made in that same room as he was in right now. And had thought at the time that, just like she herself. It would now allow not only the younger men and boys, but also the younger women and girls to at least have a taste of what was in store for them afterwards. Likely even speeding quite a lot of their sexual training techniques up by quite a rate. She suddenly sat bolt upright on the bench.

Could that be the actual problem that had caused her so much unrest tonight, she now wondered. That so many of the younger women she had herself seen entering the house earlier. Many of who she had actually known to still be in-training virgin members themselves . . . Was that it?

Was it the fact that her Douglas was going to be the very first man to sample each of *their* bodies in such a way as he had with her own? She searched inside herself deeply for the answer to that, and was just as stunned when the unexpected answer to it was actually, no. So, just what *is* my problem then she asked furiously of herself? She was becoming so confused about everything that her face was buried within her hands when her mother and sisters finally found her out there. Where they all sat down beside her on the wide bench and comforted her together as only a very close knit family can do.

'What is wrong, Kumiko?' asked her mother softly.

'I do not know, Mother. I have never felt this way in my life ever before, so I just don't know how to cope with the emotions and feelings I am having.'

'You are feeling little lost perhaps, and maybe also jealous and very envious of those of us who have already been pleased by him within our homes main room, *neh*?'

She nodded her head so gently that it was almost imperceptible in the slight moonlit darkness around them. Although they all appeared to feel it as if connected when it came from her.

'Trust me, it is only to be expected, daughter. I sat out here with both Noriko and Makiko when it was also their own pre-wedding nights too. Just as my own mother once sat right here with me on the night before my wedding to your father,' she said as three different arms somehow managed to encircle Kumiko in some way.

'So why *am* I feeling this way, Mother?'

'In a way, Kumiko, your own mind will be in an even worse state than either of your two sisters, or mine was on this particular night.'

'But why should that be?' she had to ask.

Her mother tilted her chin up so that she could look into her face, and saw the shine of tears in her eyes. 'Because it *is* very different for you, Kumiko, when your father and I talked alone upon your return here, he told me what had transpired in your Douglas's house over there. And that he actually encouraged you to share your own body with him so quickly.'

'Only encouraged, Mother, he never ordered me to do it.'

'And that is exactly my point, child. We three only made love to our husbands *after* our marriage to them had taken place. Whereas our own virgin husbands to be were allowed a night of pleasure with as many women who wished to be fulfilled by them, *before* we ourselves were able to. That is the reason why we all felt so unhappy - But for *you*, Kumiko. You have already shared something so private and wonderful with your, Douglas. That it is paining you even more to think of him inside our house with so many other women all wanting him tonight. You see, until now, you have had him all to yourself and whenever you wanted to. Just like when you came back home to us with him, and then almost went straight to your own bedroom to have sex with him.'

Spirit of a Dragon

Shinko's maternal instincts for her daughter were working full-time as they tried to aid her desperate plight.

'But I know that already, Mother. I know what we do as a clan, and what is allowed in it. So I know how things *are* done, and what takes place on nights like tonight. And just because of that, I shouldn't even be feeling this way as I know exactly just how everything *is* done.'

'Which is exactly what I am trying to explain to you right now, eldest daughter. It is only *because* you have already *had* sex with him, that your love for him has, since then I ould say, grown tenfold so quickly over what is it now, barely a week, *neh*?'

Kumiko nodded her head.

'Then do you not see what I mean, daughter? It's not simply your very closeness over that week already – it's *because* of all the time you spent having sex with each other that has bonded you to each other so quickly. We women here before you were not that fortunate ourselves, or else we may all have felt just as badly as you do now. We may have felt a kind of waiting in preparation to come, for those same bonds of love to begin with us with our own soon-to-be-husbands. Just as you yourself already have. But, you *must* also see my daughter, that sex between a newly happily matched couple, can also then bring forth other *very* powerful emotions in themselves too. This is why you feel as you do now, because you are actually feeling something akin to fright that he is being unfaithful to you.'

She shook her head in response. 'That cannot be it, Mother. As I sat and watched him having sex with Raiko on our first day here. And then I also watched Noriko and Makiko both play with him and tease him while we all lay together after the funeral when he recovered again.'

Her mother was smiling. 'I know that. But you know Raiko so well already, Kumiko. Also, that she is only a servant and not a true serving member as we are. So of course you did not feel threatened by *her* having sex with him at all. You trust her completely, just as you have to, in the same way that we also completely trust every one of our own servants. Or else where would we be? I will tell you . . . Not being able to trust *any* one of them with our husband's, or our lives, that's what! And when you go home soon---'

Her mother sighed aloud. 'We are all going to miss you so very much when you are so far away from us so soon now, Kumiko. And the tension you are now feeling all through your body will disappear when you are alone with him again once more and virtually on your own. Well, apart from Raiko that is. Who I expect, just like you, will also be hoping to be pleased regularly by him too while she is over there and serving you both. As it will surely not be much fun for her over there with so very few limited options being available to her for pleasure, especially if you do *not* allow it you know. Always remember that she is not only a servant to you both now but that she is also your protector as well if required. So she does deserve to be *well* looked after by you both, and as much as you would want the same thing for yourselves if either of you were in her shoes.'

Kumiko already knew that herself, that even though she had been well trained by other experienced servants within their clan. That her first role was to protect the lives of those she would serve, even if it meant her own death from doing so actually occurring. And to Kumiko, since she had taken on Raiko as her own personal servant to her five years ago. She had even begun to think of her more like a friend than just as a servant anyway. As she was *always* there with a bright pleasing smile whenever she had returned home from work. And at whatever time of day or night it may have been when she did come back home from it.

Her home was always spotlessly clean and tidy, a meal more often than not being prepared, or waiting her arrival. Not forgetting the hot bath she so much enjoyed soaking in after a hard day. Raiko would happily offer to bathe and massage her too. She cooked for her, cleaned up after her, and looked after all her clothing and also *her* tirelessly and selflessly. In fact to Kumiko, she was almost as close to being a second Mother to her and not a servant at all.

Her mother's arm gently squeezed her trim waist. 'I must also say now, that I myself was very pleased that your soon to be new husband is *very* well equipped *and* so virile with it, daughter. Especially for someone who is still untrained in our own special skills. He not only pleased me immensely, but both your sisters also.'

'Is that true?' Kumiko asked them both. At last starting to get over whatever she had been feeling before which had led to a state of quite terrible angst boiling up within her.

Makiko smiled and also squeezed her. 'He even gave me an impressive orgasm, sister. Which I must say without him knowing any of the pleasure points that can be used to excite a woman *during* sex, has given me even much higher hopes for my future times with him.'

She peered closely at her sister then. 'Are you saying to me that you would be more than happy to ask my Douglas for more sex now?'

Makiko chuckled in a low tone. 'Any time that it was ever possible for either of us, my sister.'

'But, what about your own husbands thoughts on that, Makiko, what of Terado?'

'My own husband understands, Kumiko. Just as he sometimes enjoys being with another woman himself at various times. So I also enjoy being with other men occasionally. I can only thank the God's that our clan allows both sexes to decide what they may want. And that's it not only the men who can do so whenever they wish.'

'But why is *my* Douglas so special?'

Noriko quickly butted in to tell her, 'I think that it's because although your Douglas at the moment cannot *heighten* our bodies sexually, in the ways that our own men can do only just by touch alone, Kumiko. It is the sheer length and width of size that he has which does almost as much for us within us. More than any of our past men have been able to offer us. He may not have the skills, but he certainly has the right weapon or *equipment* to offer a woman, *neh*, Mother?'

'Oh heavens, indeed yes, Noriko, he is very filling indeed . . . well, he was to me anyway,' she replied quite happily.

'He is probably the same for all of us, Mother,' said Makiko.

'Undoubtedly!' she admitted. 'And I hope that I am still alive when he finally gains all of our own skills and techniques too. As from then on, I would say that he really *will* become a very formidable sexual partner for any of the women in our clan to be with from then on. As we know just from what he already has to use now, to later and with everything that he will also have learned!'

'Amen to that,' whispered Makiko most enticingly. 'And when that happens, I may well be visiting England to see you a great deal more in the future than I will be anyway, sister.'

Their mother said, 'And both of you, if not more of us, will have to visit you as often as we can anyway after you return there. For us to aid him as his new family in his additional training as quickly as we can.'

'Why?' Kumiko asked her guardedly. 'As Father told me that *I* myself would be personally responsible for his training when we are in our new home, Mother. And that only *if* I ever needed help with something he would send someone over to do that.'

'Kumiko, my daughter, it is only because you have no idea of how many of the women's passions he has aroused tonight inside our house. In the kitchen after you left me, they were coming in one after the other as time passed, including both of your sisters here. With them all saying that they had never had so much *true* enjoyment from having sex with any man. And that *without* needing the various touches used to stimulate, thrill, and excite. The servant women alone mostly likened him to a lust-filled beast of pleasure to them.

'I also do know that you have watched couples having sex before, even though you were not allowed to take part in them yourself. So you had seen a man's erect penis before, *neh*?'

She nodded. 'Of course, I have not only seen my Father with you and other women, but also you with other men. And I have also seen both my sisters with other men, as well as two of my brothers doing so, too.'

'But that is also my point, daughter. Our men, who although we know are far more skilled in our arts, have always lacked one very important thing which we women also may sometimes need. Which of course, means having that special something moving within our bodies that we can all truly feel and enjoy. And *your* new man, my daughter, definitely manages that for us. By the God's daughter, he's had some of the young virgins in there close to screaming with pleasure and passion tonight!'

Kumiko blanched. '*They* have also come tonight, too!'

'They have almost come out in *force* tonight you could say, since Father's new law was given and spread around the clan.'

'My God, Mother, just how many women and girls *did* arrive here to offer their bodies to him tonight? I thought there were only about thirty of them in there?'

Spirit of a Dragon

'About eighty of us, I think?' she answered.

'*Eighty!*' gasped Kumiko in shock.

'I thought that there was more than that, possibly even a hundred,' said Noriko, as she followed her statement.

Makiko's head was already shaking negatively. 'I'm sorry but you are both wrong, as I actually managed to count everyone in the room before it began tonight. My own total came to one hundred and twenty-two.'

'Heavens above,' uttered her mother.

'That just *has* to be some kind of a record offering for our clan, doesn't it?' queried Noriko in shock.

'I think it only stands at nesr forty now anyway, so your man Douglas is well over that amount - in fact it's actually trebled the amount.'

Kumiko was almost beside herself with worry all over again, but for a very different reason now. 'My Douglas will never be able to see to them all, Mother. He will eventually tire, and totally exhaust his body in just *trying* to do this for all of them. And soon, he will just simply be no longer *able* to perform for them at all. Remember, he is not trained in our ways – so he cannot even do our most basic erection presses to aid him.'

'Then we all must go back in there and watch over him for when this happens, daughter. But you also must now realise that when an offer has been made like this it cannot just be turned away now . . . And I must admit that even I was surprised when he accepted every single one of us earlier myself! So, it means that those who have not been seen tonight *must* still be seen tomorrow evening instead.'

'But it's my wedding day to him tomorrow, and also our wedding night, Mother!'

'I *do* know that, Kumiko. Even then, it cannot be halted now, as with having been accepted, it simply *must* take place. But, my daughter, you as his new wife could be the one to enjoy him first of all tomorrow. And then, he will just have to keep his promise to satisfy the rest of them until all of his very pleasurable work *has* finally been carried out.'

'What a wedding day that is going to be for us . . .' Kumiko muttered very unhappily.

'You must only think of this situation in a positive way, daughter. Which is of course that your own new husband will have already given so much pleasure to so many of us while being here with us in Japan. That his own name will be spoken of in only high regard from then on. And then while you are both away in England together. Our own memories of him, and of either of the nights for which we were able to be with him, will linger in all our minds for a long time to come.'

Kumiko didn't actually cheer up at the news offered to her, but she was more thoughtful about it. As a lot of what they had been saying to her was very true. And the main fact was that when they did go back to England, there would only be the three of them.

She stood up. 'Come on then, we'd better go and see how my man is managing at the moment?'

The four of them then walked over to the house and through the various rooms to the main room. Yet passing the kitchen they all heard the still so very excited talking happening within it.

∞

Hyde felt utterly exhausted and almost completely drained as he leant back on to the backs of his legs to rest after yet another tiring, but ever growing shorter mating sesion had taken place. From his entering the room some time ago. Even how long ago it was now, even *he* didn't know, as he actually wore nothing at all on his body. The sheer mass of all their naked waiting bodies in the room had filled him with something akin to dread and terror. Some of them had even been turning grey-haired, but he knew that *that* had been through his own fault when he had offered his acceptance to them earlier. So they could have been aged anywhere between fifty years old to around ninety to him. And just like Carmen had said to him . . . And good god, that was barely only a few days ago too now, he thought. That it was not unusual for so many Asian and oriental women to look a lot younger than they actually were, until the final deeper wrinkles of old age eventually came to all of them.

The only reason he was thankful when he saw some of the much younger looking ones inside, was because he had been there when her father had set the new guidelines out. So those that he himself would have maybe guessed to have only been around nine or ten years old. He at least knew in his own mind that they had to have been *at least* fifteen by this rule. Which didn't help him a lot, though that was about all that saved his own sanity as he began to proceed. Right from his entrance of walking in naked at first, as they all must have done before him in readiness. He could feel his face burning redly as he felt all of *their* eyes roving over his own unclothed body, while he in turn looked at theirs.

He couldn't do anything *but* to look at them, as they were all there just waiting for him to pleasure them. They were kneeling side by side all the way around the room, in a way that they had to do, to be to fit inside it. And as such were almost packed together five or six deep. The room just appeared to him to be a heaving mass of so much bare female flesh on display to his eyes. With both young and old alike all kneeling there upright, as if patiently waiting for it to start. And he only actually knew six of them by sight, the rest of those who had arrived he just didn't have a clue about.

As he went to stand in the virtual small circular spaced empty centre of it, where just a single plain thin futon lay waiting to be used by him. And his many upcoming partners. He watched in astonishment as they all bowed very low, and literally all together in one mass group to him. This was when he was able to see their backs as he turned himself and looked around them all, and saw an overwhelming array of full-backed tattoos. Along with those who bore the other very small and larger twin emblems upon each shoulder blade, which of course denoted to him that they were servants within the clan.

So at least he had a fair idea and knew which were members and which were servants, but that was about all. Yet he'd been totally surprised by the many unmarked ones who were there, for a few moments not comprehending why this was. Until he suddenly remembered Kumiko's own words as they came into his head. That those members without any markings upon their backs were still young, and so had not yet become *fully* trained, so they could not wear the small servant, or full dragon tattoo emblem of their clan yet. This also reminded him that most, if not all of these would actually be entirely made up of virgins.

At which point he still just couldn't accept that so many of these women were here just wanting to have sex with him . . . Him, a foreign man, one who was still classed as an outsider in their eyes through his not *being* of Japanese birth. They still held this low bow as they awaited it being returned to them. All of the women in the room were patiently following Kumiko's mother's actions. What with her being, what was considered to be, the matriarchal head of their clan. He just kept turning around over and over again and looking at them all, unaware of what he was actually doing, and which was causing all of them to just have to await his final decision upon each and every one of them during this time. Although to most of those there, they were assuming that he was just deciding who could stay for the upcoming pleasures – and who would have to leave the room if not chosen by him to remain.

It didn't actually take very long before the sight of them all in here, and his own thoughts over what was about to take place in this very room. Caused his own sexual arousal to heighten, along with a certain stirring from below taking place. Within less than a minute he felt almost light-headed, as if his breathing had been stilled in some weird way. Then a previously spoken detail by Kumiko placed itself in his mind, and he bowed to her mother.

Shinko herself had waited patiently for him in her deeply held bow, but with her eyes reaching upwards to watch him. Almost understanding what the sight of all of them waiting here so quietly for him, may have done in robbing *any* man of immediate thought, and not just him. Especially after watching the bright redness appear upon his face, from when he had first seen all of them in here awaiting his own pleasure giving to them. Some of them were only fifteen, or sixteen like Masaya's second eldest daughter, Mariko. To old Junko herself who was the wife of old Ichiro. Because if she *herself* had been surprised by the amount of women offering themselves to him tonight, then she knew instinctively that poor Douglas must have actually felt utterly confused by it all.

She watched him turning slowly as he looked around the room, then again and again, each turn becoming even slower. She saw the changing movements and emotions appearing on his face as he tried to understand just what exactly was happening to him. And to her vast personal delight, she watched as the growing erection of his manhood finally began to form. She had to even wet her lips with her tongue just from it alone, as she saw it steadily growing into its glorious length before her. Then at last the memory must have risen in his mind and he bowed back to them. Which was what he had to do to formally accept any of them. And from what he had done, he had just accepted them all, and without exception!

That gave her some cause to worry now, as did he *himself* actually remember this fact or not? As all that he had needed to do, was to point at any of them he did not wish to please, and to just shake his head. Then that woman, or women, would then have left the room there and then. She was unsure herself, but now, once his agreement *had* been given by his returned bow to them, even *she* knew that it could not be taken back. Just as all of *their* offers to him were now sealed in the same fateful way as his own was. He was now duty bound to please each and every one of them, just as all of them were duty bound to him to allow him entrance without fail into each one of their bodies.

Kumiko's mother due to her own rank had naturally been his first test, and then both of her daughters. Of which he had even began to enjoy himself after the first worrying moments of it had finally started, and as such his work ahead had also therefore begun in earnest too.

∞

Kumiko and the three of them each had to undress again now before they could re-enter the main room. As that was one of the few stipulations about a pre-wedding night offering, as well as the room chosen where the offering would be carried out inside it. That no-one who was entering within it could wear anything whatsoever, so that they were all basically appearing to him in the same way: as only bodies. No hairpins, or jewellery, and certainly no watches. Even something for some of them to pass the time with as they each had to patiently await their turn of pleasure was forbidden. So all that those who were there *could* now do was to kneel there patiently, and watch as each woman took her place before him. And then after her pleasure by him, she would then thank him and quietly get to her feet and leave the room.

Some of the married woman watched over the newest single females, who had now also been given entrance to what had previously been the secretive world of the married women's one last private and enjoyable domain As he had heartily pleasured the three female family members first of his bride to be. Pleasured very much *indeed* they all knew, from the many wonderful sounding vocal expressions, with gasps and pants being emitted by all three of them, as well as actual orgasms from two of them! Which only left the rest of them feeling desperate to have their turn.

Those with previous sexual experience had listened to the whispers coming from those known as being still untouched in their group, aged anywhere between fifteen to those closer to forty or fifty if they'd never married. As they had each expressed varying whispers to each other over what they were seeing happening before them. Not that they hadn't seen it before . . . it was just that this time, they would also be *encountering* it for their own very first times too, and due to their personal offering, could not escape from its happening to them even if they wanted to.

The sight of his huge looking shaft was literally terrifying to some of these women. While others were seemingly just staring in utter wide-eyed awe at it while it did its continuing, and quite apparent enjoyable work before them.

But Hyde knew he was already starting to tire now, so much so that he'd even lost count of just how many of them he had been with already. No matter that each new body that appeared before him excited him once again. Although as he rested for a while in his leant back position and tried to ease his aching back muscles a little, he gazed around him, and still couldn't believe that so many were still here in the room. As for him it already felt as if he'd been at it for days, and not only for an hour or so.

He almost emitted a woeful cry of desperation as he heard the double doors being opened from outside after the last woman had only recently left. Though even before she had completely gone, another woman had quickly crawled over to him and on to the futon from out of the group, and was already kneeling upon her hands and knees in front of him. Some chose to kneel, while others lay down on thir backs - that was their choice. The latest one placed herself in position and was now just waiting for him on the, by now, very well wrinkled and damp-spotted futon. Not only becoming damp from his own perspiration, but occasionally orgasms from either party as well.

Even in his own extremely tired state, the sight which was placed and waiting in readiness before him, quickly aroused him all over again. Just as it had done each and every other time since its beginning tonight; but he knew that he just had to have a short rest right now at least to ease his back. And it was now that he saw just who was coming in through the opened doors. Not only her mother and sisters, but Kumiko herself was now here.

Kumiko walked straight over to him and knelt at his side and looked at him very closely, quickly noticing that his body was almost entirely bathed in a glowing sheen of damp perspiration by this time. 'How are you, my love?' she asked him gently.

Spirit of a Dragon

'Well, I myself, as well as my back are just about bloody well knackered, pet!' he said in an affectionate name to her, as she knew, 'I'm as thirsty as hell, and it feels as if I'm starving too,' he added.

'Have you not been provided with *anything* for your personal sustenance since we left, Douglas-san?' asked Shinko.

'Only lots of horny women,' he said with a grin.

Shinko turned on them. 'I cannot believe this of you, all of you!' she said harshly to them all. 'Douglas-san willingly accepted *every* single one of us tonight, and yet none of you have shown *him* any consideration whatsoever! Why have none of you gone for any refreshments for him yet? He is not a *machine* you know, who can go on forever and ever with entering all of our bodies! And if you *are* wishful of him to keep up his strength for so long tonight for your own enjoyment, then looking after *his* needs first and foremost has to be your main priority here. Many of you should already have known this from past experiences!'

She turned and knelt at his side and now bowed so low with her head to the floor itself, that it was actually seen as if not demeaning, then to be thought of as degrading by them all. And all those who were still in the room, apart from Kumiko herself who were taking part, although even *she* also had to now comply. As they all had to copy the very same gesture as she had done before him.

'I must apologise to you on behalf of *every* single female within our clan here on this night, Douglas-san,' she said to him. 'That not even *one* of them had a single thought of your own personal needs at any time is not what we would call very honourable at all. And especially because of the very enjoyable service you have willingly been providing to all we women here tonight.'

With that being said she raised her body into a similar position to that of his own, and tapped her fingers against the quite naked rump of the woman in front of him. 'Instead of you just flaunting your own very nice genitalia at him like you are doing, Yoko, why don't *you* ask him if he needs anything!'

The same woman now spun herself around slowly to face him. 'I must also express and apologise to you for my own thoughtlessness, Douglas-san. As *I*, just as all of the other women with you were. If honest, we were all just so impressed by your fortitude already with so many of us, and also the very lovely sight of your extremely large shaft at work. That I'm afraid we quite forget about our own obligations regarding seeing to your personal welfare tonight.' She bowed humbly to him once more, just as she had had to when Shinko herself had done it. Then she asked as she rose, 'May I personally go and bring you something from the kitchen to aid your health, Douglas-san?'

'That would be very kind of you Yoko-san, thank you. Something to drink for my parched throat, as well as a bite to eat would both be gratefully accepted. Though I must also visit the toilet as well if none of you ladies will mind the short interruption that will cause.'

'Heavens!' gasped Shinko. 'That is also true isn't it? That since you have not left this room since your arriving in here, you have not even been asked if you wished to see to any of those other needs either!' Her furious gaze swept over them all and their heads fell in utter shame.

'Kumiko, you and your sisters go out with your man now, and when he has finished doing what needs doing. Then I require all three of you to wipe him down with warm wet cloths and then dry him off with warm towels as well. And upon your return, possibly do your best to also ease his aching muscles for him too. As the night is now growing colder, and we cannot allow him to get a chill from his many previous exertions while he is about to enjoy a very lamented - but short rest period from them all here. And while you three *are* doing that . . . I am going to have a little talk with all of the women in here. Now be off with you!'

Hyde and the three women left and went one way out of the door, while Yoko turned to the right towards the kitchen area to get the same diligent man something to keep his stamina up near its peak condition. And she was happy right now to do that too, as she also knew that she would be well away from Shinko's vociferous tongue lashing which was about to follow their leaving.

∞

When they had left she had one of the women close the doors to keep the heat inside the room, and also to hold down what she was going to say to them from those in the kitchen now. Though she could not have cared less if the also heard her now too, as the fault could lie with any of them as well.

Shinko then began, and she harangued and chastised them all

harshly, both for their lack of manners, and also of the lack of respect shown to him so forcibly. That none of them could do little else but to lower their heads in complete and utter shame. They all knew what she was almost ranting in indignation at them for, because it was true.

But most of them were just as shocked to know that they had actually even done such a thing. Which was also why they all knew that such a severe telling off from her was not only warranted, but also in this case, fully merited as well! For as he was someone who was not even judged to be a true member within their clan as yet, those within the room were showing up the clan to him as not being as it should be to a newcomer. And that any proper courtesies that were only being shown to him now, should have been even *more* extravagant and special just because of this.

'What on earth *he* must think of us all now I just cannot imagine!' she groaned aloud, 'to think that he knew so little about us as it was when he met my daughter in England for the first time. Then he came back here with Kumiko and my husband, just so that he could be at Akiko's funeral for us, and still wished to marry my eldest daughter. And that was even *before* he found out that he would have to have the tattoo that so many of us carry with pride being placed upon his own back. Did he even change his mind. No. In fact he has accepted everything just so honourably, which is an amazing thing for *any* outsider to have even considered doing just to marry someone in our clan.

'He was not born into the clan like so many of us were, so he did not even *know* about some of our rituals we have. Certainly not *this* pre-wedding night ritual for one thing, of which *we* all take so much for granted. He did not actually find out about this until yesterday, in fact. Yet did he say no, I won't do that! Or actually deign to refuse any one of us when we offered ourselves to him tonight? No! No matter what ages we all were, from the very youngest of the virgins who are here to the much older ones of us,' she barked angrily, and all their heads sank again.

She scathed them with her very words. 'Douglas-san has conducted himself so correctly, and carried out his own part in this so well since he arrived on our shores. That all I feel is embarrassment for our entire clan right now! All that any of you thought about over the hours you were in here was only that of his large cock entering you all!' she spat at them.

'And yes, I do know that he will keep up his end of the bargain made between us all tonight . . . But, when it *is* all finally over, will he then still be so happy as to even wish to enter any of you again if you ever again desire it, *neh*? You can all now only *hope* that this will still be so after this enormous clan debacle. As I know that I *myself* would be more than happy to be entertained by him at *any* time at all from today. Just as I would think you all will be after he has also pleasured each of you.'

Her voice now softened and changed from its earlier harsh tone of only a few moments ago. To now sound more like her usual self as she then said calmly to them, 'But one thing that I must tell the rest of you here with me now is this. That not only I, but also Kumiko herself *knows* that Douglas-san will not be able to pleasure *all* of you here tonight.' She watched the show of concern as it flickered over the faces of those still remaining in the room.

'But,' she then said quickly, and followed it with, 'just as you must also remember that Douglas-san has not been taught *any* of our sexual training yet. In order for him to be able to *carry out* such a huge sexual workload as this has been tonight for him either! Kumiko herself though has since also agreed with me, that those who will not been seen, can still be with him tomorrow after their wedding has taken place. Her one and only proviso to this decision though, is that she will be with him first herself as his new bride. And then she will then be staying with him right throughout it, until you are all finally seen to.' She looked around them slowly. 'I hope that you are you all happy to comply with that?'

Their heads nodded happily at what her daughter had allowed them.

'I am pleased that you have all found some manners now, as that is a *very* generous gift being offered as well as being bestowed to you by my own daughter. And I hope that you will all now treat this man with the consummate respect that he certainly deserves. By the way, did any of you know that according to my daughter, Makiko, that there were actually one hundred and twenty-two of us women here right at the very start!

'If not, then you should all now be able to see just *how* well and how hard and unselfishly Douglas-san has been working tonight for *all* of our own benefits. So, if you are kindly to him from this time on; and give him your full respect and show him our usual manners. Then I have no doubt that he *will* be pleased to entertain any of you when he is next here, or perhaps maybe at his own home if you ever wished to visit them over there.'

CHAPTER 16

Douglas, even after a few times since arriving here in their country was still quite embarrassed about using their conventional Japanese toilet. One which lay close to the far wall and positioned as usual, well away from the large sunken bath. It was also set on a slightly lower level than the bath was. Presumably he thought, so that any unexpected overflow occurring would not find its way over into that, but wasn't sure. It just seemed an appropriate answer to him for it, that was all.

He personally preferred to use a urinal or cubicle type toilet, or one with at least a *door*, like at home. As since he came, and with eating the same kinds of food as they ate so regularly. Soon found that he had begun to fill up with far more wind more often now. And more than once over the elongated porcelain drain placed well out in the open, he had broken wind very loudly indeed. So he was terrified of doing just that right now with the three women in the bathroom there with him.

Squatting over the drain, he waited momentarily for whichever function needed to go first. Then quietly began to mutter, 'No! No! No!' as he felt the sudden build-up of pressure within his body. And of course, just as he *had* feared, it happened. His face turned profusely red at the long and interminably noisy explosion which now exited itself from beneath his body. He really didn't want to look across at any of them now, but he just had to. And yes, the three of them were still there over by the raised edge of the sunken bath he noticed.

Still kneeling and bent over to soak each of their cloths into the hot - or maybe only lukewarm water which now lay in it. Yet not one of them showed any sign whatsoever of even having heard his immense blow-out of wind. Though he knew that it would be quite impossible for any one of them *not* to have done so unless they were completely stone deaf! He even feared that it had been so loud, that surely the rest of the house would have heard it too!

In his own mind he knew that he shouldn't have been so worried about it anyway. As since he'd arrived at the house he'd seen most of them use the same drain while in front of him at some time, and with similar occurrences quite a few times as well. Which he thought might also have been down to all the bowls of noodles and soups that they were regularly eating.

It was only a typical Japanese mind set from times long past which made them ignore his bodily functions. Just as they knew that it was a also a form of politeness they also showed, as in not listening in to other people's conversations. All this stemmed from the walls of their houses being literally "paper thin" from centuries ago. So any privacy at all was also hard to find due to the sheer number of people living so close to each other in their country.

Modern times now weren't so bad as back then, as the buildings these days were being constructed, or fabricated, from more than just wood and oil paper. Steel, concrete, and brick had overtaken much of the far older Japanese building platforms. And with it, in these same cases, also brought with it their almost unknown before privacy.

But this house was not that modern. And although the house itself dated back well over three hundred years now, various repairs that were needed now and then had left little of the initial inner-structure untouched. The new wiring throughout for electricity had actually only taken place in the early seventies when Koichi's father, the last of his parents living here had passed away. As he, in his own way had tried to adhere to their much older disciplines and ways of life. Certainly no electric or gas, and no modern heating apart from in the kitchen itself from a wood burning stove. While in the main room a square-shaped lower seating level for where a brazier type of fire had once been used as another heat source.

After his death, Koichi had quickly modernised the house as much as was possible without ruining its traditional outside looks. An under floor central heating system had been fitted along with his late father's much hated electricity. Each had been required for warmth and cooking purposes. So now instead of having to heat water in a huge old metal pot on the brazier, or upon the stove for their tea, he had also had modern counters and units installed and electric kettles or large urns were now used. Instead of the original small wood burning stove, with its wood fire heated top for boiling or cooking on. A duty which had been taken over by Shinko upon his Koichi's mother's death. Happily for her, these had all been replaced to that of modern gas and electric cookers side by side.

To Koichi himself tradition was very important. But to also keep up with the modern way of life in which they now lived, was also considered to be just as important now too. As how else would they keep up with, and sometimes even surpass the West with their own new technologies that were being developed, created, and invented if they did not do so.

∞

After his visit to the weird toilet that he had lastly flushed with the small handle raised on a pipe leading to the wall from beneath the floor. He then washed his hands in the much more modern style of basin against it, then dried his hands on a very white looking roller towel. Something that seemed distinctly out of place here in a house. As he'd only ever seen them before in public toilets in factories and offices, and usually others that were located in outside conveniences for the general public to use prior to the use of warm air-driers.

Hyde was soon being carefully, if not actually gently, wiped down by the three of them, and then dried with warm towels in the same way. They all returned back to the main large room again. Where he was then given a quite skilful massage by all of their kneading hands and fingers. Yoko had returned to it before him with his ready meal and drink. And only after he had finally been massaged and had quenched his thirst and appetite. Did he again feel ready once more to carry on.

∞

The following morning as he awoke from his exhausted sleep and was kissed tenderly by Kumiko upon doing so. It didn't feel as if his muscles were as stiff as he thought they would have been. Though that could just have been down to Raiko's own amazingly long and careful massage upon his tired, if not exhausted body. And it was only when he finally knew that he simply *couldn't* manage to carry on with any of the remaining women who were still patiently waiting any longer. No matter who much he even tried to. Was at the point when Shinko herself had immediately called it a night, looking around the room to see who was still waiting to be seen to by him yet. Then she simply bade them all a good night until the following evening.

For Hyde himself, who just barely after seeing to his needs in the bathroom once again, now had to almost be led by the hand to the bedroom by Kumiko in a stumbling walk; which was where he just collapsed on the pre-prepared thick futon. His eyes fluttered open and closed occasionally as he lay there. Once imagining seeing Raiko now sat upon his groin as she kneaded his upper torso expertly. He had a very strange and quite vivid dream during the lengthy massage being carried out upon his body. Of being in one of those seedy massage parlours while he'd been in the vice squad for a short time. To then actually seeing himself laid out on a table while the woman performed what was known as "personal services" to him. Surprisingly enough though, both women could only look at each other in amazement, as a somewhat kind of tired looking erection formed yet again. From her excellent, but sometimes also sensual ministrations and manipulations to him.

Raiko was watched, and then helped now and then by Kumiko to turn him over, as she used her trained skills upon his aching muscles. She *had* indeed been sat upon his groin when he'd seen her momentarily before his eyes closed again and his new erection had formed. Her stroking, rubbing, pressing, and kneading all the various areas on his upper body with her hands were done time and time again.

During these same procedures, many times had Kumiko whispered quietly, 'Oh my poor Douglas!' at his listless and worn out body. As for what had recently passed, had certainly taken it's toll out on him that evening.

Then she had turned around on him and did his upper thighs, lower legs and feet. Then aided in turning his body, but only after Kumiko had used a deft finger press to get rid of his latest tired looking stiffness. She then sat upon him again and followed the same patterns. But now, and also just as expertly, doing the same kind of task upon his shoulders and lower torso and the backs of his arms.

Then Raiko had slid her body down until her own parted legs were kneeling on the outside of his, just above his knees. She had then kneaded and pressed her fingers into his buttocks with such deftness that he just elicited a sigh from her ministrations. With that part done, she again turned and sat upon his body, just behind his buttocks and across his spine. Where she now massaged the backs of his thighs, taking away the tightness and knotting of his muscles from so much kneeling earlier. Then she slid her body over his buttocks to finish his calves, and right at the very end, sat facing his feet so that she could perform some final reflexology upon the soles of his feet.

Which as she held each of his feet in her hands one at a time and used her thumb and fingers in varying motions. Being done as she had been trained to do, so as to benefit his entire body. Just as she had performed for her mistress on the many ocassions when *she'd* done a lot of walking some days ias part of her work.

From the nervous to his immune systems, his red and white blood cells, his heart, liver and lungs. Onto his other body functions such as the bowels and its intestines, also the skin encompassing his body and even the brain itself. Raiko left no single organ or part of his body untouched. Even the nerve stimulation of his virility and semen production were being encouraged and promoted while he lay there like a huge joint of inert meat on the bed.

When she had finally finished her time consuming work on him, and they had turned him to lie upon his back again. Kumiko said to her, 'Would you mind doing the same to him in the morning as well, Raiko?'

'If that is what your wish, mistress?'

Kumiko nodded to her in the low-lit room. 'Yes, I think it will relax him ready for the long day ahead of us that is to come. And also another one again just after our bath, before he has to perform with the remaining women. As it will no doubt relax his body in preparation for that also. And I think I will also take one from you then for myself too, Raiko.'

'As you wish, mistress,' she repeated.

Kumiko then lay down beside him on the futon. While Raiko drew the waiting coverlet up from the bottom towards her, until they were both covered under its quilted warmth.

'I know that you will be coming with us on our short honeymoon, Raiko. But are you truly happy to come to England with me? As if you are not then I will not ask you to do so if that is what you personally want.

You could even change mistresses if that may be your desire, too?'

'I will go wherever you go, mistress . . . as I have *always* done.'

'Only if you are quite sure though, Raiko, as when we go there we'll then both be a very long way from our own former homes and families here. Of course we will return to visit home now and then on holidays and such like. And I have no doubts now that some of them will also come to visit us over there. But for the most part I guess it will only be the three of us.'

'I do not mind that, my mistress.'

Kumiko looked at the man lying resting beside her. 'You like my soon to be husband, Raiko? And do you also feel you will be happy with him as your master?'

She gave a quick nod. 'Yes, mistress, from what I have seen of him in this short time already. I know that he is a kind man. Also very gentle and perhaps he will also be fun to be around since you told me of his very strange sense of humour. He is also not as dominating as most of our own men can be with any servant; and above all else my mistress, he pleased my body very much indeed.'

Kumiko smiled at that response, as she'd been there at the time so knew it to be true.

'But my main reason for agreeing to go, mistress,' she now added, 'is because we can actually speak together. As if he did not know Japanese, then I would only be able to speak with you alone. As you know that my own English is quite limited now, with my never having had to use it much here since I was first taught it.'

'Then we will both have to help you to get far better at it once more, Raiko, *neh*? As I am sure that not many of the shopkeepers over there in *England* will be able to speak Japanese with you whenever you may need to go out shopping there?'

'That was my main worry about going there, mistress. Here I can do *anything* at all that may be required for you. But over there I would not be able to do that.'

'Hopefully within a short time you will, Raiko. I also think that we should all speak English during the day to get you attuned to it more quickly. Then later in the evening we all can talk in Japanese together, so that we can carry on our own ways for a short while too.'

'I would be happy to try that for you, mistress.'

Kumiko nodded. 'And if we are both out of the house during the day, Raiko. There is an old lady next door to Douglas, called Edith. Who I'm sure would be pleased to talk with you during the day for some company if that is so.'

'So long as I can talk with someone, my mistress, then I'm sure that I'll begin to pick the language up again very quickly again.'

'Then we will all live happily together there, Raiko, *neh?*'

'Oh I do hope so, mistress,' she replied.

Kumiko finally bade her good night, and as she snuggled into his body, she saw the lighting lower even more until it went out altogether. The click from the small dimmer switch near the door meant that it had been completely switched off. The hiss of the door twice had told her that Raiko had now left, and she closed her eyes and slept beside her man beneath the warm quilt.

∞

During their privately taken breakfast together and after what he felt was an extraordinary massage from Raiko. Kumiko's father imparted to him the information and instructions about how the wedding itself would be carried out. That the very same Shinto priest who was there to carry out the funeral on Saturday, would also be the one doing their service here at the house. He told Hyde of the formal kimono type of dress code that he would be required to wear throughout it. Then of the required rituals that he and Kumiko would both have to follow, along with the priest as the service went on.

He said nothing at all about what had taken place the previous evening with all the women. He didn't really need to, since his wife had already told him everything anyway. Though he had thought that Douglas himself had actually put up quite an amazing show. Which had left him feeling very impressed with the young man's as yet untrained stamina so far.

Before their wedding had been due to begin, her father and

brother's all came to attend to him in her parents' bedroom. Just to make sure that he was dressed correctly for the part he was to play to become one of their family. Whilst his bride-to-be, Kumiko, was now being aided with her own dressing and make-up in her own bedroom. Being well-aided herself by her mother, sisters, and of course, the always available Raiko.

Luckily the day was warm, but not *too* hot for a change. Not hot or humid enough to cause your clothing to stick to your body anyway. The priest was seated on a cushion towards the rear of the veranda in the cooling shade. Two other cushions had been placed out before him, as well as a small low wooden table which had been set up there. The two empty cushions were both quite large and were also family heirlooms. Very much well used over the generations, and heavily brocaded in gold and silver and other richly coloured silks. Made so, so as to suit the formal occasions for which they had been created.

Many of the witnesses to it were already kneeling on plain coloured cushions placed upon the ground, and these were arranged in ranks. Almost like that of an audience in a theatre. They themselves were all once again dressed in the same kimonos as with the funeral. As what with it being a clan wedding, it was a similar role they were expected to be attired for.

There were only a few children present this time, vastly different from the funeral. As only those families who had travelled any kind of distance at all to be here for it had their children beside them. While those who lived near enough to attend today's event had been able to send their children of school age *to* school. So it was only those still too young, or who had already left, or had been allowed by their parents to miss a day. Who were now in attendance and waiting outside the large house.

Precisely as noon arrived, the priest rang a small bell and the wedding rituals began. Hyde was led out of one side of the house with her father beside him, and followed behind by her three brothers. Kumiko from the other side of it had her mother at her side, and her two sister's behind. With barely a minute to spare, Raiko hurried from the same side of it before the bell was rang. To take her place upon one of the vacant cushions right at the very front of the throng outside. Even some of the local inhabitants from the nearby village had again been allowed to attend. Although only because those few of them actually knew *what* they really were through their own families long-standing service to them.

Spirit of a Dragon

The ceremony itself, after they had both knelt on the two cushions before the priest, began with an almost identical no breathing monologue being read from yet another scroll. His low voice droning on so long almost sent Hyde off to sleep as he knelt in front of him. Thankfully it only lasted fifteen minutes this time though, and then after the rituals of sharing sake together from the same small bowl. The self-same priest announced to all and sundry that their marriage was completed.

As soon as he said that, close to thirty people rose from their kneeling places and hurried around to the side of the house. A good few restaurants were missing their top chefs today along with their well-trained assistants. But as they were all working within the businesses of their owners. Of who were all members of the clan anyway - their help was certainly required on such a celebratory day as this. Being that of their clan leaders daugter. As there was also a lot of people to be fed on this festive occasion.

Just as Kumiko was now raising her black veil from over her face to show it to her new husband, the low clatter of pots and pans being moved around, and that of much hasty chopping had already started. They were all now striving to create a very traditional *Kai-siki* meal for those still outside, which could be as many as ten or twelve separate dishes for each and every person there to eat. And that was without any sake or cha, or soft drinks that would also be consumed along with it.

As they returned down the steps together straight after, her father and brothers greeted him as a full family member now. Then led him aside towards where all the men had begun to stand and group together to meet him. While Kumiko was being led the other way by her mother and sister's towards all their waiting women guests.

One particular man from the male coucil meeting previously, strode out towards him with his hand stretched out in front. 'I bid you welcome to our clan, Douglas-san,' he offered. 'And by all the God's I'm so pleased that Kumiko has finally married so that I can at long last be allowed to visit *her* sweet Chamber of Joy!'

'I hope for you that it will have been worth the wait when you do visit it, Masaya-san,' he returned, just as Kumiko's father had instructed him. Then following his same instructions added, 'I hope that her chamber is as sweet for you as those of your own daughters were for me last night.'

Those in front saw the sudden tension appear to rise in his face. And then disappear almost just as quickly, as he began to laugh loudly. 'Ah, Douglas-san, you are very right and I apologise to you for my own rudeness just then.' His head even began to bob. 'Two of my daughters could speak of little else when they returned home last night, and for that I can only thank you from the bottom of my heart. They expressed so much joy for the feelings of pleasure they had with you, that they both asked to wish to see you again if possible. Whenever you may be available for their pleasure, of course. Whereas my other daughter is also very much looking forward to tonight with you, that she said that she could barely contain herself today . . .'

Douglas also now nodded his head. 'I can only offer my own sincerest thanks to them both for last night. And had hoped that they enjoyed it. As for your other daughter, I will do what I can later to offer her the very same feelings as those of her sisters.'

'Thank you, Douglas-san,' said Masaya warmly, his own mind already predominantly dwelling on asking Kumiko for his own pleasure.

Koichi saw this on his face, so said a little too happily, and not in sadness as Kumiko had told him to do it this morning, 'Though I'm afraid that any of Douglas's, or my daughter Kumiko's possible new partners may have to wait awhile longer for that additional pleasure, such as it will be.'

Masaya stood open mouthed. 'What?'

'Yes, I am very sad to say so, Masaya-san. You see Kumiko decided to be with her new husband first tonight, so as to make it her first ever time with her new husband. And then she said that she would be there to watch over him throughout it. She has also decided to take personal care over him over the next two days while he has our clan tattoo given to him.'

'But surely after that---'

'After that is done. On Thursday morning they are then going off for an almost week-long honeymoon trip around some parts of Japan. Before they then finally return here to say their farewells to us and be taken home by our private aircraft.'

Another man chuckled, 'It looks like you'll just have to wait a bit longer before you do get the chance of thrusting against *her* bush, Masaya-san, *neh*?'

Koichi grinned at old Ichiro's words as he saw how it had caused Masaya so much irritation. But he then decided to give him a return offering to console him, something that Kumiko herself certainly hadn't said to him.

'But I have no doubt Masaya-san, that if you decide to take your family to visit them over there perhaps for a short holiday. That you could probably spend some time alone with his new wife, Kumiko. *If she accepts your offer!*' he stressed casually, 'While Douglas-san here takes care of your own wife and daughters at the same time? The best of both worlds for you all then, and you could even use one of our aircraft to get there and back if you wished.' Koichi offered rather generously. While also seeing the utter consternation written on the other man's face now. Most of them knowing that he had wanted to enjoy her body ever since she was a young girl, but her lack of not being married had quite rightly halted any of his own advances. Not that he had ever known if she would even *deign* to accept his proposal of sex between them or not yet either. But it had been his wish for so many years now already, that he simply couldn't see her saying no!

Now she *was* free to do so with whichever man she pleased, but that could also be a stalling point as Masaya himself already knew. As he had hoped to enjoy her here, but without the new foreigner actually being able to get anywhere near his own wife, and also even three of his daughters. And he had lost, since *he'd* already had sex with two of his young daughters, who by their leaders changing of the laws were now deemed them both old enough to partake in it if wished. He wasn't feeling as happy as he was trying to now show outwardly to them. As with his daughters talking to his wife Saachiko last night about what they had gone through, even *she* was now thinking about it herself! And *that* had shocked him to his core!

He had also had heard just how happy *they* would both be to do the very same again with him at any time now. And due to their previous enjoyment, had even asked through him to do so again with this man - which he had, very unhappily, but dutifully had to do. Though not in an entirely happy frame of mind at all. As the real problem to him, was that this same foreigner could very well be invited to bed the entire female side of his family while his own advances to Kumiko could quite easily be rebuffed by her. Which would inevitably leave him right out in the cold, while that same foreigner who stood before him, happily pleased and pleasured himself with all but his youngest daughter. Who he also knew was *already* talking about it with them, and that was what was so terrifying to him.

'I will have to think about that, Koichi-san,' he nearly stammered in reply as most of them smiled. 'As I have heard that Douglas-sans house is not that large so would be difficult to take all of us for a holiday, *neh*?'

Koichi had felt quite smug in putting the younger overbearing man in his place for once. And now decided to add to his misery even more just because of it. 'It shouldn't really be *that* difficult to manage Masaya-san. As I know that his home does have three bedrooms---'

'Ahhh, *only three* . . .' said Masaya, feigning a loud yet sad appearing sigh.

'Maybe only three, but as Raiko will have one to herself that would still leave two to use. Of course I'm sure that your wife and daughters will be quite happy to *all* share his bed with him now, *neh*?'

Masaya quickly knew that he was becoming flustered from these events. Events now being spoken of so openly among their gathered group. Then an idea suddenly came to him. 'That, I assume, would be all and well and good Koichi-san,' he said in his sweetly sickening voice. 'But, my youngest daughter and son, as well as our servants would have nowhere to sleep themselves, would they?' He smiled slyly yet again. After finally feeling that he had at long last overcome his imperious leader at least *once* in nearly two decades.

Koichi was a fighter born and bred though, and would not give up so easily to him. 'I forgot about your servants for a moment there, Masaya-san, I'm sorry. And of course they would probably all wish to enjoy Douglas-sans services while they are there, too. Of that I have no doubt. For the moment though I am sure that Raiko would give your other younger children her bed, while she and your own servants could naturally use some futons downstairs in his house.

That is a good idea you have now given me, Masaya-san, a very good one indeed. Perhaps I should buy them a much larger five, six or more bedroomed house for them to live in, *neh*? As with so many women telling of their happiness with him last night, I am sure that their house will be being visited regularly by many of our members when they leave

Spirit of a Dragon

here soon.'

Masaya was not only beat but stood there shell-shocked. Whichever way he tried to turn, Koichi always seemed to get the better of him. All he could do was to nod thoughtfully in response and move away. While Ichiro's grin was as wide as Koichi's own as he departed.

It was his turn to look at Douglas now. 'I also express my thanks to you for pleasuring my wife and our daughters last night, Douglas-san. As few of the younger men in our clan would never even think of doing so for an older woman like she is now. And I give to you my total gratitude for the amount of pleasure you gave to her and especially *them* last night.'

'It was *my* honour to have been offered *such* a gift from your not only your wife, Ichiro-san. But the same from your daughters too.'

The old man then actually bowed to him and as he walked away was muttering, 'Remarkable!' over and over again.

Kumiko, who was now over talking with the other women, was hearing only very pleasing things about her new husband. Mainly of course about his large size, and for just how long he had more than willingly worked for them all last night. Some to her on surprise even commenting on how handsome he actually was, *for an outsider*, that is.

Her eyes picked up Masaya's sudden approach towards Douglas and her father and she waited expectantly. She watched his face as it changed regularly as certain information was given to him. Watching as his face rapidly suffused red once; and then even almost to purple too. And then after what appeared to her to be a brief, yet somewhat heated conversation had ensued between them, she had then watched him walk away.

She was then distracted by the same man's own wife and four daughters who came over in a group now, just to talk with her.

∞

Hyde did indeed keep to his word after he had enjoyed yet another very stimulating massage from Raiko in what once was Kumiko's bedroom. That would be now known as *their* bedroom from now on. With a meal inside him and just having had some tea.

Before what women still remained from last night, plus *one* other.

233

As he had pleasured Kumiko herself just so well in front of them all. That he had made those who were still awaiting their own turn there with him from the previous night. Literally becoming wide-eyed and panting and gasping aloud along with them both.

He was only about an hour into his now, very enjoyable work. When his mobile telephone began to ring where it had been left lying on the chair inside their bedroom. Raiko, who had already been accepted by him the previous day, was now kneeling patiently in the open doorway of it. She was waiting there in that place dutifully, only in case either of them may have wanted anything during his latest *workout* as he had now started to call it.

She hurried over to it and picked it up. Due to her lack of English usage at the moment, the number and name which showed on the screen itself also meant very little to her. Since she of course knew no-one from there. So, she quickly carried it with hurrying feet towards where they were, or to the *sex room* as it was now being called by her own young and beautiful mistress.

Rushing into the room with little regard to anything but her task in hand. She saw that her new master was *extremely* busy right at the moment, so fell to her knees right beside Kumiko; to who she offered the explanation of, 'My master's telephone began to ring, mistress,' she reported while passing it over to her.

'Green button,' said Douglas as she looked at it.

'*Mushi-mushi?*' she said after touching the green button. Even forgetting where she was herself for the present moment.

'Eh? I beg your pardon?' said a voice in English in return.

'Oh, so sorry, hello?' she answered in English this time.

'*Hello?*' queried an uncertain voice. 'This *is* Douglas's number that I have called, isn't it?' asked Terry from over five thousand miles away.

'Yes, you are quite correct,' she replied.

'May I speak with Douglas then, please? This is Terry from his department at work calling him.'

'Ah yes, I do remember him talking about you to me, Terry-san. I am Kumiko, and I'm afraid that Douglas is just a *little bit busy* right at this very moment in time, Terry-san,' said Kumiko. Who then had to hold a hand over the end while she gave a throaty chuckle. Since Douglas was there right in front of her and happily thrusting himself into yet another woman's desperate void at this very inopportune time.

'It is a little bit urgent, Kumiko,' Terry responded.

'I see, Terry-san, but cannot I, as his newly married wife to him, not take a message from you to give to him later?'

'Eh . . .? What's that? You're what!' She heard him give a gasp and then mutter back down the phone in response.

'We were married today, Terry-san. Has what I have just said taken you a little by surprise?'

'Bloody hell, sorry, I mean yes, you could say that, Kumiko!'

'Hold on a moment then please while I get him for you,' she replied, covering the mouthpiece by placing it against her bare stomach while she waited for him. And while *she* waited for him, Terry was already telling those in his department as he waited.

Hyde withdrew from the one knelt in front of him and sat back on his legs. He took a few moments to allow his breathing to return to normal, while the woman in front of him just sighed out loud and then lay happily stretched out on her stomach upon the futon like a pleased feline; if only to await his impending return to her. If she'd been a cat she likely would probably have purred!

When he thought he was ready, he received the mobile from Kumiko to take the call. 'Hi there Terry, how are things going?' he asked.

'Hi Dougie, bloody hell, that was a bit of a surprise mate! When did all this happen you old bugger!'

'Just the way things sometimes work out I guess, Terry,' he said.

'You're not kidding! Well, we here in the office all send our congratulations to you both anyway, even if it was so unexpected!'

Kumiko listened in like most of them to the one way, and broken sentenced conversation. Since Douglas never once thought about putting it on to its speaker option. Head slightly tilted to one side or the other as they tried to follow his speaking. Not that they really should have been doing so, and few of them, like Raiko, were already quite lost.

'Cheers, we both thank you all. So, what did you ring me up for, has some news finally come up to help us now? - What! - Jesus, you have to be kidding me! - Christ! – Well, I guess it's possible, Terry. - No, you're handling it fine from what you've told me. - No, we're not due back until next week at best, Terry. - We are? - Okay, well just keep doing what you're doing then, and if you need any help just give me another buzz. - Righto mate. - Yeah, just keep on top of things as much as you can, as that's about all you can do right now really. - All I can advise you to do right now is to have a quiet word with the Boss about it, Terry. Maybe with all our forces working together we *can* get it on Crimewatch now or something, eh? - I know. - How's Edith keeping by the way? - Good, good, and thanks for keeping an eye on her for me, Terry. - Okay, I'll talk to you later, cheers mate, bye for now then.'

Kumiko's face had been a picture of emotions as he'd watched her. Trying to work out what exactly was being said between them from a very one-sided conversation. He ended the call with the red button and handed it back to Raiko with an added, 'Thank you, honey . . .'

'*Well? Was* it important?' she now asked.

He nodded. 'It's all turning to shit over there, pet!'

'How so?' she said oddly.

'Akiko isn't the only woman that he's killed, that we *do* know now for sure.' She emitted a loud gasp. 'According to Terry back home now, there were six other women before her and have been three more since her so far.'

'Ten killings, and are you sure they were all by the same man?'

He nodded again. 'Terry said that the findings on our own reports were being matched precisely by others. Though we also might have found a clue now it seems; as at one of those scenes after ours occurred, a flask was found not far away from the body. Tests on it have already shown that it held the exact same two drugs within it as with the other victims. They're running fingerprint and hopefully DNA tests on it as we speak.'

Spirit of a Dragon

'But *ten* murdered women now, Douglas!'

'I know sweetheart. But there could be more yet.'

'What do you mean?' she asked.

'Because he's in a groove right now, my love. Getting away with what it is he *wants* to do right now, and he doesn't imagine that he'll be caught either. But the nearer we start to get to him will lead to one of two things.' He saw that she was waiting for him. 'Either he will stop, and then try and go into hiding somewhere until the heat dies down on our search for him . . .'

'Or?' she asked,

He shrugged. 'In the other scenario, he will literally go out *on* a full-on killing *spree*! Thinking that if he is going to get caught, then in for a penny or in for a pound as they say!'

'Huh?'

'In a way, it means, what has he now got to lose by killing more women, love. As for one pre-planned murder he'd get life when he's caught.'

'And for the ten that he's killed so far?'

'Ten life sentences – which matters little really, does it, since he can only ever really serve one of them until he finally dies in prison. But that's what *really* pisses me, as well as most coppers, and a lot of the public off about our system back in the UK, Kumiko. We should never have done away with corporal and capital punishment in the 60's.'

'Do you mean hanging?'

He nodded at her as they all listened and most understood, or were interpreting for those who did not. 'Hanging used to be our way back then of dealing with someone who had committed a very serious capital offence, like murder and such like. But with all these bloody humanitarian do-gooder's knocking around, and with all the new laws coming out about Human Rights and so forth now. Our legal system's just become a fuckin' joke to every criminal in our country!' He was just so frustrated at it, that he'd forgotten himself for the moment to swear luridly – a rare event for him.

'So what was this corporal thing you said?'

'Corporal punishment was a lower level that could be given as a sentence, in the olden days people were put into the stocks for a set time, and other members of the public could abuse you with insults – or even throw things at you. Or, you could be whipped so many times. Later it became mainly hard labour to be served. But now! Christ, the bastards just sit in jail and get fed better than most of the poor, or those of our elderly people trying to live and survive outside it! That's why so many people in our country want both of those options bringing back again. To finally get shot of those who by all rights of decency, shouldn't even still be alive now for what they've done. Just like the bastard who killed your sister. They should be hung along with any drug barons, and people who even just *attempt* to commit murder or violent crimes. Even carrying a gun or knife should also be allowed in with it now. What with so many people being badly injured or killed by them these days.

'For the rest, the drug dealers, the con men, the burglars, the thieves, and the car criminals. A damn good thrashing with twenty odd lashes or more with the cat would soon get all of them back into line.'

She was puzzled, as were many there. 'You mean you would use a live or dead cat to hit them with, Douglas?'

'No love, I meant a cat o'nine tails.'

'Whatever is a cat with nine tails?'

'It's just what they once used to use in the days of old wooden ships in our navy a long time ago, for troublesome or disobedient seamen. Nine thin strips of leather on a kind of whip with a small knot at each end of them. That when it was used tore the skin of a back open. Most men sometimes survived the one or two dozen that were often awarded as severe punishment. But few, if any, could survive the thirty-six or higher! Some captains were even known to give a man a hundred, and just made the crew watch as even after he died his back was almost torn away. And that's what we need to get back in law as quick as we can. Instead of our having to spend millions, or perhaps even billions every year, just to cosset all of these scum that are in our prisons all the time. Of course that's why they don't really care after being released if they get caught doing something again. As there's bugger all for them to fear by being sent back is there!

'Even some kind of a renewed compulsory National Service being brought back into use would get a lot of these youngsters. Many who are leaving school now, at least some work knowledge. And usually who only start out in crime in the first case because they've no money and nothing to do. For some, doing a three or four year stint in one of the forces where at least they'd learn some discipline. As well as a trade for if they leave after it. Whereas others who find they liked it might just stay in the services for a longer stretch.

'But it would take a hell of a lot of trouble off the streets for us to have to cope with! Drunken fights, ordinary gang related fights, muggings, rapes, car thieves, etc. So I would have capital, corporal, and also even hard labour brought back like a shot if I had any say in the matter,' he stated, finally ending his voluble oration to her and everyone else within hearing distance.

Then to their surprise, he then just tapped the leg of the woman that still lay stretched on the floor looking behind her to watch him speaking. Who then just moved back into her former kneeling position again. And then he just carried straight on from where he'd left off.

CHAPTER 17

Hyde stood beside Kumiko and her father in their large bathroom the following morning, it was now Tuesday, and the day after his wedding. Alongside them were four others, two males and two females. One of the men and women were quite, if not very old. Whereas the other two appeared to be young. Of the youngest, he thought were barely out of school, but he was informed that they were both in their late twenties now. Which only made him shake his head in simialr surprise to find that out once more.

He then found out that the youngest were just two of their many chosen student apprentices: and to where such an apprenticeship could last as long as ten years, before they were ever to be let loose on creating a fully detailed insignia of their own. Although they were, after only a few years of well structured training. Then allowed to adorn any new servants with their personal tiny miniatures and finally slightly larger tattoos, just to save their far elderly teachers more of their own time. But right now, their only duties with being only classed as trainees at such a major event as this. Was to have all of the inks and needles in constant readiness for their teachers to use. Ready to be handed over to either one of them at a moment's notice, in order to keep their teachers work rate both high and constantly flowing.

Yet that wasn't what was bothering him at the moment . . . It was the very weird and wooden-looking contraption that had been brought with them and set-up just over the end of the toilet drain. He was already stripped in preparation for the business ahead, yet still felt perturbed at the object.

'Come, my husband,' said Kumiko to him. 'Each of us with our own tattoo have had to do the same thing as you will be doing now.'

She saw that he was looking, well, staring would likely have been a better word for it, at their very strange in appearance old tattoo table. And it *was* old she knew, as it *had* been used repeatedly over the centuries by countless people as their backs were adorned with their emblem of clan unity.

'But why the straps?' he asked her.

'Only so that your body cannot move about freely while it is being worked upon, my love. You have seen upon my own now just how intricate the work which has to be done truly is. So the less movement you are able to make while they are working upon you – also makes it far easier for them to accomplish it quicker.'

'But I *thought* you said that my body would be manipulated every once in a while to keep it pliable over the coming two days ahead, Kumiko? So how can that possibly be managed if I'm tied down to that thing?'

'And so it will be, my husband. As every hour while they are here with you, even Yasuji and Miho, and their students will need to take a short rest period to refresh themselves with a drink or whatever. As it is also very hard work on their eyes to carry out such highly delicate work as this. So, while they take a rest every so often as I said, I myself and Raiko, or one or more of the other people or servants here at our home will come in to see to your bodily needs. Later, when they have both worked long enough, Hiroshi and Otoyo will also arrive with their students, and be waiting to take over for them and vice-versa. And *that* is how it can all be completed in only two days, Douglas. By four of our *very* highly skilled people and their apprentices working around the clock almost non-stop in order to do it.'

'And I will feel nothing at all you said? That I will be asleep for the entire time it is being done?'

'From the potion which you will soon be given, my love, you will almost be in a coma like state for all of that time. You will feel nothing, see nothing, and hear nothing. Your mind, if it was like my own was when I was done, will be almost in a dreamlike state of nothingness for the entire time that it is being carried out. And the reason that the tattooing apparatus is positioned here over the drain is so that your bodily functions can flow whenever they want to without hinder. As the drug that is administered, and with it being so powerful, will soon release every muscle in your body to relax you completely when it takes you over. It is also *why* your body must also be manipulated so often. So as not to cause any softening of those muscles tissues from occurring.'

'Well, that sounds okay then,' he told her. 'So what do I do now?'

'When you are ready to proceed, you must be standing right next to the table for when you ingest the drug. You have to do that, as it takes barely less than a minute to work its way deep into your system. So as soon as you have swallowed it you must quickly climb upon it ready, and then as soon as you have sank into your sleep. We will then tie the straps and check you over before they can get started on you.'

'Okay'' he said and walked to the side of the weird apparatus.

'Are you still sure that you want to go ahead with this Douglas-san?' her father asked him. 'Because as a non-Japanese. Even if you are seen as one of us now, you are not really forced to carry this through you know.'

He smiled widely at all six of them then. 'If my gorgeous new wife of mine tells me that it is all right, Koichi-san. And if in all your eyes I will also be seen as a fully joined member of the clan either way. Then what kind of fool would I be seen to be if I did not believe her implicitly?'

'True,' he muttered.

The young woman apprentice then handed over the small cup of very potent liquid to him. He sniffed at it and wrinkled his nose at the unpleasant odour from within. Then quickly placed it to his lips and drank it down in one go. At which he thought just then that it was lucky he had. Because the actual taste of the concoction as it slid down his throat, was even worse than the terrible smell. Even as he clambered up on to the strange looking frame next to him, his senses were being assailed by the imagined thoughts of what he had just accepted. That it could have been a mixture of mouse droppings and fresh sick for all *he* knew! He quickly lay face down upon its multitude of wide leather straps.

Straps which now held his full body weight in mid-air between the opened heavy wooden frame, and smiled up at his new wife.

'This feels just like lying in a hamm----'

His head just dropped suddenly before he'd even finished talking. He was out cold. As her father checked his pulse rate, which as they hoped for, was slow but very strong. But they had to check it anyway in order to carry on. Kumiko went over to him and turned his head to a more comfortable position for him for the first hour of work. Koichi nodded to the four others who now began to strap his arms and legs to the opened up star-shaped contraption with its slightly lower in height limb placements. An odd device it was, but one which had been made in exactly that way. Only so that each limb could be pulled outwards tightly before tying. This also became an aid to stretching the skin of the person who was about to be tattooed.

'They must have had some quite tall men back then in our clan as well,' murmured Miho to her young female apprentice. 'As his body only just fits the table,' she told her while tightening a strap over his now limp wrist.

Kumiko was beneath the table now and gently eased his penis and testicles through some of the strapping. Then, from a hook beneath it, she took a funnel like object with a long pipe on one end. The pipe she made sure was in the drain before placing the funnel part of it over his hanging manhood. Happy where it was placed, she clipped it to the nearest straps and let go of it. She gave a nod when it didn't swing or fall, and then came out from under the table.

She now moved to the rear of it, into the gap where his legs had been opened quite wide and then tied down to the structure. From a hollow tube underneath which she now opened, she removed another item shaped like a huge banana and which looked like a "c" shaped gutter drain form a roof. Now it was made of shining metal, but centuries before it had been made of wood. But they both, whenever they needed to be used, were always coated with some type of frictionless liquid. Animal fat or grease had once originally been the mainstay, but now modern oils were an even better lubricant than those which had once been used.

So Kumiko was careful how she handled it, never once touching the inside of the small "c" shaped pipe. Using her eye as a measuring gauge, she held the top end of it towards his spread-apart buttocks. As one hand parted them even wider, the other brought the end to a point just below his now visible anus. She released the hand on his buttocks and began clipping the pipe to the table to hold it in place, making sure that the far end of it was seated in the drain. So that just like the earlier funnel, any faecal matter emitting from him would just emerge on its own when needed. Then it would simply slide straight down the pipe and run down into the trough. From where it could easily be flushed away whenever it happened. It was, so she let go of the entire thing and checked that it was still held in the correct place to do that, it was.

She nodded to them both that he was now quite ready for them to begin. And as she walked away, Douglas's muscles were already loosening from the drug, and a huge sound echoed and vibrated around the bathroom as he broke wind fiercely. Kumiko walked around to where his head was and stooped over to look into his face.

'Douglas, my husband,' she said to his very relaxed appearing face after kissing his forehead softly. 'Where on *earth* does all this wind of yours keep coming from?' Then she gave a deep sigh, knowing that he would almost remain in this same positional comatose state for close to two full days while they worked upon him. And lastly, right at the very end of it, they would liberally cover his back with the ointment which would begin to heal his back very rapidly afterwards.

∞

For close to thirty-six long, yet unknowing arduous hours, Hyde remained strapped to the table. Except for around every hour when Kumiko, Raiko, Shinko, Koichi, or one of the other five servants of the family house took their own allotted turn to look after him. Either before or after his body was flexed and manipulated, he was fed liquid to drink and a mushy based substance to ingest. It just depended on *whose* turn it was to look after him. And throughout it all, either sleeping or resting as she occasionally even watched them at work upon him, was Kumiko, just as she'd promised to be.

The water within their sunken bath was kept at a hot enough temperature to create steam all the time, yet only as an aid to keeping his inert naked body warm. While the rest of those working or watching within the bathroom perspired profusely in the constant heat which rose upwards from it.

Occasionally he urinated or defecated, since unbeknown to him right now, he was constantly being fed food and water to keep his body's nutrients at their peak all the time. A few times while Kumiko had been standing very near, so as to watch their usual, but still amazing skill upon the flesh of his back, she had flushed the drain. At other times, when she was either asleep or only resting on the quickly changed futons when they grew too damp, either one of of her parents or the apprentices, or possibly the servant seeing to him at the time flushed it. And just as was said to him, throughout it all he knew nothing at all . . . His mind didn't even wander or dream once during his long respite. For him, it *was* just like being in a deep black coma-like existence of being nowhere at all.

The final nine hours that he lay there after his back had been liberally smeared with a mixture of a typical foul smelling ointment that promoted rapid tissue healing. Which Kumiko was thankful for when she'd seen his blood trailed back. From where the continual pricking of the old style needles had each drew separate spots of blood. That in time met another and another, until a larger drop was formed and it ran down his spine or over the sides of his body. The busy tattooist's, of course, had taken no notice of this at all, unless needing to remove some of it in order to see what they were doing. As their own lengthy task was to etch his back, and that was it. The apprentices were the same, their main role being to have the waiting ink covered needles ready to pass across to either teacher instantly. So they barely had time to move at all during their sessions with him. Only as an hourly break arrived did cramped muscles and tired eyes, from their long hours of bending over and staring fixatedly at their work finally enjoy some brief movement.

∞

When he finally did come round again, he found himself not upon the apparatus any longer, but laid out on his front upon a futon on the same bathroom floor. But now with Kumiko asleep and snuggled in beside him. Only when Raiko saw that his mind was back in full working order did she awaken her mistress. She then followed as Kumiko led him across to their bathrooms long wooden bench where they both washed and rinsed the well-hardened dirty grey coloured gunk from his back, along with the rest of his body. Raiko was always ready, so as soon as she had helped Kumiko finish with him, Raiko then saw to the needs of her mistress. As was normal now, they both then went over to step down into, and then to sit and relax in the heated water of the waiting bath. With Raiko herself joining them within it a few minutes later after seeing to herself.

'I've already pre-booked the rooms where we'll be staying for the first three days of our travelling honeymoon, husband,' she told them as they all relaxed together. 'And just as you hoped, we should be able to visit most of the places which you wanted to go to.'

'Where first?' he asked.

'We will leave on the Bullet Train at noon today and we'll begin at Kagoshima, then stay the night at Nagasaki on Kyushu. The next day we begin to travel back this way again, and the ferry will take us across to Shikoku, to visit either Kochi or Kagawa, or perhaps both if we have time enough. We'll then take another ferry from the other side and stay the night in Hiroshima. On the third day we'll stay a while in Kobe, or for the entire day if you prefer, before going on to Kyoto. But I would recommend Kyoto to stay so we can also enjoy a lovely walk together around the gardens of the old Emperors Palace.'

'And what will you be doing, Raiko?' he asked.

'Waiting for you both to return to wherever we will be staying for the night, master.'

'No, I don't think you will be you know,' he told her. 'You will come along with us wherever we go when we are out.'

She shook her head quickly. 'I am but your servant, master, and you will be on your honeymoon.'

'That makes no difference, Raiko. Outside for the next week we will only be seen as three people travelling together. And I just cannot see any enjoyment in it for you, if you are always stuck in some hotel room or other just waiting for us to come back there to it. No!' he said very authoritatively, 'you will be with us!'

'I would also like that as well, Raiko. As we have never really been out together as such have we, except when maybe shopping.'

'Well no, mistress, but it is not right for me to do so is it?'

'From this day on it is.'

Her frown was quite apparent, so Kumiko said to her, 'I can believe that just like me, Raiko. You have also never visited many other places in Japan either, *neh*?'

'Not really, mistress, apart from when you went anywhere in our country on holiday, or due to work commitments.'

'Then I take my husband's point as well now. That as we will all be moving to England very shortly. So we should *all* enjoy this visit around our country together, Raiko. Just to remind both of us of what we are leaving behind us soon now, and of what we can enjoy whenever we return again.'

'If that is your own wish of course, mistress, then I will obey.'

'As my husband has just said, that *now* it is, Raiko!' Kumiko confirmed. 'Anyway, our fourth day will be spent heading for Hokkaido, which is also a long trip just like today will be for us. There we will stay and visit Sapporo and Hakodate. The fifth day will begin in either Akita or Iwate, if the former then we will go on to Shibata and stay there. If the latter, then we will later go on to Sendai and stay there, the choice will be yours, my husband. But at Sendai we will already be on the eastern coast of Japan, and also back on the correct side for the next day's Bullet Train which will be running back this way. As Shibata you see, is on the western side of Japan, so we may have to travel across country in order to get our return train back.

'Our last two days will be spent closer to Tokyo really, at Yokohama, Kanagawa, and Mishima. We can decide which one, or which two of them you want to visit if you still want to have a look around Tokyo on our very last day. Though if lucky we may just fit all three of them in, but we'll need to know this in advance so that we can book rooms. As just hoping to find any rooms for us when we're only going *somewhere* could lead to some difficulties at a later time. Though we *could* get lucky and do so without any worry at all. Or perhaps if none are available for us – then I'm quite sure that any of our clan members in those areas would allow us to stay with them for that small period of time.

'And my father has said that if we arrive back home in plenty of time for the plane to take us over to England. Then we can have a farewell meal with all my family and say our goodbyes before we do leave.'

'I would even miss a place out altogether on our trip if it meant that you could do that, sweetheart. As I know just how much you want to spend a bit of time with them before we do have to leave.'

'Thank you for thinking of me, my love.'

'And you Raiko? Will you be seeing your family too?' he asked.

'Probably not until I come back home again at some later time after we have left, master. My own family lives in Shizuoka.'

'Where's that?' he asked Kumiko.

'It's on the same line between Kanagawa and Nagoya, perhaps about up to one hundred miles from each one, all depending upon how you're actually getting there.'

'Then why don't we all just drop in there for you as we come back up this way, Raiko? Or pop over that way on one of our two last days? If on the last days we can visit your family first with you before we go on to see some of Mishima, Kanagawa or Yokohama. How does that sound to you, eh?'

When nothing came from her after that offer was made, they both looked over towards her. She was sitting there with tears streaming down her face.

'I'm sorry Raiko, have I said something wrong?' he asked her softly.

Her head shook from side to side.

'What is it? Please tell me Raiko,' insisted Kumiko.

She sniffled loudly and attempted to dry her eyes with a wet hand from the water. 'You are both being too kind, and wonderful, to even be thinking of *me* at all on your honeymoon,' she whispered between many sniffs, and lowering her head, 'when I am in fact only your servant.'

Kumiko looked at him sadly, then her eyes widened and she gave him a remarkable looking wink. 'If you carry on like this Raiko,' she said quite brusquely to her, which brought her head up quite sharply. 'My husband might not decide to have sex with you even *once* this week!'

'I would not expect so anyway mistress, certainly not on your *honeymoon*.'

'Why not if you both desire it, as it is only for pleasurable sex, Raiko, though I do feel that I may even join you both, and use some of my own skills upon each of you while we are together.'

'Do you mean a threesome?' he asked gobsmacked.

Her slim shoulders rose and fell quickly. 'I suppose so, unless any of our clan hear that we are in a city or town near to them, then you could be much busier than expected most nights still, my husband.'

He grinned at her, and Raiko. 'I think just the two of you together would be fine by me.'

Kumiko leaned over and kissed him, hard. Then he looked steadily at Raiko and tapped his lips with a finger. 'And what about you, Raiko?' he asked her. 'You also seemed to like doing that if I remember?' Then he began to wiggle a finger at her.

She actually swam over to him to do so, and when she reached him, he grabbed her and pulled her hard against him. He kissed her so hard that she felt almost faint from the lack of air in her lungs.

'That's me getting my own back on you for that afternoon after the funeral!' he announced as their lips finally parted. She sucked a great deal of air into her lungs and could do nothing but smile widely at Kumiko after it.

'Come on then,' said Kumiko, 'there's only two hours or so now to the train leaving. It won't wait for us, and we all still have to eat yet before we leave.'

They left the bath at the same time, and while Raiko dried Kumiko off, he used the drain. Then it was his turn, and after it they went to dress. Raiko as usual, and as expected, saw to her own needs last of all. Yet she still felt remarkably happy in both mind and body after doing so.

∞

The private plane belonging to Hirano Electronics left Tokyo right on time the following Wednesday evening. While two quite tearful farewells had been done. Since they had also called in at Raiko's family's home, just as he had said they would for her. And the meal at Kumiko's rural home had been a quite lavish full family affair. With all of her brothers and sisters and their children, as well as any of their nearby close relations who were invited. Which of course also involved them being there to say their goodbyes to them both too.

Even as it took off the runway, Kumiko was still waving her hand through the small window aperture to them. Not that she could see any of them standing near the same hangar, as they were just *too* far away now. And only because her eyes were distinctly misted up with tears. She was squeezing his hand so hard he thought some of the bones in it might break. Although he said nothing during it, and allowed her get over it in her own way if she could.

It had been the same pilots and stewardess as before. He of course not knowing that they were the only aircrew ever used on that particular plane. While additional crew were also being trained to do the same tasks, in case any were ever needed due to any unexpected or unforeseen problems. But at the steps outside, as they had waited for them to embark, all three had given him the same low bow as they had given to Kumiko previously. Word travelled fast in their clan it seemed, he thought. Once in flight, the very attractive and smartly attired stewardess began to do her work within the tiny galley area. Preparing meals for them all, and what drinks she had been told by their leader to provide for them on their flight back to England.

As she served them their first drinks, Douglas was studying her face very thoughtfully. 'I'm almost quite sure that I've seen you somewhere else apart from in this plane you know,' he told her.

'You have indeed, Douglas-san.'

'Where was it?'

'If you think of Sunday evening, you may just have call to remember me,' she answered.

'Ahhh, now I see.' He smiled. 'I do remember you quite well now, and you seemed to be as pleased as I was that night . . .'

Her returned smile was soft and warm in response to his. 'You pleasured me *very* much indeed that night Douglas-san, thank you.'

'Well, it's a long flight isn't it?' he said. 'And I'm also not yet even a full member of the Mile High Club yet,' he told her.

Her eyes glanced curiously at Kumiko.

Who said, 'It means that my husband has never had sex on a plane while it was in flight yet, Yuki.' She then thoughtfully added, 'But then again, my husband, neither have I in that case!'

'I have never ever thought of doing so, Douglas-san,' said the stewardess now. 'But of course, I would very much be very pleased to accept your offer this time, or at any time in the future that you wish to do so.'

They all watched with smiles beginning as he started to rub his hands together, his grin spreading all over his face as he said, 'Well now, three new members of the Club to join, eh? Or should I say four?' he said with a very flirtatious look and wink at Raiko over at the other side.

'Four does *sound* like a much better number than only three to be used by you, master,' she answered happily.

So it wasn't unexpected air pockets that caused either one of the three women during the long flight to feel their bodies rising up and down more than once to Hyde's newly found enjoyment. Just as the Mile High Club also soon had four new very happy members within it.

∞

In the week that Hyde had been away in Japan, not only Terry, but also other forces around the UK now began to think that a plague of killers had descended upon the British Isles. As one new murder was following another in a seemingly unconnected and totally haphazard way, which also gave each one of them further days of endless worry.

The grey van went from Cardiff on the A48 and then used the M5, M6, and M60 to Bradford, then back down on the M6 and M5 to Gloucester. From there it went to Bristol and Weston-Super-Mare. Leaving a trail of death behind it everywhere that it stopped that week, and it was still moving as Hyde, his wife, and Raiko finally came in to land at Newcastle.

The next two finds were in Colchester and then in Maidstone. Now, Terry finally thought he had the killer's strategy all sussed-out now. Which was that he kept to the main motorway's of the country so as to get around it quickly; even if it was done only for him to carry out his sickening tasks. The next body that was found proved his new theory utterly wrong and left him both floundering and swearing in more doubt yet again. As how the hell did he get right down to Eastbourne so fast! Then, on the first day of August he struck again at Winchester. By this stage in the hunt, Terry was not only losing his temper, he was also close to losing his mind! As for him even now it was just impossible to know where - He shook his head in a daze. Not even where, but which country he'd be in, or where and when he would strike next!

Their task seemed not only arduous, but endless at the same time. As it appeared that he was just casually driving about from England to Scotland, from Scotland to Wales, and now from Wales back to England in a way that was so utterly haphazard. That it would be damn hard for anyone to know *where* they should be looking for him. And that was even if they knew who, or what vehicle he was using, and even *where* to look for him in the first place!

Terry's own sanity was only just retained only by the knowledge that Hyde would be in the following day to take full control again. Though what he would think of the rapidly building, and completely chaotic scenes occurring in here right now, even he didn't know. As there were now two complete walls lined with crime fact boards of the killer's work. All *eighteen* of them!

∞

The plane landed at Newcastle after its long but also very enjoyable flight. Just as a quite typical dull, cloudy dawn was breaking over the UK. And Hyde couldn't very well use the same method as last time when Kumiko and her father had arrived. Which was by his Boss using his infuential position to gain the same unusual courtesies for them all again with immigration and customs control. Since he couldn't exactly call any of them VIPs, nor were they on a similar type of mercy mission as previously. So this time as they disembarked from the stairs of the aircraft. There was no car waiting to pick them up, only an electric cart with a driver. As asked for by the pilot at his own request via the airport police on duty. He could have asked Terry as a favour to do so for him. But he had then decided that due to the events which had taken place since he'd left, from what he'd heard from him. Terry had too much to do, that it would be far better just to allow him to get on with the work in hand. Not actually knowing right now, that Terry would just as happlly paid good money in order to get away from that same crime room for an hour or so.

He returned the bows of the flight crew with the same slight bow that Kumiko herself now offered to them. Unlike Raiko, who gave a similar deeper bow in return to them, as he now also knew that they were all clan servants. Then in his own way, he still shook the two men by the hand and thanked them for the good flight. And as for Yuki herself, he kissed her on both cheeks and whispered to her. *"But only until the next time we meet again I hope, Yuki".* She gave him another low bow as the three of them placed what hand baggage they were carrying on to the cart, and then climbed back onboard to arrange the usual things on it before it was parked. Hyde took the awkward backward rear facing seat on the cart for himself.

But just as they were about to pull away. A fast motorway saloon patrol car in its blue and yellow chequered livery and full set of roof lights, quickly sped up to them and halted right alongside the cart.

A uniformed figure then emerged from within it, to ask 'Detective Inspector Hyde?'

'That's me!' he said in response, wondering what was going on.

'Sergeant McMahon, sir, from our regular airport duty roster here. Chief Constable Ramshaw himself asked me to pick you up here when you arrived.'

'There's really no need, as we'll have to wait for our luggage to be cleared through anyway.'

'Again, not necessary, sir,' said the sergeant as he raised the boot of the police car. 'The Man himself also personally called through to the Airport Manager, and so to the customs people here and vouched for both you *and* your companions. This is why I am here right now, sir, to pick both yourselves *and* your luggage up at the aircraft, and to get you away from here as soon as possible.'

'And what about our passports sergeant, as I do know the immigration people won't just let any of us walk through unchecked?'

'John here will take them back to them, and then they will dropped off for you at our office in the airport, sir. We'll then see that they're all taken care of properly for you, and someone will drop them off over at HQ for you later today for you to collect them at any time there.'

'Well okay then, if it's all been sorted out like that,' he answered.

'It has, sir.'

The two pilots had heard what was being said so quickly began to unload everything again.

'Hold on a minute!' muttered the officer with a grunt. 'I can't get all of *those* in my boot!'

Hyde looked in and saw that he was right. His own duty police car had little room to spare, and this traffic one had even less. As it even held a small row of flattened portable traffic cones stacked inside, unlike his.

'Probably only get one case in here and one or two of the smaller ones on one of the rear seats at best, eh?' Hyde guessed.

'That's about it.'

'Can you radio your office to have a taxi sent round here then? An estate or mini-bus type would probably be better to fit all the rest into it.'

'I will see what I can do, sir, if you will just wait a moment,' the sergeant responded. He then leaned into the open door of the car, turned a small knob on the radio at his shoulder to increase the volume a little so that he could hear above some whining jet engines. Then spoke into it, 'Alpha Tango 9-4-1 to airport control?' Static and crackle came back at first, then a few indistinct voices.

'Alpha Tango 9-4-1 to airport control?' he tried again.

'Go ahead 'Alpha Tango 9-4-1?' a reply now came back clearly.

'Alpha Tango 9-4-1 to control, I'm over at the plane with DI Hyde right now. But as my own car can't transport all the luggage they've brought with them. He's asked if you could get an estate taxi, or mini-bus taxi to come around here to where we are to load all the rest?'

'I'll see what I can do Alpha Tango 9-4-1.'

As they stood and waited, the man identified as John on the electric cart was given their six passports and finally left with no baggage and no people on board. It was another ten minutes before they heard over the radio. That an estate type taxi had been found, and was just being allowed over to them through the security gates.

When the said taxi finally arrived at the plane, it pulled up beside the stacked pile of luggage to transport. From the passenger seat, someone from the airport in a fluorescent yellow overall climbed out. Then after giving them a wave walked over to where some other planes were on the ground.

'You wanted a taxi mate,' queried the driver as he got out and looked at the pile of luggage stood there. 'Bloody hell, I think you should've asked for a bleeding truck instead!' he moaned loudly.

'You just can't win can you, sir?' said the sergeant with a wide grin. 'Complain when they've *got* no work on, and when you do give 'em some work to do - then they do nowt *but* complain about it anyway!' The two pilots, Hyde and the sergeant brought the cases and smaller baggage over to the taxi as the driver finally got them all into the back.

'You'll be following *my* car when everything's ready, mate,' said the sergeant.

'What if I lose you though? Where the hell am I supposed to be going with these then, eh?'

'62, Gulliver Road, do you know where that is?' asked Hyde.

He jerked his head. 'Oh aye, I only live a few streets away from it in Thompson Road myself. So I can get them there no bother now.'

'Okay, then we'll either see you there when we get there, or meet up with you there if we get parted for some reason.'

'Right you are then mate, no problem.' Then he let the rear door hatch drop until it clicked shut and climbed into his taxi.

Hyde looked over at the crew from the plane. '*Arigato gozaimasu!*' he called out to them. Thank you.

'*Do itashimashite*, Hyde-san' they replied. You're welcome, Mr Hyde.

'*Dewa mata nochihodo*,' he ended with. See you later.

'*Sayonara*, Hyde-san,' they each said with a bow. Goodbye, Mr Hyde Then looked over at where Kumiko and Raiko stood and said the same and bowed again, which was returned.

The taxi just managed to stay with the police car for around two to three miles after leaving the airport, and that was it. As where the marked police car was basically shown much politeness and a general good attitude by other road users - just so they were left alone by it. The more ordinary looking taxi was basically ignored as it tried to keep up with it. So in the end he just had to give up and make his own to Hyde's house. Although even then with knowing a few short-cuts, he only arrived at most five minutes behind them. And after he'd dropped their luggage off and was paid, along with a nice tip for his trouble. He drove off, but only for another few streets further away. To where he then called in at his own home to have a short break and cup of something before going back to the airport rank.

∞

Hyde, as he had sat in the passenger seat beside the sergeant on the drive back to his home began chatting with him about his work. Asking how his regular duties at the airport compared to their more usual work on the streets. Where they were more likely to always be looking for drunk drivers, burglars or thieves, or just those who had no actual legal documents at all; No insurance cover, MOT certificate, or road tax disc.

'Same as usual sir, as you yourself know. Here, we may get illegal immigrants appearing occasionally, drunks trying to fly more often than not, and even the same car thieves trying to steal them from the long-stay car-parks. While when you are out on the roads, the normal crews contend with those who don't have the last three, and are either disqualified drivers, or typically youngsters. As well aslikely haven't even had any lessons in their life, never mind a test. Who when they *are* stopped and asked, always tell you that they're safe drivers anyway, which really doesn't account for why they're actually driving now. No test, no papers, so no licence to drive. They're just a danger on the roads to everyone else, but they just can't see that for themselves for some reason. That they're an actual liability to other road users with not being insured, but they just don't seem to care.'

Hyde nodded and said in reply, 'And there's little we can do even after catching them either, is there? Sure we can take the car they're driving away from them and impound it. Probably where it'll then end up being crushed when it's not claimed. Due to it likely costing more than the car was actually worth in the first place. They'd each likely get a driving ban for being caught. But what use is doing that to them when they've already *been* driving like that, and some of them for many years already! All they will do is to go out and buy another cheap banger and then carry on doing the very same thing with that one until they're stopped again, and so we're back to square one all over again.'

'Putting each of them away for a few years could help, I suppose. As at least it *would* get them off the roads for a while. But even I know that there's just so many of them doing it that it would fill the prisons up in no time. And anyway, it would still leave thousands more of the buggers out here that we could do little about,' said the sergeant.

'Is this one of the cases where that cat with nine tails of yours would come in handy, Douglas?' asked Kumiko from the back seat.

'Aye, something like that being used now would *soon* cut those numbers down, bonny lass!' agreed the sergeant even before Hyde could speak himself.

'Yes,' Hyde now finally added. 'I was telling my wife about the justice system of our country back in the sixties and well before then. That we've never seen so much trouble and problems since those times when capital and corporal punishment were metered out.'

'Quicker they're brought back the better eh, sir? Soon sort some of these young car thieves and worse out, wouldn't it!'

'Scare almost them all to death would be a fairer view, I'd say.'

'Too true,' agreed the driver with a wide smile. 'The penalty of having your back torn to shreds just for committing a minor crime. Would probably cut our problems now by at least three quarters.'

'I was thinking more on the lines of about ninety percent myself,' said Hyde to him.

'It's possible, sir, but highly improbable,' he said as he turned a corner, 'don't forget that druggies are *always* needing money to feed their habits. So I can't even see a threat like that stopping *them* from trying to get the money they need one way or another - though if caught *doing* something now, then *that* might just stop them from trying it again afterwards ...'

'I see what you mean, sergeant. That there's always the hardened element of criminals, isn't there? Those who will still try to find their money the easiest way possible. Rather than attempting to work for a living like ninety-nine percent of this country would always do.'

He nodded as they approached the turn off to Hyde's home. 'The criminal's we do have up here in our own patch may only be a small number. But by God they cause enough trouble for thousands more don't they, sir!'

Hyde pointed. 'Three houses past the red car on the left hand side, sergeant,' he informed him. 'And pull right up to the white garage door if you would, please, thank you?'

'Right you are, sir. By the way,' he said, 'do you know that there's a countrywide alert out for a killer?'

'Is it the same one as when I left a short while back? The one who'd killed around ten young women?'

'Ten . . . Hell, no, sir, even from what I've heard over at the airport station it's already up to eighteen now.'

'Jesus!' gasped Hyde. 'So he *is* on a killing spree now.'

The sergeant looked over at him just as the patrol car turned into the short driveway and halted in front of the garage. 'You know the case well, sir?'

'I was actually *running* the investigation until I left for a short break, sergeant. And I had hoped that he would've gone into hiding for a while and not went on a wild killing spree instead.' He sighed aloud, 'Looks like I'll have even more work cut out for me when I do go back in later to take charge again.'

'Well, the very best of luck to you, sir, that's all I can say. Apart from I hope you catch the bastard quick before he kills any more of them.' He then hastily looked back into the rear seats to apologise for his language to the two women seated there.

'We have heard far worse language than that before ourselves, sergeant. I've even used some similar choice words myself occasionally when the problem merited it,' stated Kumiko with a smile for him.

'My wife is an Inspector in her own police force in Japan, sergeant. But you may rest your fears, as I will do whatever I can to catch him,. You can count on it!' he said as he climbed out.

'Well we'll all be behind you one hundred percent to help to catch him, sir, and *you* can count on that!' he then smiled in return.

'Thanks, and thanks for picking us up, too.'

'It was no problem at all, sir, especially not if it gets you back on this job of finding him a little quicker now.'

After extracting the three suitcases from the boot and rear seat, they waved to him as he reversed and then pulled away.

CHAPTER 18

Edith, his next door neighbour had seen the police car as it had arrived next door with only as she had been looking out of her window at the time. Seeing that, she had then popped her head out of her own front door just to check who was in, or getting out of it better. And upon her seeing Douglas seated in the front seat and now opening the door. She had retreated back inside again in order to return his front door key to him.

'Hi Douglas!' she said brightly. 'Oh, hello again Kumiko, it is so *very* nice to see you back here so soon.'

'Hello Edith, keeping all right are you?' he asked her, as usual.

'Fit as a fiddle with just two strings to my bow, as always, my lovely lad,' she said as she approached them, while looking keenly at the third member of their party now.

He gave her a hug and then kissed her on the cheek as she stood before him holding out the key. More like a son would have done rather than that of just a neighbour. 'It's good to see you again, and looking so well, Edith.'

'Well I haven't had as much company to chat with since you've been away for those past two weeks, Douglas. But your friend from work, Terry, has been to see me every few days. Or when he was not able to come over - he did give me a ring to do the same. Which I know was down to you keeping an eye on me still, so thank you.'

He smiled. 'No problem as always, Edith. Have you met my wife yet?'

Edith looked shocked as Kumiko smiled at her.

'It seems that you were right then, Edith, *neh*? That we would *indeed* make a good couple when you saw us earlier?'

'What's that?' he asked.

'Oh just something Edith and I spoke about when I was here previously, my husband,' she told him.

'That's news to me . . .' he replied looking from one to the other.

'I did do a bit of dusting and hoovering for you last night, Douglas. As I knew that you would be home today or tomorrow by what your friend told me last night when he came over.' She smiled warmly at Kumiko. 'I've also left a plate on your kitchen table, just in case any of you were maybe feeling just that tiny bit peckish at all on your return, too?'

'Are there any of those scones of yours on that same plate, Edith?' Kumiko asked eagerly.

'There are *always* some of those. And as to be honest, Terry did tell me that you were married now, but not who to, Douglas. So I wasn't really as shocked as I led you to believe. Though I was really very thrilled to hear that you were, really I was. Even then, I wasn't actually sure if it *was* Kumiko who you had married or not while over there, but I had hoped it was.'

'You are very kind, Edith.'

'Nonsense Kumiko, I told you what I thought when you were here before, didn't I? So I'm feeling happy knowing that I was quite right about it now,' she said with a very warm smile at her. 'And who is this other lovely young lady, another of your younger sisters perhaps?'

'No, Edith. My other two sisters are both married with families back home. Though they have now said that they may visit us here occasionally. Along with some of my other relatives. But this is Raiko, my maid from back in Japan who agreed to come here with me. Though I'm afraid her English is very limited at the moment, as she has had to speak so little of it during her service to me over the years.'

'Years . . .' said Edith. 'From where I'm looking it looks as if she's barely just left school!'

Kumiko smiled now. 'Raiko is already twenty-one now, Edith. And she has been my maid since that time, for five years now.'

'Well I never,' she mumbled. 'She certainly doesn't look it at all. But then again you never looked thirty either when you told me how old *you* were.'

'You are being much *too* kind now, Edith.'

Edith sighed. 'I just wish I looked as good as either of you. Both in age and in shape, as your bodies are both so slim.'

'Well mine won't be for long if you keep sending round those lovely pies and pastries of yours for us, will they?' she chuckled.

'Do you want me to stop making them then?' queried the old woman.

'Good heavens no, Edith! I can barely wait to get inside and start eating a few of those that are waiting in there already now,' she answered. 'As I am afraid that both my father and I have acquired quite a taste for your baking skills now.'

'Mistress, do you wish me to go inside and start unpacking your things yet?' asked Raiko of her in their own language.

'What a sweet young thing, and so polite, too,' said Edith.

Both he and Kumiko stared fixedly at the old woman. 'You know what she just said, Edith?' he asked her.

'Of course I did,' she replied, then just remembered that the young girl had not spoken English at all.

'How?' he asked again.

She shrugged. 'I may tell you later, then again I may not, Douglas.'

She then handed over his key to him. 'But it is good to see you both back here again,' she said as she walked away back to her own house again.

'Well I'll be buggered!' Hyde stated absently.

'I take it you also did not know that she could understand Japanese, Douglas?'

'Never even gave it a thought, Kumiko. She's never told me if she could or not since we became neighbours. Then again, her late husband Bert never said anything about it to me either. That is if he even knew about it himself?'

'It does seem strange, I suppose,' admitted Kumiko. 'So, shall we all go inside now Douglas?'

'Sure,' he said, moving towards the front door. 'Do you want to see to the alarm, Kumiko?'

'No, I think we had better get Raiko here used to it as well now, I feel.'

'Good idea, you show her then, eh?'

'Very well. Follow me Raiko while I show you how to switch Douglas's house alarm system off and on.'

Hyde opened the front door and the two women stepped inside. Raiko followed Kumiko over to the small box on the wall where the small red digital numbers were already flashing its twenty seconds countdown sequence.

She showed Raiko what to do, and then said to her, '*Ichi, shi, zero, go, go, hachi,*' she told Raiko. 'His alarm system is controlled by the date of his birth, Raiko. Which over here is my husband's day born, then the month, and the final two are of the last two digits of the year.'

Raiko fed them in as the small box beeped along with the countdown. And only when she pressed the enter button at Kumiko's next words, did the display go blank and a small green light come on.

'You follow the same routine before going out and closing the door as well, Raiko. The lit button beside it . . . the red one will then appear in its place to show that it has now been re-armed.'

'Does that mean that my new master is forty-two years of age then, mistress?' she asked.

'Yes, he was forty-two on May fourteenth, Raiko.'

'He doesn't look that old, mistress.'

'I know, just around his late thirties maybe.'

'He also appears to have kept his kept his body in *extremely* good shape, too, mistress.'

Kumiko grinned. 'Of which you already know about so well, *neh*?'

'Oh yes indeed, mistress. For someone of his age he is indeed still very vigorous when it comes to having sex.'

'That you do like so much already, and will also be wishful of enjoying a great deal more of too, *neh*?'

'Oh, very much so, mistress, I'm even looking forward to each time that I do so with him now.'

'Maybe tonight we may both be lucky again, *neh*? But only if he's not too tired after going into, and then coming back from work so soon already.'

'He is not staying here with us today then? He will be leaving for work very soon now, mistress?'

'I expect so, Raiko.'

The young woman nodded. 'Then I had better go and look for his uniform to check its condition in that case, mistress. As I would judge it to be most improper for him to wear it if has not been carefully looked after and ironed; not for almost two entire long weeks now, *neh*?'

'You don't need to do that, Raiko. As Douglas wears only plain clothing while on duty, sometimes he even wore jeans while we were here last.'

'That sounds a very odd way when working in a police force, mistress. I mean how would people know that he was a policeman and be able to find him if he is dressed like that? Surely they should always be smartly dressed as you always are when you are on duty, *neh*? Just the same as that man who drove us here today?'

'They are called uniformed officers, Raiko, and they also drive around in cars like we were inside. Douglas on the other hand, uses a car that is very discreet, with no markings or lights upon it that you can see. Which I suppose is also why he dresses as he does so that he can blend in more with the ordinary public outside.'

Their conversation came to an end as Hyde entered with the three cases of luggage, just as the taxi came into the driveway with the rest of them.

'If you give Raiko the grand tour of our own humble mansion, Kumiko, I'll get the rest of your things inside and then we can have a cuppa together before I head off see what's happening at work.'

'You won't eat all Edith's baking before we get back will you?'

'No!' he said guardedly. 'There will still be a *few* things left when you come back.'

Kumiko gave a groan. 'Come on Raiko! What he means is that we must be quick or else he will leave us none of them!'

Kumiko then did give Raiko a very quick tour of the upstairs of the house. In her own attempt to get back down to the kitchen; in case true to his word, he got started on any of the freshly baked new foodstuffs now waiting there for them. As from remembering how she and her father had just kept eating them. And that was even before the home-made jam and marmalade came out. She could only assume that Douglas himself would also eat them in a quite similar quick manner as well.

The only slow part of the tour was at the two spare bedrooms. Where Kumiko had said to her that she could choose which one of them she would like to have as her own. Then showed her their bedroom and the bathroom, before almost hurrying back downstairs, saying, 'I will show you the downstairs later after we have eaten something ourselves and he has left Raiko, all right!'

And she rushed into the kitchen just in time to see a large glob of that similar delicious jam just being spread over an already cut open and liberally buttered scone. Kumiko sat down in the chair beside him, and then simply looked up at him in a patient way. Then with a smile, happily accepted the first piece that he had just prepared to eat himself. He gave a low sigh as his wife murmured many pleasure filled sounds as she tasted that half of the scone. So after coating the second half just as before, he just passed it over to Raiko. And then, finally began on one for himself.

Kumiko chewed her piece of jam coated scone with quite some vigour. Savouring the taste that she had missed for nearly two full weeks now, even as a huge blob of jam had appeared on the upper lip of her mouth after escaping from it, and Hyde leaned over and kissed it away.

She stared at him under beetling eyebrows. 'I could have reached that with my tongue easily, Douglas! You have stolen some from me now!'

He shook his head, then placed a dollop from off the knife onto the edge of his own lips, which she quickly now took back. 'Are we even now then?' he asked her.

She could only nod her reply to him, as any speech with such a large chunk of scone in her mouth was quite impossible for her to do.

'I hope that if you become pregnant you don't get a compulsion for this jam, Kumiko. As I only get about eight jars once a year off Edith, and I've only got three full ones left after this one.'

'When does she make them?' she mumbled through her full mouth, crumbs either dropping or flying from between her lips as she tried to speak.

'It depends on what amount of berries she gets given from some people around here, pet. Those who collect them for her, in return may get a few jars back, it just depends on what quantity they have offered. For this strawberry jam, she gets the strawberries from an elderly man who has quite a large allotment and greenhouse just down the street. The others, like for the blackberry and raspberry jams, depend mainly on what people might grow in their own gardens. Or if they have picked them from the various bushes that are growing wild quite near here.'

'Maybe we should all go and do this picking too then, Douglas, *neh*? I mean if it will allow Edith to make even more jars for us?' she said quickly, again losing more falling crumbs from her mouth.

'I try to do that anyway love, which is also why I usually get so many jars from her already. You see, the old man who mainly grows all of the strawberries can't get around very well now, nor can he just eat the one same type of jam all the time. So while he receives some jams made from my own blackberry and raspberry gathering. I in return also get some of his. She makes jams and preserves, all kinds of stuff from all sorts of things really, Kumiko. Just like she also makes her own wine as well. She kept that part of it going after Bert sadly passed away, as he was the home-brewer originally. You could almost say that she's almost like a small market garden what with so much to offer. She could probably evwen open up a shop and sell everything she makes every single day if she really wanted to.'

'Have you got some of those wines, too?'

'Only a couple of bottles left now, as I've become quite partial to those myself when relaxing at night after work.'

'I think that I'm going to enjoy living here with you very much indeed, my husband!' she smiled at him, her jam stained teeth then causing him to laugh merrily.

With some sadness she then asked him, 'Was what I heard in the car also true my husband? That there are now seventeen more dead women attributed to this very same murderer of my own sister, Akiko?'

'It seems like it, Kumiko. But I'll only know that when I go in soon and find out for myself.'

'And when will you be leaving?'

'Only after I have taken a quick shower and changed. As my own car is still here in the garage, so I can drive straight to work after that.'

'And what time do you think you will be coming home?'

'Maybe around five, though it could be as late as six if I get far too deeply involved with it so soon. But I'll try and give you a ring before I leave work so that you know I'm on my way back, okay.'

She gave a nod. 'That will be fine, Douglas. I still have your address on that piece of paper you wrote out for us last time. So if we do need to go out shopping, at least we should be able to find our way back here again.'

'Have you had any money changed to our currency yet?' he asked her.

When she shook her head, he pulled out his wallet from the pocket on the inside of his coat, and from it withdrew all the notes that were inside. He replied to her offered words to him after seeing the money being taken out, that she had brought her credit cards over with her. Until she could open an account over here, to then transfer some or all of her money across into it.

'I only have a hundred and ten pounds on me right now, Kumiko. So I'll give you that to use just in case you, or both of you may need something, okay. You'll need it since almost any taxi won't take credit cards, unless it's been a very long trip! For myself, I'll just stop somewhere and draw a bit more out from the cash point machine on the way into or out of work. But if you do go out and then get a taxi to bring you home, then make sure to ask him before he drives off that he knows where this house is himself. As you won't be able to direct him yet if you all get lost looking for it.'

'I will remember to do that, my husband,' she told him. Then also told Raiko so that she could remind her if need be when the time came.

Hyde went up to have a shower only after carrying all the cases upstairs. While Kumiko and Raiko followed him a few minutes later after setting the kettle to boil again for something more to drink. She showed her where he kept his clothes, trousers, long and short sleeved shirts and t-shirt's, some even totally sleeveless, and his underwear - when he wore any. Raiko watched as her mistress took a pair of dark trousers from a hanger in his wardrobe, then a light blue shirt from off another hanger at the other side. From the chest of drawers she chose a folded black cotton t-shirt, and socks of which it seemed were numerous.

'I do not know if he will wear the same jacket as he is wearing now though, Raiko. So I will not take one of them out for him. Now, while I make some tea for us to drink downstairs, and perhaps also one for my husband before he leaves. You can go in and see to drying him. If there are no towels in the bathroom then there will be some in what he calls over here, his "*airing cupboard*". At least I think that was what he called it when I was here before. It is also where he said he usually placed any of his latest ironing that he had done after washing and drying them for a while, sometimes even overnight.

As Raiko went in to see to her new master's requirements, Kumiko headed downstairs to the kitchen.

Spirit of a Dragon

∞

The first words Hyde heard as he entered the department on walking in, was from his second in command Terry, who said, 'Thank God you're back, Dougie! Though I guess you've just turned up when I'd just got everything finally sorted out!'

'Oh, well then,' said Hyde. 'If you've got everything under control here, then I can go back home again to rest after my long flight?' As he then turned to leave again.

'Hold on there you bugger!' he called out to his boss. 'When I said sorted, I didn't *mean* sorted the way you think!'

'So what did you mean then?' he asked turning to face the younger man again.

'Believe it or not Dougie, but we've had a bit of a breakthrough!'

'Have we now. Well? Come on then - Spit it out!'

'It was paint flakes Dougie; as three different coroners or pathologists found a few flakes of paint which was almost buried into the skin of three of the newer bodies.'

Hyde took a quick glance around the room. 'Still at eighteen are we? Or have any more been found already?'

'Still eighteen so far, but I guess you were right about the spree side of it, eh?'

'I wish that I hadn't been right, Terry. Anyway, what were the results of these flakes?'

'We're actually waiting for much more detailed testing being done on those, boss.'

'For their colour, as well as a make and model, I hope?'

'Under their microscopes, the pathologists, or their assistants said that the colour looked *greyish*, but that was the best they could do for us. That's why they've all been sent to specialist laboratories. Who through their own testing equipment may be able to tell us what the paint make up in them actually is. Not only to give us the true colour of the vehicle being used but possibly also its make and model, too. Maybe even the year itself if we're extremely lucky! But that can only happen when they have their findings, and by speaking to the various car manufacturers.'

'So we're waiting for them to get back to us. Is there anything else helping us out yet, like as in what about the flask that was found?'

'We did get quite a few fingerprints from it, but sadly we found out that they only came from some of the women we already knew about. Apart from that, and the positive results of what residue had been inside it, nothing else has come in to help so far.'

'So what have you done since hearing that?'

'Nothing yet, we're still collating everything from all the victims, Dougie. We've even had to take over department M4's room next door.'

'Why? Don't we have enough space in here still?'

'The Boss was down.'

'*What, again?*' said Hyde in wonder.

'He's been down a few times while you were away, Dougie. And when I told him about your idea to use the Crimewatch programme on television, but only when you had more facts for us to use. He said that we'd better have a bit extra room in place ready to handle any of those calls as they were coming in. So he allocated M4's office to us.'

Hyde slowly nodded. 'And who will be in there taking the calls?'

'Mostly some of us from here in our department, as we are going to work odd shifts during and after the programme when its shown. Though he did mention that he'd try to give us a few more extra bodies just to help us out for a while, too.'

'Okay. So until we get some word back about the paint itself, or the make of vehicle, we'll just have to wait now, I guess. Do me a favour will you Terry, Run me off a comparison report so that I can go through the details of all these murders myself.'

Terry grinned. 'I've already done it boss, since I knew you'd be back soon. It's already over there on your desk waiting for you.'

Spirit of a Dragon

'Smart arse!' he said as he then went over to it.

Terry smiled widely. As it certainly did feel *so good* to have him back in the saddle again. In the room, it even felt as if a new lease or breath of life had come to them all now at his return. Although even Terry knew it was nothing to do with him personally while in charge, as he was just a novice leader compared to Douglas. But, they already all knew about Douglas's skills and capabilities over recent times. He simply had an air of superb control about him; something which always made you feel as if he was never in doubt himself with any decision.

Terry knew he was still learning these qualities and technicalities, even now. Learning slowly but surely was how he stated his own case for it. While at the opposite end of the scale was Jenkins. And when he came to take over, it appeared as if he had gained none of that same level of skilled experience from all of the years behind him. His own particular summary and opinion in the matter of it all was; that even if Douglas could not be called a teacher in the widest sense. He was certainly always learning from him the variety of ways to think things through. To work yet more out in his own head of what was what in each case as it happened. That both he and the team around him, thought of him more like as being something of a savant in looking through the eyes, and into the brain of any particular criminal to be caught.

Any enquiry they were typically delegated to work on needed a good, strong, and natural leader to do it. Not a by guess and by God one. But one who had an apparent natural talent for the work. And Hyde was certainly one of those people who was just like that – and *could* do it with his hands tied behind his back. That was what they all knew after a few years working together. Simply put, he was a natural for the job, and his earlier successes had shown his aptness for it.

For nearly four straight hours as the rest of those in the same office moved around him. Hyde, as he usually always did. He carefully scrutinised every detail of each and every report that Terry had placed on his desk ready for him to peruse. Some of them occasionally cast an eye, or turned their heads to watch as his right hand moved over to a pad beside him. As he scribbled something else down on it as an idea, or maybe even just as a thought came to him from what he was reading. Which may come to nothing anyway, that they knew. But he did just appear to have one of those deeply scrutinising, analytical minds. One that could pick out almost insignificant details which others had already seen and missed. This was also one of the reasons why they were all so glad he was back in charge again.

At four-thirty, a request came for him to report to Ramshaw's office upstairs, through a uniformed messenger appearing in their office. At which to its deliverer, the entire room as a combined unit emitted a low "Oooooo!" altogether.

'Shut up and get on with your work you idle bunch!' Hyde chuckled back. Their heads turned to do just that, but the grins on their faces remained as he picked up the pad he'd just been scribbling on and left.

∞

'Good to have you back, Hyde. Sit yourself down lad. How's married life treating you already? I've got all of your passports here for you to collect, too? What's happening downstairs right now?' asked his Boss. But all fired at him so quickly that Hyde couldn't get a word in edgeways until he stopped.

'Thank you, sir. It's fine right now. Kumiko's maid came with her, and I've noted down what can be done if you don't mind giving me a few minutes of your time?'

'Not at all, glad to help if I can. Fire away!' said his superior. As he then leaned back in his chair to listen. As Hyde outlined what he thought was happening, what he expected to happen next. And lastly what they could possibly do about certain things, all being dependant really on what the results were when they finally came back from the flakes of paint which had been discovered.

'So, it's really all down to those three tiny bits of paint at the moment so far then, isn't it?' said Ramshaw thoughtfully.

Hyde nodded. 'That's dead right, sir. If they all match up as being from the same vehicle, and this specialist place can even give us a make and year of vehicle at least from the colour. Then we can get a full record from the DVLA in Swansea of who owns such vehicles. That would be our starting position after that. Narrowing it down from what we already know by where it has been used in the past few weeks, or months at a push.

'Which I must say will be very hard going indeed, as every force in the country will have to help out now. In order to narrow down the field of possible suspects in their own perspective areas. But, if the results can show up an actual model type that used it, along with the correct colour and year, then we do have a very good chance of finding it far more quickly than without.'

The tips of Ramshaw's fingers on his left hand were beating a slow rhythm on his desk as he listened to the man before him. Who by his actually starting this enquiry off in the first place, was now in sole charge of the entire investigation. And of one which now stretched throughout the whole of the United Kingdom. He had wondered at the time when he'd first heard the news telephoned to him by the Police Commissioner from London. Whether Hyde *could* actually handle such a complicated issue like this himself, or if he should place a far more experience Inspector or Chief Inspector in charge of the entire investigation instead.

As Ramshaw also knew that if Hyde coped well under the arduous circumstances that he had now found himself under; and with a bit of luck actually caught the person involved. Then his rise to Chief Inspector wouldn't be long in following either. Indeed, it would be less than most would expect from solving such a brutal case as this was. And Ramshaw knew that he was already due for such a promotion very soon after his previous good work anyway. As these very same assessments, which were for any candidates for the purpose of being promoted were already being asked for by those at a higher level in the force. Including from their own Divisional Chief Constables.

But even he knew that it always depended on how many vacancies there actually were to fill each time. Depending sometimes upon retirement's or ill health, possible transfers to other areas. Or just through those Chief Inspector's themselves who would soon be gaining further promotion. Ramshaw had three possible candidates to put forward from his own division, with Hyde being one of them anyway. So he knew that this case could well be the making or even the breaking of his career and future promotion here and now.

'I'll go along with what you said,' he told Hyde after some study. 'If the results from the paint flakes are positive enough for us to use, then I'll see about getting an urgent spot on Crimewatch for you as soon I can.'

'Thank you, sir, although I'm quite sure that *I* don't need to be the one to go on the show.'

'Oh yes you do, my lad. As you're the one in overall charge of the full investigation right now. But don't worry about it, Hyde. You do have a way with you that the public will find comforting. So I think that they will be trying even harder to aid you when you do ask for their help.'

'Well, if you say so, I suppose, sir,' he responded, not that happy at all about having to be seen on National television himself; as it really just wasn't about who he was.

'Well I *do* say so, Hyde. Have you never watched the programme yourself? It's nearly always the person leading the current investigation who gives out what details can be allowed to the public. As he *should* be the one who is most up to date with all that is going on anyway - otherwise someone junior doing it could just let slip *something* or other that shouldn't really be known to anyone outside of our force. And a mistake giving tip like that could change the whole balance of things, Hyde. We may then be helping the *killer* out instead of ourselves with doing that! Do you see what I mean?'

Hyde nodded. It looked as if he *would* actually have to do it himself now. There seemed to be no way around it.

'One other thing while you *are* here, Hyde.'

'Yes sir?'

'I've been informed from London that your new wife has been seconded to us from the Tokyo Police. For two months at least, at the moment, to work with you up here.'

'She has?'

And he had looked more astonished at Ramshaw's words than how he had felt himself when hearing of it.

'She has indeed, Hyde. So I want to see her in here at nine sharp tomorrow morning to advise her personally upon what she can, and to what she cannot do while she is seconded to us. You yourself must also remember that she is not a member of our own Police Force either. And as such, she has also not sworn to defend the lives and properties of the Queen's subjects like we have all done. I won't mind if she goes wherever you go in your role as a detective, Hyde. But she cannot arrest someone herself formally over here. Athough she can of course use her experience to arrest someone just as one of the general public are allowed to by means of a citizen's arrest.'

'I will explain all this to her when I go home, sir. And I will also make her aware that she is to see you at nine on the dot tomorrow morning.'

'All right, Hyde. We know what we're up against here right now. So just do what you can to keep things ticking over downstairs as sweetly as possible until the paint result comes in.'

'I'll do just that, sir.'

Ramshaw nodded to him. 'Right then, off you go then and look after your department now.'

∞

The two women's shopping trip had taken them to almost the exact same area of stores and supermarkets as those when Kumiko and her father were last here for foodstuffs. Though they did also wander into a few of the other shops on their look around, and by using one of her own four credit cards, she was even able to purchase some new jeans, t-shirts, shorts, and trainers for them both. Already knowing of course that whatever she bought for Raiko to use personally. She could soon claim back through their servant procurement team of accountants who worked within their clan. Or that Raiko herself would pay her back for them herself.

As the four people that ran that part of it daily for the clan, had literally thousands of servants to pay wages to each month. As well as to oversee their general welfare, whether it be in the way of feeding or clothing them if they worked in a specialised area. Or if any kind of personal health care was required for any one of them. It was basically, a huge widely tasked amount of work involved with it. But one that had been very well and dutifully managed over a great length of time now.

Their return was easier than expected for them, as she had taken a business card from the taxi driver when he had arrived at the house to pick them up. So, she just used her mobile to ring him back up, and for them to be collected again and be taken home. And since he already knew the way to her new home, she was quite happy to do it that way.

Kumiko was out relaxing in one of the bamboo chairs in the garden while Raiko prepared their meals, when Hyde arrived back home. He had waited until five, but with no word having been sent back from the specialist lab, he decided to call it a day. He was home by five-thirty, a little later than he thought due to having been caught up in some of the late rush hour traffic.

Entering the kitchen first after leaving his car in the garage, he found Raiko stirring around the inside of a pot on the stove. He came up beside her and placed an arm around her shoulder, then lowered his head towards the large pot to have a sniff at the aroma of it.

'What is it, Raiko? As it smells lovely?' he asked her in Japanese.

'A seafood stew my mistress sometimes likes, master.'

'Is there enough for me in there as well?'

'But of course, master.'

He turned his head and kissed her full on the lips. 'Good evening, Raiko.'

'Good evening to you also, my master. My mistress was becoming worried about you since you had not called us here yet.'

'Damn, I forgot about that, Raiko,' he told her. 'Just shows how unused to being a married man I still am, eh?' He grinned at her.

'My mistress was previously sitting out in the garden relaxing while awaiting your return, master.' He nodded, kissed her on the lips just as pleasantly again and then left.

Kumiko was quietly humming to herself as she sat in the garden on the chair, enjoying the sheer tranquillity of it as she sat there among the wonderful smells and aromas. As well as the soothing, peaceful, view of it, whenever she decided to look that is. A shadow passed over her closed eyes and then she felt a pair of firm lips press against her own, that she responded to quickly.

After they had parted, he moved around to face her, squatting on his haunches with his arms resting on her thighs. He tutted at her, then said, 'You are quite shameless woman! You didn't even look at who was kissing you there - It could have been the milkman, or anyone!'

Her smile was wide. 'I know your kisses very well already now, Douglas, so I knew that it was you who was doing so to me. And no one would have got past Raiko to come through the house anyway, my love.'

'Your seducer may have come over the back fence after seeing your desirable body just sitting relaxing here, my girl, and not through the front door,' he answered, as she now stretched and yawned, then leaned forward to return his initial kiss to her.

'How was your work today?'

'You'll find that out yourself when you come in tomorrow yourself?'

'And why do I need to go in there tomorrow, Douglas?'

'Because I think your father's been up to his tricks, Kumiko, that's why. The Boss told me this afternoon that he'd received a call from London, to say that you have been seconded to our division here for a few months, and, also even into my very own department, dear lady.'

'I had hoped for that to happen after a little while, my husband. But with not knowing if it *was* actually possible or not to do, or to choose which area you wished to be in. So I thought it not worth mentioning just in case it never happened.'

'Okay, I'll go along with you on that. Anyway, the Boss told me today that he wanted to see you at nine sharp tomorrow morning in his office, Kumiko. So it does appear that your secondment to us is complete for the time being. Though how the hell you managed to do it like that is--- Yoshi! The man I met at the plane after we landed in Japan. He was the one who managed to arrange it for you, wasn't he?' he asked her just as a question.

She nodded. 'As he works in our government over there he is able to pull certain strings for us occasionally, which also does have a few advantages for our clan in other ways too.'

'He's a clan member just helping the clan out then due to where his position lies, is that it?'

She nodded again. 'He is a very honest and resourceful man on the various occasions that we may need to use his skills. You must also remember though, that from where he is based for us, his knowledge of who to contact about different things can also help us out enormously sometimes.'

'Well, you're in with us now. And after you have met the Boss tomorrow I'll take you down to meet the seven members of my team that I have.'

'Of which this Terry-san of yours is one of them, yes?'

'Yes, he's second-in-command to me within the department, Kumiko.'

She chuckled. 'I can still picture him speaking with me on your telephone while you were plunging your happy shaft deep into Hisako!'

'Give over woman!' he grunted. 'If I've told you once, I've told you ten or more times already now. Which is to stop talking about sex so much when I'm near you; as just thinking about only a *few* of those nights spent in Japan always gives me quite a quick erection now.'

'Then I hope you will have one later as Raiko and myself are both hoping to enjoy it with you tonight . . . '

'Separately you mean?' he asked.

Her mouth widened in a warm smile. 'Oh no my husband, we shall all be *together*, of course!'

He emitted a low sigh. As it seemed as if yet another night of hard work lay ahead of him - again . . .

CHAPTER 19

After their meal together, which Hyde found delicious both to his nose and   taste buds alike. They retired to the living room to relax for the evening while Raiko now began to clean up. She replying to him that she did *not* require any help *whatsoever* when he had offered to do so. And stating quite firmly that it wasn't his place to even *ask* her about such things as that now. That it was *her* duty to see to anything that needed doing within the house, and that she was *quite* capable to do so by herself. He had left the kitchen suitably admonished with a widely grinning Kumiko.

'Do not worry, my husband,' she chuckled sweetly, and then whispered, 'on more than one occasion since employing Raiko. I myself have been suitably told off by her in the very same way too!'

As he flopped into one of the two large armchairs and lay back, the footrest emerged from beneath him at the front and rose to support his lower legs. He sighed in an immense state of happiness. While Kumiko stood in front of his bookshelf to see what he had on offer for her to read. She could see that he had quite a few large collections of paperbacks by some highly acclaimed authors like James, and Frank Herbert, Clive Cussler and Alexander Kent, the latter ones having a row of possibly between ten or twenty in very one long line. And some were there with only a few books in a united row, like, Patrick Robinson, Marc Olden and Alan Evans. One writer that she had heard of herself stood close to hand,

James Clavell, of which she saw six of these were quite thick, and one, named King Rat, was small by comparison to them. Though she had recognised one book immediately by the title name of it, *Shogun*, as even she had seen the serialised and dubbed television film of it at home.

The James Herriot line of books about the life of a country veterninarian she saw were almost like old friends to her, As even she had read and loved many of them when much younger. Though her husband appeared to have far more of them in his row of books here, than what she had ever had read herself at home on his shelf. So it was a collection that she *would* happily now read all over again.

She bent down to now look at the shelves below, ones that she wasn't able to see when standing, and then decided just to kneel instead. More authors' names came out to meet her eyes from that level. Some that she had heard of and others that again, she had not, with the likes of single books by Graham Masterton called The Manitou, and Richard Herman Jnr's being entitled Mosquito Run. And then appearing to lean quite tiredly against those two was a book by Richard Cox. That going off its warped shape, seemed to have been well thumbed through over many years, by the name of SAM 7. Not that she knew that of those latter two, the first one had parts with the SAS in the story, and that the second was a story based around the police in London during a terrorist threat and an aeroplane crash.

'So of the books you have here, what do their writers actually write stories about. Apart from your one called *Shogun,* and the many James Herriot ones? only as I've already read quite a few of his books back home when I was just a young girl.'

He climbed out from the chair, and helped her to her feet with his hand. He pointed some of them out to her. 'The Alexander Kent row here starts with, and is a kind of maritime sea saga about a young boy, slowly maturing into a young man. And then as he grows into adulthood and then middle-age; it takes place back in the days of wooden sailing ships and before and after the Revolution with America.' He then pointed at a row of three others. 'Patrick Robinson's another like that but mainly deals with modern thrillers about submarines and American SEAL's. Really both of them are like war stories written about the sea.'

'James Herbert is my favourite thriller writer though. While I read Clive Cussler just for the different types of adventures he writes. I think you would like those by Marc Olden yourself though, Kumiko.' He grinned at her then.

'Why?' she asked cautiously, looking at him, and then at the only two books there on display by the writer he had pointed out to her on the shelf.

'Because, it seems that he usually likes writing stories about ninja's, just like you, my love.'

'And you now, my love.' She smiled back.

'But I'm not a full one, sweetheart, only a novice ninja at best when compared to you,' he said with a low chuckle.

She gave him a gentle punch on the arm for his sarcasm. 'In time, and with the right training my love, you will soon know everything that I do. And with your own record, will then be well above me.'

'How can that possibly be?'

'Because you have killed before, my love, while I have not.'

'So what, killing isn't a great thing really you know. It's only what I had to do at the time. And even your father told me that not many of you have actually had to do much of that for many decades now, have you?'

'What you have said is true, Douglas. Though I have told you that we must always *be* ready for if the call does come . . . if ever. As that is what we have all *been* trained for in this life! And until then, I myself and others will train you in all of our ways as best we can, with much sex being involved to teach you in those ways, too. Raiko will also be happy to help you with *that* part of your training I'm sure!'

He tried to change the subject of sex quickly. 'All right, but what kinds of books or films do you personally like to read or watch then?'

'Well I do like some thrillers and action style books, as long as there is a good bit of romance or just plenty of sex in them.'

'Good grief, why is that?'

'Because until I met you I'd never *had* sex of course. So until then, the best I could do before that night here was to either read about it, or watch it.'

'On a video film or television you mean?'

'We have sex videos of course, but they are really just for the older children to watch and to amuse them sometimes. The same reason my father had our country's own pay as you view sex channel for us to watch. If we, or anyone ever wished to, by using the satellite dish for us. But most of what sex I have seen is by what I've watched happening in our own house since I was a young girl.'

'You have to be kidding me!'

'Of course not, Douglas, I only speak the truth to you. I've watched both my married sisters enjoy themselves many times with men there. As well as my father, mother, and brothers; well, all except Kazuo as he was unmarried like me. But now he can also sample the same delights as we have due to my father's new laws too now, *neh*?'

'I suppose so. But it just sounded strange to hear that *that* was how you actually first learned about sex.'

'It is the usual way for the children in our clan to learn about it so early, Douglas. Though as you now know, what *was* learned by us could not actually be truly enjoyed until marriage. So how did you learn about sex?' she then asked.

'As a youngster I was like all the rest of the children over here, I guess. A young boy who wanted to know what a girl's got, against a young girl wanted to see what I had. So before too long we just gave each other a good look at what we both had.'

'That is a very strange, and I must admit, *unusual* way of learning about sex to me, I'm afraid,' she answered sadly. 'As not to grow up in a house where such sexual freedom occurs must be difficult for everyone but us, Douglas. Just think that while your children over here are doing that, we have already watched sex happening not only on television, but also in the flesh too. So of course this is why we have never had any such worries over seeing naked bodies, or couples performing together, or even being part of one. As I have already been so with you in our family home, and then with Raiko on our honeymoon trip, and lastly in the plane on our way here.

'To us you see, we must actually begin to learn, or be taught about sex at an early age. More as a means of good knowledge for our clan's children than anything else really. And also because it was taught to us that we could watch it as much as we liked, but could in no way do those very same things until we were married. So perhaps this is why our own ways work so well, while everyone else have such hang-ups about their bodies, or even sex. A thing which causes so many problems in the world these days, *neh*?'

He thought over her point and found somewhat quite unexpectedly, that it actually made some kind of sense to him. As the way that they had been taught about sex, was usually just so vague as to be almost worthless in all reality. In fact it was stupid when he thought about it now. Since even young children here in this country, could actually watch animals on most nature programmes on television regularly humping away at each other openly. Yet that was only if their parents didn't turn the channel over, or shoo them out of the room, of course. But when it then came down to *humans* having sex together, the thought of allowing children to see that in the same way was an almost abhorrent thought to every adult.

Yet they all knew that it was only a basic need as in nature itself, as where animals typically mated only to provide more of the same species. Humans, and occasionally some other mammals it must be said, had since evolved to use sex also in the way of pleasure. As well as just as to the usual means for reproduction or procreation. His wife's way of looking at it was definitely the right one. But still, he just couldn't accept it right now, or ever imagine it ever becoming the same way of teaching in the wider world. The thought of a couple of sex education teachers humping away on a desk or table in front of their class of children at school. Only so as to *show* them, *exactly*, what it was all about caused him to laugh out loud. So he had to tell her what he was laughing at when he eventually ceased.

'And that, is the real problem facing every youngster all over the known world today, my husband,' she stated. 'Except for those wo may be abducted, and who are then forced into – or sometimes just sold into prostitution by their parents or whatever. Only in order for the rest of them to be able to survive themselves in some cases. The children these days basically know so little - or literally, nothing at all about what the act of sex really *is*, or what it should be about. So of course, when they do become old enough to begin to become more interested about it. And then start and *think* about what this, *so very secretive thing is*. Which as we know, most adults definitely will not tell them about it completely and honestly. Is also about the same time when two young people then just decide to *try it* in order to see what all of that fuss *was* about.

'That, is likely also the true reason now why you end up with so many young children actually now *having* children of their own when they are still far too young. It is mainly *because* they have not been given the correct information regarding it in the first place by these so-called adults. As it can only be the adults who are at fault. Why is this you may well ask? Well, they are ones who are supposedly there to give them any such basic fundamental knowledge and guidance towards that very learning. And that is also why the percentages of young people with sexually transmitted diseases are forever increasing too. And all because none of them appear not to know any better themselves, Douglas!

'Just think of other subjects which are taught in a typical school curriculum, husband. English, history, chemistry, and so on and so forth. If these very same subjects were taught and explained in the same way as sex is. Then what you would learn about all of these other topics could be biased, meagre or very sparse in detail. Possibly even being completely hopeless to an extreme. All of their minds would be filled with the exact same information as each other. Hence, leading to them basically becoming robots with no additional knowledge included in their mind-set. No initiative, no personal drive, no imagination . . . Now that would be a boring existence for anyone!'

She was spot-on yet again. As he'd heard just recently on the television or radio for himself just a short while ago, that underage sex was increasing in the UK all the time. And from what he could recall, he was sure that it had been an eleven-year-old girl who had just had a baby last time to the barely older father of it. All likely due to that same lack of awareness or knowledge. And this was happening in so many other countries around the world as well, and not just the UK.

Only in families who rigidly regarded sex outside marriage as a sin. Being labelled as a basic kind of evil on earth within their religion, were where such things rarely happened. But Kumiko's clan, or those also in *his* clan, as he should now say, was where basic sex, and in both graphic and detailed live forms when carried out. Had actually been openly watched as it took place by these same young children. And yet not one of them had ever broken their own laws to do it. Until they themselves were finally married to a partner. To him as he thought about it all now, it just showed who had the right ideas about the teaching structures of sex. And it was them.

Spirit of a Dragon

'I guess you're dead right, love. The way that you have all continually taught it to your children over generations, I think, must be the right way. Especially if those who are being taught it in that way, still also held back their virginities for a far longer time, or as you stated, when their marriage finally took place. While our own kind of almost Victorian way of doing it has been quite useless.'

She nodded to him. 'Even I who have only enjoyed true sex from the age of thirty with only you have not really missed out on it, my husband. As I still also had my career to enjoy while I patiently hoped and waited to become married. Yet *because* I was always able to watch such simple acts of sex for pleasure, and at times even for love taking place. I always knew – well, I *hoped*. That one day, I myself would enjoy those same feelings that I was seeing before me. Which would be to experience both the ordinary pleasures which can be found from it. To the far deeper intimacy that can be shared between a true loving couple while others openly watched them. And of course, what more fun it could also be to share together when completely alone too.

'This is why we are also not so prudish about our bodies, my husband. In this way old and young alike can see each other for what we really are. For the old, it is what some may all miss and wish to return to being once more; And as for the young, they can see what their own bodies will end up looking like in the upcoming distant years that lie well ahead of them. The very young of both sexes under eight or nine, can clearly see what puberty actually does and causes to happen to those who are only a little older than they are. So they will also have advance knowledge of it, and *know* already of what will happen to their own bodies quite soon. From the breasts that will sprout from the chests on the young girls and her pubic hair below. As well as to the enlarging of a young boy's penis and the hair that will be appearing around it, with his testicles finally emerging fully as their puberty beckons.

'And we also fully approve of personal masturbation anyway you know, husband. Either done alone or with someone else. Just so that we can all learn to enjoy our bodies in the correct way. As sometimes we are taught how to do so, without any fear or recrimination, or additional worries of scorn or shame being thrown back at us, simply for trying to do so. As not only young people always have this basic need to explore not only themselves, but also that of the other sex, my husband. Even I from a young age have constantly used masturbation as a means of keeping myself happy in all the years that I was without a partner and husband. And what way is better to learn this, than from someone who will actually teach you how you can please yourself if you do not already know . . .

'Take yourself for instance, husband. If as a young boy or girl, would you rather be *shown* by someone more experienced. Of *how* something should be performed correctly to give yourself what stimulation, and pleasure, you may desire to reach a certain point? Or to hide away in an unlocked bedroom or bathroom alone, while trying to find these things out all on your own? Literally scared to death that someone will come in and catch you while you *are* doing, what they'd say is such a despicably vile thing to your *own* body? And that is my actual point, my husband. As it is *your* body to do with it as and when you please, and no one else's. So why should what you do with it bother anyone else?

'As you yourself know, the rooms in our family home are quite open and easily moved through, *neh*?' He gave a nod to her. 'Well when we were all younger we occasionally walked through each other's bedrooms, as we all still do even now with very little thought. I did this many times and saw either my sister or brothers masturbating themselves, just as they sometimes saw me.'

'Did it not even shock you to see them?' he muttered.

'Of course not, husband, why should it? Have you not been listening to what I have been saying to you? Or is all my talking about sex making you horny again and you have lost all thought now?' she asked, then placed a hand at his groin. 'Ah, I see,' she giggled sweetly, 'well, I'll see to *that* very problem you have in just a moment for you, my husband.'

She said that with another smile, and then continued, 'We were actually encouraged to watch and help each other out if we also wished to do so even at that age. So I sat and watched each of my brothers as they played with their erections, just as they have sat and watched their sisters do the same with their vaginas.'

'You aren't going to tell me that---'

'Certainly,' she interrupted him. 'As children we played with each other quite openly. Even together a few times to help each other with new ways that we thought we'd just thought of. And we were not always alone when we did this, my husband. As often other children of our clan would be there with us, or we would go over to their homes now and then also.

Spirit of a Dragon

'More often than not, any of our parents, relatives, busy servants and whoever else also passed through at unexpected times too. Just as it may have been like in your own youth, it was all a matter of simple experimentation for us; though as you now see, for us it was much better. As where in your own life as a child, it would have been considered filthy, disgusting, and likely also being a very, very, unnatural thing for you even to be thinking to be doing. Whereas in our own lives, it was actually encouraged to be done for our main need to learn, and so, it soon felt quite natural to do.'

She pressed a stiff finger into his groin, and with a sigh, he felt his erection subside instantly. She lifted up on to her toes and kissed him. 'How do you think we were able to learn things such as that? You do not know how to do these things as yet until you are taught But I have already told you that our training began at around five years of age, give or take an extra year or two, didn't I?'

'Aye, I remember that part.'

She pressed him again and his new erection smacked against his trouser leg. 'I had learned *how* to do this to a young boy, or man even, by the time I reached puberty at the age of eleven, my love. And as I practised my finger techniques on giving and taking away erections from them as well as other things to excite them; as well as also being able to make them ejaculate immediately from another point and by other means too. They had to use my own body as an aid to learn where similar pressure would also not only cause arousal, but even to give me an orgasm only from a similar type of touch. Including a variety of other ways that would also excite my body into a heightened state, too! But only from when I was old enough to achieve one.

'Since as you already know, full sex of *any* kind was certainly forbidden and not allowed in any form at all for young novice servants or members. So even though our unmarried men and women may not have had sex before and were still virgins. They could still please each other in so many various ways. That it did not ever need to involve total penetration occurring between them to take place. Since there are many more ways than just having full sex to achieve pleasure!

'And until I finally reached my full training at nineteen, and received my own tattoo like the one which you also now have. I have had to learn so many sexual techniques, that I will now also have to begin to teach you these over time. It is going to involve you having to learn a great deal about the various muscle and nerve groups that all lie within the human body.'

'I can't wait to start and learn all of these things if it will make our sex life even better for you, Kumiko.'

'It was also be a great deal better for you too, my love. Be sure of it. As we will be able to please each other in so many more ways than we can now. And not only before, but also *while,* and then even after we have had sex. Enjoying them all fully could then make it last for as long as ten or more hours.'

'Now that *is* something to look forward to!' he told her.

∞

After a few hours, of which Hyde lay on the chair and Kumiko decided to just lie upon him, to be as close to him as possible while they watched some television together. Raiko arrived with a cup of tea for each of them, and then used the other unused large chair to great measure, although she appeared even tinier when stretched out upon it only by herself.

At close to nine-thirty after the BBC News had finished. Which he'd now began watching ever since the murders had begun to take place. Really, that was only in case of any newer developments happening somewhere else in the country while he wasn't at work. After that, and with nothing new to concern him, it was soon time to bathe before their last meal and retiring, so he asked them both to come upstairs with him.

They followed him in their bare feet, since they didn't wear any similar kind of slippers as he did on their feet when back home. And his floors were carpeted, unlike their own, so that was also easier for them. As they'd been more used to only wearing a kind of old fashioned style of clog. While he as usual had ever only worn his slippers after work at home; even after staying in Japan it was still an almost everyday thing for him to do without concious thought.

'I've got something to show both of you upstairs now,' he said as they all went up the staircase.

Kumiko smiled at her maid. 'Now I have been waiting to hear you say that for many hours already, my husband. How about you, Raiko?'

'Oh yes, mistress, I have been waiting ever since we arrived at the house to hear *those* words being spoken by, my master!'

'You two must have sex on the brain!' he said from in front of them.

'You mean you are not taking up us here for a good long while of lustful sex?' she asked, and saw his head shaking before her. She sighed, 'What a waste of both our desperate bodies this climb is going to be then . . .'

'I'm actually going to show you something now which you've both never seen before!'

'I've never seen your tongue anywhere near my vagina yet, my love. Or near Raiko's either for that matter?'

'God help me,' he groaned, 'you two women and your ever continual lust for more sex!'

'It is only because we both really like having sex with you so much, my husband,' she also then happily added, 'and of course such enjoyment also benefits towards the health of all our bodies too! Is that not so Raiko?'

'Oh yes mistress that is so true, and very much so?'

'Stop all of this sex talk and just come with me for a moment, okay?'

'Only as long as it will not take long, so that we can all have some sex together with you short---'

She was cut off abruptly by him. 'Kumiko, pack it in will you,' he said becoming a little short with her as he reached the landing upstairs. He turned to them both as they joined him. 'Look, I will give you both a good shagging soon enough, okay? I just wanted to show you something in the house that no one else knows about or has ever seen before except me.'

'Very well, my husband, since the enjoyment of our having sex tonight is now certainly assured with you. I am all ears to what this secret of yours now is.'

'Well thank the Lord for that!' he said.

They watched as he gave a small jump and caught a very small loop that hung from the ceiling. As he came back down, so did quite a wide door following him, and then they both watched as a metal counterbalanced ladder slowly slid down through it until it rested on the floor.

'Come on . . .' he said to them as he began to climb.

'Why are we going up here, mistress?' she whispered at her.

'Maybe my husband has a hidden sex den up here, Raiko!' she answered in the same soft way, hearing her maid elicit a low gasp.

They followed him up the wide rungs of the ladder, though it was far more comfortable for him in his slippers than it was for their bare feet on the cold metal. He waited until they had both climbed up to him, and they all now stood in the semi-darkness of his attic. An attic which was dim inside only because the sun had already began setting by this time, and any moonlight there could have been, was little or none at all right now. This didn't really matter much anyway, because soon enough his knowing fingers touched the switch that suddenly bathed the entire floor in a warm glow.

They just stood looking at it, as it *was* almost like a secret lair they had now discovered and had been brought into. And if as he had said no one else knew about it, then he must have done all of this himself.

'Is this your real training area then, my husband?' she asked him.

'Aye, it's where I keep myself in shape I guess you could say. Only I couldn't use any of it when you and your father were here, or else you may have heard me doing it up here.'

Kumiko went for a walk around his large attic now with Raiko. The only barrier being the large, central, and very thick roof joist's that held up the weight of the roof and almost halved it in the middle. On the side where they were now at, there was a heavy looking punch bag hung, as well as a ball like one that stood affixed to a pole. Another was attached to a vertical board and was stood out via a strut, and then hung beneath it. There was a wooden dummy with quite a few knives sticking out of it, so they assumed that it must be used for that purpose.

And then yet another wooden dummy, though she could tell that it could revolve from its smaller spindle on the base. Though she knew what this was with its many thick pieces of wood jutting out all over it in various lengths and angles. It was for him to practice his own martial arts against. Not only to toughen up his arms, hands, legs and feet, but also to use while he practiced his attacking and defending moves against it. Kumiko was very impressed. Until she went to look over at the other side of the wooden barrier, and then quickly called her maid over to see as well. As he even had a number of thick cushioned mats laid out for using to practice his falls on.

Kumiko pointed to them. 'These will be certainly be being used quite a lot now in your coming future, my husband. As both Raiko and I can both help to teach you new styles and such like on this. Just as your own servant will be able to help you when they arrive too.'

'My servant, Kumiko? Why on earth do I need my own servant when we have our wonderful Raiko here already?' he asked her worriedly.

'Because, my love, it is usual for each adult member in any house to have their own personal servant so as to see to their own needs. I contacted my father about it this very afternoon while you were at work to ask this, and he agreed wholeheartedly. In fact he felt a little ashamed of not having remembered to make the actual offer to provide you with a choice of one, especially after your clan tattoo had been given to you back in Japan. If he had done so, then your own personal servant could just as easily have travelled back with us here on the same flight, and so would then have been here in order to begin their duty to you already.'

'A choice, do you mean you are allowed to choose a servant?'

'But of course. He is going to have our servant bureau send what details and pictures they have of any servants not in use who are waiting for personal work on their books at the present moment. Perhaps even some of those who are wishful only to have a change of master or mistress, or both for a while. They may well be added too now, seeing as we're now a married couple. There are actually both male and female servants in our clan, husband. Though my father will tell them to send only the female availablilities to you.

'You must understand this though, my love. I do not *own* my maid Raiko here. So, if she ever wishes to leave my service then I cannot stop her. Just as if she ever did something unforgivable that I wasn't happy about, then I could also relinquish her services to me. If that ever happened, then she would need to find a new work position, master, mistress, or family to serve. Just as I would also then have to find myself someone else to serve me. But after five years together now, I think we have both become quite attuned to each other's ways of thinking. She has done her very best for me *always*, and I hope that I do the same for her.'

'But why do I need one myself?' he asked. 'As there certainly isn't enough housework for both of them here.'

'I've already told you of all the skills a servant *must* have before being allowed to be assigned to someone, Douglas. So, just imagine that if Raiko is ever sick at any time, then this other servant will be here to help out. And if I am ever out somewhere shopping or have gone home to Japan on holiday to see my family without you, possibly even for a week or two. In either case Raiko would be going with me. And in that way, your own servant would still be here to look after you and our home while we are not here. Also,' she said quite happily to him. 'By choosing a female maid as I have, you will still be able to enjoy sex with her whilst I am not with you. Unless you would like or perhaps even prefer a male option as a servant instead?'

'Err, no, I think a female maid will be fine! But why is it *always* about sex!' he muttered once more.

'Because, sex is simply a basic function and often an important need for our bodies to stay at their optimum health levels, my love. Never forget that in any way, as it is not only used for training purposes with us, but it also includes both a natural means of pleasure and relaxation as well as for any stress relief. This is also why you are allowed to choose your servant beforehand, just as they can agree or refuse to serve you after being asked. So that you will like how each other may look. Which always makes any sex that could occur between them much easier, *neh*?'

He sighed, as it was the best he could do right now and then said to her, 'Whatever you wish, Kumiko.'

'Good. We should have a few options on my laptop for you to view in the morning or tomorrow night when we return from work.'

'You are going to work tomorrow, mistress? What work is this that you are speaking about?' asked Raiko nervously. Knowing that from what she'd just heard spoken, that she could well be here in this new house all on her own tomorrow.

Spirit of a Dragon

'I'll be going with my husband into his police station of work, Raiko. It has been arranged that I will work within his department with him for the next few weeks or months, or whatever . . . Afterwards, when that is over, I'll just have to think of what else I can do to keep myself busy over here.'

'In that case I had better go and see to your uniform, mistress, as it will definitely require an ironing. And perhaps even a little brushing and be allowed to hang after being inside the suitcase all day now.'

'That can be done in a little while Raiko. As first of all, we can all bathe and then have our late meal together, *neh*?'

∞

The three of them slept together in just the one bed that night, and then woke up together as his alarm clock greeted them at six. An hour earlier than Kumiko herself had expected, as it had always been seven when she was here last. Douglas lay in the centre, with them on either side of him. He had changed its setting the night before. As he already knew her predilection for enjoying a busy morning with him, just as it was also the same reason that he had arrived late for work for the first time in almost three years. And for him, being late once was already one too many to him.

Kumiko, who was lying nearest his bedside table raised her body up and leaned out from the bed towards the wailing alarm. A quick look and she quickly silenced it by using the off button she recalled. She then turned on to her side even more, and lifted the pillow taken from one of the spare beds higher against the headboard. Then turned again on to her back and edged her body upwards until she was soon in almost a sitting position. And just sitting there quite bare breasted like that, she looked unusually beautiful to him this morning as he joined her in a similar position.

Her arm reached down beside the bed and found her laptop. Plugged into the mains throughout the night by way of the brought over voltage adapter of her father. Which she'd remembered to borrow from him, due to her father needing it on their previous visit. And she had left it switched on – but on sleep mode ready for using it this morning. Upon raising the upper half of it, he saw that it was still waiting to be selected on to her personal e-mail account ready for her hopeful viewing.

'Twenty-five messages have been delivered since we went to bed, my husband,' she told him. Forgetting that he could read the Japanese character script on her display screen just as well as she could, and also noted that each message had an accompanying photo attachment icon beside them. At her spoken words, Raiko finally now awakened, yawned, thenand rose from her previous flat position to join them by leaning over him slightly. This now meant that all three of them were now looking at the screen.

Hyde eased his arms out from beneath the duvet and placed one around each of their shoulders. As his wife began to open the first message which had been delivered, Raiko's own small hand then appeared to be searching for something to do around his groin area.

'What do you wish to know about them first, my husband?' she asked him, 'their age, their height, weight, or perhaps just their pictures?'

'If as you say they are *all* considered as being fully qualified and as experienced maids. That they can each do the exact same tasks as Raiko here does for us, or you I should say. Then everything but their time of experience means more, I think, doesn't it?'

'They have all been very capably trained with the very same skills that Raiko herself was, my husband. So in essence, how long they have been doing it really makes no difference. This is the only reason why their details have been sent to us. If only an apprentice who is as yet still under training, then they would not be allowed to offer their services to anyone yet.'

'So, as I just said, what they can all do matters little then, eh? Since all of these here can all provide the *same* thing just as well each other?'

'That is quite correct,' said Kumiko as she gave her own left breast a gentle scratch.

'Well, ages don't bother me much at all. And I guess their heights and weights mean about the same to me, too. So how about just seeing each of their pictures first then, hmm? And I'll just go off those that I might fancy the most from what they look like, and I'll try and get down to choosing only one of them from that?'

Kumiko's head bobbed and she selected the first picture, and then the next and the next. It was almost mildly pornographic to his eyes and former sense of prudishness about open sex. Only since each one of them was quite naked while appearing to him on the screen. Each message contained five pictures of each woman, with a close up full face one being the first she showed him, and then she waited to see his reaction to it. Those women that he didn't find himself instantly attracted to were left behind as she then moved on. While those who he said that he found were okay, she then clicked on each of the other four photographs to show him.

'Why do they need to send five pictures of each woman for you to view?' he asked her.

'So that any of their future masters or mistresses can see them as they truly are in life right now, my husband. The big close-up photograph of them allows you to see their faces in much closer detail. As some members prefer to go off their looks, just like you have decided to do right at this moment. The other four are to show them from the back and front, and both sides. The back shot of them allows the member to see their general body shape, and that they have gained their full servant tattoos. So anyone who is looking at them will know just from that alone now, that they are now ready to serve someone within our clan.

'The main front one allows you to view their breast size, pubic area, body shape again, and frontal servant tattoos. While the two opposite side shots allow you a side view of them as well. In this way you would also see if they had any birthmarks, moles, bruises, scars, or whatever.'

'And is this how *you* also chose our lovely Raiko here?'

Kumiko nodded again. 'Yes. It was her cheeky grin at the camera that caught my attention when I first saw her picture in my option list. So I knew that she would be a cheerful person to have with, and to be around me. Which is really why I picked her. And we have been together now for five good years Raiko, *neh*?'

'Yes indeed, mistress. The time seems to have flown over since I joined you,' stated the young woman, who right now was quite happily massaging her master beneath the covers.

By the end of all twenty-five being shown, only ten had caused him to view their other four pictures. And after that, he had felt really only attracted to five of them. He'd gave her the five numbers, which she'd flagged, and so they all looked over the same five again, but he looked much closer and even harder at them all this time.

'Well?' she asked him.

'I'd say number eighteen probably makes me feel the horniest of all, love, and she also has a nice smile too. Although to be honest, the other four weren't that far behind her by very much at all.'

'All right then, now we'll see what details there are here about her for you, *neh*? Kumiko said as she clicked on her report information.

'Oh, now she's just a little *too* young, don't you think?' he said worriedly on now seeing her age appear on the screen.

As Kumiko stared at him Raiko offered a small chuckle. 'But you just said to me that age meant nothing to you, my husband?' she responded with arched eyebrows.

'Jesus, Kumiko, I never thought that any of them would be *that* young for heaven's sake!'

'Why not, I already told you that Raiko was the same age of sixteen when I asked *her* if she would like to serve me.'

'I know *that*, woman!' he moaned. 'But you weren't expected to have sex with her were you! Hells teeth what do you think my neighbours will think if they see *her* here. Eh? Their own female children of around the same age will be in the road talking about boys together, while I could well be in here having sex with someone almost from their same age group!'

Raiko chuckled again at his consternation, even while her hand continued its enjoyable ministrations upon his now hardened member.

'But you must not see her in that way, my husband. Like all of us you must see them only as a servant first of all. Only later, when you have come to know them much better as a person; like those of us who have had the same servant for a few, or perhaps even many years. Then you may come to see them almost as a close friend, maybe even a confidante .. . as I now do with Raiko. So age doesn't really come into it at all, Douglas. Whatever the age of the woman is that you choose to have, she will serve you to the best of her abilities, and in *every* way possible.'

'But---'

Spirit of a Dragon

'No, I won't allow you to change your mind now just because of that! You chose young Hiroko only from her picture first of all, telling me that any other details about her wouldn't matter to you. She is fully trained, my husband, and that is all what counts! So I am going to arrange for her to be asked to see if she would be happy to come here and serve you now. And we will speak no more about it!'

Raiko finally, after waiting for them to stop talking to each other, managed to at long last say, 'Please, you must not worry about her age, master.'

'Why not, Raiko, this isn't Japan you know, where so many of you live that no one cares who the other people are. This is England my dear, and there aren't an awful lot of Japanese over here to start with. I'm only worried about what people here may start to think!'

'About what exactly may they think?' Kumiko asked him.

'Well, seeing me living here with three hot young Japanese women for one thing. Their tongues will soon be wagging straight away . . . Offering strange comments like, 'is he, a policeman, actually running a brothel or massage parlour over there in his house,? And just *look* at *that* young oriental girl, why she can't be more than only ten or twelve at most - so what on earth could *she* be doing there with *him* at his age!'

They both began to laugh at the attempted outraged high-pitched tone of voice that he had tried to use to do it.

'Please, you must not worry about her age, master,' Raiko said again when her own chortling high laughter died away.

'But why should I not worry about it, Raiko? When I know how it could be going to look to some of them here already!'

Her smile was wide at him. 'Why, master . . . because you have *already* had sex with her.'

'I have . . . when?'

'It was on the night after your wedding to my mistress, master. As I saw her when she came from the sex room, after having been pleasured by you as she passed by me. And yes, I do know that she very much enjoyed it too!'

'How is this, Raiko,' asked Kumiko.

'Because *her* smile was even wider than your own was on the plane coming here mistress. And so, I must just say that she looked *very* happy indeed when she came out of the room!'

'Ahhh, I see, well then, that is certainly good enough for me.'

'Hold on a minute,' he muttered quickly, and hopefully it must be said, 'another two files have just come into your mailbox now.'

They viewed them as well, but Kumiko noticed that they had not affected them as much as the picture of young Hiroko had earlier. He gave off a low quiet sigh.

'Is something wrong, my husband?'

'Nothing . . . Well to be honest, I was just hoping that Yuki might have been on here to view.'

'You like Yuki?'

He nodded at her. 'Though God knows how old she is! Probably only *nine* knowing my luck just now,' he exclaimed.

'No husband, as I do know that Yuki is in her twenties at least by now.'

'Well thank the Lord for that!'

Then he watched her hand move to the table to pick up her mobile. She looked at the clock, and turned it on. 'That's good, it's only about three-fifteen in the afternoon at home now,' she said to herself as her finger hit one of her speed dial buttons.

'Who are you calling, young woman?' he asked her, but she didn't answer him.

'Father, hello, yes it's me. Oh, we're all fine thank you. No, we've really only just woken up over here.'

Now it was Douglas's turn to listen in to a one-way conversation and try to work out what was being said at the other end.

Spirit of a Dragon

'You were? - How many of them? - Three this time? - All right, Father.' She turned to him. 'Father asks if we could purchase another three of those chairs of yours for our plane to take back with them.'

'What colours though, and only if they have them in stock?' he asked, forgetting about what they'd just been talking about for the moment.

'One like your own, another of black, and one of a burgundy,' she said to him.

And as he nodded, she went back on to the phone again. 'Douglas say's that that should be all right, Father *if* they can get those colours for you. Though as we are both required to go into work today shortly. As I have to meet with his Boss before I can work with him now. It will mean that we may not be able to get them ordered and taken to the plane today. Unless the shop is still open after we have finished work this evening – Oh, they will?'

She looked at him again. 'My Father has said that he will just ask them to stay at the hotel here until they receive the chairs from the shop, and then they will leave for home again. He has also asked if we will be at work on a Saturday or not?'

'I may be, but I doubt you would need to,' he replied.

'No Father, perhaps only Douglas. So if we cannot get there before then, then I will take Raiko with me and get them bought or ordered for you then, all right? Of course it is no problem for me to do this, Father. But would it not be better if I took one of the aircrew with me to this shop this or next time. Then if you still ever require any more of them, then at least one of them would be able to go and see about any more straight away after that for you . . .

'Of course, I would be happy to do so for you. – What, why was I calling you? Oh yes, it was only because Douglas has a little problem over accepting the maid that he first chose from those we have received here via my e-mail box. It was Sato Hiroko, Father. - Yes I know that she is, and that was the actual problem for my husband. - Very well, I will tell him that for you. Although he was also asking about Yuki from the plane too, but really that was only because he did not see her picture and details on offer here with the others this morning.

'Do you think so? - Well, if you are quite sure about that, Father. - Very well, I will tell him about that as well now then . . . Good bye, Father, until we speak again.' Kumiko then hung up.

'You are a very lucky man indeed, my husband,' she told him.

'So, he also agreed with me why Hiroko may not be suitable then, eh?'

'Oh no, my love, he has told me to tell you that you can have them both if they are willing to agree to it . . .'

'God Almighty!' he breathed.

'You *can* thank Him if you so wish, my husband. But it is actually my father who has allowed this very unusual state of events to take place. As it is usual for only one servant to be designated to one adult person at any given time; unless of course some kind of an illness comes up. But, he said that because you still require so much training in our ways still, and also that so few of us are over here to help you out. That you may *well* need two maids in order to help you out -- and so, he has allowed this for you. He said that he will telephone Yuki at the hotel very soon himself personally today to see what she says. As if she does agree to it, then he will have to find a replacement for her to become a crew member for the plane.'

CHAPTER 20

Answering the knock at his door, Ramshaw was quite astounded by the well-groomed and very smartly turned out woman who had just entered into his office. Raiko and Kumiko had done their very best to make her look good and to create a perfect impression for her first meeting with his Boss. And this had proved positive if his reaction to her presentation was anything for her to go by. The close fit of her uniform appeared to be just as well tailored as his was, if not actually better. He'd also noticed her highly polished patent leather flat-soled shoes, and the shine from the brown leather belt positioned around her slim waist. As well as the same one that crossed over her chest diagonally, had all been so well-polished, that they could easily have reflected a face in them.

At each of her hips, there were a few small similar coloured carrying pouches to the belt. Probably one for her handcuffs and one for her notepad or other things, he presumed. Only since he couldn't see any notepad - or a single pen sticking out for that matter, or protruding from any of the squared off pockets of her dark blue tunic. As she reached him, Kumiko simply offered him a deep bow.

'Please, sit down, Mrs *Hyde*,' he said with a faint grin after gently shaking her hand.

'Thank you very much, sir,' she responded just as politely.

Ramshaw looked her over as he would any officer as she approached the seat and then sat down. He also gave a hasty look at her slim legs as she crossed them one over the other as she settled before him. He *almost* began to nod then, but just managed to refrain from doing so in front of her. Dr Stone had been right, that she *was* an extremely attractive woman, just as she'd said when he'd called her up on the first day of Hyde's leave to ask about her.

At which Dr Stone herself had seemed almost at a loss to hear that Hyde was soon going to be married, within only a few days, and to the very same woman who now sat in front of him. But from his viewpoint right now, he thought that Hyde was indeed a very lucky man. He had of course heard over the past few years, that Hyde and Dr Stone had shared the odd drink together sometimes after work. But it had always been told as if it was more of a social event between work colleagues, rather than anything serious being between them. Since others from the various departments were typically there as well. He, as well as many others, had no idea whatsoever that Carmen herself had been *very* interested in him n a more personal way. As she'd always felt that she had got on so well with him. But then again, neither had Hyde.

'I hope that everything went smoothly over in Japan for you Mrs Hyde?'

'Very well indeed sir, thank you for asking.'

'I also hope that you will find it easy enough to settle into our country as the wife of one of our officers.'

'I will find it very easy to do so, sir. As my maids will look after our house while we are both at work for the time being.'

'Did you say *maids*, Mrs Hyde?'

'Yes, sir, you see it is quite customary for *some* of us to have maids to see to our well-being and even our homes in Japan while we are out working.'

'It is?'

'But of course, sir. In various professional professions like ours, some people come home after work feeling quite exhausted from working such very long hours. So to have your home already cleaned, any shopping bought, and a meal ready and waiting for when you return at the end of work is extremely popular with some. Although only one of them has come over here with me right now, I am hoping that either one or both of my two other maids will also wish to join me here very soon as well, but at the moment, they are dealing with my own furnishings and such like back home.'

'But that would make five of you, and where will they stay over here anyway?'

'They all lived with me at home, sir. So of course they will do so again if they all agree,' Kumiko answered him directly eye to eye. Doing her very best to *artfully* get Douglas's Boss into her *own* way of thinking.

Ramshaw gave a low cough. 'I'm *quite* sure that your husband does not own a large enough dwelling to be able to satisfy *all* of their personal sleeping arrangements, Mrs Hyde . . .'

Kumiko smiled at him. 'In my own two-bedroom *flat*, sir,' she stated carefully to him, 'my maids all slept in the only other bedroom that it had.' She was right now lying through her teeth as deftly as she could for the benefit of her new husband's position. As well as also protecting him from any possible outcry later.

'But how can they do that?' asked Ramshaw quickly falling into her expertly set trap.

'Because at home we mostly still use futons to sleep on and not the similar fixed placements of beds as you do here, sir. At night, just like I did myself, we each just simply unrolled our futons as a bed and we go to sleep on them along with a covering quilt. And in the morning, any futon and quilt is very easily rolled up again, and then can be removed to create more living space during the daytime.'

'I see,' he replied, now convinced by her entirely.

Kumiko knew this, so added also, 'Which is why my husband has allowed me to offer them the use of one or both of his other two bedrooms. So now and then they can use one alone if they wish for a period of time before exchanging places with one of the others.'

'I understand, Mrs Hyde. And thank you for taking the time to explain it to me in such a way.'

'That was of course no effort on my part, sir. All that it will mean is that my husband and I will have no housework to do. Very little shopping, if *any* at all to worry about . . and so we can therefore just relax at whatever time we get home again.'

'A very excellent idea, my dear, I only wish that I could afford something similar in our own home to help out my own wife and family life in the same way,' he said thoughtfully.

She thought he was up to something now, so needed to discourage him the only way that she knew how to do so. 'In a way, I am also very lucky sir, as my father is the one who has always paid their salaries for me. Of which he said that he would be happy to continue doing so even *after* my marriage to Douglas. And that is really the only way that *I* too could ever afford to have one, if not all them all coming here to be with me myself.' Ramshaw emitted a low sigh. His hopes of doing something similar to aid his wife at home had just fallen by the wayside now.

His mind returned to the very elegant woman seated before him, and he now began to explain to her exactly what her role in this country entailed. And all that she would be allowed to do and also carry out. After hearing from her that occasionally, or more often than not, her work in Tokyo involved handling a lot of cases concerning tourists in her country due to her personal English skills. Ramshaw knew that she was capable enough of carrying out some similar duties within Department M3. A department which, of course, was very effectively run by her husband downstairs. Though he also now told her what he had told him previously. That if possible, *he* would prefer it much more that if she did happen to go on any outside task with anyone while she was stationed here with them. That it would be with her husband, and to dress accordingly at the time. To which Kumiko gave him her own full agreement.

∞

It was nearly forty-five minutes before Hyde received a call from Ramshaw to go upstairs to pick her up and take her back to his department. And every minute that he had to wait while she was being interviewed had felt like a prison sentence to him a few floors below. Wondering what he was asking her, and wondering *exactly* what his wife was managing to think up to tell *him* at the same time. As she n her own way had told him simply not to worry, and that she would soon have everything sorted out to their own benefit.

304

Spirit of a Dragon

By the time he got upstairs and went into his Boss's office to collect her in person. And then had to answer a few questions asked by him as Kumiko listened on attentively, it was a further fifteen minutes gone. The time was only two minutes after ten that morning when they walked into his department with the six investigation members under him, and Terry, who had all now been waiting quite impatiently for her imminent arrival.

As soon as they entered the door a low murmur rose from most of them. The women at how beautifully *dressed* she was, the men at just how *beautiful* she really was.

But it was Terry who spoke first and not Hyde.

'Bad news already, Boss. We've just received a call from down in Bournemouth . . . It seems that he's chalked up his nineteenth now.'

Kumiko's introduction to them all was then quickly forgotten about as he turned straight to the job at hand. 'Damn! Have any details about her come through yet?' he asked Terry straight away.

Kumiko said nothing, as she stood there quietly, waiting to see how her husband reacted and did things here. She wanted to know before too long, *how* he thought and how he considered details and worked them out for himself. Really it was her just wanting to know how his mind actually worked and rationalised anything. From any given details and how *he* then worked them out, if possible. As even now, she still knew so little about the real *him*, since all that she really *did* know about him had come from the report Yoshi had sent to her father. Though even she knew herself already that it was likely a great deal more than any of those here in the room with them had ever known about him. Or would even suspect about him if it came to that . . .

'She was only found about half an hour ago, Dougie,' said Terry. 'And it was only because of the bulletins that you had sent out to every other force in the country of what to watch out for. That they gave us a call when their own Path person, and who on the spot said she'd been found just like all the rest, and strangled.' He said the last word cautiously, as he knew it was also how the woman now standing quite close to his sister had also been killed.'

Hyde saw his glance. 'You okay, Kumiko?' he asked her. 'I'm afraid Terry didn't know any other way to put it but straight like that.'

She nodded to him. 'I am perfectly fine my husband, thank you. But I had thought that you were going to introduce them all to me, *neh*?'

'Oh, sorry, of course I was.' So he gave off a loud throat clearing cough to make everyone, (who were all supposedly very busy), look up from what they were doing and to him. He gestured form her to them, and then from them back to her again as he said, 'Team - Meet Inspector Kumiko Hyde of the Tokyo Police, who has been seconded to us for the present time . . . Kumiko - Meet, my team!'

Terry stuck his hand out to her. 'Pleased to meet you Mrs Hyde, I'm Detective Inspector Terry Boyne. And thankfully only second-in-command of this department again now!' he said to her.

Kumiko gave him a quick bow then stuck her hand out to meet up with his own. But Terry was already halfway through returning her own unexpected bow that had just been given to him, so there was no hand for her to hold right now. Until he had straightened up again that is.

'There was really no need for you to return my own greeting, Boyne-san. As it was a customary Japanese greeting to you and not a western one, which I should have remembered to do for your own personal comfort.'

'That's okay Mrs - Inspector Hyde---'

'Please call me Kumiko if it any easier for you, Boyne-san.'

'Okay, Kumiko, but what's this Boyne-san?'

'Oh I am sorry, then how should I address you?'

'Terry'll be fine, Kumiko.'

'But it surely cannot be polite for me to do so, Boyne-san.'

He gave a frown, since he still didn't know what was implied by what she was calling him.

'Again I apologise for disturbing you, *Terry*. But it is typical of Japanese people to call someone by their surname only first. Certainly if we do not consider having known them well enough to use their Christian name yet. So in fact I was only being respectful by calling you, Mr Boyne . . .'

'Oh?' He was just about to add something further when the phone on his desk began to ring. He excused himself and hurried over to it.

'Come on Kumiko I'll introduce you to them all properly then.'

'That would very much be appreciated by me as you know, Douglas.'

Since she now knew Terry, he took her around the other six waiting members of his team, introducing her one by one to Gary Mooney, Marie Crosby, Colin Monteith, Charlie Anderson, Brenda McGuire and Andrew Golightly. Although not doing it in any special order at all, just going to the nearest table to where they were each time. And of course, to each and every one of them, Kumiko offered a bow before shaking their hands – to then address them by their surname whilst adding *san* to it.

'Boss,' Terry called out to him with his hand clasped over the mouthpiece, 'it's one of our lot down in Bournemouth. Saying from what was in her handbag that, which they've since had a good look in now. That she was, twenty-three and called Jill Moran.'

'Jot every detail down that they can give you for her right now, and then set another board up on the end to follow the last one when you're through, Terry,' said Hyde with a tired sigh.

'Righto!' he said, then sat down with the telephone to his ear and began quickly jotting notes on to a waiting A4 writing pad, handily placed beside an open file on his desk. Something else he'd learned from Douglas. Which was always to have something handy nearby to ne able to write on it a hurry.

'So this newly found body of the poor woman now makes it nineteen murders in total now, my husband, am I correct?'

'So far!' he grunted.

'You still expect even more?'

'Aye, until the bugger's been caught I do.'

'Why? Should he not be worried about being caught easier if he keeps on doing these terrible things now?'

'Come and have a sit down at my desk with me, love. And I'll then try to get you into how we're all thinking in here, okay.'

He pulled a spare chair from against the wall over next to his own chair at his desk and they sat down. Then as she waited, he called out to an older detective, Gary Mooney. One who now looked back over at him, and with a somewhat expectant look waiting there upon his face.

'How many people, and vehicles, do you think are out on our roads every day travelling around as we speak, delivering, picking-up, salesman, and people just driving about?'

'I haven't got a clue, boss, a good few million, at least!'

'Throughout the UK today, probably two to five or more million people and their vehicles are doing just that right now, Kumiko! And for us to start to catch whoever it is doing this, we need at least one decent clue for us to try and find him. As we don't know what he's driving, if anything. Neither do we know so far, if it is his job that's taking him all over the country or not. For all we do know he might just be bumming around the country all day long and doing nothing but killing a woman wherever he ends up that day.'

'Unless we can get something positive from the specialist lab in order to help us out now, Boss!'

'That's right, Gary. If in some way they can come up with a true colour, or possibly even a make and model of the vehicle from the flakes found on three of the victim's bodies so far. Then the millions we have at present could be narrowed down for us by a hell of a lot. But, if they can also give us give us a *year* to it! Then we could very well be down to a few hundred, or a few thousand at most with that extra detail. And then, only then, could we really begin to make some decent inroads into our work with that sort of help - although it will also involve a lot of manpower to do it. But if we want to catch him, then we may just have to pull out all the stops to do that between all of us.'

Kumiko, after listening to what they had said, had also now began to see the enormous task that lay upon her husband's broad shoulders in finding her younger sister's killer. And by not even having to stretch her imagination at all, was she finding out the real difficulties that they were all facing. To her way of thinking, it would be almost be impossible and would need a lot of luck to find him. Not really actual skill right now, for whoever was involved at leading this investigation.

Spirit of a Dragon

As a new board went up, and its own findings were being written or pinned on to it, the day wore on slowly, very slowly indeed. Everyone in that room was waiting to hear something from the specialist laboratory. Literally anything at all. Since only from this evidence would it then give them something to use as a base to begin working from. A few of the team waited there until close to six that evening for the telephone call they needed, but it still didn't come ...

Hyde left the two people from another department who had just arrived to start their shifts to take over from them. While he told those with him to head for home and get a good night's sleep. As tomorrow could be the day when they might get word back, and then the hunt for the killer would finally begin in earnest!

Hyde and his wife drove straight to the shop first of all, but it was already closed. Kumiko though, decided to leave a message for the manager of the shop anyway. So wrote it out on the back page of her own notepad, telling the manager what chairs were required this time. And also left the telephone number of the hotel where the flight crew were all staying over at. So that they could see to it themselves, as she would likely be back at the station with him tomorrow again. Though she would also give them a call when she got home shortly to tell them that, too. Only so that any call they received tomorrow from the manager would not come as a complete surprise to them.

When they did get home, Kumiko said that they might as well carry out some of his training first before they ate or bathed. And for the next hour in his attic. No matter how hard Hyde tried, and he was trying! He was always being casually tossed or thrown around on the padded matting up there by them both. Which also told him that the way her sister Akiko had died just *had* to have been premeditated, and as such had left her with no way of being able to defend herself at all. Since he already knew from her tattoo now she had been just as well trained as Kumiko herself had been, and that also meant much better than Raiko. Who were both very slippery customers indeed he soon learned, as he constantly tried to grab hold of one of them over and over again; in a rather vain attempt to deposit one of *them* on to the thick matting for a change, instead of it only being him each time.

For the entire hour, only once had he successfully caught and thrown the young maid. And that was only through luck, and because she'd lost her balance when her foot slid in a patch of his own damp sweat on the mat. Which had came from one of his many repeated falls.

He never once even got *close* to throwing his wife. As she changed her styles of attack and defence so quickly, and in so many ways, that he was left floundering every time and just grabbing at thin air. Where he would then find himself in the same place, which of course was usually flat on his back on the mat.

After his personal bout of aerial gymnastics in the attic was finally over, and after they had both bathed the only sore body between all three of them. He sat down at the kitchen table with Kumiko, as Raiko served the foods she had prepared to serve them for their meals a little earlier.

'It's no good,' he told them. 'I've just got to have a fry-up tomorrow morning or evening.'

'You do not like my cooking, master?' Raiko asked of him, while also looking very sad indeed at his words.

'Oh, it's not that at all, Raiko,' he explained. 'Both you and my wife can cook very nicely indeed. But I really need something that is far more substantial to see me through the day. Not like what you two little birds eat every meal to keep your bodies so trim and thin. You just can't beat a good serving of bacon, eggs, and sausage for breakfast.'

'But that is not a very healthy meal for you if you have it every day, my husband,' she said. 'Our own foods contain everything a body requires to keep it in peak shape.'

'More than likely they do, Kumiko. But in that case, why did your father tell me that you also prefer many western types of fast food yourself?'

She gave a shrug. 'It is only because they are readily accessible foods as a snack when I am at work, or out on the streets of Tokyo, my husband. And as such, I probably also burn any of those calories off due to it too, But I still very much enjoy coming home to whatever Raiko has arranged for me to eat day or night.'

'I know, it is very nice, but I'll have to get both of you used to my own way of cooking as well though, eh? As if like me you don't try different foods now and then. Then neither of you will ever know if you would like them yourselves, or not. Especially barbecues in the summer months like I usually have out in the garden when it's this warm.'

'I agree, husband. But it is only because your foods typically come in such huge portions that we just cannot eat everything. This is why we keep to our own foods as much as possible whenever we can.'

He nodded. 'I'm not saying that you have to eat them *all* of the time. Neither do you have to eat everything that is given to you on a plate. I'm only saying that you should try them out just to see what they taste like to you.'

'Kumiko looked at her maid. 'I think we could do that for you husband, *neh,* Raiko?'

Raiko bobbed her head. 'Though I do only know how to mainly cook our own foods, master. But I am willing to learn how to cook your kind for you if you will be happy to teach me?'

With their meal finished and the kitchen tidied up as usual. They made their way into the living room and relaxed in the two chairs. It was where Kumiko also told him of her meeting with his Boss, Ramshaw. And of what he had told her she couldn't do while working with them. While also what she had told him about the possible two other maids who would soon be living here with them now too.

'He even told me that I did not even have to wear my uniform if I did not want to, my husband. As he said to me that in departments such as yours are, a more casual look can be much more acceptable at times.'

Hyde gave her a smile. 'It's one of the main reasons why those of us who work in them try so hard to get into them in the first place, my love. So that we *don't* have to wear our uniforms so much afterwards. But if you're coming in tomorrow, and in those new tight jeans of yours that you bought. Well, I can easily see a few of the blokes in the office not being able to stand up after they see your gorgeous little bum swaying around in front of them!' he said patting her thigh as she lay on his lap in the chair.

She kissed him, and then snuggled even more into him as they watched the film on the television set together.

∞

It was on the Friday afternoon when they finally received *some* good news from the specialist laboratory, although it certainly wasn't as much good news as they'd hoped to get. As the news which did reach them, from the initial testing phase, was that the paint flakes appeared to be of a metallic light grey colour - and that was it. Even after Hyde had almost barraged them with further questions over what else he needed to know. But that was all they could give him right now; as even they themselves were now waiting for updated specimen samples to arrive from the manufacturers to identify the actual paint source. And this would be the only way that *they* could also get any further than they already had.

Hyde wasn't too happy at all at this outcome, and at the additional delay being involved now. Indeed he was almost fuming at the delays. Delays that could ultimately cause yet more deaths to occur as further precious time passed by: and for any quicker solution being found each day by them in what had now become a manhunt.

Kumiko did her best to appease him by reassuring him that *everyone* who was helping on the case was already doing their best, just as he was doing to help to solve it. Since no one else was going to say anything to him, when they guessed how he'd react. Seeing that he was still barely only managing to hold his anger in check. He actually sat and watched her as she openly flicked a finger out, which then caused a pencil there to roll, and then fall over the far edge of his desk.

'Oh silly me!' she said to him. 'I must go and retrieve it now!'

Which is also just what she did, and right in front of his desk while now wearing those same tight jeans he'd mentioned, that stretched and clung to every curve of her bottom as she bent for it. Hyde caught more than his own eyes watching her display. As all those other male eyes quickly left when they found his on them. He could do little else but feel a grin somehow emerging from his tight lips, which then changed into a loud laugh when he suddenly worked out just *what* she was now doing.

'Now that is much better, my husband,' she told him upon retaking her seat beside him and replaced the pencil. 'You must never let things get on top of you so much or it will of course also affect your blood pressure!' Then she leaned over to him and dropped her voice. 'As the only things that *should* be allowed to get on top of you right now, are myself and Raiko of course!'

A bellowing laugh from him almost rocked the office. And as they all looked over they could see his wife smiling widely, while he was just laughing away at something she must have said to him.

'All right, I give up,' he replied. Then he went back to work in a far better frame of mind. 'Terry, you get on to the DVLA for me. Tell them that we need to know for our investigation purposes of just how many cars, vans, trucks and HGV's are registered with them under that colour at the moment.'

'You must be kidding, Dougie!'

He shook his head. 'It's the only lead that we have right now. And as it is at least finally some kind of a start for us. So all we can do is to get on with that, and gain just as much info on them as we can. It may all help out later when, or *if*, we get more details to work on soon.'

Terry did what was asked, was passed from one manager to another, until he finally reached who he apparently needed to speak to on the other end. Though his talk with him soon became short and heated, and feeling utterly frustrated, he had to hand it to Hyde. Moment by moment they watched as his own face begin to change colour, as the man at the other end of the telephone literally refused to waste any of their own staffs resources on such a huge scale piece of work.

They watched him as he clenched his teeth, and almost spoke through them as he said, '*And your name is?*' His breath was almost hissing from between his teeth as he waited.

'Right you are then, *Mr* Ferguson, someone else will be in touch with you in a few minutes again I would expect.' He exhaled a deep breath and then slammed the phone down. '*Bastard!*' he muttered aloud.

'Will you calm yourself down, my husband, or should I roll yet another pencil off your desk for you?' she asked in a low tone. Which almost brought another smile to his mouth, but only almost, as this time what she said just didn't quite make it.

He sat down, since he'd ended up standing up by the end of his heated talk with the manager. He took a few good breaths of air, then picked up the telephone and dialled two digits.

'Sir,' he said after being passed through by Ramshaw's secretary. 'As you probably know already, we only received the most basic of details about the three paint flakes. Yes, sir, I just did that and the manager there actually refused point blank to help us with what he called a flimsy, and utter waste of his own staffs time! Thank you, sir, if you would. His name was Ferguson by the way . . .' Hyde added for him and gave the extension number that Terry had also used in order to reach him.

They all waited, including those who were doing other things in the department. Five minutes passed by, and then ten. Twenty, and then thirty finally went by too. Kumiko herself was almost ready to slap his hand, as when his fingers weren't tapping on the desk. They were heading over to pull his jacket sleeve up his wrist for the umpteenth time since they'd both sat there and waited.

And then Ramshaw himself sudden'y just walked in to their department.

'*That bloody man!*' he barked so loudly that one of the women sat there jumped in alarm. 'Pardon me, Mrs Hyde, ladies,' he muttered to the women. Though they knew that they'd heard far worse on any one day of work, so it must have been to his wife being there which brought out his rather sudden apology.

'I couldn't actually *believe* the damn man's behaviour myself, Hyde!' he stormed. 'I had to call the Police Commissioner for some help with him! And even *he* couldn't get any help from that Jobsworth either!'

Kumiko looked at her husband for help with that.

'Some people in charge of some particular places often feel that they carry more authority than they actually have at their disposal, Kumiko. And if you ask them for something which they don't really wish to do . . . It soon becomes a saying like "It's more than my *job is worth* to do that!" . . . So this is now why these same people now are known by the title of Jobsworth's here.'

'I see,' she said, though she didn't really.

'So what will happen next then, sir?' he asked Ramshaw.

'Well, the Commissioner finally got as pig sick of him as I did finally. Then he called me back to say that he'd had to get on the telephone to one of the government chappies to sort all this damn mess out for us.'

'And, do you think that we'll get some help now, or not, sir?'

Ramshaw smiled. 'Oh yes, Hyde. Now we're finally getting some help. I think the Minister for Transport, or whoever it must have been, must have put a rather large flea into this man's ear to tell him exactly what *is* what now! And also what would be best for this man Ferguson to do. As this man Ferguson then actually called me back and apologised, saying to me that he didn't know the seriousness of what we were doing at the time. He then said that he'd get his people right on it.'

Hyde looked across the room. 'You did actually tell him *why* we needed the information, Terry?'

'Sure did, boss. But that's when it all began to go pear-shaped and I had to let you take over from me with him.'

Hyde nodded. 'And I explained the same thing to him also. So he was a right Jobsworth then, wasn't he!'

'And I also told him the reason for the request myself too, Hyde. So if all three of us told him why it was required, then he must have known the importance of it anyway!'

Ramshaw glanced at the clock on the wall and then intervened, 'You've all been working hard on this case for quite a while now as it is. So, since he said that they'll have to sift through their computers for what could be a few days to get what data we'll need. I'd say that those of you who aren't on late shift might as well go home early now. You can't do any more until you get something further to help you. So, you may as well get away and rest up ready for the weekend, and week ahead to come. As I have a distinct feeling in my bones that it is going to be quite a hectic one!' Those of you who are on late duty, or who are working over the weekend can respond to any pertinent requests or calls and get any further information that may come in from them.'

∞

In the four interminably long weeks that followed, the grey van and its single occupant happily wandered around the south of England. As he only needed to stay at two locations during those first two weeks, since he was mostly parked-up in overnight lorry parks to spend the night before doing his deliveries. But even then, at these other two places he had struck yet again. Notching up new victims in Hammersmith and Oxford. Those being where another two women had fallen victim to him, and making his body count rise again now to twenty-one. In the next two weeks, while the details regarding *those* two fresh attacks had been received in Hyde's department, and were going up on to new boards in the large office. He was again on his travels, from Cambridge up to Leicester. So he was back in the Midlands again; while leaving yet more trails of death in his wake.

Hyde wasn't happy. No one in his team was thrilled right now, and neither was Ramshaw at just how easily he was moving around the country to commit all of these same capital crimes not only regularly - but also just so easily or so it seemed. As they weren't strictly crimes of passion that he was committing since the beginning - It was now really only premeditated murder in its purest, darkest, and most sinister form. They all knew that what he was on was definitely just a killing spree now, in an attempt to rack up as many victims of his own desperation as he could, before they hoped he would be caught. But, even with what scant information had finally been supplied to them by the DVLA at Swansea, the sheer numbers that had been involved had led to a feeling of almost utter defeat.

As with no make, model, or year to base their search on yet so far, the multitude of lists that had been finally sent to them seemed almost endless. Since all the DVLA *could do*, was to give them *whatever* information they had based on what vehicles were registered with them at the time, and of that certain colour which had been asked for.

From vehicles that had just came out brand new. To those that were much older. Some pages even had vehicles that even dated back to as far as the old vintage models, those made sometime around nineteen-thirty or earlier. And this is what had caused the problem, as with such a long time frame between them. There were still close to two million ordinary grey coloured vehicles. Out of the twenty plus million or so that were on the roads right now on their computers from between those seventy intervening years. Even if not all of them were roadworthy at the moment, or being used for delivery's, or for travelling salesmen. Though a few things could have helped them come to a lower total.

One being that any heavy goods vehicles on the road were listed on one long sheet of data all on their own. As vehicles such as they were, had to have different MOT tests done upon them, and pay higher road taxation duties annually due to their road weight, too. So, they were therefore monitored by a different department at the DVLA. For that reason, there were only a few thousand such vehicles on the list. But light vans and cars that came under a certain weight restriction. These were all lumped together as one type within the main vehicle licencing department. Which was where the real trouble occurred. As this was the majority of the total, and a far more likely area from which the killer's transport was hidden.

All Hyde could do when the lists came to him was to ask his team to do whatever sifting they could to separate them into various years and makes first of all. Leaving the various types of models until later, when hopefully any further - but much more specific in nature information might come back from the laboratory to aid them even more.

∞

When Douglas and Kumiko finally returned from another tedious brain-numbing day of work that evening, a surprise lay in store for them both. As not only were both Yuki and Hiroko actually just sitting in the kitchen happily chatting away to Raiko after having arrived. But so too was Kumiko's mother, Shinko. Who had decided to visit her eldest daughter and husband on the offchance. Since her own husband offered the use of their company jet to ferry them both over to England to their new master anyway. As always, he was looking after *the* welfare of two newly re-assigned servants, just as he would have done for any clan members who were going to visit another country for business or otherwise.

This was why Shinko had decided to travel with them, mainly in the event that she may not see her daughter again for many months, if not a year or more. So she took time out herself in order to make her own first visit over to see them. As well as to see in exactly what standard of lifestyle she would be living over there. Her husband had tried to give her as many details about the house they had stayed at from memory. But for her mind, it wasn't the same as being able to see it for herself with her own eyes, and then judge its compatibility.

Kumiko could do little else but to gasp aloud and then fling her arms around her mother. As her being in their house had come as such a shock to her. Whereas Yuki and Hiroko both stood up, then smiled and bowed from their waists to the man who had asked for them both personally to come to this country, and to serve him.

'We are both now here for you, master,' announced Yuki with a very genuine smile at him.

'So I see!' he replied, smiling back. 'Not that we knew you were all coming *today* though, as if we had of known that we could have met you at the airport.'

'Raiko told us of the problems you are now facing at work, Douglas. What with so many more new deaths being added to that of my youngest daughter,' said her mother sadly from over her daughter's shoulder. 'So we decided that we should not bother you in that way. And anyway, we have all taken taxis before, so knew that it would just as easy to do for us.'

'How long are you staying with us for, Mother?' asked Kumiko as their embrace finally broke up.

'At most only a few days this first time my daughter, since as you would say, it was only a spur of the moment idea that caused me to come over here to see how you were managing. As you know, the crew will need at least a full day's rest before being able to fly me back home again. And of course, since the new stewardess has now taken over Yuki's duties from her, only after she had helped teach her most of the duties that would be required . . . So, with your father using the aircraft to get Yuki and Hiroko over here to tend to your husband Douglas's personal needs. Maybe two days, possibly three at most I would say.'

The older woman now stepped back from her daughter after their embrace. Then hugged and kissed her new son-in-law on both of his cheeks. 'Both of them have been talking of little else but of their new roles here with you on our way over here.'

Kumiko said to the now ex-stewardess of her father's plane, 'You are happy to become purely a servant in our home, Yuki? Instead of being able to fly all over the world as you have been doing?'

The twenty-five-year-old woman nodded and beamed at her. 'Being part of the crew on your father's private company plane was a very important role and duty for me to do in my clan life, mistress. But my actually being *requested* to become a personal servant to the master, as well as a house servant to you both. I felt, simply offered more to me than being a flight hostess had. Now I hope I have found a more permanent role in my life as I serve you both every day. Instead of only being required for duty as and when the plane was needed to fly somewhere.'

Kumiko smiled back at her. 'I didn't request either of you to join us actually,' she told them. 'My father, while we were in Japan, simply forgot to offer my husband the actual services of a servant of his own. Upon remembering, he decided that my husband should indeed have his own servant here to personally take care of him. This in case I ever went home for a holiday or whatever. Because, as of course you both know, Raiko would have went with me, and that would then have left my poor husband here being and feeling very much on his own here then. And after a while with Raiko looking after the house and everything else for him, my father and I both knew that he would probably find it quite strange having to cope with doing it all on his own again. So, I asked him to have the servant office send me an e-mail as to which servants in our society were looking for work, or wished to change houses.'

Yuki gave a frown. 'But I was not on our work list to change, mistress.'

She smiled again. 'I know that, Yuki. My husband was hoping for your own record to come up on the screen to view, I think. But when it did not, and we had gone through about thirty of them that had been sent here. He said to me that he liked Hiroko the most from those he had seen on there, but afterwards, then also asked me about you also. So with *him* suggesting two servants' names like that, I naturally had to call my father up to ask about that being at all possible.'

'And as I am also now here with Hiroko, then he must have allowed it I take it, mistress?'

She gave a nod. 'He allowed it, only because he said that my husband had a great deal of training to learn now, and two extra helpers might well be better than one. Especially since if I'm ever away, then he'd still be able to practise with both of you. And, also knowing that if he only had the one servant looking after him, then if she ever requested a holiday period to return home – or even worse fell ill, then he may not have anyone here doing that for him then! He may have ended up having to stay off work to look after her instead!'

'What types of training does our master still need to learn, mistress?' asked the young Hiroko of her.

'Well our different styles of unarmed combat for one thing, Hiroko. As my husband knew some already, and is doing quite well right now, but he still requires as much help as we can possibly offer him in them all.'

'Doing *well*?' Hyde said aloud to her with a laugh. 'The only thing I'm doing well at right at this moment in time, is constantly being thrown to the mat by the both of you!'

'You have also done the same to Raiko twice now, my husband,' she answered with a grin.

'Aye - twice,' he chuckled, 'but both times only when she slipped on the sweat that came from *my* own body on to the mat though. Apart from that, not once, and you! You, I can't even get a hold of yet to try and throw you!'

'That time will come, my husband, as you steadily gain more experience, knowledge, and techniques from all of us. That you will indeed, I honestly know, soon be able to manage what I can do with you right now. Then it will be *we* who will be ending up down there soon.'

'And the sooner *that* happens the better!' he muttered.

'Only time can give to you what we each already know so well, my love. We have all had to train for many years ourselves from a very young age to be able to do with you what we can do. Even with your greater levels of strength over us. You nowk now that it is not actually about a body's strength itself. It is about how a body is positioned, and what form of defence or attack is used to counteract your own movements upon us. And things like that can only come in time, training, teaching, and most of all, patience, just as they had to for us all. When learning these same things, *we* were the ones always being thrown down on to the mats, my husband. As those who were teaching us were, as you would expect, already very skilled. So, when you have finally learned what we four can now begin to teach you together here. Then your own skills will continue to grow at an even more rapid pace, if we can manage to keep up our nightly practise structure.

'What other training could *we* possibly help our master out with, mistress?' asked Hiroko of her. 'We are but servants as you already know, and apart from what you have just said, we have no further beneficial skills to offer our new master here other than in unarmed combat?'

'I also have to teach him our innermost sexual skills, Hiroko.' She grinned both at the young girl, and Yuki. 'And for that side of things, he will need some *very* willing volunteers to practice them upon as I teach them to him.'

'Ahhh!' they both uttered softly, and then just smiled up at him.

CHAPTER 21

Hyde's weekend wasn't really what he would ever call *relaxing* in any sense of the word. As not only were there now five women who openly enjoyed themselves, as seemingly with almost casual ease they threw him around the attic space. And down repetedly on to the proactive floor matting far too many times to mention. Apparently also without much effort being involved either, or so it seemed to him.

And then Kumiko, along with her mother were also now attempting to teach him some of their own basic versatile sex techniques. Not that he was much good at them for quite a while to start with. In fact he was so bad at the beginning that no matter how many times they showed him how to gain an instant erection from nerve pressure in his groin alone. He continually hit the wrong part of those nerves, which only caused his own manhood to keep shrivelling smaller and smaller.

It was Sunday evening before he managed the first one of his own. With both women sitting beside him on the bed nodding as it finally came right for him after so many attempts. Though he had hit the wrong one so often to dissipate it, that he knew *exactly* where that was now. He was asked to keep it up, and to learn where both groups of them were. Watching, just as they both did, as it rose and fell in odd jerky movements before them.

Happy with that being taught and learned, they proceeded to show him where a woman's own nerve groups lay in their groins, to also allow him to give *any* woman an orgasm, and by only touching, or pressing upon that highly stimulating part of her body alone. When he'd got that sorted correctly by trying it out on them both until they were happy. As well as ending up feeling quite light-headed from how many they had each received as he was being instructed. They both took a break downstairs for a snack after they had called the three maids into his bedroom. For him to continue practising his new skills upon them for a while now instead.

Though he had, before they had begun to teach him any of these, asked why none of the maids were with them. He was told by her mother that, basically, any servant within their clan was not raised to *be* trained in these adept and sensual and sexual acts in any way. Or even in any of the very secretive arts, which were only gained to add on to any of their *own* personal skills. That *their* own skills were very different to those of any of their servants. As theirs lay only in what training they received by learning a few of their own erotic masseuse techniques. Which when known, came close to giving such pleasure to others.

∞

On the Friday night following their arrival, after some further teaching and training in the attic had been taken with them. He had just walked into the bathroom, at where he found his small mother-in-law almost struggling to climb over the side of it into his own different bath. Since at home, she was more used to her own sunken one where you had to walk down into it, by means of a few small steps, whereas with his. As basically with western ones, you had to step over the side into the water, and do the reverse when you got out again.

Since he had been coming for a bath himself to rest in after his workout with them up in the attic. He just scooped her off her feet and carried her within his arms, then lifted a leg over the side into the water before allowing her to regain her feet. His own bath was large enough for two and a very tight fit for three. But Kumiko soon made it three when she turned up there herself. After pressing the button on the side of it, the powerful hidden jets surrounding all of them, quickly turned it into a frothing, bubbling, Jacuzzi.

∞

The Saturday afternoon was warm, dry, and showed few clouds in the sky once again. So it looked as if it was going to be another quite warm one. The unexpected downpour that had come down on Friday night had acutally been quite refreshing after so many endless days of humid heat. It's arrival was also something which saved him, or more in particular, any of their maids from any plant watering in his garden. Or Edith's being required to be done. As of course Raiko had initially taken on those same duties upon her arrival there too. The morning air had felt fresh and renewed after the coolness of the previous rainfall. Although the risng sun had began to quickly dry out whatever moisture remained. Even so, Douglas got his barbecue equipment out of the shed and set it up. Where of course, the well-known aromatic smells of the chicken, sausage, and burgers being cooked upon it, soon reached out to the nose of his elderly neighbour. This brought Edith out of her house and over to the fence to look over it. As she, and her husband Bert, had always been invited around whenever he had made the effort. Just as she had since also been to most of them on her own since he had passed away.

Yet as her eyes rose above the fence, she saw much more than only his new wife and her maid over on the other side. Now there were six of them all told. And where all but Douglas was wearing their kimono type of clothing.

'They'll be about ten minutes yet, Edith!' he called over to her after seeing her hair catch the sunlight as it rose above the fencing.

'I really wouldn't like to intrude this time, Douglas,' she answered back as they all now looked at her.

'You are as welcome as always, Edith,' said Kumiko to her. 'And it will also give you a chance to meet, my Mother.'

'Oh! And are *these* two your other sisters this time then?'

'Oh no, Edith. Both Yuki, and Hiroko there, are additional maids who have also come to look after us over here. As she mentioned their names to her, each of them turned and offered her a bow.'

Edith's head shook slowly. As she wondered to herself, just whatever were they all needed for? As it certainly wasn't as if Douglas had a very large or dirty house that needed so much taking care of, since it was only the same basic size as her home next door . . . Of course she had seen Raiko out watering both his and her own gardens daily. Sometimes she had even come out to talk with her as she did so. The young maid seemed more than capable of doing everything on her own, or so it seemed. So why two further maids were also required had baffled her.

'Are you quite sure that it wouldn't be any imposition, or an inconvenience to you?' she asked again. Not wishing to disturb Kumiko's mother while she was here with them.

'Hyde gave a laugh. 'Come on in, Edith! Since I know that you are just as partial to my barbecues as I am to your own pastries.'

Edith chuckled aloud as she knew that was indeed very true. Within a few minutes, a click was heard as the fence opened to admit her into his garden. Hyde gave everything a quick turn on the grill, then hurried past her to her own side and returned with her garden chair. That he quickly placed beside his own two bamboo chairs as well as four dining chairs, which had been taken from the around his kitchen table and brought out to use by them.

A small sized plastic circular table, along with its pre-opened large shading parasol through the central hole, had also been brought from the shed where they were always stored for such times. Each item had also been given a quick wash with an antibacterial agent to rid them of any dust or dirt after being in storage. Since it was the only table he had to use outside on days like these, for the placing any of the cooked food on, as and when they were ready to eat.

Edith sat down on her own chair beside Kumiko and her mother with her usual sigh. Her eyes then moving to watch the three younger women as they all stood quietly while bending over slightly, with their hands behind their backs. All were very close beside Douglas as he worked at the hot grill. The one maid there, who she now knew as Raiko for almost close to two months now, was stood watching him beside these two other newer ones. She discreetly observed them all from where she now sat listening, as the girl Raiko asked something of Douglas in her still halting English tones. Though by now, it *had* begun to get much better since her arrival at the house. Just as had Edith's old Japanese skills as she had talked much with the young girl since then.

Her mother, she decided, looked just like a slightly older version of her daughter beside her. Similar bone and facial structure, as well as their similar long jet black hair, though neither of them seemed to be wearing any make-up. She glanced over at the three young girls beside Douglas again . . . and neither did they from what she could see. As her hands clasped together over her ample stomach, she thought that they were all very striking, and quite elegant appearing women to look at - even *without* any make-up on them.

Edith watched as Douglas placed a few sausages and burgers, as well as a chicken leg onto a plate, and then handed it to the smallest of the three young women, who gave him a small bow before heading over towards them with the filled plate.

'My master has said that this meal is for you, Edith-san,' said Hiroko in far better English than Raiko as she placed the plate before her. Edith thanked her, even as Kumiko and her mother's heads then turned so quickly at what she had just said to her, that Edith was surprised neither of them had been injured, so sudden was it. She also caught Kumiko's fierce-eyed glance at the young girl, and Hiroko's face blanched from it, and who also now just as quickly left them.

Very odd, thought Edith as she saw both women obviously studiously looking at her for some reason or othre. Though she herself deigned not to notice it from them. As with her calling Douglas by the somewhat old-termed and imperious sounding title of *master* was quite unusual to say the least! But then she did recall that Raiko had always addressed Kumiko as mistress whenever they talked together anyway. So perhaps it was just something they did to those who they served.

But, if that was *so*, then why were they both watching *her* so closely and intently right now? Did they think that she had interpreted what the young girl had said in a different way? It was possible. Though it still didn't account for why they were concentrating so much on her.

Edith cut her three buns open from the plate in the middle of the table and buttered them. Then put the two thin burgers in one of them, the sausages in another. And for the third bun, she used her fingers to tear the tender chicken of the leg into smaller pieces. Which she now placed into the last bun before licking them clean and wiping them off on one of the pile of waiting paper towels set out on the table for such use.

Allowing her eyes to gaze upwards at them, she asked, 'Penny for your thoughts Kumiko? Is something wrong?'

'Of course not, Edith, why would you think that?'

Halting herself from taking a bite out of one of them for a moment. She looked at Douglas's wife and gave her a smile. 'Just from the way that you were both watching me, my dear. Did your young Hiroko unintentionally perhaps make some kind of mistake before me a moment ago?'

'Mistake, Edith?' Kumiko asked watchfully alert.

'By calling Douglas her *master*, perhaps, could that be what is bothering you both so much now?'

'No, of course its not, Edith,' Kumiko offered rather quickly.

'*Kumiko*, my dear,' Edith expressed gently. 'I may be an old woman, but I'm not blind *or* deaf yet you know!'

Kumiko caught her breath from making a gasp, and also only just managed to stop her hand from rising to her mouth for the same thing. 'I an sure I do not know or understand what you mean, Edith?' She asked, as she was feeling caught off guard right now, and just wasn't used to having to think up unplanned lies so suddenly as this to cover up what they all were. She was feeling flustered and knew it!

'Coffee, Edith?' asked Douglas as he held a cup out for her and placed it beside her hand upon the table, breaking the very inquisitive look being given to his wife by his elderly neighbour.

As she took it from him with a guarded smile on her lips, which revealed very little, Hyde saw the momentary look of panic starting to vanish from his wife's face.

'You can't imagine how helpful they all are around the house, Edith,' he interjected to give Kumiko some time to recover. 'The house is always spotlessly clean when we come in now. The gardnen seen to, and no shopping for us to do at all, nor is there any washing or ironing. It's almost like living in a top hotel with its room service.'

Edith cast an eye at him. 'You're fudging, Douglas.'

'Who *me*!' he responded in a great deal of mock alarm.

Her eyes squinted at him. 'I know you are! As I've known you for far too long now, my dear. And long enough to just about recognise what you are now doing on your wife's behalf.' Then she smiled and added, 'which was of course, to save her from having to answer my last question to her.'

'And where and when, and how, did you learn your Japanese, Edith?' he returned just as succinctly to her.

'I've already told you that I couldn't tell you that, Douglas.'

'A government secret is it? Were you a spy before you retired . . . or something?'

She gave a loud throaty chuckle. 'Me - A spy . . .! Heavens, Douglas, some of the things you come out with!'

He had seen the surprise in her eyes though. 'I think *you* are the one who's fudging now, Edith?' he chided her in return.

She shook her head. 'I cannot say anything about it, Douglas, I'm sorry.'

He nodded, then rested his hands upon the table and went into some deep contemplation about whatever she herself did not want to discuss. He first took in her age as she was now. That she was eighty-five he already knew from her last birthday, so she was born in or around 1915. Too young to do anything in the First World War, so that only left the second one for him to consider now. In 1939 when it began, she would be only a young woman of about twenty-four years of age. And around that age, that somehow or other, she had learned and could speak Japanese!

Edith began to worry when she saw him so deep in thought. Knowing that he had one of those quite deep analytical minds, and one that she knew was quite capable of anything, since he helped to solve murder cases with it. She was not in any way unhappy about what she had done during the war, but knew that it was still almost held as Top Secret by those in Government. Even though many television programmes had already been made about what she had done, and had also even included some of those people who she had worked with. She watched as a minute smile now flickered over his mouth and began to fear the worst - that her own very long, and tightly withheld sixty-year-old hidden secret was about to come out into the open right now.

'Douglas, *please*,' she whispered.

His eyes flickered to her, seeing her worry and sudden alarm. But it was already now too late. 'From what I can surmise of you, Edith,' he began, 'it comes to my mind that you have been one of three things which has caused it to remain a secret for so long now . . . Either you were a member of Churchill's inner staff during the war. Or you were a member of SOE; or else you worked at Bletchley Park doing code work on the Enigma machine?'

'I can uderstand two of those. But what was this SOE, husband?' asked Kumiko of him.

'In short, the SOE stood for Special Operations Executive. That was the group during the war who handled all the agents and spies. And who also sent out and recieved the coded messages either way.'

She seemed to shrivel even smaller before his eyes as he said these to her, and his heart went out to her. Now knowing that he shouldn't have pried as deeply he had into her former life.

'Edith, love . . .' he said softly. 'We don't care what you were, or what you even *did* that long ago now; it's all in a long time ago in the past. We *all* have our little secrets that we have, or try to hide from others,' he said with a glance at Kumiko and her mother. 'And if you would like to tell me yours - then I will tell you mine,' he offered. 'Even mine first if you'd like me too?'

'You have a dark secret, *too*, Douglas?' she asked in a low whisper.

He nodded to her. 'That I do, love.'

As they had begun to speak so quietly amongst themselves, and seeing as there was nothing more on the grill to keep an eye on right now. Their three young maids all now came over carrying the rest of the food from the barbecue to place them on the table. They bypassed the waiting chairs, and all knelt on the grass nearer beside them so as to listen to what was being said. As from going by what they had heard already, it somehow had seemed quite important information that none of them should miss out on hearing right now.

'And who else knows of *your* secret, Douglas?'

'Kumiko and her family, probably these maids here now, and those who I worked with at the time. As well as some others in the military, my Boss at work . . . And since then, very few other people know.'

Spirit of a Dragon

She nodded. 'Only my Bert, and those above me or who I worked with knew what I did during the war.'

'And because I trust *you* to keep *my* secret safe, Edith . . . Is the reason why I am willing to tell it to you now.'

'In exchange for my own, you mean?'

'Only if *you* would like to do the same in return for me, Edith. And there will be no pressure on you to do that, if you do not want to!'

She sighed slowly, and then gave a short nod towards his new wife and mother-in-law, then to the maids as well. '*They* may not like to hear what I may have to say though.'

'Then we will give them all the choice of staying here and hearing it from you, or going inside the house for the moment. Where they then won't be able to hear anything of what you tell me at all.'

'And do you trust all of them with your own secret, Douglas?'

'Implicitly!' he stated for her benefit.

She nodded. 'All right, but I have warned them, okay?'

She watched them all nodding to her, even Raiko who had also had only just been able to follow her words that were said.

'All right then, Edith. You and Bert both knew that I served in the Royal Marines, yes?'

She nodded again.

'But afterwards, I then joined the SAS and took part in quite a few operations with them. Some of them were classed as "Black" operations even, as they involved my having to kill people, and some by these very own hands of mine.'

'How many?' she asked in a rather brittle sounding voice.

He thought he was detecting a little hate from her at this point, but shrugged it off to say to her, 'About twelve, maybe as many as fifteen people have died through me, or as I should have said, personally by my own hands, Edith.'

'Only *twelve* or so, Douglas,' she whispered. 'I may have been responsible for *hundreds*, if not *thousands* of people dying!'

'You may have actually done this, Edith?'

'Yes, me Douglas . . . your very own little old friend and neighbour Edith Glover who is sitting right here.' She looked at the five women quickly. 'Are you all staying?'

Shinko nodded at her. 'Yes, Edith. Whatever you can say will shock none of us here, I can promise you that.'

'Very well then . . . if you're all quite sure of this?' And from all their nods she decided that they all were. 'In that case, I will begin at the start for you all to understand my story and how and why it came about.'

She eased herself into a far more comfortable position on her chair and allowed her mind to roll back over the lost years.

'When I was only a young girl of around eighteen, and mostly by my own private studying being carried out. I was allowed to enter university a little later in order to further my studies. On what was my favourite subject in those days which was the Far East - or perhaps more in particular, about Japan, its people and its culture. Although in no way knowing what lay ahead of us all within only a few more years, which was to be yet another World War!

'While there I also learned your *Kanji* and *Hiragana* characters, only finally learning your much newer *Katakana* style of writing some years later after the war ended. Just before and after learning the latter, both Bert and I had two holidays over in your country together in the mid 1960's.'

'So *that* is how you could understand Japanese, Edith, *neh*?' Kumiko said very gently to her.

Her silvery head bobbed an answer. 'Anyway, the war started in 1939, as you know, with Germany invading Poland and then various other countries after that. Well, I was only starting at university then, wondering what to do to help out when they started asking for us women to begin help out at home for the war effort. So, very early in 1941, when our own professors and lecturers began to leave quite suddenly. I also left and became a Staff Car Driver for the War Department. Though I wasn't kept in that driving job for very much longer as it happens, especially not when a rather very fateful day occurred in the December of 1941 in that same year.'

'I can almost imagine that you are about to say the words Pearl Harbour to us all now, Edith,' said Kumiko's mother, Shinko.

'You are quite right, as that is just what I was about to say, it is also the reason why I didn't want to discuss it in front of you five women here.'

'Why not?' asked Kumiko.

'Only because it may have brought back some very sad or painful memories to you of any of your relatives. Of those who may have died during that war of course.'

'Many families endured such things as those, Edith,' said Shinko. 'Not only we Japanese, but those of your own countrymen too.'

'I know that, Shinko.' She then gave what they all thought was a low drawn out sigh of remorse, endurance . . . possibly even forbearance. They were not really sure at all, as only Edith knew that it was a sigh of happiness --- Happiness at finally being able to speak to someone else about what her younger life had entailed, apart from her own now dearly departed husband.

'When that day happened, and Japan declared war on the United States and England after it, and then sided with Germany and Italy. I was quickly taken from my driving duties, in the same way that others were who I had been studying at university with. As our lecturers and professors had already began to prepare a list of names ready for two reasons. One being if *your* country ever came into the war against our country, and the other was if you came in on our side. As in both matters, translators and linguists would be needed either way.

'And yes, you were right, Douglas, when you said Bletchley Park aloud earlier as one of your guesses. Only I didn't work on the German Enigma to help crack German codes. I was there to do that with the Japanese ones that they had been given to use by them, and we began to receive and decrypt those.'

Hyde was slowly nodding. Thinking as he'd listened to her story. That you just never knew what anyone that passed you in the street anytime had done. As what Edith had done had even surprised him!

'We even sent a team over to help the Americans set-up a similar team for a little while, before we came home to our own work again.' And when she had said *we*, they all knew that she had been one of the many skilled people who had been sent over there to help the Americans to get their own code breaking departments up and running quickly after it had started.

'So I, along with others in my group, and as we quickly began to crack your codes. Soon had your naval convoys and army details located, and then these would be passed on to our own forces to use. Which of course led to them being attacked and people were killed during these times.' She then looked at all the women before her there.

'So I'm sorry if I caused any of your relatives to die, but that was the war we were fighting back then. So bloody, that it was a case of kill or be killed. And we had to look after our own people.'

Shinko nodded her understanding as Edith's final words trailed off. 'I understand your feelings, Edith. Indeed I do. Yes, even our own families lost quite a few of our relatives in that war. But please, do not worry yourself about it anymore now. *You* were not the cause of that war, so of course you were only doing your duty to your country, just as our relatives fought for theirs.

'And we all know *now* that it wasn't even that of our own Emperor's fault at the time either. As he was just misled into starting a war by the leaders of military factions. Mainly one man called General Tojo deserves the true credit for taking our country into such a senseless war, and in order to only gain extra resources for our country. But we do all thank you very much for sharing your trust with us, which of course we will all keep silent about just as you wish.'

'Thank you,' Edith whispered.

Douglas squatted in front of Edith, and said to her. 'No matter what *you* may personally think you have done to these other people during the war, love. You have to remember that it was *none* of your doing really! You didn't tell them which targets to select, nor did you send any of our men out to attack and kill any of their men either, Edith. Your own job was to crack the codes and pass them on to those higher who then made the final decisions about them, and that's all. It was our military staff who then decided what to do with any of that information you and others found out, love.'

Spirit of a Dragon

'Douglas is, of course, completely correct in that, Edith,' added Shinko.

'Mother . . .' murmured Kumiko, '*a secret for a secret*, can we also do this with Edith, or not?'

Shinko gave an undisguised shrug in return. 'For myself, and from now having met Edith, I would now say yes. But you also know where our problem will lie by doing so, I hope?'

Kumiko nodded straight away. 'Most assuredly, Mother. But cannot you ask Father what he may also think? We all know Douglas's secret now, and now we also know Edith's, too. So if both he and she can trust *us* to keep theirs, can we not also offer her the same knowledge about us too?'

Shinko gave a gentle sigh and then stood up and walked off into the living room to ask her husband exactly that. He was their clan leader, so it was of course it was his responsibility and decision to choose. Though he had told her when he came home before, that Douglas's elderly next door neighbour was not only a very adroit old lady. But still also retained an amazingly sharp mind as well. While he didn't know why this was at the time, Shinko now did.

Her call to her husband on her mobile was brief and to the point. As was his own answer to her when she had told him about Edith's almost epic in its time of hiding it, long kept secret. As only by his having met her himself, did he judge from what he had now heard. That she would also be able to keep their own secret life untold, just as safely as her own had been kept for so long.

Shinko was to be honest quite surprised at her husband's actual response, although she was also pleased in a way. too. As just as her daughter had said to her in the garden. A well-kept secret like that had been, truly deserved a similar secret being told back to it in reply. Just so that both sides had learned something quite unknown about each other. A thing like that could also only forge a stronger bond, and bring them much closer than they already were now. And so, with her husband's acceptance as he listened to what she had said. Along with his full approval and blessing at backing her own judgement. She replaced the phone and went back out into the garden. Whereupon she said nothing at all to any of them until they had all sat and eaten some of the foods which had been prepared on Douglas's barbecue.

It was only after they had all finished and everything had been put away again into the house and shed. Did Shinko ask them all to come into his living room with her, which also included his elderly neighbour. And there, Edith soon came to learn what those around her were all a part of. Even to that of her next-door-neighbour, Douglas, now too. When Shinko had asked him to show her his back first of all, Edith had been very surprised indeed at what now lay etched upon it. As she knew that not so long ago when she had seen him working in either of their gardens bare-backed. That he certainly did not have such an amazing decoration as that upon it then. Then she, and her daughter had followed suit, with finally the three maids.

Either Kumiko or her mother had then answered each one of Edith's' many questions as she began to ask them about their clan. Some they had found quite deep and profound, and were as always, answered with total honesty by them. Even of how they had all begun to learn such teaching and enjoyment. Not only of their own bodies at a very young age, but also of other children's. Edith didn't look shocked, or even surprised, when they had told her about some of their more intimate clan rituals.

She in turn replied to them that she herself *had* actually heard some very strange noises coming from his bedroom – what with her own being just through the wall next to his. And had wondered how Kumiko had been able to manage for so long with him all by herself through all that time. But now, she knew different, and what it had all been. She was also quite breathless when they had also told her of Douglas's' two nights of major passion back in Japan with so many of them. And of just how many women had been involved, and could be coming here to stay now and then to receive something similar from him again whenever it was possible.

They had all seen the, very brief, but fleeting look of sadness appear and disappear from her face. While she was being regaled over her younger neighbour's newly opened sexual appetite and prowess. Knowing that she now only felt a little jealous of all the women that he had enjoyed sex with. And that some of those who had were here, which meant that he was still enjoying it with them even now - all five of them actually! She was now a little bitter at her own age, and not being able to enjoy some of that herself anymore.

'Why the long sad face, Edith?' asked Kumiko about then to her.

She gave a loud sigh. 'All this talk of sex that you are all having so much of in here. And there am I next door not young enough to do so any more.'

'But why not, my friend?' asked Shinko.

'Why not, because I'm eighty-five now Shinko. And I am certainly not the vibrant young woman of twenty or thirty-five as I once was so long ago!'

'But why is that stopping you from enjoying any of the same pleasures, Edith?' she queried. 'We have even older men and women who still enjoy such pleasures as we vave been speaking about back home . . .'

'My God!' she gasped.

Shinko smiled at her warmly. 'I know that you feel that your age now could be a problem for any man who may be as young as Douglas here is to wish entertain you, Edith. But older men like my husband, Koichi, and those even older than he is if they came here to stay for a short holiday. I feel *would* happily accept any offer of such enjoyment that you may ask of them.'

Edith's eyes were like saucers as she looked at them all. Then she began to shake her head after some further thought. 'No, I couldn't do something like that against my dearly departed Bertram's memory. It would be quite shameless of me to even think of doing such a thing after the amount of time we spent married together.'

'Perhaps, but why should your body miss out on such enjoyable pleasures now, even if there is no one to aid you in this way?'

Edith sighed again. 'Because I would only be thinking purely of myself then, Shinko. And not about what all those wonderful times and years that I *did* spend with my husband were like. And what it really meant to me . . .'

'Memories are, and can be a truly wonderful thing for us to remember. Including those who are now sadly departed from us, Edith,' she replied. 'But, pleasure for our own *self* is always needed now and then, myself included! I cannot even *begin* to tell you of how my other two daughters, and myself, enjoyed our time with Douglas on the night before his wedding to my Kumiko. I am just happy that he will still *consider* my own offers while I am here with them now. Just as I know both Makiko and Noriko are also already desperately making plans to come over soon to enjoy more with him. *As well as to visit and see their sister, of course,*' she added with a cheeky smile at her daughter.'

Shino added, 'Though many of our clan members back home are already speaking to each other about the very same thing before I'd left. As what our Douglas here does not know in the ways and nuances of so many of our various skills, as yet. He certainly makes up for that with the sheer length of his beautiful shaft, and the pleasure that he gives to us all like that!' she stated as four other heads began to nod rather quickly to affirm what she had said.

'And what do you say about that, Doug---?' Edith started to say, and then stopped when she saw the flush on his face from Kumiko's mother's own frank words. 'Are you all right?'

He gave a nod, though barely able to look at his elderly neighbour right now. 'I'm okay, Edith. It's just that I'm *still* not used to the way they talk about sex so frankly and openly between them all yet.' His red flush began to dissipate as he answered her, 'not like that anyway!'

Until Yuki made it come back again rapidly by saying to them all, 'But we *all* love the size of your beautiful penis, master!'

Edith chuckled at his consternation. Though why, she didn't actually know, since it shouldn't have been that funny, even to her. But it may have been that it was just so refreshing to hear such things being spoken of so openly and carelessly between them all. Not even counting how many different women her younger neighbour had pleased while in Japan. And of how many he was also pleasing; and right next door to her now, too.

'Please think over what I have said to you, Edith. As if any of these older men are over here at any time, and you feel that you ever really *do need*, or would *like* to enjoy such pleasure again. Then some of them, I have no doubt about that in my mind, will be happy to help you out. Even some of our trained women could offer you almost as much pleasure as that also, if you ever wished . . .'

'But I am not a member of this clan of yours, Shinko,' Edith remarked. 'I don't carry any of the marks that you do, do I. and I think I'm just a little *too* old now to go in for getting tattoos, don't you think?'

'Only because of your age now would I agree, Edith. As I don't think you would get through the one day process for a servant or the longer two day process for our kind of tattooing now. Something which you possibly would have been able to do, if you had been maybe only twenty-years younger than you are now. But as my husband, Koichi, said to me when I called him. That because of this, we are now classing you as not only an honorary, but also as an honourable and venerable member of our clan from this day on.'

'I feel so proud just to have been told your secret, never mind becoming a part of your clan - even if only an honorary member.'

Shinko smiled widely at her. 'So now, Edith, as a kind of member within our clan, you can also enjoy the same pleasures that we all do!'

'I understand what you have said, Shinko. But I will still have to have a very *long* think over what it is that you are now offering to me.'

'The choice of course is yours to make now, my friend. If you do wish it to be so, then someone will likely happily do so for you. But if you do not wish to, then of course you don't have to ask them.' She smiled again. 'Though of course some of the men may well *still* ask you for pleasure themselves . . . Then you will be the one who will have to turn *them* down formally at such times. And also do not forget, that if you would ever like to take another holiday over in Japan – that you could now just come and stay with me and my family at our country home too!'

Many other details and clan information was then offered for her to digest. Some of which she took in, and thought over. While with others that she was given and took in, she didn't expect to have to ever recall again. But with everything, as before, it was all spoken of very openly and honestly to her.

∞

Early on the Monday morning of the new week, Hyde and his wife dropped her Mother off at the hotel where the crew of the plane were as usual staying. So that she could travel to the airport with them from there. They were now leaving her there while on their way into work. While also hoping at the same time, that some new developments may have came in over the weekend for them to be able to study. Whereas Shinko was going to head back home after what had been a brief, but very happy stay with them.

She had even stayed her last night at Edith's, and with her invitation for that given option to her, there was just the two of them. So neither he nor Kumiko had any idea at all yet what they had talked about. Since neither one of them had mentioned anything about it to them that morning. All they *had* noticed before leaving Hyde's home before driving away this morning, was that the two women apparently parted on *very* friendly terms indeed.

CHAPTER 22

Hyde and Kumiko were little more than five minutes late in reaching the office that day after a short delay from dropping Shinko off. But when they did reach work and enter, they found it almost buzzing like a hive with utter excitement!

'It's here, Dougie!' Terry called out loudly over all the other excited tones there. 'It just came in after we got here barely a few minutes ago!'

'So what's the best news?' he called back while also taking his jacket off at the same time.

Terry shook the paper in his hand at him. 'They can now state that the paint came off an *metallic* light-grey *Ford Transit*, Dougie.'

'What about a year? Did we get a year for it as well?' he asked hopefully.

Terry's grin said it all. 'It's an almost new W reg one, Dougie!'

'Yes!' he bellowed, while also smacking a clenched fist into his other palm. 'All right everyone,' he called aloud, 'get yourselves cracking on those pages that we already have here, and then we can also begin to get our possible list of suspects narrowed down for us. We'll have to do this as quickly as we can now!' he informed them, almost if not enthusiastically, then ecstatically. 'And when you *have* got all these Ford Transit's that match this new description marked, then I want them sorted out into their various areas for me too, okay!'

'Surely with this info the DVLA could run a fast printout off for us, Dougie?' said Terry to him.

'They *might* well be able to run a printout off for us, Terry. But how long it would be before they can also sort it all out, and we *get* the printout back from them to check is another matter entirely! Though I'll give them a call anyway while we get cracking on what we already have here in our hands. Either way, we can then use theirs as a *bona fide* checklist against our own work whenever it finally does arrive.'

Kumiko watched them all getting to work, and apparently with a far higher will and expectancy now too. As where before they had had little to aid them in their earlier searches. Now, they finally had something to sink their teeth into and chew at. As well as making it much more progressive search also! Each of the team she now saw were coming over to the centre table that held all the earlier pages sent to them. Where after grabbing a good handful each, they went back to their usual desks and began to *"get cracking!"* as her husband had just said.

'Why do you need specific areas, Douglas?' she asked him.

He looked at her with a huge smile on his face, then grabbed her and hugged her tightly, which lifted her off the floor, before swinging her around until finally releasing her again on to her feet. 'Why? Because we're going to need help from other forces around the country to start checking them all out aren't we, Kumiko. With everyone co-operating like this, we can soon start to narrow our search down even further and much quicker now.'

'How is that so?'

'Easy. Because we only need to check up on them to see which of these vans are being used for nationwide runs all the time. Any of those which are only being used locally all the time by companies or individuals can be readily dismissed from our search. And in *this* way, we might even be able to get our most likely suspects down to a few hundred, or a few thousand at most! A hell of a lot better than a million or more, isn't it?'

She nodded, even to finding herself already becoming caught up with his excited enthusiasm and energy, just as all the rest of his team had minutes previously. As she now knew that he was a born leader. His personal enthusiasm for a task, however hard it may be, had been instantly passed over to those working with him quickly. And as such, had galvanised them, and caused them to work just as hard themselves.

'Then I had better lend a hand, too, my husband, *neh*? Since that is also the reason why I was allowed to be here in your *team* with you.'

'Go for it, my love,' he said, acknowledging her own eager willingness to also help out. Then he nodded towards where Terry was working at his desk. 'Watch Terry for a few minutes as he does some first though, until you get the main picture of how it's done yourself, and then just dig in with us.'

She nodded rapidly and then walked away towards where Terry sat with his finger running down the page in front of him. Leaning to look over Terry's shoulder, Kumiko watched his finger going quite fast down the page. As he apparently quickly collated whatever information he needed to see or know, She was wondering just how he was able to do it at such a rate of speed, which seemed beyond her for the moment.

'How do you search so quickly, Terry?' she asked him. The adage of the *san* she had always used from their initial meeting had by now been dropped more than a week ago. 'Are you looking for anything specific to be able to do this checking of it so fast?'

'It's easy, Kumiko,' he told her, 'let your eyes follow your finger down as you look for the title Ford here in the first left column. If it says anything other than Transit in the second column after it, then ignore it. If those two *do* match up, then you can pass over the third column, which is the year of manufacture, and just look at the fourth. As that column only has the year of manufacture letter printed. If you see a W on its own there, then take a glance at the earlier column just to be sure that it was made in the nineteen ninety's. If that also matches, then use a highlighter pen and mark through it all.' Terry's own finger stopped just about then as she watched. Where she saw it move from Ford, to Transit in the second column. Then over to where a W was, then back to the one before it to make sure. Now she watched as he laid a thick pink line through its entire length.

'But there is no address showing on it for whoever *owns* any of these vans to help us out more, Terry!' she remarked suddenly.

His finger tapped the last column now illuminated in pink and easily visible to her eyes. 'No, but there's a reference number, Kumiko. And if you give one of those to the DVLA, they can look it up straight away on their computers and get that information back to us quick enough. Even our own PNC, which stands for our Police National Computer, can do the exact same job that is required now. Though probably just not as quickly as the DVLA's own can. As their computer only deals *with* this kind of data, while ours includes various others, such as fingerprints, stolen vehicles, stolen items, as well as information about criminals. So their sysytem will not only be able to offer a quicker search, but it will also leave our own network free to continue the work that it's already doing at the moment all aound the country.'

'But then we will end up with even *more* of these data pages being sent here to look at!' she gasped.

'Yes, but it's a hell of a lot better than us having to try and trace each and every single owner of *every* one of these vehicles already sent to us, Kumiko. As if we had done it that way, instead of this way, then we would have had literally *thousands* of extra pages to check just because of that!'

She finally made sense out of what he had just said. That with so many having been cut out from the original number they had been given. That a far fewer number could be asked for from this Government Transportation Department of theirs. And this also meant that only *definite* matches to the new criteria involved could be pursued for the suspect woh was involved. As she walked away from him to the central table to gather up a handful of these same pages herself to begin to work on. She saw that her husband was already speaking to someone on the telephone. Possibly that *Jobsworth* man again as they'd called him, Ferguson if she remembered correctly . . .

Kumiko was sliding her finger down the first list she had brought over to his desk. Having, with some luck it had to be said, already highlighted two lines with her green highlighter pen.

As Hyde came off the telephone after giving a thank you to whomever it was at the other end. He called out to everyone in the room nearby, 'They are going to try to get the new information we need to us just as soon as they can!'

Then after putting the telephone down, he went over and picked up a handful of the pages himself before coming to sit beside her. He sat down and opened his drawer, but not finding what he was looking for, since his wife now already had it in her hand. 'Brenda!' he called over to one of his team members. 'Have you got a spare highlighter over there?'

The policewoman detective left her finger at the place where she'd had to stop checking. Then used her other hand to open the drawer beside her to rummage around inside it for a few seconds. 'Only a red one, will that do you, Dougie?'

'Sure.'

With an almost casual appearing sideways toss, she threw it towards him and he caught it first time. Thanked her, and then got down to work on the pages laid in front of him, just as everyone else was doing. For four solid hours they worked through them, occasionally answering a ringing telephone at one of their desks as they worked. Until Ramshaw himself entered, walking straight over to where their team leader Hyde was seated.

He saw Hyde's new wife beside him also doing a similar task to those of his group and was pleased to see that she was also working in an active role for them so quickly. Halting beside their shared desk he asked, 'How's it going, Hyde? And have we had any more information come in yet?'

Douglas, just like the rest when being made to halt his search, left a finger in place as he looked up at his superior. 'Had some good news from the specialist lab already, sir. With the help from the manufacturers. And they were finally able to give us a make, model, as well as its year of manufacture.'

'So what are you all doing now? You should have just rung up the DVLA again to get a new list printed out for you.'

'I've just already done that, sir. But I thought that while they're coming up with that new list of data for us to use . . . We could use our own time at the moment to go through those that we already had, and then begin to make our own up from them.'

'What on earth for?'

Hyde grinned. 'At the moment, to use as a kind of back-up list come checklist against theirs, sir. I've already spoken to Ferguson again at the

DVLA---'

'*Him* . . . Was he any more helpful than last time for you?'

Hyde nodded. 'A lot better, sir. I've asked him for a new list covering every Transit Van of that colour, and also for that specific year now. As well asking for the names and addresses of their owners included.'

'That could take a while to do . . .'

'Which is why I've got all of us doing this right now, sir. Since we still can't do a lot more yet until we do get much more exact details from them. And as we're not getting many calls from anywhere to help us right now; so at least if we do this it will keep us all busy for the moment.'

'You may be getting more calls than you'd ever hoped to get shortly,' stated Ramshaw.

'How so, sir?' queried Hyde.

His superior gave a smile at the solemn face below him, and then offered, 'Because you will soon be heading off down to London. Well, actually *today* Hyde, or tonight anyway.'

'Why?'

'Crimewatch, Hyde . . . Have you forgotten about it being on tomorrow night? Their monthly show will be on live as usual this Tuesday night, and as we've managed to get you bumped on to the show due to this actual investigations importance! So, you'd better take whatever notes you think you may need to put over to the public while you're on. But don't forget what I told you earlier about it, eh? Just stick to what *facts* we do have, no surmises or guesses, and for God's sake don't give out any unexpected information or rough summations out on air to the general public. Especially about what they *don't* need to know!'

'But we mightn't need it now sir, what with the new information we have received now,' he said quickly, and still trying to get out of it somehow.

Ramshaw shook his head slowly and stubbornly. 'You know just as well as I do Hyde, that the public still need to be informed about our killer's *modus operandi* of thought process and attacks. As even now, some of them may even have an idea of his true identity at this very minute from what we can give out to them tomorrow night. But because of the very limited information that we *have* decided to let out so far in the various newspapers. They've been unable to make any true guess as to his identity. For Heaven's sake, Hyde. Even the tabloid newspapers have come up with a damn name for him already now, did you know that yet?'

Douglas nodded: 'Mac the Ripper.'

Ramshaw grimaced. 'Yes, that! Since they couldn't very well call the bugger Jack the Ripper 2, could they?'

'They did that so it would have the same type of tabloid jingoistic sound to it I think, sir.'

'I know that Hyde, damn it! And that's my point entirely! The sooner we get some information departed to those outside our own establishment. Then *any* extra lead from them, be it big or small - could well be about the person that we're hunting for. The Police Commissioner agrees with me. Don't you agree too?' he asked, now staring down at the younger man.

'Yes, sir,' sighed Hyde. 'But I still don't think that I'm the right person for that particular job.'

'You don't have any choice in the matter, Hyde. *You're* the man who is in charge of the whole investigation involving all of these murders. Murders that have kept rising throughout your investigation too, I may add.'

He quickly held a hand up in the air, as Hyde was just about to respond to his statement. 'I'm not blaming any of you for that happening, Hyde. As without any facts or actual leads to help you out, we all know how difficult it has been lately. Even the Commissioner said that to me when we talked about the problem last time. But that's my point, Hyde. Since you now actually *have* some decent facts with which to offer to the public about this serial killer. Being on television is also only a small part in it of helping us to catch him. Only so that the quicker this devil *is* caught and brought to justice. Then the quicker all of the killing's he's doing will finally come to a full stop.'

Hyde gave a low sigh. 'All right, sir, I'll go and do Crimewatch for you just as you said.'

Ramshaw nodded, far happier now. 'I *know* that you don't want to do it, Hyde. But it just has to be done. You can even take your wife down there with you as a travelling companion if you like?'

Kumiko looked up at that point. 'My husband knows that my work is to be here to help out, sir. Whereas If I had *not* been offered a position to work in uniform beside him, and had arrived here only as his wife, then of course I would have gladly gone there with him . . . But, as I was actually seconded over here to *help out* in this department towards this task, then he would also fully understand why I could not do that.'

Ramshaw was impressed to say the least.

'Will I need to wear the *uniform*, sir?'

'No, detectives wear what they like on the show so long as they make sure that they look *smart*. And you *are* representing the force. Our Force in particular, Hyde. So for God's sake at least *try* to look smart for us on it, eh? And a nice shirt and tie to match it certainly wouldn't come amiss either!' he added with a look at his wide-open collar.

'I'll choose something suitable for my husband to wear, sir,' said Kumiko before her eyes dropped back down to her list.

'How am I travelling, sir?'

'By what means would you like to go?'

'I've driven down there by car before, sir. So if I can use my department car, then I'll go that way.'

Ramshaw worked out the various costs and journey times in his head. Between that of using a plane, train, bus, or car, and quickly decided that it would be much cheaper the way that he had offered to go there, even if using a police car would take longer. Not that he was miserly in any way, but he was the one who had to account for any unnecessary expenditure when they were audited every year. Via train or plane could mean additional transport being required; possibly even if using a bus too. And he knew that using a taxi down there certainly was never cheap! So he decided that the car would take him there and back with far less fuss.

Spirit of a Dragon

'Very well Hyde, since I suppose I can't expect you to use your own car when on police business like this.' Then he placed his hands flat on the table, and leaned over to look right into his eyes. 'But *nothing*, and by that, I mean nothing *whatsoever*, should prevent you from getting down there just as if you were only driving on the road like a regular traveller, right!'

Hyde nodded and cursed inwardly. Ramshaw was remarkably adept. As he had been hoping that any kind of minor or major incident on his way down there. Might *just* have helped him delay the inevitable, a little, if not a lot.'

'I'll get my secretary to book a room for you as near to the BBC studios as I can for tonight then, Hyde. And a meal or two on the way down and back can be reimbursed if you wish also.'

'Thank you, sir.'

Kumiko looked up again. 'And as *I* am not going there with you, my husband, I will of course send one of our maids down there with you.'

Ramshaw gave a low cough. 'I'm afraid that we will only be booking one room, Inspector Hyde.'

'That in itself is not a great problem really, sir. As the maid chosen can take her futon with her and just roll it out on the same bedroom floor. They are all used to doing that anyway, so it would not be an inconvenience for her. Nor would it bother *any* one of them to have to do so. And at least my husband will have company both ways, someone with who to actually talk to on the drive. As he has already told me that it could take eight or nine hours to get there, and back again when I asked him about my having a shopping trip down there previously. So any company of course would be nice to have on such a long journey, *neh*?'

'Very well,' said Ramshaw giving in to her with a low sigh, 'we'll even reimburse you for *her* meals as well, Hyde.'

'I'll also have her iron out your clothes just before you leave for the television studios while down there, my husband. So that as the Chief Constable mentioned earlier to you. That you will represent your police force here very well on the actual night itself.'

Ramshaw's indignant manner died in his throat, as Kumiko had hit on the one button that smoothed his feelings. That of a smartly dressed officer who would soon be representing their local police force before the entire nation on national television.

'I'll get my secretary on to sorting all of that out for you straight away then, Hyde. While you leave the others to get on with what you told them to do. I want you to begin to get everything you need collated together. I'll even get my secretary to run off a schedule note for you as well. Just so that you will know where you'll be staying and where you also have to be, and by what time.'

'Thank you, sir.'

Ramshaw was just about to walk away, but paused. 'Are you eligible to drive yourself in our country yet, Mrs Hyde?' he asked her.

She shook her head. 'Not yet sir, I am still awaiting my testing date to procure a full United Kingdom driving licence so that I can be allowed to drive here in England. My husband has been aiding us all to get to grips with the driving over here much easier. And being a policeman as he is, he is also very thorough with us all when he teaches up too!' she stated. 'I know that we all could have used our own Japanese licences for a short period of time. But, I would rather be seen as being proficient enough to be able to pass your driving examination standards, before even wishing to do so in my own mind.'

She had impressed him again, so about all Ramshaw could say after that was, 'Then you'll have to leave your own car here for tonight and tomorrow Hyde. Your wife will just have to come in by taxi tomorrow, unless I can arrange something for her.'

Hyde looked past him. 'Terry. Can you pick Kumiko up at our house in the morning and then also run her home again tomorrow evening for me too?'

'Sure, boss.'

'Then that's all nicely sorted,' said Ramshaw as he strode away in his usual marching gait.

'Who're you sending down with me, Kumiko?' he asked softly so that no one else would hear them.

'I was thinking of sending Hiroko with you. But I felt that right now, her actual youth could pose just too *many* risjs, as well as questions for you to have to answer. And as Raiko is actually my maid, and still a little nervous when she is speaking in English to other people. That really only leaves us with our, Yuki. Who I would have to say between them all, has a better age look to her. And she already has far more knowledge of the world anyway from her previous flight duties and hotel stays. Her English is also quite excellent, so she would be much easier choice to move around in your country with you, and she is also mature enough not to let anything slip-out unawares.'

'And she'll be taking her futon with her?'

'Yes, but only in case you really *are* given a room with only a single bed within it, husband. If it is a double then she can sleep in it with you to save her having to lie on the floor.'

'But if we're both in the one bed . . .'

'If so, and you wish to, then you can also have sex together if you both require or desire it. Please do not worry about it, my husband. We both know what goes on in our *own* house now anyway already, don't we? So, if you aren't too exhausted from your drive down there, then you can try to practise some of your new techniques upon her if that is your wish.

'I already know that *Yuki* would be more than happy to help you out at *any* time you wished to do so. As she has already spoken of this to us since her arrival here. In the very same way that Raiko and Hiroko would both also offer to do the very same for you. But anyway, just see how you feel when you get there, husband, as you already know that there is no actual pressure upon you to do anything with her that *you* personally do not wish to do. Always remember that you are *her* master now while she stays with us.'

∞

Darkness was arriving as Hyde and Yuki were preparing to leave, and both gave a final wave to the three women who now stood outside the front door to their home. Also only after having eaten a large enough meal in order to sustain them for the long journey ahead. Well, at least for most of the way down there, if not all of it. The two maids left in the house with her after they had departed, and his car vanished from their sight. Has watched as their mistress walked from one room to another, now seemingly at something of a loss at just where she should be herself right now.

349

As for Kumiko, she soon found that she was missing him quickly. what with having spent nearly every day beside him since even before their marriage. And with not being near him right now in some way, even so soon, it had left her feeling that a distinct part of her was already missing. Which had came as quite a surprise to her she found, especially after their only being together and married for such a short time to him. As with the long years of her lonely single life now left behind her, those same days had been now placed only into her distant memory.

She now knew that she loved Douglas utterly, and without reservation. Even to having loved him as much from when they had seen each other, she also now knew in her own heart. With both maids still in the house with her, she wasn't actually alone in that sense, thought she *still* felt unusually lonely. Which was a very strange and very new feeling to her. Since she and Raiko had lived almost like flatmates in her Tokyo apartment for so many years together. Not like mistress and maid in feeling, even if it was fact. But Raiko wasn't Douglas, and even she couldn't make up for that new feeling which she had found emerging with him. He wasn't only her mate, but her partner, her own husband, a true soul mate. She emitted a sigh in a low whisper. He was now, she simply knew, her whole life!

She lay in *their* chair with an opened book on her lap. Yet even with her latest James Herriot novel, she just couldn't concentrate enough to get into its story properly. So closing the book, she turned the television on to watch that instead. Only to find that nothing on it, as she flicked through its channels, was interesting her enough to keep her watching it. After a few more minutes of not knowing what else to do with herself, she went upstairs and took a bath then went to bed early. Of course, as his body wasn't there to lie beside her tonight, to touch, or snuggle into, she suddenly became oddly tearful because of that. It was a feeling akin to akmost being quite single and being on her own again. After a few minutes, she called out for both Raiko and Hiroko, and only with them both lying very closely beside her within it, did she finally manage to at last fall asleep.

∞

It was September by now as Kumiko slept, and Hyde and Yuki drove southwards in the dark down the A1 towards London. At the same time, and not really that far away from where Kumiko and her maids now slept. A greyish hued van was parked-up at the unlit end of an Industrial Estate in Sunderland less than ten miles from the sleeping trio. No lights showed on it from either front or back. And only if anyone had walked by near enough to it that evening, might they have heard the groans and feverishly low lurid calls coming from behind its closed rear double doors. As well as the slight rocking motion of the van. Sadly, victim number twenty-four was already in dire peril.

∞

It was almost five in the morning when Hyde finally pulled up outside the small hotel only a few streets away from the television studios themselves. His eyes practically feeling raw and red-rimmed from having gone so long without any sleep by now. And since he had now been awake since seven the previous morning. So what with him almost going a full twenty-four hours without any sleep now. He was almost ready to crash-out and collapse just about anywhere at all. Even on a floor somewhere, or here in the car itself if need be! He gave the lucky sleeping figure in the passenger seat beside him a gentle shake and Yuki's eyes opened, even as a long yawn came from her mouth. A sound which only caused Hyde himself to utter one straight away in a joined response to it.

'We're here Yuki,' he told her. 'Remember now just what we planned on the way down?'

She gave a nod, and even after the last two hours of their journey in which she had managed to sleep on and off. She still looked just as tired from it as he did. Not surprising at all really, as she had also been awake for as many hours as he had himself, too. 'You may be assured that I will remember, master.'

'Be alert inside to whatever might be said, okay? As I may even have to call you my girlfriend or wife if need be.'

'I will be very wary and watch out for any problems that could occur, my master,' she said with a dutiful nod to him.

'It may not even *be* necessary,' he told her. 'As they may just think that you are a girlfriend of mine . . . or *something*,' he added with a genial wink at her, which brought a wide white-toothed smile to her mouth. 'But, it's always best to be prepared and ready for any eventuality, Yuki. And we especially do *not* want to hear any of your, *master's,* being said in front of anyone down here either!'

She nodded, affirming that she understood its true relevance, and then they both climbed out of the car together. Each of them stretching their bodies as the doorman come porter peered out through the still closed hotel doors. He began to smile as he waited to see if his help would be required in any way by them. As that of course would benefit him by being offered a tip of some kind at least in what was still the most boring and dead time of all hotels. But what he saw them taking from the back seat and then from inside the boot before it was closed, caused his hopeful smile to disappear.

He opened the door for them as they entered inside though, and closed it again when they had passed through. As that was besically his job, with a nod of the head as a thank you from Hyde was only tip he received.

As Hyde and Yuki walked straight over to where yet another very bored looking receptionist sat behind the counter. Apparently dispiritedly on with filing her long fingernails to pass the time. More than likely as working the graveyard shift in the early hours of any job wasn't a very enjoyable duty or task at any time. He already knew that himself from his own changeable work times. Though at least it was warmer inside the hotel, which helped them somewhat.

'Douglas Hyde, there should be a room booked for us in my name?'

The young girl behind the counter placed the emery board on the desk and then slid along behind the counter in her wheeled chair. Up to the computer console without the need to even stand up to move, where she then scrolled down the screen. 'Only for one night isn't it, sir?' she queried.

He gave a nod, and yawned as he actually said, 'Yes, just the one.'

She saw the exhaustion on them both as she looked up at them. 'Room 69 on the fourth floor, Mr Hyde, only a single room was requested to be booked by telephone. But I'm afraid we only had doubles left by the time we were called, so that was all we had to offer. But we are pleased to have you with us even for such a short time, and do hope that you enjoy your stay here,' she said almost automatically in her receptionist patter. 'We do also have room service in operation if you may need anything.'

'Thank you, but sleep is about the most important thing that is very much on our minds right now.'

Spirit of a Dragon

He took the key from her as she handed it to him, and then she gestured to where elevators stood side by side. They walked over and entered inside its bare metallic cabinet. He pushed the button with the four on it and the doors closed. After some unknown music played inside, it opened on to the fourth floor. Where it then took them a few minutes to locate their room at which point they entered inside.

Yuki, who was very much used to staying in variety of hotel rooms due to her previous work. Placed her futon and small items of baggage on the floor before moving straight over to the waiting kettle. She checked its water level was high enough before setting it to boil. While he quickly deposited both of their cases at the bottom of the bed, then almost slumped down in a sitting position wearily upon its edge. While it boiled she came over to him, kicked her slip-on shoes off, and climbed up on to the bed to kneel behind him. To where her deft and well-trained fingers or elbows, quickly began to massage first his shoulders and then neck, taking some of the deep aches and pains from within his tired body almost instantly.

'Master, please go and enjoy a hot shower while I prepare a hot drink for us both before I come in to help you. When you come out, I will also give you a *proper* massage to ease your body into feeling much better before we go to sleep.'

Hyde's sagging head gave a nod and he began to undress. Yuki quickly got off the bed and came to help him. Only when he was sitting back on the bed to take his socks off did she leave and enter the bathroom. She went in and turned on the tap which set the shower to emitting a warming spray. A hand into it felt to check the temperature, then she came back out again to him. She emitted a quick gasp at seeing other tall lit buildings out of their window. Then hurriedly went over to close the curtains and turn the ceiling light on. She shook her head as she watched his naked body almost stagger into the bathroom.

Removing her own clothing even faster, she then quickly made two cups of coffee from the tiny packets and sachets of coffee, milk and sugar that lay on the little tray. Stirred them both, and then headed into the bathroom to see to her usual duties.

She found him leaning against the wall with his head under the spray. Eyes closed and not even moving. Which quickly made her wonder if he'd actually fallen asleep in such an awkward position as that. In her hands she now held a small bottle of full body shampoo made by a pharmaceutical company owned by one of their own clan. Which she knew from prior use herself, mainly from the many long and tiring flights she had been on in her time. That it not only cleansed very well indeed, but that it also rejuvenated and invigorated any of their tired bodies for a short while whenever it may be required.

She looked around the small bathroom until she espied a small, four-legged, plastic square-shaped stool. One that she thought would be ideal for what she wanted it for, and went for it. She took it inside the cubicle and placed it on the tiled floor behind him, feeling many splashes of the warm spray from the water as it hit her.

She got him to sit down, or rather almost slump down on to it, while she then began to personally bathe him from head to toe. Her own touch must have awakened him a little, and as she came around and straddled his thighs to bathe his front. So he did her own for her at the same time. Then she turned around at his suggestion so he could do her back. With that done she completed the rest of him after first thanking him for helping her with her body. After washing his groin, thighs, legs and feet, she quickly washed her own hair and legs. Then holding the shower in her hand, she rinsed him off quite thoroughly before copying the same action upon herself.

With her body's own needs also now seen to, she turned the shower off and led him out into the bedroom with one hand while holding both of the large bath towels in the other. Spreading one of them over the end of the bed, he then sat down and she proceeded to dry him off thoroughly with the other. Happy with her work, she then placed one of the still hot cups into his hands while she saw to drying herself off. Also to using a rapid blow dry on each of their hair from a small travelling hairdryer extracted from within her suitcase. It had only been included and brought for that one purpose due to her former work. His hair drying took barely a minute due to what it actually was – while her hair took far longer with it being so long. With the large damp bath towels soon hanging back on their rail in the bathroom, and one of the smaller ones wrapped around her still damp hair. Their empty cups were returned to the tray.

She then got him to lie stretched out on the bed, and massaged him thoroughly both front and back. With what he had since became used to, which was their usual very adept skill at so many things.

After that had been carried out, he then climbed slowly into bed and she drew the covers over him. Yuki then went over for her futon to unroll it for herself, until he asked where she was going. He shook his head at her, and then lifted the covers over the empty side of the double bed and asked her to join him in it. She removed the towel from her head, giving it a final quick and brisk rubbing before returning that to the bathroom as well.

As she settled into its still unusual high off the floor position, she turned to face him to ask, 'Do you require any need of sex from me, my master?'

'God no, not right now, Yuki, its sleep that I need most of all,' he said.

'I am also pleased master, as I am also feeling quite tired too.'

'Maybe in a few hours though when I'm feeling a lot better. Or maybe just when we get home again, eh?'

'Whenever you wish it of course, my master,' she responded quickly with a wide and bright smile at him.

He leaned over and kissed her full on the lips. 'You will know when the time comes, Yuki,' he told her with a tired smile himself, and then relaxed into a soft sleep with her head on his arm. Yuki then happily cuddled up to him, draping half her body, which included a breast, one arm and a leg across his own body for extra warmth for him.

∞

After they had both awakened later in the afternoon after an amazingly good long, and much needed refreshing sleep. With only Hyde's small travelling alarm clock there to do the job of waking them up. They went to eat a meal together down in the hotels dining room, before returning back up to their room. There after quite an enjoyable and lengthy sexual session happened between them to Yuki's personal vast happiness. Yuki then just stood in the nude humming to herself as she re-ironed his brought down clothing by means of the bedrooms own offered ironing board. The tiny iron she used was yet another of her own travelling devicies. Preparing him ready for his appearance on television soon, just as she had been instructed to do by her mistress, Kumiko. While he also took another hot shower and had a good close shave in preparation for his television debut.

With yet another superb massage from her skilled fingers, he felt that all was well with the world again. As she had managed to relax him totally before he started to dress ready for the task ahead. And with a further kiss on her lips, he left her there to do whatever she wished to do while he was out. As he then left and walked the short distance required from the hotel to the television studios. Using the schedule which had been typed and printed out by Ramshaw's secretary for him before he'd left work the previous afternoon.

Yuki, only after her work was done and after he had left. Had then taken a shower herself and wrapped a towel around her body as well as her hair, before telephoning her mistress, Kumiko. As had been arranged between them, just to give her a report on what had happened so far, and of how he was feeling before going on live television before the public.

∞

In Hyde's house after work the following evening, and many hours after her husband had left with Yuki. Terry had dropped her off just as he'd promised Douglas that he would. And was invited inside for a coffee for doing so by her. Where he was more than a bit surprised to find two other young attractive Japanese women in the house already when he entered with her. He left after having coffee with them in a rather peculiar state of mind it had to be said. As he had not asked who they both were, nor of why they were there in the house, so of course with Kumiko being Kumiko - she did not offer to explain either.

As the evening wore on, Kumiko, Raiko, Hiroko, and also their visitor from next door Edith, were all sitting in the living room chatting. All waiting rather impatiently more than anything else now, as they waited for the Crimewatch programme to begin at nine. And Kumiko had asked Raiko before leaving for work with Terry. To ask Edith if she would like to join them for it. For the single reason that, they could all watch his actual performance together, before then being able to discuss it afterwards.

After Yuki called her up, at which point they all kept silent until she had finished talking with her. Kumiko had ended their call with a, "Well, we'll see you both whenever you get back home again very soon then, Yuki". And had then informed them all what had had taken place down there.

'Douglas should at least be feeling a little more relaxed for tonight now than he might have been otherwise,' announced Kumiko to them all.

'I know that I would have been feeling relaxed if *I'd* just had more sex again with our master!' stated Hiroko with a happy smile. 'As his touch given in *any* way to my body is *always* very pleasing and relaxing to *me*!' she said to them in their usual very open way of speaking.

As the four of them watched the television together as they waited for it to come on soon. Many of Hyde's own team was doing the exact same thing. While some were at home ready to watch it. Others had gone back into the department to help out with any telephone calls that would come in from the public. Yuki herself though was back in bed, watching the television against the wall at the foot of the bed from beneath the covers. All of them were doing a variety of things as Hyde was being prepared by being led through the procedures for the show, as well as getting a dab of make-up on his face for the cameras to take the usual natural shine from it.

∞

The grey van was again hidden in darkness. Although this time, now stationary in an overnight lorry park in Leeds. The young man lying comfortably in the rear of it was watching the small television set from a prone position, with his head raised up by the aid of a few thick cushions, ones which he used as pillows when he slept there. He was also waiting for Crimewatch to start, just as he had every month since his roll of killings began. Only now they were more in earnest than ever before.

As he waited he munched noisily upon a recently bought pack of sandwiches while going through some of the national papers. Grinning almost dementedly as he picked out his new title here and there of, "Mac the Ripper". Where the very name they had chosen, had given him a great deal of pleasure. And so far, still nothing of what he'd done over the past ten months had been on any of the Crimewatch show's so far yet. So to him, he'd began to think that his lost flask had indeed been found and carried off by some unsuspecting fool for their own personal usage anyway. And they may have thought that it was their good luck in doing so; if such had been the outcome. Then the good luck involved was definitely that of his own!

So, as he sat and ate, and read through some of the extremely sparse details of the crimes which he had already committed . . . he waited. Just like everyone else was now doing who watched or worked on the programme. But with more of a way of utter contempt in his thoughts that were churning inside his brain than of anything else. As *he* still felt that he was untouchable. Even now. And as such, still free and able to go around and carry out his same hideous atrocities just as he had been doing for so long.

Just before the programme was about to come on, a tiny bit of the theme music from the show was being played. And as he lowered his paper to watch it, Edith herself was humming along with the tune. As she was a regular viewer and fan of the programme anyway. While Kumiko and their maids had only seen two of them so far with Douglas up to now.

The main male presenter of the show appeared for a few brief seconds, to ask the public for their help after the last programme finished, and to watch the show. He said that, "With members of the general public's help, and with information that they would all soon be hearing for the first time. They could indeed help the police to finally catch, and convict, the serial killer of twenty-four young women over the past ten months." Then he faded from the screen while the remaining end titles of the previous programme scrolled past.

Within the van, the killer sat upright there and then, almost shocked, his fingers nervously playing with the newspaper. As he began to wonder exactly *what* information they could have found to finally be able to come on Crimewatch with it. He wondered worriedly, at just how good *was* this information . . . if they expected to catch him with it now?

Hyde had less than half an hour now before his own stint near the very end of the programme would begin. And the same feelings that he shouldn't be here at all, or be the one to do it. Continually ran through his mind every few minutes even as the shows signature tune began.

'I do hope that my husband is all right?' said Kumiko worriedly to the others around her. 'Maybe I really *should* have gone down with him when his superior asked.'

'Why?' asked Edith, who was just as nervously waiting for her own friend and neighbour to appear on national television.

'Because where Yuki could not go with him to the studios. At least I could have done with being a policewoman and also as a member of the team working on the same enquiry with him. Perhaps, I could have also offered him some moral support if I had been there, too!' she admitted.

Spirit of a Dragon

'It's too late to think of that now, my dear. Douglas will be fine, I'm sure of it, Kumiko. I know he doesn't seek or enjoy the attention whenever these things come up. But he does have a certain kind of attitude that surrounds him you know. Almost a kind of magnetic mystique which persists and draws you to him - even you must have felt that from when you first saw him?'

She nodded. 'It was what made me do what I did on the very first night my father and I stayed here with him. He does have a strange . . .' she sighed. 'I just cannot think of the word in English. About a full minute later, she finally said, 'Disposition or nature is a possible word for it.'

Edith nodded. 'In a way, Douglas is a very self-assured kind of man, Kumiko. And I can understand even better why this is now, especially with my knowing what he has done in his past previously; and which I didn't know a thing about for so many years. He has a kind of coolness, as if nothing could ever faze him at any time. But that is also possibly the way he must have come to have to think about such things, when he was confronted by having to kill someone . . . and sometimes, as he has said, in cold blood.

'As if he didn't have the right attitude or mentality to be able to get over those things as they *were* done. Then he could well have just ended up as a psychological wreck. Or maybe with just a massive guilt complex along with it. As killing someone accidentally, unintentionally, or even unexpectedly may not carry the same burden of guilt with it – although I am sure that there would still be some. But to have to carry out a killing as a planned duty or necessity must be much tougher for someone to have to do. Yet he's a very stable minded man from what I have seen of him over the years. Even my *Bert* would, never in a million years, have guessed he'd *ever* done something like that either.'

As they relaxed waiting for it to start. The two remaining maids went off into the kitchen to make some refreshments that would see them all through the length of the show soon to come on. Whereas the man waiting in the van, was not in a relaxed state of mind at all now, as he was not only becoming very nervous, but also highly agitated as the time drew ever nearer for it to begin.

∞

When the theme tune finally began to herald the proper start of Crimewatch UK. All who knew Douglas personally were just starting to get a little anxious themselves by now. Most wondering how he would manage to come across to the public at such an initial thing. Could he manage to pull it off? A first appearance on any television programme was likely scary enough, but this was one that was about to go out *live* into the homes of millions of viewers! It was lucky that he knew nothing about the worries everyone else had about his television debut.

The killer, as he now sat there, having got up from his earlier lying position due to his own nerves getting the better of him. Could do nothing but wait and see *how much* they actually knew about him already, if anything at all really. Just to see exactly how tight the search net around him now could soon become.

One by one the different stories came out. The first was of a stabbing. Then of the mugging of an elderly man for a few pounds, who now still lay in hospital battered and bruised after that cowardly attack. They then did their photo parade - showing pictures of people for a variety of reasons, and who they were very interested in knowing their whereabouts. Finally, that of an attempted rape of a fifteen-year-old girl in a park at Bury St Edmonds.

All of these were seemingly appearing to be leading up to the last and final one, which was of course always the major event of the show. And which was always done last of all, only so that when it came back on the air after its short break for the news which followed it. This way, the millions of viewers around the country would have seen and heard *those* details last of all. So this would allow the last item to be retained in their memories for a far longer period of time, while the break was taking place between its two parts.

Nick Ross finally came on again. 'Now we come to out final case of the night. This is Detective Inspector Hyde of Newcastle CID. Who is the person in charge of the full and on-going nationwide murder investigation for the criminal who has perpetuated so many of these terrible crimes right now . . . Detective Inspector Hyde?'

'Thank you, Nick,' said Hyde actually very calmly. The most surprising thing was, he was apparently looking to be in a far more relaxed state than those who knew him, and who were also watching his effort, would have expected.

From that moment on, Douglas began to give an almost commentary like story based on what facts they had at their disposal so far. He did not mention any of the young women murdered by name, as there were just too many of them now to give out in such a short time. Anyway, the newspaper in there bid for more sales had already done that. For himself especially, he wanted to give various but so far unknown details out tonight. He also knew as well, that the brutality of their deaths could still have a terrible effect on any members of their families if they were also watching this.

From within the van, the killer listened as the man he could see on his small portable television, had both traced and tracked each and every one of his own killings up and down the country. From his very first in London in November a year earlier, right up to the one he'd just carried out in Sunderland only the other night. So he also now knew that she'd already been found and added to his list of killings quicker than most of them had. And he told them only what they could be told on television as kind of in a basic statement way. Leaving out exactly *how* the women were killed, with it being *too* grisly for them.

'And how can our viewers who are watching right now help you to find this man, Detective Inspector?' said Nick Ross quickly and right on queue - after having also seen the floor manager of the show making his, five minutes remaining, gesture at him. Which told him that their time was already starting to run short and to get what they could out now before their time limit was up.

Hyde gave an odd smile right about then at the camera, one which everyone saw who were watching their television sets right then. To nearly all of them it appeared to be one almost of hope and also of utter determination. While also needing their help to do it. Whereas for the killer, it just looked totally menacing. But *his* brain was working on a very different level to any of theirs.

He gave a small croak as Hyde lifted his original flask, now wrapped in a plastic evidence bag on to the table. And the same odd smile came from him again, which stretched his nerves even tighter. He told them beside which murder it had been found, what it had contained, which was why he had been able to do his *sick* work on all of his victims so far. And that until caught, any young women out there should be very wary of accepting lifts from anyone they didn't know. Not forgetting to also add, that any offer of a drink from this person should never be accepted, but quickly refused; even if they did happen to do so.

Then even to the killer's total shock, he announced that due to some DNA tests which had been carried out. He said to those watching that the killer was male. Likely with fair hair and was quite young, fir or strong looking. Probably aged between thirty to forty years old. And that he once drove, or was still driving around in a metallic light-grey Ford Transit Van, which brandished a "W" registration plate. And from their departments own summarising, he was either a courier or a delivery driver. Probably one who was either self-employed, or drove for a company which did this type of regular everyday kind of work.

The floor managers hands were now moving at Nick Ross even quicker now, as only a bare minute was left before the credits were due to roll.

'Do you have anything further to add, Detective Inspector Hyde?' he asked, seeing the hasty gesture, and from the voices in his earpiece.

Douglas leaned forward over the desk on his bent arms and looked directly into the camera with the red light on above it. Again, what he said next, sounded not only promising, but apparently also quite determined to the watchers. For the killer it was even more menacing and threatening, as his eyes appeared to look right back into those on the television in front of him.

'I hope he decides to turn himself in right now without any further problems!' said Douglas in his low but resonating voice, 'Because, we are certainly going to catch him very soon now. Mainly because each and every member of our force throughout this country of ours is now duly involved with seeking him out for his imminent arrest and capture.'

The camera stayed fixed on his face for a few more moments, as everyone watching it, wherever they were. Either in the studio running the programme, or outside somewhere watching it. They all saw the utter *matter of fact* determination etched upon his face as he stated his last and final fact to all of those who were sitting watching it right now.

The presenter after an additional call on his earpiece said to get him to say something now, quickly said, 'We'll be back in forty minutes for an update after the news on what you have all seen tonight on the programme. So we'll look forward to any of your calls to us here at the studio, or to the represented police station numbers given out already. If you missed them, they will be shown at the bottom of the screen as we leave for the moment – but we will hope that you will all join us later, to see what developments may start to appear.'

At his final word, the producer had the theme tune began again to bring it to an end for the time being.

Kumiko and those gathered around her were feeling very proud of him. While Ramshaw and his wife looked at each other in surprise by how he'd carried such a difficult thing off. Carmen, with her legs nestled beneath her on her own settee at home. Had not only been intrigued, but amazed at his way of capturing the watching audiences mind set. While his colleagues who were at home went to use their kettles for a cup of something to drink and maybe a bite to eat as the break came up, until the following part began. Were cheered-up enormously by how he had put it over on television for their group. Even those now waiting in the department for any calls gave a round of applause to him after seeing it on their own office television. Before some of the phones beside them now began to ring.

The public always had a choice as to how they wished to offer any information they thought may be helpful. They could ring something called Crime stoppers whenever they liked. Or that of the Crimewatch studios themselves and ask to speak to a member of its staff in confidence; only if they didn't want to speak to the police personally for any particular reason. Elsewise, they could always call the shown on-screen number which would get them through to the actual police force involved. Wherever the main enquiry was already taking place, which was Douglas's department for the last casde shown.

Although Ramshaw had also helped out, by asking his opposite number if he could borrow a few willing officers from the London Metropolitan Police. To act as his professional call taking team while he was on the air down there. So as to leave all of their own people to answer any incoming calls back at the department, where the actual murder enquiry was based and being worked on.

The killer himself right then, just didn't know what to do! They knew his van's colour, make, and year. Well most of it, apart from the rest of the letters and numerals which it had on its licence plate. Though how they could know even that much was getting to him already. And worst of all, that he was between thirty and forty with fair hair. Were they only guessing with that? Or had they also found something else, left by him as another clue somewhere, somehow?

He was almost about to drive out of the lorry park, when his thinking brain finally decided to kick itself back into gear again. And he now thought more calmly, that if he left now, the other lorry drivers who had seen him arrive might begin to wonder about this. And even more so if they had also just watched the show. Whereas if he did nothing for at least an hour or so, he suspected that they probably wouldn't connect him with it at all. Possibly? He was also pleased that he'd decided to drive down to Leeds ready for this afternoon's very late pick-up, instead of parking up in Sunderland as he had initially thought of doing at the time.

As his van, as well as the matching details to it, may just have caught someone's attention. To then cause him to be spotted by some sharp-eyed passer-by. Anyway, since he had the package for delivery already in the back with him, all he needed to do was to drive to Prestwick tomorrow morning. Then he grinned rather evilly, thinking to himself that just maybe. In an hour or so perhaps, he could go and have a little drive around for a while before he actually went back on the road.

He thought that, if they *were* going to close in on him very soon from what he's just heard - then why not *go out with bang*, and with a few more of those wonderfully sweet young beauties under his belt too . . .

CHAPTER 23

Hyde couldn't leave the studios as the break commenced for the evening news. Only as he had to be there for the very start of the sort follow-up to the programme to come after it. So while he hung around waiting for that to happen, he drank a few cups of almost tasteless coffee. And and then just wandered aimlessly around the studio set to see what else was happening there. Until at least *some* details from the constantly ringing telephones came to him. He read through the handed messages one at a time, not looking at whether the incoming call had been handled by a BBC member of staff, or from a locally borrowed police officer.

But he found that mostly, they were all giving details of owners of similar registered metallic light-grey transit vans; who members of the public thought may be of help to them. In its own way they were, but he could get the same from the DVLA also. From a separate telephone line there in the studio, he called his department up at his own desk, and was quite surprised to find out that Terry was there, and being the one who picked up his phone to answer his call.

'How's it going up there then, Terry?' he asked.

'It's buzzing something fierce right now after your great report, boss!' Not too much in the way of detail though, apart from just owners of the vans.'

'I know, it's the same here as well, and we would have got any of them from the DVLA anyway! But you never know, lad, we may just get someone giving us names of some fair-haired drivers on some of them as well?'

'I hope so, Dougie. Otherwise we're just going to become snowed under up here with even more lists of grey vans than we already have now! And a lot of them could just be repeated ones over and over again!'

'Stick with it, Terry. It's just the price we have to pay for looking for the public's help I'm afraid. And as I said to you before, any one of the calls could very well be the missing lead we've been waiting for!'

'Will do, Dougie, will do!'

They both ended their calls, as Hyde was already being offered another sheaf of new messages to read. While Terry, who was at their HQ had just been called over to help out one of those manning their telephones in the department, with something that required sorting out.

Hundreds of calls were pouring into both places, although many more into the studio itself, as it was dealing with many lines of enquiries. But back at Douglas's office, they were mostly giving the exact same thing. Less than a quarter were giving an occasional name to match them. Even a few grey van owners had already rang up on their own initiative; in order to give their own details just to be helpful. As well as just to eliminate themselves from the actual investigation, only hopefully of course. The only reason for doing that, of course. Was to take away any sudden visitation from their own local police force coming to see them. By their means of telling them that they only delivered locally and not nationally.

As the follow-up part to the programme returned to give fresh updates on some cases mentioned; Hyde continued to collect new details and keep in touch with Terry. Then when he was asked right at the very end yet again to offer his own update to the camera. He simply told those who were watching that some good leads were already being called in to them, and left it at that. This wasn't particularly true by any means, he just wanted to add more tension to the killers mind of his getting caught.

By then, the grey van that had been parked-up in a Leeds lorry-park, had slowly crept out of it. Just as some heavy rain began to fall, which also aided his odd departure. Yet even by the time the short add on to the main programme had ended, the van was already driving along with two occupants inside it . . . One of them being that of yet another unsuspecting young female. Another who had taken no notice of the recent warnings that had been given out by the various media.

Hyde gave Yuki a call from his mobile after his update and before he left the television station. Advising her to be ready to leave as soon as he arrived back at the hotel. And to have a drink of something and a quick bite to eat as well if she needed to. As he was just about to do the same himself before heading there to her. That they would then be leaving for home as soon as he reached the hotel.

An hour after the second part of the programme had ended; they were already thirty miles away from the hotel and now heading back home again at a far better speed. Only after they had eventually got through the packed traffic of central London. To where he could then put his foot down on reaching the motorway, as they began heading northwards where the travelling was easier.

In Leeds by then though, yet another naked body was laid outside in the darkness and just waiting to be found by someone. The grey van was already leaving the latest murder scene to its next destination of Prestwick.

∞

As he and Yuki finally got back to the house, it was almost six the next morning when they did so. She with tired eyes once again, went straight to the kitchen to make them something to drink. While Hyde went upstairs and sank his tired body into a quickly ran hot bath. A bath which began to relax him almost as soon as the small jets within its sides began; with each watery jet blowing streams against his submerged body, caused the surface of the water to bubble and froth up with the pre-added bath foam.

He was enjoying it fully when he felt a gentle touch upon his arm. His eyes opened and Yuki was kneeling beside it, holding a mug of coffee out for him, her own steaming mug clasped in her other hand.

She nodded at the water. 'May I join you to relax also, master?'

Taking the proffered mug from her hand and resting it on the wide edge of the bath. He gave an affirmative nod to her, whereupon she placed her own mug upon the same edge of the bath; except her own was over towards the other end of it. She then quickly divested herself of her own travelling clothes. And then sank slowly and happily into the bubbling water opposite him with a great sigh of contentment escaping from her mouth, even as she sank fully within its warming embrace.

As they were finally able to relax like this after their similar very long return journey. The driver of the grey van had reached Prestwick many hours before them, with his being a much shorter drive time. And he was already asleep in the back of it. Taking pleasant respite from yet another night of sickening mischief, and as such, recovering his own energy for the day ahead of him.

Kumiko was sure that she had heard something which she thought had woken her, and after a few more minutes did wake up fully. Then she slowly slid her body down the middle of the bed between the two maids, to emerge from the bottom of the warm duvet covering her. She did this slowly, only so as not to wake either of her sleeping partners of the previous night. Who at her own call, had dutifully climbed in at each side of her to keep her company throughout the seemingly long night until her own sadness only left her when as she then fell asleep.

After finally sliding feet first from the bed, the bare feet of her naked body made no sound at all on the floor as she walked over the thick shag-pile bedroom carpet. Over to where she thought she had heard the noise. From the net covering the bedroom window, she could see plainly espy Douglas's unmarked police car now had returned. And that it was just sitting parked outside the garage. She was quitely elated, as he was back!

She hurried from the room and down the stairs, quite forgetting in her actual haste, about her still unclothed condition in her own happiness to see him again. But then, she also quickly realised that none of them were anywhere around, or within her hearing downstairs at all. She cautiously unlocked, opened, and then peeped her head out of the front door, only to see that neither one of them were still sitting inside, or in front of the car. The interior and front of which she hadn't been able to see clearly from the upstairs bedroom window due to the acute angle and positioning of it.

She looked into the kitchen again and just barely noticed that a hint of steam was still rising from the kettle's spout. So they were inside the house she now knew . . . somewhere? A step inside on to the padded floor of the lino, and a quick feel of her hand at its cooling plastic side told her that it must have only been boiled barely minutes ago. She looked around again, and saw that two mugs were now also missing from upon the countertop. Then, knowing that she hadn't checked the garden in her haste, she hurried through the lounge to check there. She parted the long, closed, and loosely slatted vertical blinds apart with her hands to peer through the gap. But the garden appeared just as empty as everywhere else was.

With a shake of her head she made her way back upstairs again, wondering where on earth they both could have disappeared to. And then, as she again passed the closed door to the bathroom, she heard the now familiar low thrusting sound of the Jacuzzi jets at work. Though she couldn't understand how she'd missed it when she'd gone past it on her way down. Her own excitement at his return home had literally masked her usual senses and dulled her ears to it the first time, she thought.

Entering the bathroom quietly, she was soon stood at the side of the bath and just looking down at them. Two as yet still full mugs of coffee stood on its edge, while the two people lying prone within it looked asleep; even with all the noise from the bubbles around them. Dipping a hand into the water they were in, she could feel that the hot heat which they must have started off with, was already going from it already. So after flicking her hand to rid the excess water off it, she moved both of their mugs over to the windowsill, and then returned to them. With great difficulty she leaned over, one hand upon each side of the bath and planted a soft kiss on his mouth.

Which she quickly knew she shouldn't have done, because as his eyes opened and his hands rose to hold her to return her kiss. His pulling grip made her lose her own, and she fell over the side right into the bath on top of him. Her legs caught Yuki as she entered within so suddenly that it woke her with a start from her drowsy rest. Then a slow smile formed on her mouth as she watched them kissing each other, with only the head and upper wings actually visible of her mistresses beautiful clan insignia to be seen out of the bubbling foamy water.

∞

After they'd bathed, and Yuki had of course done her duty in drying them of first of all. He knew that he didn't even have time to have a short nap, so as to catch up on his lost period of sleep from that morning until they retuned home again. He gave a low sigh, knowing that it would be later tonight before he could finally enjoy a long rest.

With their drying off completed, Douglas and Kumiko headed downstairs. To where they found the newly risen Raiko and Hiroko already pottering around the kitchen, preparing breakfasts and hot drinks for them all. Yuki being the luckiest one of them all, as Kumiko had advised her – if not actually ordered her, to just go to bed and get some extra sleep after she had had hers. So while she was lucky to be able to catch up on her much needed sleep. He himself would just have to wait until he returned later from work.

With little or nothing really for him to do now, just like most mornings since his bachelor house had literally changed into that of a full five person, and mainly female one. Hyde went back upstairs and dressed ready for work. Joining his wife in their bedroom who was already doing that herself. He even managed a grin when he saw her struggling, and then jumping up and down, in her aim to wear yet another pair of her newly-purchased tight fitting jeans. Though today was the first time that he had actually seen the lilac coloured t-shirt she had laid out on the bed ready to put on over her bra.

She smiled back at him as he looked at her tight clothing. 'I am really still not used to being able to dress in such a way as this for work you know, husband,' she offered, 'As I always had to wear my uniform back home, as I was never allowed to work in any such casual attire as this.'

'It certainly suits your hot little bum love, that's one thing I can tell you anyway!' he stated to her, gaining yet another smile from her. As she also now knew that *bum* was his term for her behind. She had certainly been learning many strange new words ever since she had met the man who had dince become her husband.

Once back downstairs again after he'd also shaved. He had then phoned Terry to tell him that he was back home, only so that he didn't have to bother driving over to pick his wife up this morning. Which Terry gave an okay to, and then gave him a quick rundown of what had he knew had came into the department last night. So that he would be more up to speed when he did get in.

Just as he usually did, he and Kumiko arrived with a good ten minutes to spare before their shift began. Luckily also able to park the used police car beside that of his personal car. Which had been quite safe overnight since it had been left inside the secure compound. He logged the mileage done on the smaller gauge on the dashboard, before finally climbing out. All the receipts from fuelling it and for what they'd eaten there and back, along with the hotel bill, were in his wallet. Everything was ready to be handed over by him so as he could be reimbursed for them shortly. His credit card had been used for the hotel and petrol bills, while what cash he had carried on him had easily paid for the few refreshments he had bought at some of the required toilet or petrol stops they' had needed to take.

Kumiko headed for the department while he went to put his receipts in for repayment. Then he made his way to it too. The room looked just as busy as it had been on the Monday afternoon when he'd left. And he soon found out why, when Terry walked up to him.

'We're still getting some calls in after the last night's programme even now, Boss,' said Terry just as he came in the door. 'Some from the public and other updates are still coming in from those who must still be at the television studio themselves. Even the DVLA must have got their finger out this time for us. As we've been sent a complete list of the owners, along with all the addresses of those with any W registered metallic light-grey Ford Transits.'

Hyde nodded after listening to him, as little by little now, all of the missing pieces in their jigsaw were now *finally* coming together to become complete whole. Bit by bit, the larger picture of it all had enfolded as each murder had taken place. At the very beginning they had known little, or actually nothing about the killer's method of operation. But now, well, now things were taking a very different direction indeed.

The finding of the flask itself, had defnitely been a bonus. And had quickly given them the knowledge of just *how* it had been possible for him to violently attack so many of them. And almost without leaving a trace behind upon them, except for that of his semen, and only recently the odd pubic hair after having raped each one of them. It was likely, also without their actual knowledge of any of the events which were taking place at the time. Though this fluid and hairs only gave them a DNA lead on the killer.

Not much use unless you could corroborate it against someone who was already on their computer system - sadly of which he had not been, of course! He was an unknown to them right now. Or from any future test taken by the killer at some point in his life if he was ever arrested later for something else. Which could even be for some crime completely different to these now at the time . . . And only then, at which point they would get the almost one hundred per cent match to show them exctly *who* had been behind all of these rapes and murders.

But at Carmen's laboratory's slightly later after their own local murder of Kumiko's youngest sister Akiko had taken place. A much more thorough toxicology test on the two substances had proven beneficial too. The barbiturate he'd used, which had made them all drowsy, was little more than an easily obtainable dose from those off-the-shelf low dosage sleeping tablets from a chemist. These were probably crushed down into a powder form before being used for a faster working mixture so she'd said.

While the aphrodisiac had all the elements and characteristics of a drug they now knew more commonly as Rohypnol, or as alike as to its other used names also, such Spanish Fly. A name which to anyone in any police department in the country, possibly even the world. Knew that it was being quite often invariably used in what was becoming known as Date Rape cases. Where mostly women, but sometimes even men too, were given such a substance in a term known as a spiked drink. These would then be hidden within any alcoholic liquid, or other strong tasting beverage in order to hide any possible taste. Especially from their new *dates* at some point in their being out together. Which was one way of saying it for what they were just out to do. It would lead to whoevers drink it had been added to, quickly becoming very sexually aroused. Or to act quite unlike their more normal reserved selves, or so it had been said.

Then, the actual break of finding three exact matching similar flakes of paint being found upon three separate bodies; again had luckily proved to be identical, and all coming from the same vehicle. That, along with the similar markings occurring around their necks. But it had been the three so very tiny flakes of paint had been their one major lead, as to their being able to find the transport which was used in these ongoing violent acts of the same growing crimes. Although this had only been known *after* this very desperate and urgently required information had finally been returned to them.

Also, the DNA which had been gathered from the various semen samples. Appeared as if he was totally unconcerned about leaving any such evidence behind. A little late, the addition of a few very insignificant appearing pubic hairs. Which could not have come from any of the victims' own bodies due to its colouring. Some still had to be keot as origina; evidence in case of an arrest.

Spirit of a Dragon

DNA research was allowed only a few pieces of them for the various forensic teams who had found them. Due to the DNA of the hair matching to the semen, it was an additional aid to come up with a rough age grouping, and now probable hair colouring of their suspected killer as well. It was finally all starting to add up.

So with all of those at hand, they now had his means of transport, its colour and its year of manufacture. But even so, just as they had had to wait for each tiny added clue to come in to help them, more murders were still taking place. Causing them not only extra grief at how slow everything was to get back to them, but of it allowing yet more women to become raped and murdered while they *were* waiting for it. Some young women, so it seemed, had apparently still not taken any heed at all of his dire warning to them on Crimewatch. Or from the covering of his details in all the national newspapers following it the next morning!

Sadly, everything as always, took its inevitable time to get, and then start to be pieced together. Nothing was as straightforward as they would ever wish it to be. And the killer was seemingly now hell bent on a total rampage even as they were drawing ever nearer to hopefully locating him. His body count was now up to twenty-five already, the last two reports only recently coming in from Sunderland and Leeds. So, it now seemed as if he was he was still just travelling around and raping and killing further young women whenever and wherever it suited him. Or really just whenever he wanted to do so, or so it appeared to them.

A few of them in the room, Kumiko included. Had looked at him now and then as if wanting to ask him something or other. But the visible tell-tale gaze on his face, had quickly told each one of them that he was in one of his own deep thought processing modes right now. And at times like that, they all knew that it was best just to leave him at that until he snapped out of it.

Hyde as he thought, with his head tilted back, and eyes not even seeing the ceiling above him. Knew that from experience, that it would all be down to lots of paperwork having to be checked, as well as the ordinary legwork to be done could be huge. As they would have to start and formulate search plans around the country for each area wherever such drivers lived. Of course, when they did begin, it would also certainly entail them having to use personnel in other police forces areas to check up on all of their newest hits, too.

Not an easy task to do at all, even from the smaller, but still very bulky printout that had come to them via the DVLA's own database. As even he did not know how large the amount of manpower it was possibly going to take to try and get through all of this work. But, there was really little else for them to do now. Time . . . everything just took so much time to get anything moving with a good rate of speed behind it.

All that they could do now was to try to plan accordingly, and by sending so many pieces of information off to each police force to start their own checks out. While here in the office, they carried on as quickly as they could in getting more lists prepared for them all. Though he hoped that with any luck that may well be due to them by now, that they might just get to him right at the very start. Rather than right at the very end of it! As the longre it took, gave him yet more time to do even more damage out there to so many other victims.

∞

The grey van had left Prestwick many hours ago, and was on its way to one of its more regular pick-up places, Manchester. Where upon almost reaching the outskirts of the city itself, it then sudden;y broke down quite unexpectedly. The whining and thrashing noises as the gearbox, as well as the driveshaft both failed nigh on simultaneously, was not only loud but unstoppable. Not a usual occurrence for him, or for such machinery by any means. But travelling at regular high speeds constantly upon motorways could take quite a heavy toll on any machinery. And so then lead to further faults happening after only one might start to take place.

It was due to this kind of heavy workload that he tried to keep it regularly serviced. Though this never always worked when it could be some major fault steadily building. So now, what with his hazard lights put on and flashing a regular warning to any other road users coming up from behind him. As the vehicle itself emitted a small plume of smoke from underneath, as the failed machinery still ground away and the smoke trailed behind. He carefully steered it over to the hard shoulder on the left-hand side, even as its speed continued to decrease before finally coming to a complete stop.

Roadside assistance, when it did finally come thirty minutes later, involved the van being dragged up by a thick wire tow cable on to the back of a trailer. Then while it was taken to a local garage in the city for repair, the technician dropped its driver off outside one of his more frequently used stop-overs. That of a lower-class, cheap hotel.

Spirit of a Dragon

Where he quickly got a room, as expected, as being a kind of regular guest, *almost*, most of the staff there even knew him by name. Although it certainly wasn't his real one that he used by any means. And that was easily done since he always paid his bills in cash.

Of course, he always had to pay that way for everything, since he didn't own a single credit card or cheque book to his name, nor did he have any bank accounts either. The only reason for it being like this, was that he had no true fixed address for any mail, bills, or statements from them to be forwarded to. So of course because of that he couldn't actually get one. As even credit card companies weren't that stupid to offer their cards to someone who only used a key-locked PO Box for all their personal mail.

With any amount of cash he made, he could only carry it around with him all the time until it grew into a decent enough total. In a very similar way, what with having nowhere to bank it either. He used an accountant to handle all of his work receipts, van bills, self-employment taxes and VAT bills, and his PO Box payments for him. This kept everything running smoothly in that way. Yet he could also get him on the phone if need be too, seeing as he also handled most of his correspondence regarding any of that as well. Elsewise, he could just as easily drop a note into his private PO Box which he regularly looked in. Only if something was not so urgent for him to know about.

Yet only by going through his accountant, had he been able to get a key locked Post Deposit Box. Which is what he used whenever he was back at home down in London, and over the many years of his working as a courier, he now had many thousands of pounds placed and hidden away inside it. By his own choice, all his savings had been changed at a bank into the higher denomination of fifty pound notes, and these were then kept neatly rolled for space within small plastic bank bags at an amount of one thousand at a time. Just so he could easily count whatever he had stored there. As they were also stored in groups of five using an elastic band. An amount that was only added to, or in times of emergencies, had some taken out from it each and every time he visited the capital. Right now, he was carrying close to another four thousand in cash on his person from all of his more recent deliveries and payments. Quite a bit of that he now knew, would soon end up paying for these upcoming repairs.

Only with this hotel becoming a more regular overnight stay for him since he had begun to kill. He had still kept to his same falsified name. At any other hotel, or guesthouse, that he might stop at out on the smaller roads and byways. And with only expecting it to be a very rare one night thing than at these other places. He would actually give them his real name, as he never expected to to use any of them ever again.

The call from the garage where his van had been dropped off, to his mobile at the hotel only told him of his worst fears. That not only his business would have to wait and suffer now, but so would he. As his van would be off the road for at least three days to a week. That of course due to everything being dependent upon how quickly the new parts were delivered to them, and then fitted. As he had insisted on only brand new parts for the repair, so that they would not only last longer, but also come under a full guarantee for a while also. And if no short-term faults happened, it would allow him to work more to bring in what money he'd just spent carrying out the expensive repair work.

He also now knew that he could do nothing at all now, but to wait until it was fixed and available to use again. He'd had to call-up his latest pick-up for a local company, to notify them that his van had broken down on the way to them, and that he would be unable to do that job for them. After using him for so many years already, they had of course accepted his word at face value, as always. Stating that they would arrange for another courier service to do it this time. From knowing that he had done their work well for them over the many years which he had transported so many items for them, and all without any problems. So he was asked when he'd be back on the road again, but he could only be vague about it himself, just as those at the garage had been. Though he had said that he would give them a call as soon as it was repaired, so that they knew he was in once more back in business.

∞

For three whole days he waited, while having to pass up on four possible well-paid contracts which he could have done otherwise. He had also been cursing his own luck at breaking down *here*, as with living under a false name at the hotel, he couldn't even use the bills he'd get at the end of it against his yearly accounts. Although with the van repair bill he could do so as usual. Losing only one day he wasn't that much bothered about at all - but three days and still counting, was now starting to get more expensive for him daily; even if it were a relatively cheap place for him to have to wait it out. Money was still money to him.

It was only later on the Saturday afternoon when he finally got it back. Just too late to recall those who had only rang him that morning to accept any of their offers. As he knew that he wouldn't be able to get to any of them quick enough now to collect and drop-off later before closing time. Due to where they were at, and where they wanted their items taking. So sadly, even with his van back in service, he knew he would have to wait until Monday morning to get back to work.

Unless he received a lucky work call shortly. But, what with his being so long at it now, and knowing the companies he dealt with well. He doubted any such task, amd was not expecting a lot of action on a weekend when most were closed. For him, it was the just the usual part of the week where he could rest and relax more from the past weeks exertions. All that he could do, was to call those up who had rang him already, just to tell them all that he was back on the road again and ready for any work. Something which he now did straight away, only so that they would all know that he was ready and able to work again from the coming Monday ahead.

After returning from the garage and parking his van at the side of the hotel, he took his highly prized sick name list from his inside jacket pocket and reattached it back on to the sun visor again. As he'd taken that off in readiness, even while he'd waited for the breakdown vehicle to arrive for him. He certainly did not want anyone in the garage who would be working on his van to possibly see it anyway. Since he had already known from what he'd heard on the van as it had broken down that it could be a long repair. And from what the breakdown driver had told him when he'd also looked at it upon his arrival, that it would definitely have to go in for some major repairs.

So he was not taking any chances like that. A small risk like picking up a girl on her own was one thing. While someone actually seeing *this* same damning and utterly incriminating bit of evidence due to his own stupidity, was another thing entirely!

He had a meal then watched a little television on the much larger set in his room instead of the van. Before finally deciding to give the van a short run out to check it for any work ahead of Monday onwards. Yet before he did that, from his small travelling case he extracted a flask, as well as a small leather pouch, which he opened and tipped out of it two small plastic bags. Both of which that were barely about a quarter full now. His tablet stocks were running quite low, he thought. Then grinned maliciously as he recalled exactly why that was now so.

He re-boiled the electric kettle in the room ready to use after warming the inside of the flask with its first supply of boiled water, after a few minutes he poured it out again. Then taking some of the tablets from each bags supply, he began to crush them all together on a newspaper with the curved bottom of a spoon. When it was done, he used the paper with its end folded like a funnel to pour them into the almost empty flask. As the only thing in there right now were his usual measures of coffee, sugar and milk. When the kettle was boiled he filled it to around the usual half full level, placed the screw top on it, and then shook it like a cocktail shaker for a few seconds, just to make sure that it had all become infused properly, and then topped it up a little more with water.

On going downstairs to the reception desk, he advised them that he was just going out to give his van a good run, to make sure that everything was working on it all right after being repaired. Also adding to the receptionist at the desk and almost as an afterthought, that he would be staying at the hotel tonight. Until very early on the Monday morning now before settling his bill with them. It wasn't an exact lie, as he *was* going to give it a run tonight. But he was also hoping to find some further fun for himself while he was out.

Which he did, but it was not of the more usual kind that he normally found when on the lookout for a victim. She *was* quite young just as he liked them to be, but there the similarity ended, as she was also a prostitute. He had found that out after asking her if she needed a lift, and she had climbed into the passenger seat much quicker than any of the others had ever done so. He still didn't have a clue as to what she was, since most young girls that he had seen on weekends going "clubbing", or as it was termed, "being out on the pull", were often dressed just as she was right now. With a very short skirt showing ample amounts of bare leg, and more often than not, plenty of thigh. That, as well as wearing a very deep V necked t-shirt, which showed more than enough cleavage to any prospective viewer of what lay beneath it.

His own shock when she had quickly stated her various prices for her sexual services as he drove away from the kerb, soon told him just what he had picked up. It had caught him slightly flat-footed. Not the usual kind of more innocent type of girl he always looked for. Though he knew that he couldn't very well just say no thanks to her offer and drop her straight off again. Or she could easily be left wondering *why* he had pulled in at where she had been standing in the first place. And due to that, might well remember not only his van, but also *him* later on. Which he knew wouldn't be a good thing for him. Which meant there was only one course of action for him to take.

His brain quickly took over, and decided that she was still good enough for him to use. He stated to her that he wanted the full works at least once from her tonight, and then accepted her price given for it. She told him exactly where he could park the van while they did this act of business. He not telling her that he almost knew the city just like many other locals to it, almost like the back of his own hand. Maybe even better than she did after so many years anyway, but he was simply trying to lull her into a false sense of security.

On the way to her chosen area for them to "work it out together" at her stated price, she actually asked if she could have a drink from the flask if there was anything in it as she was thirsty. Since it was a cool night, the garments she wore were definitely not worn for keeping her warm. To which he happily stated that she could, but that he didn't use a cup himself . . . and that he just drank it from the open flask as it was. She offered no complaints of having to do anything like that. And so as they drove towards her designated destination. He watched his flask being raised from where she was resting it on her fleshy thigh, up to her mouth more and more frequently as he drove.

He began to chat away to her like a friend, as he did with them all usually, only to hear what their replies were like as its contents took effect. And when he thought that she was far enough out of it from the crushed tablets. He turned the steering wheel and then went a completely different way altogether, until he ended up at the place where *he* had known that he wanted to take her to.

Not to very long after that, Tiffany the prostitute, was yet another victim to become abused and violated by him; and in the very same ways as all the rest of them had been. *He* had given her a quick release from her recent few years of prostitution, done only to pay for her drug habit on the streets of her city. Whereas Tiffany responded to that in her own way by giving *him* not only the clap, but also a dose of chlamydia too. He returned to the hotel not knowing what he had taken with him from his last encounter . . . Or victim twenty-seven as he thought of it now, with a throaty chuckle. Though her first name, and his pleasures with her were already scrawled down on his almost filled piece of cardboard on the sun visor.

Saturday night passed quietly after that for him, Sunday too had little to worry him either. Monday morning however when he went down to check out of the hotel, he soon received something of a shock. The manager, upon coming in to work barely thirty minutes ago that morning was surprised to see that his work van had already left their private car park. So he had assumed that he must have already received a business call and left. Only when checking on the computer of who was still staying there, and barely only a few minutes ago. Did he see that he was still classed as residing as a guest within their own hotel. Easily spotted, seeing as no bill for his stay had yet been paid, just as his room key had not been returned either.

And to him right then, it could only mean one thing to his mind, so he'd informed the police straight away as to the theft from one of their guests. That of a Mr Stedman, who it seemed, had had his vehicle stolen from right outside their own hotel and car park as he had stayed with them. He was informed that someone would be on their way over to deal with it very shortly.

Upon his hearing this from the manager when he came down. This time he *was* literally panic-stricken. As he was going to actually have to talk with the police, face-to-face *in person*. And he had not forgotten what was now hung up in the driver's compartment was there to be seen by the opportunist thief. Or by the police if they found it somewhere and checked it out.

∞

The incident room had worked away both relentlessly and meticulously at the massed amount of paperwork in front of them. By the first day, close to fifty of their own lists had been compiled and were being sent out to their own and other areas for verification. The second day it was almost a hundred as the speed increased due to Ramshaw's own involvement. Who had sent five additional people to work with Hyde's own department team. So as to help them to save a little more time with the very large-scale search procedure they were now co-ordinating. By the third day they were close to the one hundred and fifty mark for each area. And with every day that passed, hoping that their killer would be found from one of these lists.

The nationwide search by every force that was now being conducted throughout the country for the infamous Mac the Ripper was using much manpower. Officers who had had to be taken from other duties, and so far it had led to nothing at all. A few close ties when a delivery driver was found being the owner or company driver of such a vehicle had already come and gone. Luckily for them, actually being able to prove in some way that he had *not* been anywhere near one of the murder places at such a time when the killing had happened or an arrest would quickly have taken place.

Neither Hyde nor anyone else in the police force had any idea that the killer would never be found in this way either. As he had no home address for them even to visit. The only link they might have had had been one caller to Crimewatch. Who had left details that a similar van and with all those similar kinds of details mentioned; often did courier work for the company where he was employed. But with just *so much* information coming in after the programme, most of those who rang in earliest now had their information resting at the bottom of those stacked piles. And the search and matching-up work they were doing at the moment, was also taking precedence over everything else. Only one person was left on checking out all of those – and those much needed details were still a long way down that pile as yet.

The killers own details were located in the alphabetically produced surnames in the M's of the DVLA's list they had been given. But so far Hyde's team were just barely at the end of the B's and just touching on the early C's of it, so they were a hell of a long way off it still by any means. It needed a bit of luck, a helping hand in some way, or just some kind of a fluky mistake to finally get them on the right track.

But none of their own work was the instigator for their luck until that Sunday evening. As when it did happen, it was only due to a young car thief and his even younger girlfriend accomplice who had stolen a grey van from outside a hotel in Manchester. Then things seemingly began to turn into what was almost a headlong rush for them all just to try and keep pace with all the new events which began to take place.

CHAPTER 24

With living in the van almost all year round, except for when it was being repaired or he was on the occasional cheap holiday abroad. His holidays were of course typically taken when it was receiving its annual major overhaul. He had since buying it, considered the expense of adding any additional alarms or devices; other than only the basic central locking and immobiliser that it came with when new. As being not only needless, but really just a waste of his own money due to how much time he actually spent in it. So, while he was lying resting upstairs in his hotel bedroom. A skinny seventeen-year-old spotty-faced youth, was walking cautiously around the grey van while looking it over. He had already noted a long time ago that the cheap hotel *still* did not have any security cameras installed on any wall, or corner of its building as a deterrent to the likes of him, or others. So he also knew that only by some freak bad luck occurring would he *not* be able to get into a vehicle from within its small parking area.

While he did that, his one year younger and rather full-breasted accomplice, who was also his girlfriend just turned sixteen. Was herself keeping a furtive weather eye out for anybody who might intrude upon, and interrupt his theft of any of the vehicles. From his quite quick walk around the limited twelve or so that were parked there. It showed him that only this van had no sign of aany working alarm showing on it, so it would be the best one for him to try to take.

Spirit of a Dragon

A look over at his girlfriend was returned with a wave from her, and from a lengthy vertical pocket in his coat a long but thin flat and flexible metal bar was extracted. It wasn't very stiff as it quivered and began to bend even as it came out from it. But it was so thin, pliant, and springy, that it quickly slid down the outside of the driver's side window past the rubber seal. Until a few seconds search with it caught on to the door locking mechanism within. Then virtually within a matter of a few seconds, the small button on the door inside popped upwards. Just as with all central locking mechanisms of that time, the driver's door controlled any others in use. So, as this took place, it also meant that the passenger side, as well as the twin rear doors to the vehicle were also now all unlocked.

Sliding the same bar back into its slim and lengthy hidey-hole pocket, he opened the door and now climbed inside the van. Hurriedly he clicked off the interior courtesy light as it came on, to keep his movements well hidden and unobserved from anyone who may be passing out the street. Yet another tool, that of a thick flat head screwdriver, was then brought out and used to break the ignition switch. A good few well learned very hard yanks on the steering wheel finally broke the lock to it. Whereas now, with only a few deft wire pulls from beneath, and having their ends twisted together made the vans engine start. All of this had been quickly done in under three minutes. Which showed that even at seventeen, the same young boy was actually no novice at doing such things as this by any means.

A signal to the young girl brought her running over, to where she then climbed up into it beside him. Both of them grinning at each other at just how easy it had been for them to *borrow* yet another means of transport for another night of just driving around together. Slipping the gear stick into first gear and then releasing the handbrake, the grey van began to move quietly but purposefully, until it slowly crawled out of the hotels small unsecured car park.

The steering wheel moved beneath his gloved hands as he took it out towards the main road. Leaving all of its lights switched off completely, until they were almost turning out on to the main road itself. Where they now began to drive away from the hotel. And where only now did their joint laughter finally start between them. As they left the scene yet another one of their crimes, and once again in another stolen vehicle.

Over the next few hours they drove wherever they wanted to around the city. Until what fuel which had been in the petrol tank showed on the petrol gauge as it steadily began to sink lower and lower, until it reached well under a quarter of a tank showing up on the gauge. At which time they just headed towards one of the many favoured haunts used by young criminals like themselves for disposing of any recent gains. A place which more often than not, ended up with the same vehicle that was stolen being torched afterwards. Doing that was basically to prevent any means of either of their identities being found out. But since they both had worn gloves during all of this, only a dumping of it was thought to be necessary right now.

What might actually happen to the vehicle once they *had* just walked away from it after leaving it somewhere like this. Was of course of no real concern to them, and not their problem either. Other people after they'd had used it may well do the same and then torch it, or it could be well be simply stripped of anything valuable that could be sold off to known buyers. There were certainly other thieves about who he knew who sometimes stole various vehiclles to order, possibly for shipping abroad. They would try to hide its old identity and attempt to pass it off as a second-hand sale to an unknowing buyer. Others would quickly take it to a hidden chop-shop somewhere and remove all of its parts, engine, wheels and tyres; literally whatever looked in a good enough condition to sell on.

But these two were only takers and users themselves, and they did it only for the kick they got out of it at the time. So they rarely bothered to set any of them on fire if they had used their gloves throughout their short driving use of them.

He drove them to a place barely a mile away from the housing estate where they both lived. Passing a few other lumps of scrap metal on each side of the trail, which were some that had been stolen a good while ago and had later been left burned out.

For one thing, where they were heading to now, wasn't that far for them to walk home from, of which they'd already done so quite a number of times by now. But also if they found anything that they could carry off with them, then it wasn't too far for them to do that either.

He had soon parked it in one of their favourite places, which lay within a tree and bush-lined area. Up on the small raised plateau of a small hill, not really more than around one or two hundred feet higher than the land around it. But even so, this extra height offered such a view from it that they could easily see the lights of their own estate; and even the illuminated streets where they lived from its position.

As she rummaged through the large glove-box compartment to discover what it held inside. Her boyfriend checked the driver's door pocket. Where apart from some well-thumbed maps of places all over the country, and a small packet of tissues, it was a small magnifying glass-come-torch that he pocketed. Which was all there was to find in the way of bonus items. It was he knew, rather remarkably uncluttered for a normal work van.

With nothing much available in the cabin itself, they got out of it and went around to the back and opened the twin rear doors, of which caused three small interior lights to come on inside and soon showed them what was in there. Both of who were quite surprised to find the entire floor of the van fully carpeted, and even included various additional accessories. Spotting the controlling switch for the lights, they climbed inside, where after they closed the doors and the lights went off. He was ready to switch them back on again instantly. Then after a careful search through the toolbox and another few carry boxes in there, of which he took a few of the tools out of the former to take with him for later usage. They ignored the small television and microwave as being too bulky to hide or carry easily. He then gave her a leering grin to her, and gestured with his eyes to the carpeted floor.

Their lovemaking was not only hurried, but very short and action-packed. Quite frenzied, mainly due to the thought of their ever being caught in such a compromising situation by anyone else in a place like this, and also with doing what they *were* doing. It was not only exciting, but also felt quite thrilling to them both at the same time.

When it was all over, and after she was pulling her underwear back up her legs while he dealt with his zip, she wanted to check her face out after they had both put their clothing into some semblance of order again. So they returned to their positions back in the front cabin. She pulling down the passenger's sun visor, where she knew there was nearly always a small vanity mirror there to use, though it showed nothing but a blank piece of plastic this time. So he pulled his own down to see if he had it on his side, and simply sat amazed as a long piece of cardboard stuck on by a length of adhesive tape, suddenly began to unfold itself before his eyes.

Her young boyfriend chuckled to her, 'No mirror here on this side either, Mand. But from what I can see on this, he must use the back of his van for the same reason that we just did!' He gave a low laugh suddenly, and muttered, 'The dirty bastard!' Then began to give off to her what information he could read that ran down the long list.

He missed her short gasp as he began to do so, and it was not until he'd finished reading them all out, and said, 'A real lady killer this bloke, ain't he? Just look at all the women he's probably screwed in the back of it!' That he turned to her and saw her young face, a face that now looked deathly pale to him.

'Wassup?' he asked her, wondering why she was looking so . . . well, just so odd to him just now, he thought? Either one of the two words he'd been looking for were, terrified, or just plain frightened, but he couldn't hit on either one of them right then.

In a very small voice, she replied, 'Don't you *ever* read the main news in the papers, Johnny?'

'Not if I can help it, babe!' he said sarcastically, 'usually only the footy pages in them at the back of course.'

She shook her head slowly from side to side at his admission. 'When you said the words "*lady killer*" Johnny, you couldn't have been more right at the time you said it! As I *do* read the papers, and I can *remember* seeing most of these women's names in it, which also means that we've just stolen and screwed in that frigging killer's van!' she moaned.

'You've gotta be taking the piss, Mand?' he said with a grin.

Her head began to shake even faster. 'No. I even remember the name that he's been given by all the papers now, Johnny - Mac the Ripper! It was that bad it was even on Crimewatch the other day about the twenty-six women that he'd raped and murdered!'

She saw his brow crease up as his mind now turned that over inside it. Of course he'd *heard* about that . . . as who hadn't by now what with all the extra publicity on television and radio that was surrounding it. Some of the stories of his killings had even made the front page! A page which he'd only glanced at of course, before turning to the back ones. As he was more of a sports minded kind of lad whenever his beloved Manchester United were involved. Then his thoughts began to make the same link, finally. Then his mind clicked into place as he looked back at the cardboard hanging before him - there were actually twenty-seven names itemised down its entire length.

'According to this then babe, he must have done another one of them in since the last one then. Maybe even last night going off this here! We'd better think about torching it this time just in case now as we leave here, eh?'

'What!' she almost shouted at him, 'what *we're* goin' to do is call the bloody cops up when we *do* leave this time!'

'Like fuckin' hell we are!' he stated angrily, quite shocked at what she'd advised.

'We bloody well *are* goin' to do that, Johnny Jones! An' if you haven't got the balls to do it, then I will! For God's sake, he's not only *raped* but also *killed* all these women, Johnny! And one of these people that he's killed could just as easily have been one of my girlfriends, any of your sisters - or *me!*' she implied to his now almost stricken face. 'So I'm not letting *this* bastard get away with all of that . . . not when we can even tell them *exactly* where we nicked the van from.'

He began to nod. 'All right, all right, but you know that we'll get done for stealing it just the same when they come here.'

'But we won't actually *be* here when they do come, Johnny, as I'm goin' to ring them up on my mobile when we're a little way off the van. Then we can watch from a distance, or do a runner as soon as we see them coming. Just so long as no one else comes along here before they do come and do anything else to it. Okay?'

He gave his assent to her suggestion, though hating that he might finally be caught. But even he was at long last also finally thinking of the larger and much fuller picture now. That *they*, in all actuality, would really only be considered as being very small fry to the police. Whereas this bloke whose van it was that they had just stolen. Was already being looked for on a nationwide kind of manhunt for what *he'd* been doing over the past months.

They left it almost as they had found it, except for the few borrowed objects in their pockets which naturally, they'd already forgotten about taking from it now in their shock. Then, from a point where they could see the van very clearly, while they were able to remain as hidden as they would want to be. He watched and listened as his girlfriend did something completely abnormal for either of them to ever want to do, as she rang their enemies, the much hated police. He heard her as she gave the location of the van as to where it was now, and from where it had been stolen earlier. Also to her adding just for their benefit, exactly what they had unearthed in the cabin of the van later on mainly by chance.

It was barely more than five minutes later before they saw the usually dreaded sight of the flashing blue lights of a police car as it sped past their own estate. To then watch it as it slowed down to take the almost invisible to the eye unmarked turn. One that was always especially hard to see at night. Then it disappeared from their view as it began to make its way up the twisting dirt track to reach where they'd parked it. It was only when they saw the blue lights flashing on the trees around the track did they know that the patrol car was about to reach the crest of the incline. Moments later, not only the blue roof lights, but also the headlights of the police car could be observed as it carefully followed the track. They watched the same headlights veer to left or right occasionally, as they attempted to miss some of the major potholes that were on the dirt track. Not always succeeding however, as they did see the headlights bounce skywards more than once. But finally, it did come to a stop right beside the van and they saw two figures quickly clambering out from it.

They were going to leave right then, but something, they didn't know what, held them back. Probably curiosity more than anything else - as they both wanted to know just what *would* happen next. And it wasn't very long after that that they saw just what kind of a stir their help had now caused. Only when he decided that with so many coppers around it now that they might be spotted or get caught. Did they both then finally agree to head off into the night towards their own homes lower down.

Both of them knowing in their own minds that what they had done that night for themselves had as usual been illegal. Though they were also now aided by the following thought that, they may also have just made up for about all of their own past misdeeds. By helping the police in the capture of the much feared woman killer; the one who had been so hard to catch, or maybe on the run from them for so long, and who had caused such heartache to so many families already.

∞

When the worried call from the hotel manager was received that morning by the police operator and only about a guest's vehicle being thought of as missing from their car park. Those there already inside the hotel, had no idea that the building itself was almost surrounded by that time. But that was where they had encountered another problem, as the van that they now held in their custody after an anonymous telephone call and tip-off had been received earlier from a female caller. On their PNC, or Police National Computer . . . it was soon found to have been registered by someone by the name of Mark Merrachion, who was listed with the DVLA as its owner and with that, likely its driver too.

But even after feeding his name into the computer it came up blank. There was only a PO box number as an address to forward him any Road Tax or insurance payment reminders. Just as there was no trace of a single fine or anything having been given to him for it either. Which only told them that it proved that he'd never been in trouble before. And the hotel manager stating that a, *Mr Stedman's* vehicle seemed to have gone missing from the car park, while also adding that his room key had not been handed in at reception yet. Only seemed to make the situation even more troublesome, as they weren't sure just who *was* using it right now.

Had the killer already sold it on to someone else in case of them spotting it, and of his driving it due to the details of it emerging on television? Or had it been stolen by this person at some place, and had then yet again been stolen by whoever had called them up earlier?

They still weren't sure, even when a quick thinking detective after seeing its owner's name on the screen in front of him, immediately rang-up the very same hotel to ask them if a Mr Merrachion had left their the hotel yet. Only to be told that no guest of that name was actually staying with them at this time.

So, not knowing just what to do for sure, or what they might encounter. They had placed what vehicles they had at their disposal at the time at strategic positions around the hotel. Just in case the actual one they were after *was* there; and only if a chase may have ensued from his seeing any one of them if he did come out.

∞

The two uniformed policemen that finally entered the hotel after answering the manager's call to them were in fact actually detectives, hastily changed to dress and act just as ordinary policemen for the part. Detectives who were more used to searching out, and gaining facts from usually unwilling people when they were talking to them.

'Good morning, sir,' said the first one of them to the reception desk. 'We hear that you rang up to report seeing one of your guest's vehicles missing from your parking area earlier?'

The manager behind the desk gave a nod. 'I'm afraid so, officer. Just as I've also been telling Mr Stedman here the very same thing, and who is the owner of the same vehicle in question.'

The policemen took out their notebooks, just as would have been expected of them to do. One went straight over to the mentioned guest, while the other policeman began asking questions of the hotel manager since he was the one who reported it missing.

'And when did you last see your vehicle parked safely in the parking area outside, Mr Stedman?'

'I'm not quite sure what time it was when I came in last night. As I'd only taken it out for a run to check the new gearbox and drive shaft repairs that had just been carried out on it, officer,' he answered not only carefully, but politefully and correctly. Yet no matter how hard he tried, his nervousness was already showing.

He leaned into the detective a little. 'My real name is not actually Stedman by the way, officer. It's Merrachion . . . Mark Merrachion. But I don't use my real name when I'm here.' His voice then dropped even lower. 'I just use the name Stedman when I'm here because I meet up with a married woman for a few nights sometimes. It's just in case her husband ever found any messages or letters from me to her - well, *you know how it is*?' he whispered while beginning to sweat quite freely.

'I understand, sir . . . But whatever you might do while here in your own personal and private life, has actually got nothing at all to do with me whatsoever. Your vehicle however, has been reported missing to us by the manager here. And as such I'm afraid that we are duty bound to carry out these obligatory checks now.'

The killer gave a shrug of his shoulders, hoping that his totally fictitious story had been accepted. And from what he could see on the police officer's face, and by the way he had spoken in reply to him, that it was still looking good for him.

The detective questioned him thoroughly about his vehicle, its make year and colour, and when he'd last seen it. What he did for a living and where he lived, in other words, his home address. As the killer did his best under his desperately worried circumstances right now, and in the calmest tone of voice that he could manage. His hopes began to slowly rise more and more, as the policemen in front of him barely even looked at him as he continued to scribble down each item of information from his own answers on his notepad.

Then he clicked his fingers in a snapping sound. 'Bob!' he called over to his colleague. 'Isn't this the same van that some of our lads just managed to get to before some youngsters were about to torch it earlier this morning?'

His colleague came over and looked at the vans details and licence plate number in the others notepad. 'Yeah . . . That's it right enough as it's got the same registration, Barry! By God you were very lucky man with that, Mr Stedman. Another few minutes and I think only the Fire Brigade would've been needed.'

'Can you remember what happened to it, Bob?'

The killer watched the second policeman's face become a true study of well-faked deep thinking as he racked his brains. Without him having any need to do so really.

'I'm sure that it was took back to the compound for safety, wasn't it?' he finally muttered in response.

The first began to nod. 'That's right, I remember it now. The wiring had been pulled out of the ignition. That's how whoever it was started it, and because of that we had to get it took there for safety.' The detective looked at him again, 'It'll cost you a bit to fix that up again I'm afraid now, sir, but from what I heard no other damage was actually done to the van, was it?'

'Nope, just the ignition and wiring as far as I know,' said the second. 'Hey!' he said almost as an afterthought. 'We were heading over that way anyway, so if you'd like a lift over there to give it a good check-over yourself, and then to sign for it and get it released back to you again, then it'd be no trouble at all . . . Kill two birds with one stone as they say, eh, Barry?' he laughed. 'We'll have solved a case quickly and that would allow us to get one of them off our books already!'

'I don't want to put you to any more trouble since you've already found it, and at least I know it's in a safe place now.'

'No trouble, sir. We're more than happy to help a member of the public out at any time we can these days. Anyway, it also allows us to show people that we actually *do* take our work very seriously indeed.'

'Well, I was about to check out of the hotel and get to work, but maybe with the ignition being as it is, it could prevent me from doing that now. Do you think that would be the case?'

The two detectives looked at each other for a moment. Then the one called Bob said, 'It might, sir. We could probably start it up for you the way it is now, but only if you would agree to take it straight to a garage to have it checked out by them properly. Maybe *they* could do something to it today to let you get away to work, and then you could have it fixed-up later if it needs to be? Just so long as it's completely roadworthy and any repair is done professionally of course.'

'That would be fine by me. And I can only thank you for your help,' said the killer with a smiling, yet unknowingly smug grin.

'Fine then, sir. We'll wait outside in the car for you to take you over there. All you have to do is check out now and also to bring whatever luggage you had here with you - You don't have a *lot* of luggage here at the hotel I hope, do you, sir, as we can't actually carry a great deal in our own vehicle?'

'I've only got two small bags.'

'Then that'll be no problem, sir. You get all that sorted out and we'll wait for you outside then, all right?'

'Yes, thank you very much.'

'Oh you're quite welcome, sir.'

He walked back to the elevator with an almost insane smile of his face as he returned to his room to pick his waiting bags up and then pay his bill.

He heard one of them then say to another, 'Hey Barry, at least that's one nicked vehicle off our books already today, eh?' Then they both laughed.

Spirit of a Dragon

Something which had of course only been said by them both as he had left them. They hoping of course that it may further allay any suspicions of the man they were both very sure that they were now after.

Merrachion himself though just couldn't believe it, at what stupid bastards they were. And knew that they would surely kick themselves when they finally found out just how close they'd been to catching him. Not only that, but that they had also even *helped* him at the same time to escape being caught. Those two idiots would soon be in for one hell of a bollocking for this cock-up. He laughed uproariously at the thought.

He gathered his belongings and returned back to reception. Handing his key over and then paying off his bill. Seeing the waiting marked police car through the doors he headed straight for it. A grin came to his face as the one he knew as Bob climbed out to actually open the boot for him to stow his luggage inside. As Bob climbed into the passenger seat beside his colleague, he climbed into the back through the waiting opened door for him.

The next thing he knew, he was being pushed very rudely from the side into the car. Then the two rear doors slammed shut in rapid succession. And he suddenly found himself sitting between two very muscular, either that, or they were very well-padded men.

The one on his right said, 'Mark Merrachion, I'm arresting you on twenty-seven charges of murder. You do not have to say anything which may harm your defence---'

He sat stunned into a shocked silence as he was read his legal rights, and handcuffs were being suddenly snapped on to both of his wrists. Only now did he understand that it was *he* who had been the one tricked, and not for any of that time back in the hotel had it been them.

EPILOGUE

The news when it broke in Hyde's department later that morning, which was that of an arrest of a suspect who used a similar kind of van to that of which the wanted killer used. As well as some *very* incriminating evidence having already been found inside the van itself, led to a feeling among them of something akin to a celebration of utter relief and joy going around.

Within a matter of only four hours from that first telephone call to them from Manchester. The van itself, completely covered with tarpaulin, was brought up by means of a low-loader and was soon undergoing the usual forensic tests. While the suspect himself was driven up by car, and by the same four officers involved in his arrest. Until he was handed over into Hyde's teams own custody there at Newcastle.

He was placed into a cell, though not before being deprived of his belt and shoe laces just in case of any possible suicide attempt. He was now awaiting the appearance of a requested lawyer. A definite requirement under his legal rights, especially whenever a charge as serious as murder was going to be initiated on someone. Hyde by now was getting all the information from the Manchester officers of how he had finally come into their custody.

When his thin-faced lawyer finally did arrive on the scene, he himself could almost imagine their grouped moans of disharmony echoing within their ranks when they found out that *he* had been the one requested to advise their new murder suspect of his rights.

Spirit of a Dragon

Gordon Braithwaite it was, or as most of their usual criminal suspects involved in some of the harder side investigations. Who often just called him by the sobriquet title of "Jesus". A title given to him by them, mainly for the amount of times he performed some kind of miracle for all of them. By somehow being able to manage to find even just that one single *tiny* flaw in the police's usually very detailed evidence, which nearly always led to his client's case becoming thrown out of court and their walking free.Or being classed under a far lesser crime instead. To the police who saw him enter the station that day, word quickly spread that, "The Fox", or "Foxy" as he had become known as to them, had now appeared to offer his aid to the man held in custody for multiple murders.

And not just because of his sometimes cunningly sly ways of working either, it was also because he had a thick mane of red hair and a full bristling beard and moustache. One which was also had the same thick and bushy kind of red tied ponytail that lay between his shoulder blades. That was really what had earned him his nicknames more than anything else from them. And to them *because* of that more than anything else, he appeared to bare an uncanny resemblance to that of the very same animal to which he had been named after.

'We've got to do our *damnedest* now to make these charge stick on him if he is the one behind all of these murders!' Hyde stated at the group meeting of his team within the department.

'But why will it be so hard to do this now, Douglas? And when we also have just so much evidence . . .?' asked Kumiko of him.

'Hard! Well, if it *was* him who's been doing them all, Kumiko. Then Foxy'll soon have him saying nothing at all just so as to make him look as innocent as a cherubic baby, even *before* another hour has passed! He's like a bloody plague to our police forces up here as a whole that little red-haired sod is!'

'You mean he is a good lawyer, my husband? Perhaps even *too* good?' she asked, her head tilted to one side as if in thought.

'Good? No, he's not good, Kumiko. He's bloody *amazing* at finding just that one missing piece of evidence; or some unseen discrepancy in a single huge statement that leaves us wide-open to failure in court and our suspect walks free or doesn't get what he should deserve. I just wish he worked for us in the Crown Prosecution Service, instead of in his own private and very expensive way against us. If he did, then we'd probably have more of our dangerous criminals who he does get off - off our streets and serving at least a few good years in prison!'

'And are you going to interrogate him shortly, Douglas?'

He actually grinned at her right then. 'Being allowed to actually *interrogate* suspects sadly went out of date many years ago now, my love. These days we have to call it *interviewing* them. Though most of us would still prefer the older interrogation methods used way back then with suspects like this. But with bloody Foxy in there with him, about all we'll get from him over and over again now. As we all already know to our cost. Will be him just saying the same words of *"no comment",* to probably just about everything that we will be asking.'

'Would I myself be allowed to possibly sit in on this *"interview"* that you will be having with him, Douglas?' she asked.

'Maybe, Kumiko, though I'll have to check that with the Boss beforehand. But why would you want to do that when he'll say next to nothing to us anyway?'

It was her turn to smile now. 'Perhaps the sight of my being there might just provoke some kind of response, or memories in him of my sister that he may forget where he is and give himself away to you?'

He shook his head at first, but then gave a sigh. 'I doubt that very much with *Him* being there to guide him now, Kumiko. But I'll still ask the Boss for permission to allow you to watch an interview in progress here.'

'Thank you, my husband,' she said with a beautiful smile. 'As I *would* still like to see if in any way, the inner workings of your police force over here in England may differ in some way from our own style of working in Japan if I can.'

∞

With Ramshaw's permission gained for their seconded officer over from Japan to attend the initial interview stage. It was still a while before the interview could take place, as time had to be given for his lawyer to speak in private with him. With that, there was more than enough time for Douglas and his wife to return home, shower and change their clothes before it would take place. Even after a change of clothing, Kumiko only added one additional item to herself. which was her waist belt with its attached pouches. Also having her husband stop at a shop on the way back while she went inside for a few brief minutes.

Hyde and his wife entered the room along with Terry following behind them. Merrachion and Braithwaite were already seated side by side at the farthest end of the table, away from the door and next to the small rectangular barred window behind them.

Douglas placed a chair carried in by him over against the wall at the side for his wife to sit on while she watched. Whereas he and Terry then sat down across from the two who had been waiting inside the room.

Spirit of a Dragon

Kumiko watched as her husband inserted two new cassette tapes into the empty compartments of the dual recording device beside him. And then after receiving a nod from the lawyer in attendance, simultaneously pressed the two separate buttons which set them both on to record mode.

'In this interview room at the moment we have Detective Inspector Hyde, who is now speaking, a Detective Inspector Boyne, and an Inspector Hyde of the Tokyo Police Force. We also have Gordon Braithwaite, the lawyer of our suspect in custody by the name of Mark Merrachion.

'The time and date at the start of this first interview with the suspect is 2.53 p.m. on Monday the 8th of September 2000.' Douglas looked across the table to the young man with the fair hair. 'Is your full name Mark Merrachion for the record and for the purpose of this recording?'

'No comment!' he said, then grinned back at Hyde.

The Fox was already smiling at the two detectives across the table. 'It's all right for you to give them an answer for your name,' he said to his client, then gave a nod for Hyde to repeat the question.

Douglas did, and got a single "Yes" from him in return for it.

For almost the next entire fifteen minutes which then followed that initial brief answer to his name. The rest of it was entirely made up of exactly the same offerings of "no comment" to every single query or question asked of him. So Kumiko now saw at first hand just why they all despised the smiling red bearded man at the table just so much.

'I'm thirsty, I want something to drink!' barked the suspect loudly.

Terry was about to get up himself, but Kumiko stopped him. 'I will go for it since there seems to be very little happening here for me to actually watch,' she said to them.

'There's a good girl!' said Merrachion with a leer.

'You behave yourself, boy,' said the lawyer quickly to him, and which quietly surprised all of them at the time. 'The lady here has made a generous offer to you by doing so, and she is *also* a police officer in her own right, Mr Merrachion. And *as* such, *anything* depreciating you may or *could* say to her, or them, *can*, or *could* be used to help in their case against you,' he stated very clearly and carefully just so that his client understood his meaning perfectly.

Merrachion did understand immediately and smiled nicely. 'I

apologise for my last words to you Inspector Hyde . . .' He then he looked quickly over at Douglas. 'Hold on, are you telling me that you are both called Hyde?'

'She's also my wife.'

'Ah.'

'Do you also require some refreshment, Mr Braithwaite?' Kumiko asked pleasantly.

Kumiko took their orders for tea or coffee and left the room. Just hearing her husband saying as she did so, that, 'Inspector Hyde has just left the interview room at 3.22 p.m. to organise some refreshments.'

She was back within five minutes carrying a tray in her hands, with the door closing behind her as she came through. With only the hand of the officer standing outside the door able to be seen as he pulled it closed after her. Her return back to the interview room was quickly announced by Douglas for the benefit of the two evidence tapes still rolling. Just as procedure dictated that it must be done. Two tapes that were even now still turning and recording even as she walked over to the table.

As Kumiko reached them and placed the small tray on the table, then began to pass a plastic cup to each of them. When she handed Merrachion his, she said to him, 'I'm afraid I got bumped on my way back here Mr Merrachion and lost some of yours. But if you require any more shortly, then I will be more than happy to bring more in for you.'

The words "stupid bitch" quickly died in his throat as he remembered what the lawyer had told him just a few minutes ago. And he was able to see the damp stain on the left leg of her jeans caused by the spillage that she had just mentioned. So he just nodded instead and mumbled his thanks.

Kumiko removed the tray while they all began to drink from their cups and went back over to sit in her chair . . . already giving a slow thirty second count in her head. She hid the anxious smile on her face as she now carefully watched who she was now very sure was her sister's killer. As he then quickly drained the half-filled cup that she had handed over to him.

When she had reached her own count of thirty, and not one of them had spoken a word since they'd begun to drink from their cups. Just as she knew they would not from what she had put in them all. But his cup had had to be only half full to give her the necessary time to do what she now had to do. And with her deliberate slow count of thirty now finally reached, and while three of the four there were still taking remarkably enjoyable refreshing drinks from their cups. The young man at the table with them still looked parched from only having a half-full cup.

Kumiko asked of them, 'Would it be all right if I was also allowed to ask you just one question, Mr Merrachion?' As she looked at the lawyer, he raised an eyebrow questioningly at her. But eventually nodded for her to go ahead and ask anyway, knowing that his client had already been instructed by him to say nothing at all to anyone. So she would just be wasting her time.

'Thank you, Mr Braithwaite. I would like to ask Mr Merrachion to tell me the reason *why* he decided to kill my younger sister, Akiko?'

Douglas's, Terry's, *and* Braithwaite's jaws all dropped open at her open audacity, and at what could only be called, a quite unexpected question. And even before the lawyer could think up a suitable response to his client, it was taken out of his hands altogether.

'Do you mean to tell me that that damn hot young Jap lass I screwed and killed up here was actually your *sister*, Akiko weren't it you said?' said Merrachion almost carelessly, and on tape. At Kumiko's own nod, he added somewhat happily, 'God, what a really damn hot screw she was!' he breathed. 'I just couldn't stop myself from coming in her!' Then he eyed Kumiko herself up quite adroitly. 'I really wouldn't mind giving you one hell of a fuckin' like that right now either!'

'Shut up! For God's sake shut up!' wailed Braithwaite as he now came to his senses, although it had been very slowly. Just what Kumiko had intended by adding a few drops from one of her small vials into his, her husband's, and Terry's cups when she had prepared them earlier. Into the young mans, instead of a the same two drops of two separate potions that would dull the mind for a short time while making them want to drink continually. He had only got the same drinking one as they had, just to make him need to drink his own even more quickly than they had.

But, into his had been added a second potion. One which was almost just as powerful as the manufactured drug sodium pentothal was, and known everywhere as being a truth serum. Though her own that was used was even far stronger than even *it* was. What with it being concocted in such a natural form by those in her clan. But *unlike* that of the injected form of sodium pentothal. Their own naturally based one only lasted for a very brief and short period of time after it was ingested in some way. At its best, only for two minutes after a thirty second count had been made. Then it would it come to a sudden end. As it quickly seeped its way into the brain and left it unguarded to any questioning. So, anything had to be done quite quickly before it did the exact opposite and began to dissipate from the victims system.

'But why did you have to kill so many women?' she asked sadly.

'Because I *wanted* to, *that's why* you daft bitch! Just as I wouldn't mind getting myself into you right now, and in a few different ways just as I did with all of them; and then to watch you as *you* slowly choked to death as I strangled the life out of your body as well!' Then he suddenly began to shake his head slowly from side to side, as if trying to clear a fog from his mind.

'Do you smoke Mr Merrachion, would you care for a cigarette?' Kumiko asked him softly now, and with no sign of hatred or shock upon her face from any of his spurious sexual or otherwise statements. And at the slow motion nodding of his head, she got to her feet and crossed back over to the table. When at the side of it she produced a packet of them from a breast pocket and opened the flap of a full packet of ten. He pulled one out from the full packet and waited as a lighter burst into flame in her hand. Leaning forward, the end of it glowed as it was placed into the bright flame and was almost greedily being sucked upon.

As Braithwaite muttered over and over again, 'Oh you fool - you bloody daft fool!' to him. He continued to inhale and exhale the nectar tasting smoke in and out of his body as if without a care in the whole world.

Even as he did that, Kumiko returned to her chair again. She crossed one slim leg over the other in just the right way to hide what she was going to do next, which was to slip her fingers into the tiny pouch inside the leather belt she wore over her jeans. A pouch barely a few inches in length, and so small that no bulge would be seen, since it was also attached to her handcuff pouch on the outside by a thin looking strap. This allowed the one inside it to be held in place by the other far larger pouch on the outside in a firm position there.

Her fingertips ran quickly but surely over the row of tiny ceramic vials that were held in place inside the miniature pouch. And at the fifth one she touched, her knowing fingertips withdrew it from its concealed place, then, with the open cigarette packet hidden behind the raised leg crossed over her knee. Kumiko quickly used the small rubber top to suck something from within the tiny bottle.

From the dropper out of the vial, she allowed just a single drop to fall on to the very centre of each white tipped filter end on the remaining nine cigarettes in the box. This new drop rapidly nullified the deadly agent she had laced all of them with. So that whichever one he cared to choose, only if he did accept one, then the final effect would soon give the same result. As for herself, she just had to make very certain that he *had* been her sister's killer before offering him one of the prepared cigarettes as she had made their drinks earlier.

With all of them taken care of in quick succession, she deftly replaced the vial back into its hidden compartment, then closed the cigarette box and placed them into the empty breast pocket of her shirt again. Then she sat back in the chair, and watched the man at the table as he still sucked at the rapidly diminishing cigarette between his fingers.

The lawyer, who was sitting there, still literally stunned at his client's own open admission of guilt at what he had done. Was sitting with his head leaning into his hands, as he now tried to think of some way with which to counteract what he had already said. And now of what was all firmly stated on record as personally quoted evidence by him.

Merrachion suddenly gave a loud gasping cough then slumped forward so quickly that his head literally bounced back up from the table even as the bang was heard as it hit it. Just as where not one of the men at the table were quick enough to prevent it from happening either.

'Jesus!' gasped Douglas as he almost jumped up from his seat at the massive thud. Terry almost fell over backwards in his chair, as he thought that he was being attacked. While Braithwaite sat shocked and open mouthed at what he'd just seen. Kumiko herself of course, quickly feigned utter horror and sheer fright on her face at what was happening right before her eyes. Her father was so right she now knew, and he would have been proud of her performance too . . . As her father had indeed been quite correct to say that, their own training regime *was* indeed *everything*.

'Kumiko, hurry, get them to call for an ambulance outside!' said her husband as he raced around the table to help the inert young man.

His wife rushed out of the room in what appeared to be a panicked state, and alerted the officer on the door outside that an ambulance was needed immediately. And as she watched the officer race away to do what she had asked, through the door behind her that had now been left ajar. She heard her husband mutter aloud, 'Come on you son of a bitch - *Breathe!*' After he had dragged him down to the floor, Terry was trying to revive him with the Kiss of Life while her husband massaged his chest in between Terry's breathing into him.

Both of them were sadly fighting against something Kumiko already knew . . . that *nothing* upon this earth could save him now, whatever anyone may have tried to do to alter it!

As the second potion, even though only a single drop of it had been used. It was just so incredibly potent that the *only* outcome of its usage was that of a huge and severe heart-attack. Her mouth began to turn upwards inro a little smile, as her head tilted up in a similar manner towards the ceiling of the corridor.

She suddenly whispered in quiet Japanese, and in a very calm hushed tone of voice. 'You have now been fully *avenged* for your own death, my little sister! Your own Spirit of a Dragon within our clan has finally been given its true release. Now, you can finally leave this earthly realm of ours, while your life-spirit is allowed to truly become one with the God's themselves at long last!'

Her last movement was to offer the very smallest of head bows to what was her own first ever victim.

THE END

If you enjoyed this book

then watch out for the upcoming first sequel to this series when it finally appears - entitled, "*Angel of the North*"

A Note from the Author:

I thank you for purchasing/borrowing my novel, the Adult Erotic Crime Thriller entitled, *Spirit of a Dragon*, and I do hope that you have enjoyed reading it? There may be a sequel to it coming through soon, if the reader/fan demand for it is high enough.

As both a writer of various genre stories, and as a reader of them myself. I do enjoy stories that appear to flow naturally without having any great difficulties in following the plot, or story line in them. I call these *"immersive"* books. In a way, I like to feel as if I am there seeing it happen in front of me as I read. This is also the way I try and write my own books for others to enjoy in the same way too.

To me, personally, you should be able to just pick up a book and read it from start to finish. Without being caught in a maze of words you cannot even begin to try and understand, or need a dictionary at hand in order to work any of them out. I like them, as I like my own, to be plain and simple, and easy to read.

Perhaps my own may not be not as technical as some you may have already read. Or as filled with an array of characters who are detailed to their utmost, offering a complete warts and all biography of literally everyone and anyone who plays each part in them. That is just my style of writing, and I concentrate more on the main principal characters involved, and on the general flow of the story itself, rather than on too many character descriptions when I don't think they are needed.

I have a Website available, where you can find out what types of novels are already written, (with links of where to find any of them) - and any others which I am currently on writing at the present time. Please feel free to have a look at it if you wish. You may even be interested in some of my other ones perhaps., too? My page on Goodreads.com is also up and running if any of you are interested - or already use it.

http://www.keithgardnerauthor.co.uk

I do have a Facebook, Twitter, and Goodreads page if you would enjoy joining any of those to keep up to date with any messages or news, or to perhaps just to say Hello - or even have a chat. You are more than welcome to join, and can easily link to any of those simply by using their auto links offered at the bottom of my website. Just as I also now have an Author page on Amazon to show what books are listed there and now available to be purchased.

http://www.amazon.co.uk/Keith-Gardner

The only thing I would like to ask you to do after you have read any book however, would be to leave your comment and a star rating for what you thought of it afterwards from wherever you purchased it. As I really do appreciate any responses such as these from readers, as your own thoughts and insights on them will tell me how you personally viewed any book.

Other Books by the same Author:

Little Haven:

Little Haven is a fictional story of the Wild West.

Julian Armitage, an Englishman who had once served in the army, and by no means any slouch with a gun himself. Against all odds decided to settle in Indian Territory alongside the Cherokee in 1775.

A lonely life was not for him though, so he slowly began to build his own town from the ground up.

From wagon trains and those who were simply passing through, he soon had a small nucleus of inhabitants living within his town. It was actually a peaceful place, which is also why he had given it such an unusual name.

That only lasted until the Hill's arrived. A Father and two sons whose robbing, plundering, and murdering were almost legend at the time. And who were not averse to seeking an opportunity anywhere, and from anyone if it could be had.

They were only looking for a hideout over the winter, after they had recently committed a number of deadly robberies. And Little Haven when they decided to stop there, so they thought, appeared to be just the place for them to take over with their brutal regime. Little did they know what would happen when they tried . . .

Honour The Star:

Honour The Star is a fictional story of the Wild West.

Daniel Goest was a well travelled man. Over the years his name became spoken of in the West, especially when a town needed Law & Order brought to it.

Now, much time had passed, and he wasn't getting any younger. So his thoughts of being a lawman had changed to that of retiring.

His arrival in the small town of Windy sparked little interest, at first. As not everyone noticed the two tied-down guns he wore, which appeared to blend into his clothing. It wouldn't be long before those who were there, would soon see exactly what they could be used for when a call to action was required.

This novel was originally planned as the finale story of his life - but there could yet be a further one after it to end it in the way that I really want.

N.B.

The 1st prequel of this actual story series - "Goest Goes West - The Early Years, Part 1" is already on with being written right now (April 2015).

Which will both detail and chronicle the time and events in his life from when he first left home at the age of sixteen - to finally lead up to his becoming the man and legend which you will you have read about in the actual novel above.

A Silent Land:

A Silent Land is a fictional Western Adventure Novel

Is suitable for both Men and Women, who enjoy Westerns, Action, Adventure, Romance, and Drama.

The story is set in the 1700's and being told through that of a young poacher by the name of Sam Hope. A young boy from the North-East of England, who aged sixteen found himself press-ganged on to a visiting naval ship.

Torn away from his former life and family, as so many others were in the day and age of wooden sailing ships, simply to serve the needs of the fleet and its large navy. He soon found out that despite having far worse food to eat, as well as fewer options allowed. His new life aboard was also showing him a lot more than he could ever have once imagined. Far away from the local forests, where he had once both roamed and hunted.

Finally, upon being left marooned upon the almost unknown coast of America by the jealous captain of a pirate ship. Older he may have been, perhaps even by now a little wiser than when young also; but he was also about to find himself beginning yet another new way of life. Although this time, one where he knew very little at all about anything to do with the peoples and country which would lie all around him. Would he even be able to survive in this harsh wilderness ...

N.B.

There is also at least one planned follow up sequel to this book - if not more than one on this particular story as time unfolds with it.

Keith Gardner

The Magical World of Cassie Carey:

The Magical World of Cassie Carey (Book 1) - is a Fantasy/Science-Fiction novel.

Do you believe in Witches and Wizards?

Elves and Fairies?

Dragons and Goblins?

Troll's and Ogre's?

That Animals are able to talk?

No, did I hear you say?

Well neither did Cassandra Carey, until she reached her thirteenth birthday. As on that very same day, everything that she had known or thought possible before soon changed for her as well.

N.B:

Cassie Carey will also become a series - if the demand is there for it too.

An Unexpected Christmas:

An Unexpected Christmas is a fictional Christmas story for all the family.

With the mixture of Santa Claus stories and others, like that of A Christmas Carol - it should offer readers a pleasing book to enjoy over holiday periods for many years to come.

It is only a few days before Christmas and Santa has become ill. His Elf Doctor, and his Head Elf, Gabriel, had already told him that there was no way it will have cleared up in time for him to be able to do his present deliveries this year.

A rapid, but thorough search of the Claus archive records dating back to when the role of Santa first began. Only showed up one distant relation in them so far, who had already had suffered from the same illness - and who may be the only one possible to be able to assume the role.

Leonard Claus, a wealthy Banker in the financial capital of London was his name. However, his own lifestyle and personal thoughts and ideals on what Christmas had since become from his own youth, were far different to that of a budding Santa Claus. The only thing he did have going for him at the time, was the inherited Claus laugh.

Would he be able to assume this highly regarded role, and carry out the task required of him? Or will his own background simply turn Christmas into a complete mess and leave a disaster behind him!

Once in a Lifetime:

Once In A Lifetime is a Romantic Drama . . .

True Love . . . Does it really exist, and does it actually happen?

Well, Roger and Suzette were sure that it had for them. From their first ever meeting at school in this heart-warming story when they were both only ten years of age.

They would soon become inseparable, beginning as childhood sweethearts, which would then lead up to much more as the following years unfolded.

Life as we know it though, is never always a bed of roses. There are highs, just as there are lows. There can be happiness, just as there can also be sadness.

You can follow their story, seen from various viewpoints. Will it be a very happy one, or one tinged with sorrow. What you will read, could make you smile, bring you to tears, even just to laugh, or offer a huge sigh. A lump in the throat perhaps, or the simple sensation of complete enjoyment.

How you will see this story for yourself is what will matter the most.

The Brotherhood:

The Brotherhood is an Adult Erotic Supernatural Crime Thriller

(It can be seen as both raw and brutal to some readers - so please note that you have been warned in advance!)

In the fight against an occult group which practices the purest form of Occult Black Magic, one man alone, Tom Jones, stands between all that is good and evil.

Magic against magic is needed when it comes to such fierce battles as these will be.

But can one man endure in this fight against, The Brotherhood . . .?

Keith Gardner

Spirit of a Dragon